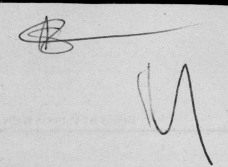

HIS FAVORITE COUNTESS

"I . . . I don't want to sit," she protested.

"You need to rest," he said, stroking his long fingers down the side of her neck. She fought back a tremor, furious with her lack of self-control. An hour ago, she had wanted this . . . wanted him. She still wanted him, but not all the complications that would come with it.

Scowling, she crossed her arms across her breasts.

"Well, we're alone now. Nobody can overhear us, so answer my question," she said. "Why did you decide to stay?"

The smoldering fire in his eyes sucked the air right out of her lungs. His fingers slid up her throat to capture her face in a tender, but unbreakable grip. Moving in, he took her mouth in a hard kiss—raw, punishing and glorious. She whimpered under the onslaught and he pulled back, still holding her face between his hands.

"This, Bathsheba," he growled. "I stayed for this . . ."

Books by Vanessa Kelly

MASTERING THE MARQUESS

SEX AND THE SINGLE EARL

MY FAVORITE COUNTESS

AN INVITATION TO SIN
(with Jo Beverley, Sally MacKenzie, and Kaitlin O'Riley)

Published by Kensington Publishing Corporation

My
Favorite
Countess

VANESSA KELLY

ZEBRA BOOKS
KENSINGTON PUBLISHING CORP.
http://www.kensingtonbooks.com

ZEBRA BOOKS are published by

Kensington Publishing Corp.
119 West 40th Street
New York, NY 10018

Copyright © 2011 by Vanessa Kelly

All rights reserved. No part of this book may be reproduced
in any form or by any means without the prior written consent
of the Publisher, excepting brief quotes used in reviews.

If you purchased this book without a cover you should be
aware that this book is stolen property. It was reported as
"unsold and destroyed" to the Publisher and neither the
Author nor the Publisher has received any payment for this
"stripped book."

All Kensington titles, imprints, and distributed lines are
available at special quantity discounts for bulk purchases for
sales promotion, premiums, fund-raising, educational, or
institutional use.

Special book excerpts or customized printings can also be created to fit specific needs. For details, write or phone the office
of the Kensington Special Sales Manager: Attn. Special Sales
Department. Kensington Publishing Corp., 119 West 40th
Street, New York, NY 10018. Phone: 1-800-221-2647.

Zebra and the Z logo Reg. U.S. Pat. & TM Off.

ISBN-13: 978-1-4201-1483-6
ISBN-10: 1-4201-1483-2

First Printing: May 2011
10 9 8 7 6 5 4 3 2 1

Printed in the United States of America

ACKNOWLEDGMENTS

To my husband, both my writing partner and biggest fan, thank you for all your support and love.

With many thanks to Debbie Mazzuca, Manda Collins, Kris Kennedy, Sharon Page, and Teresa Wilde, for all their advice and support. With much gratitude to my agent, Evan Marshall, and my editor, John Scognamiglio, and the cover artists at Kensington for giving me another fantastic cover.

Thanks also to Roy Waite of the Ripon Historical Society, for answering my questions and providing much useful information about that lovely town in Yorkshire.

Finally, with grateful thanks to librarian extraodinaire Franzeca Drouin, who helped me research the fascinating but often horrifying history of obstetrics in Regency England. Mostly especially, my eternal gratitude goes to Kim Castillo, whose organizational skills and wicked sense of humor are second to none.

Prologue

London
June 1817

John had failed and another woman was dead. Soon the rumors would begin again, whispered through the sooty laneways and alleys of St. Giles, spreading fear and ignorance like a foul contagion.

The Angel of Death.

That was the name some of the locals called him. He could hardly blame them, although cold logic told him they were wrong. Still, Death trailed in his footsteps. No matter how fiercely he struggled to best it, in these dark places he rarely emerged victorious.

John dropped his scalpel into the tray lying on the floor next to the rough-hewn bed. A battered wooden table, a few mismatched and broken chairs, and an old trunk made up the rest of the tenant's furniture. In the fitful light cast by one old lamp and a few smoking candles, the room testified to the hardscrabble life eked out by the wretched souls in the London stews.

Roger Simmons, his assistant and medical student, carefully drew a tattered, grime-encrusted blanket over the body of their patient. Patients, rather, since John had been unable to save Mrs. O'Neill's baby, either. The stillborn infant lay in his mother's arms, joined with her for eternity, which John hoped was a more forgiving place than this dreary pest-hole.

"There wasn't another thing you could do to save her, Dr. Blackmore, and you know it." Roger's rough voice, still bearing the faint traces of his upbringing in Spitalfields, broke the unearthly quiet of a room that had vibrated with a woman's screams just a short while ago.

"So you say."

The words scraped raw in John's throat as he rubbed the blood from his fingers with a scrap of cloth. Once it had become clear Mrs. O'Neill was breathing her last, he'd cut her open in a futile attempt to save the babe. But, as usual, he was too late. The poor of St. Giles rarely sent for a doctor or surgeon to deliver an infant—not that most doctors would even set foot in the place—and put their trust instead in neighbors or relatives to assist in the birth. If they were fortunate, they could perhaps afford a midwife, but in this benighted part of London even that was an unusual occurrence. So by the time someone became desperate enough to run to St. Bartholomew's Hospital to fetch him, the unfortunate woman was often beyond help.

"Sir, you know her pelvis was too small, too disfigured." Roger carried on doggedly, wiping medical instruments clean before stowing them back in John's bag. "Her life was slipping away by the time we got here. A caesarean was the only chance we had to save the infant. You know how many of these women have rickets. Christ, we've seen it often enough these past months—especially among the Irish."

The certainty of that knowledge offered John little comfort.

He bit back a frustrated oath and threw the bloody cloth into the tray. It would take more than a few bits of cotton to scrub the gore from his hands and arms. And God only knew what it would take to wipe clean the stains that marked his soul.

He turned away from the bed, rubbing his neck, searching for the knots that felt like pieces of lead shot under his fingertips. Exhaustion leached through his veins, and he suddenly craved the solitude of his study. And a brandy. A very large brandy.

Roger gave him a sharp look as he shrugged back into his coat. "If you don't mind me saying so, sir, I'm thinking this would be a good time to make that trip up north you've been talking about. To visit Dr. Littleton. Why don't you leave tomorrow or the next day? Dr. Wardrop will be happy to see to your patients while you're gone."

"You know I haven't the time to spare," John replied as he retrieved his unused forceps from the tray and handed them to Roger. His assistant had an annoying tendency to fuss over him like an old hen, but John couldn't seem to break him of the habit.

Roger grimaced. "You need the rest, guv," he said, slipping into his old pattern of speech. He only did that when frustrated. "You've been working flat-out for months, trying to make those old chawbacons at Bart's change their ways."

John started to answer when a heavy thud sounded against the only door leading into the room.

"What's happenin' in there? I ain't hearin' my Mary screamin' anymore. Is the babe come?"

This time John didn't bother to hold back his curse. Derek O'Neill had been openly hostile when they had arrived an hour ago, fetched by a local woman who had once been a patient at St. Bartholomew's Hospital. O'Neill had made it abundantly clear that the last person he wanted to entrust his wife to was an English physician—and a swell bastard at that, he had growled, flinging the epithet in John's face. Only the fact that his wife continually shrieked in agony had finally convinced the belligerent man to let them into the room.

John cast one quick glance over Mrs. O'Neill's body. He and Roger had cleaned her as best they could, but the woman's blood was everywhere. There hadn't been enough water or time to do a thorough job of it.

"Shall I let the man in, sir?" Roger looked almost as grim as John felt.

"A moment, please." He buttoned his waistcoat, shrugged into his coat, swiped his fingers once more in a useless attempt to better clean them, and then nodded to his assistant.

Roger had barely cracked the door open when O'Neill shouldered his way into the room. The big, dark-haired immigrant, loud and blustering only a short time ago, took two steps before stumbling to a halt, his face turning pale as milk. His horrified gaze fastened on the bodies lying in the narrow bed.

John crossed the small space to stand in front of him, blocking out the gruesome scene behind.

"Mr. O'Neill, I'm very sorry. Your wife labored too long, and she was too weak to survive such an ordeal. She died before she could birth the child. We attempted to save your son, but that was beyond our powers, as well. I grieve that we were not able to help them."

Eyes the color of mud—dark pools of anguish—shifted to meet his.

"A son?" O'Neill's brogue was a shattered whisper.

"Yes," John replied, his throat pulled tight with bitterness and guilt.

The big man stepped around him and fell to his knees beside the bed, a low moan of pain coming from his throat. The sound rose, gaining intensity until it became a howling wail that raised prickles along the back of John's neck.

Drawn by the awful noise, Mrs. Lanton—who had fetched him from the hospital—and several other neighbors crowded into the doorway. Sadness etched the features of some. Others displayed the avid and morbid curiosity so often evoked by an agonizing death.

John held back the sharp words that threatened to fall from his lips. It would be cruel to reprimand them for using their curiosity as a defense against the calamities that so often befell them. He had come to understand it was a way to distance themselves from the mundane horror of daily life in the rookery.

He gestured to Mrs. Lanton. She crossed swiftly to his side.

"Does Mr. O'Neill have any relatives in London who could assist him?" he asked quietly.

She shook her head. "He's all alone now, sir, except for the likes of us. He and the missus," her gaze drifted to the appalling tableau by the bed, then jerked back to him, "they only arrived in London six months ago. She was a love, but he's a bit of rough trade, if you get my meaning. Still, he was devoted to his Mary, that's for sure."

"Is there anyone—"

John broke off as O'Neill surged to his feet. The Irishman turned from the bed to confront him, his face contorted by grief and fury.

"You killed 'er." His voice was guttural and thick with hatred. "I hear what they say about you, what you do to our women. They don't survive once you get your hands on them, you bastard. Do they send you here to kill us, your mighty lords and masters in the City?"

Mrs. Lanton drew in a shocked gasp, but the growing crowd now jostling in the doorway began to murmur with anticipation. John ignored them, focusing on O'Neill, flexing his tired arms as he prepared for what might happen next.

The distraught husband took a menacing step forward. Roger circled around behind him, his hands clenching into sturdy fists. His assistant might have left the streets of Spitalfields long ago, but he was always game for any fight.

John gave his head a slight shake, signalling Roger to stay where he was.

"Mr. O'Neill, I am truly grieved for your loss," John said gently. "I swear to you that my assistant and I did everything we could to help your wife and child. But we do not possess the power of life over death. Only the Lord can affect such a miracle. Your wife's soul is now in His hands."

The platitudes stuck in his throat. Miracles tended to be in short supply in St. Giles, as they were in his own life.

O'Neill's face went from dead white to mottled red in seconds. "I say you killed 'er, and now I'm going to kill you."

He lurched at John, his massive fist a blur in the air. John smoothly blocked the man's punch but didn't strike back. The man deserved his sympathy, not a beating.

His momentum carrying him forward, O'Neill staggered past John and tripped, crashing to the floor with a bone-jarring thud. Roger threw himself on top of the Irishman and wrapped his forearm around his neck. O'Neill twisted violently as he tried to break Roger's punishing grip.

"Don't just stand there, you fools," yelled Mrs. Lanton to the men gawking in the doorway. "Get in here."

Three or four neighbors rushed in and helped restrain the raging man. They pushed O'Neill to the floor where he continued to struggle, crying out his grief in wrenching sobs. Cursing, John grappled his way through the tangle of limbs and peeled Roger from the pile of writhing bodies, hauling him to his feet. His assistant shook himself like a dog coming in from the storm.

"We best be off, Dr. Blackmore," he said. "Not much more we can do here." His gaze shot to the door, and to the rapidly growing mob out in the alley. "And it looks like things might be getting a bit ugly."

John followed his glance, noting the suspicious looks directed his way and hearing the hostile tones in the build-up of voices outside.

"You would appear to be right," he responded, trying to keep the bitterness from his voice. His failure slashed like a blade through his gut, as sharp and unforgiving as death.

He retrieved his medical bag and headed for the door. Mrs. Lanton followed him.

"You mustn't mind sir," she whispered. "Some of these folk don't know any better. But there's plenty who do know all the good you do for our sick women and babies. And I don't forget what you done for me over at Bart's, neither. You saved my life, you did."

He forced himself to smile into her careworn face. "Thank you, Mrs. Lanton." He extracted a guinea from his pocket. "For Mrs. O'Neill's funeral."

She pocketed the coin. "I'll take care of it, sir. Now you best be on your way."

John took one more look at the anguished man sobbing on the hard-packed dirt floor, at the tiny, foul-smelling room, and at the pathetic, slight figure with her lifeless baby in her arms. Clenching his jaw, he pushed his way through the crowd at the door, eager to be gone from this squalid place of grief.

He and Roger strode along the dingy, narrow street toward Drury Lane, doing their best to ignore the scowls and muttered comments that followed in their wake. Bitterness still pulled at his gut, along with a low throb of something akin to despair.

He glanced over at his assistant. Roger had a small cut on his cheek and what would soon be a spectacular black eye.

"Blast you, Roger," he growled. "I could have dealt with O'Neill. You needn't always try to protect me. You're just as breakable as I am."

Roger shook his head. "Sorry, sir, but we can't have you damaging your hands. Besides, what would Dr. Abernethy say if you showed up for hospital rounds looking like you'd been in a brawl? You know he's waiting for any excuse to report you to the Board of Governors."

John gave an irritated grunt in reply. Roger was correct, of course, but the knowledge still stuck in his craw. Abernethy was an idiot, but the chief surgeon would take the first opportunity to toss him out on his ear. If that happened, John would almost certainly lose his growing practice in Mayfair.

He strode into the bustle of Drury Lane, suddenly disgusted with all the messy compromises that made up his life. Perhaps Roger had a point. Perhaps it was time to get away from London, away from the politics of the hospital and the demands of his aristocratic patients.

More importantly, he had to get away before he had to stand by and watch another helpless woman succumb to an agonizing death.

Chapter 1

Compton Manor, Yorkshire
July 1817

It was so much worse than she'd imagined.

Bathsheba Compton, widow of the fifth earl of Randolph, stared in horror at Mr. Oliver as he outlined her dire situation. Ruination loomed, and no matter how hard she taxed her brain she couldn't see a way to avoid it—not without a wrenching sacrifice on her part. The very thought of what *that* might entail made her stomach twist into knots.

Matthew also stared at his land agent. Not with horror, but with his usual befuddled expression. With his wrinkled brow, balding pate, and droopy eyes, the current Earl of Randolph looked like a basset hound emerging from a sound slumber.

"I say, Oliver," he exclaimed. "You've been droning on about the accounts for the last half hour, and I can hardly make heads or tails of it. What do you mean, bankrupt? I can't be bankrupt. I'm an earl!"

Mr. Oliver cast a long-suffering glance in Bathsheba's direction and tried again.

"I regret to say, my lord," he replied, enunciating very carefully, "that the estate is seriously encumbered with debt and, at this juncture, the small crop yield at the end of the summer will do little to alleviate the problem. Coming on the heels of last year's crop failures, the situation is little short of disastrous."

Bathsheba closed her eyes and held still, hoping the roiling in her stomach would subside before she became physically ill. The day of reckoning had finally arrived, in spite of her desperate efforts to save her family from disgrace.

"Do you mean we're at a standstill?" demanded the earl, finally waking up to the urgency of the situation. "I thought all that retrenching we did last year was supposed to pull us out of dun territory? What was the point of all that cheeseparing if we're still in as bad a shape as we were last year?"

Mr. Oliver's mouth opened just a fraction as he stared at his employer in disbelief. Matthew glared back at him. The beleaguered land agent sighed and pulled one of the leatherbound ledgers from the pile in front of him.

Hunched over the old walnut desk in the library of Compton Manor, Bathsheba and Matthew peered at the account books Mr. Oliver had spread before them. She had grasped the miserable state of their finances instantly. After all, she had kept her father's books for several years preceding his death. Numbers were one of the few things that never lied, especially when recorded by an employee as meticulous and honest as Mr. Oliver.

The land agent flipped through the ledger until he found what he wanted, then shoved the book in front of his employer.

"My lord, you have very little income, and certainly not enough to support two households. The town house in London," he glanced again at Bathsheba, "requires significant upkeep and maintains a full complement of servants. You will recall that you and her ladyship agreed some time ago that it was imperative to keep up appearances in town, so as not to draw attention to the considerable debt left by the previous earl."

Matthew rolled his eyes. "Of course I remember. I'm not an idiot. But we've spent next to nothing these last three years on the improvement of the estate here in Yorkshire. Nothing's been refurbished or replaced. I can't even remember the last time I bought a book."

Mr. Oliver didn't even blink. "My lord, you obtained several rare volumes just last month. I have the bills right here."

Bathsheba snatched the papers from Mr. Oliver, quickly scanning them.

"Oh, Matthew," she groaned. "How could you? You spent over five hundred pounds on books just last month." She riffled through the bills with growing disbelief. "Did you really need another edition of *The Canterbury Tales* to add to the three you already own?"

The earl's long face drooped with guilt. "I suppose not, Sheba. But it has such magnificent illustrations."

He lurched from his chair to retrieve the text from one of his carefully organized bookshelves. Returning, he cradled the large volume in his arms as tenderly as an infant.

"See?" He pointed out an elaborate and beautifully drawn illustration of the Wife of Bath. "The workmanship is priceless. I've been waiting years for Samuel Thompson to let go of this." His eyes pleaded with her to understand.

Bathsheba had to swallow twice before she could answer. "Yes, dear. It's lovely." But not as lovely as paying off some of their mountain of debt would have been.

He beamed, but his smile faded as he examined her face. He sank into his chair with a sigh.

"Is it really as bad as all that?"

She reached across the desk and took his hand in a comforting grip.

"Matthew, we were forced to retrench last year because all the crops failed after that horrible summer. We hoped the harvest this year would correct the situation but, according to Mr. Oliver's figures, we will not be so fortunate."

Matthew still looked confused. Though the sweetest man

she had ever met, he had the worst head for business in Yorkshire. Never expecting to be a lord—after all, everyone had assumed Bathsheba would give her husband an heir—Matthew hadn't trained for it, and still spent most of his time with his nose buried in antiquarian texts. He had always been more than content to leave the business of managing the Yorkshire estate and the town house in London to her.

His face suddenly brightened. "But what about our investments? You've done a bang-up job managing them these last few years. Surely Oliver exaggerates. Why, you're the smartest female I've ever met. You always take care of everything."

Guilt burned through her veins like fire. She hadn't managed things well at all, not since the Earl of Trask abandoned her as his mistress two years ago. That had been the first disaster, and more had piled on ever since.

"I'm afraid there have been problems with our investments," she admitted. "I was forced to fire our man of business just last week. Mr. Gates saw fit to invest the vast majority of our funds in speculative ventures, all of which came to naught. I didn't realize how risky these schemes were until it was too late. We have nothing left. Nothing but debt, and I have only myself to blame."

Disbelief slowly replaced confusion on the earl's kind face. She couldn't look at him, so she pushed out of her chair and began pacing the threadbare carpet. More than anything she wanted to run from the library and from this house full of never-ending responsibilities and bitter memories. She wanted to run all the way to London, never to set foot in Ripon or Yorkshire again.

Mr. Oliver rose from his chair and began stacking the ledgers. When he had completed his task he turned to Bathsheba, watching her with patient sympathy. She and Mr. Oliver had worked together for years. He was one of the few men in her life she had come to respect.

"Will there be anything else, my lady?"

She stopped in front of the old chimneypiece, painted with a bucolic but sadly faded scene. She had to resist the temptation to lean against the mantel and burst into tears.

"Thank you, Mr. Oliver," she said, dredging up a smile. "That will be all for now."

Silence fell over the room after he left, and for a moment it seemed imbued with the peace of a warm summer day in the country. She let her gaze drift round the library, her perceptions sharpened to painful acuity by their impending disaster.

The late-afternoon sun streamed in through the mullioned windows, casting gentle beams on the old-fashioned Queen Anne chairs, the venerable but scarred desk, and the cracked leather wingchair stationed in front of the empty grate. To others it might all look old and worn, but the weariness of the room was lightened by bowls of yellow roses on side tables, and by Matthew's collection of antique globes, polished to a high gleam. The servants had to make do with very little, but they were fanatically loyal to the earl and did their best to transform the run-down estate into a home—more of a home than it had ever been during the time she had resided there with her husband, Reggie.

"Sheba, what are we going to do?"

She jerked around. Matthew hadn't moved from behind his desk, paralyzed, no doubt, by her incompetence. But a moment later he leapt to his feet and hurried over to join her.

"Don't look like that, my dear," he said. "You'll think of something—I know you will. You always do."

He gazed at her with perfect confidence, and her heart almost broke under the strain of his trust. Unlike most people she knew, Matthew had never lost faith in her. And he would do anything he could to help her.

She straightened her spine, disgusted by her momentary weakness. Matthew could no more help her than he could help himself. As usual, she was the one who would have to make things right. If that meant giving up her freedom, well, that was infinitely preferable to living in poverty and disgrace.

And there was Rachel to consider. Bathsheba would slit her own wrists before she let anything happen to her sister.

Pinning a confident smile on her face—marriage had taught her never to appear vulnerable—she led Matthew back to his desk.

"I do have a plan, and I must return to London on the morrow to put it into effect."

"Capital! I knew you'd have some trick up your sleeve." He sank into his chair, looking enormously relieved.

That made her laugh, but even to her own ears it sounded bitter.

"Hardly a trick. I see only one way out of this mess, and that's for me to find a rich husband. I'll demand—and get—a very large settlement. That way I can help you alleviate your debt, and you'll be able to rent the town house in Berkeley Square once I move out."

Her heart contracted painfully at the thought of leaving her elegant mansion, but Matthew had let her live there on sufferance. After Reggie died, the new earl would have been well within his rights to ask the widow Randolph to vacate the premises.

Matthew stared at her as if she'd lost her wits. "No, Bathsheba. I won't hear of it. You don't want to marry again—you vowed you wouldn't after—after—that is to say . . ." His words died away as he fiddled with a lump of sealing wax.

"After Lord Trask abandoned me to marry Sophie Stanton? Go ahead, Matthew. You can say it."

His soft brown eyes filled with sympathy, but he remained silent. She sighed and lowered herself into the wingchair, ignoring the crackle of ancient leather.

Her skin still crawled whenever she thought of those terrible weeks in Bath almost two years ago. Trying to come between Simon and Sophie—to wreck their engagement—had been a cruel and wrenching task. But she'd had little choice. Simon was one of the richest men in England, and if he had married her, all her money problems would have vanished like smoke. But after that episode she had lost her appetite for husband-hunting and had vowed to rescue the Randolph finances on her own. Instead, she had seen their investments—not very healthy in the first place—vanish under the weight of her own carelessness and a hired man's greed.

Matthew stirred, interrupting her gloomy ruminations.

"You don't have to marry just anyone," he said. "You could marry me."

His abrupt offer startled a laugh out of her. "My dear, please don't be ridiculous."

"I'm serious," he said stoutly. "I'm very fond of you. Always have been. And you're a beautiful, intelligent woman. Never thought that bastard cousin of mine deserved you. I understand your worth, Bathsheba, and I would never betray you. Only say the word and I'm yours." He finished his unexpected proposal with a shy, earnest smile.

Bathsheba's eyes stung. Lord, she hadn't felt so much like crying since her father died.

"Matthew, you're a dear man and I'm very fond of you, but we wouldn't suit. Besides, that would hardly solve our problem."

"But if we married we could consolidate households. Sell that bloody great barn in London and retrench here in the country."

Anything but that. She would throw herself into the Serpentine before she moved back to Yorkshire.

"Darling, you know I would go mad if I had to live here all year 'round. And I would make your life a misery. My mind is made up. I'll return to London right away and begin looking for a husband in earnest."

She smiled at him, seeking to ease his anxiety. "I'm not completely without resources. I don't think I'll have too much difficulty finding someone who will suit. He simply needs to be very wealthy, and to bother me as little as possible."

Matthew bristled. "Of course you won't have any trouble. Never meant to suggest otherwise. Just snap your fingers and every man in London will be falling all over you."

"Yes," she replied sarcastically. "But this time I have to persuade one of them to actually marry me."

He shushed her and rearranged the papers on his desk, but Bathsheba couldn't fail to notice his relief that she had rejected his proposal. No wonder she had turned so cynical. Men didn't want to marry her. They only wanted to bed her. Well, at least she could acquit Matthew of that charge. He didn't even want that.

"Bathsheba, what are you going to do about Rachel?"

Her heart jolted with a hard, extra beat. Why did Matthew have to bring her sister up now? Didn't they have enough to worry about? "I'm not going to do anything about Rachel. She's fine just where she is."

He fiddled with his papers some more. "I was thinking we could bring her here—to Compton Manor. I could look out for her, and I've more than enough servants to tend to her needs. That, at least, would relieve you of the expense of her upkeep."

She stared at him, stunned by the suggestion, fighting back incipient panic. To the world, her sister had died long ago. The scandal of her reappearance would surely doom Bathsheba's chances of securing a rich husband.

"Absolutely not." Her voice came out sharp as a blade. She cleared her throat and tried again. "Thank you for the offer, but Rachel is happy where she is. The Wilsons love her and would be very sorry to lose her."

That much, at least, was true. On her visits to Rachel, it was obvious to Bathsheba that her sister was happy, and that her caretakers were genuinely fond of her. No matter how much it cost—and it cost a great deal—she must keep

Rachel safely hidden away in the countryside. A rich husband could help her do just that.

The earl gave her countenance a thorough inspection. She calmly met his gaze, refusing to squirm or show any discomfort.

"Don't you think it's time for another physician to examine her?" he asked abruptly. "Perhaps something could be done for her."

She took a moment to quell the stab of anger and guilt that pierced her. "There's nothing that can be done to help. She's like a child, Matthew. The fever robbed her of both her speech and her wits. Rachel will never recover, and no one will understand why my father insisted we hide her away, or why I maintained the fiction of her death after Papa died."

Because you were a coward. The words whispered through her brain, but she ruthlessly beat them back. She might have been a coward, but Reggie had left her no choice.

"But . . ."

She leaned forward in her chair and glared at him. "Leave it alone, Matthew. I mean it."

As always, he crumbled before her will. "Well, she's your sister," he conceded. "I just wanted to help."

"Thank you, but she's my responsibility, not yours." She knew she sounded heartless, but Matthew's sentimentality—and naiveté—tried her patience. She was too weary and discouraged to pretend otherwise.

Bathsheba rose, smoothing down the silk of her skirts, taking comfort, as always, in the slippery, rich feel of the material draping her body.

"If you'll excuse me, I must speak to my abigail. We leave for London first thing in the morning." Now that her mind had been made up, she couldn't wait to shake the dirt of Yorkshire from her slippers and return to the city. Where she belonged.

Matthew rose, too, but suddenly looked as if someone had stuck a burr down the front of his breeches.

She sighed. "Is there something else?"

"Sir Philip Dellworthy and his lady heard you were back and sent round an invitation to dine with them tomorrow."

Bathsheba closed her eyes. Of course they had. She had arrived in Ripon only twenty-four hours ago, but she so rarely came north that her visit was bound to cause a stir amongst what passed for the local gentry. They would all want to see the Countess of Randolph and hear the latest gossip from town. And there was nothing she hated more than having to hobnob with a drawing room full of vulgar mushrooms, beefy squires, and disapproving, countrified matrons.

"And you told them what?"

He gulped. "That we would be happy to dine with them."

"Matthew!"

He cut her off. "It won't do to run away, Sheba. They'll think something's wrong, and that will cause gossip." He gave her a placating smile. "Must keep up appearances. That's what you always say, isn't it?"

She flung herself back into the creaky leather chair. "Yes, that's what I always say. Pour me a brandy, will you? And make it a generous one. I'm going to need it."

Bathsheba wedged herself into the corner of her luxurious carriage, resting her throbbing head against the squabs as the vehicle bumped over the appalling country roads. She let her eyelids droop, allowing herself to slip into velvety darkness. Sleep began to thread its foggy tendrils through her brain. Worries slowly dissipated as she drifted into welcome oblivion.

A loud thump, and then her head slammed into the side of the carriage as a wheel plunged into a hole the size of Westminster Abbey.

"Oh, I say, old girl," said Matthew, peering at her with concern. "Hope you didn't hurt yourself. The roads are ghastly, what with all the rain we've had lately."

She stifled an unladylike curse and raised her hands to smooth her coiffure.

Another twenty-four hours of country living had done nothing to improve her humor. After an intensely boring dinner with Matthew—who had brought the new copy of *Canterbury Tales* to the table with him—Bathsheba had retired to bed early. She had tossed and turned most of the night, kept awake by the quarter hours of the casement clock outside her door and by her gloomy thoughts. Sleep had finally come near dawn. A few hours later she had been awakened by a cacophony of birdsong, which somehow seemed a great deal louder and much more annoying than all the tumult and bustle of the London streets.

Her day had passed with all the speed of a hobbled tortoise. After thoroughly depressing herself with an inspection of the overgrown gardens and shabby manor house, she wrote several letters, read a book, and went over the ledgers again with Mr. Oliver. By the time she and Matthew set out for the Dellworthys at the absurdly early hour of four P.M., Bathsheba was ready to shriek with boredom and frustration. When she was young she had loved the country. Now she had no idea how it had ever appealed to her.

"Where in God's name is Dellworthy's estate? Scotland?" she groused. "We've been driving for ages."

Matthew smiled, ignoring her miserable temper. "Not much farther, my dear. And it's not really an estate. More like a smallish park. But the house is only a few years old, and Dellworthy spared no expense in the building of it. The man made a killing in the wool trade. Rich as Croesus, they say."

Bathsheba hated him already.

A few minutes later they bowled up a graveled drive through a small park, trimmed and landscaped to within an inch of its life. As the carriage pulled into the sweep in front of the house, Bathsheba jerked upright to stare out the window.

"I thought you said they built the house a few years ago."
Matthew nodded.

"It looks like a castle," she said. An absurd, miniature
castle. Loaded down with battlements, chimney stacks, and
what appeared to be a small Gothic chapel sticking out into
the front courtyard.

She looked at Matthew. "You must be joking."

He shrugged.

Sir Philip and his lady greeted them in an entrance hall
crammed with Roman statuary, then escorted them into
a red drawing room festooned with elaborately draped
curtains—also red—held up by gilt carved eagles. Large
pier glasses, bright crimson sofas in the French fashion, and
an Egyptian chimneypiece added up to a stylistic assault. I
the late afternoon sun, the entire room seemed to pulsate an
throb as if it were alive. Bathsheba surreptitiously rubbed
her temples, feeling the building ache of a migraine.

Lady Dellworthy introduced her to the other guests, including the vicar and his wife, some other respectable and
boring local worthies, and Miss Amanda Elliott, a middle-
aged spinster whom Bathsheba vaguely remembered from a
previous visit. Miss Elliott, however, clearly remembered
her, and not with fondness, if her coldly correct greeting was
any indication.

Lady Dellworthy tapped Bathsheba's arm with her fan.
"And here is our local physician, the worthy Dr. Littleton. And
his friend and former student, visiting from London. Perhaps
you have met him already. Dr. Blackmore, may I present Lady
Randolph, cousin to the current earl, Lord Randolph."

Bathsheba turned away from the chill of Miss Elliot. She
looked up, looked higher, and felt the breath clog in her
throat as she found herself staring into the compelling gaze
of a very tall and very broad-shouldered man. The throbbing, wound-colored drawing room faded away, as did the
pain in her temples.

Like an untried schoolgirl she stood motionless, fascinated by the color of his eyes—a shivery, wintery gray. They were hooded and penetrating, with a weariness that called out to her, sneaking past her defenses, setting off a bittersweet ache in her chest.

He didn't speak or move. She let her gaze drift over toolean features that were beautiful in a starkly masculine way. There were deep lines around a sensual, generous mouth, and a hard jaw shadowed with the hint of a night beard that matched the black of his unfashionably short hair.

Bathsheba blinked hard and tried to look away, but she couldn't. She had the bizarre notion she could stare into Dr. Blackmore's face for days on end, and never once feel bored.

Amusement began to replace the weariness in those amazing eyes. The doctor bowed, then straightened to his considerable height. She felt like an awkward child standing before him.

"Lady Randolph," he said, his deep, smooth voice sending a velvet hum up her spine. "It is a great pleasure to finally meet you. I have seen you at routs and concerts in London, of course, but have never had the honor of an introduction." His smile grew knowing, as if he sensed her discomposure and found it entertaining.

She jerked herself to attention, irritated by her uncharacteristic loss of control.

"Why, Dr. Blackmore," she replied in her best seductive purr. "How remiss of you not to secure an introduction. I'm sure I should be insulted. Perhaps if I bother to think about it long enough, I will be."

He looked startled. Lady Dellworthy squeaked and fluttered helplessly beside him.

Bathsheba turned away to address Dr. Littleton. Fortunately, she did remember him, and took refuge in asking questions about the general health of the local villagers. The physician happily obliged her, launching into a detailed recital. But Dr. Blackmore still loomed over her, a disturbing presence that set her nerves jangling like a steepleful of demented bells. She ignored him, studiously listening to his colleague. After a few minutes—although it felt so much longer—he walked away.

She gradually let out her breath, doing her best to pretend she was listening to Dr. Littleton drone on about Mary something-or-other's consumptive complaint. Why had she reacted so strongly to Dr. Blackmore? Certainly, he was a handsome man, but she had known dozens of handsome men, and taken a few of them into her bed. No. There was something else. Something that plucked a chord deep within her memory—something her conscious mind wanted to push away.

She dared a peek across the room, where Dr. Blackmore now stood talking with Miss Elliott and Matthew. As if she had tapped him on the shoulder, he glanced over, meeting her gaze with a direct, hard look.

Hard, but not cold. In fact, she felt burned by the heat in his eyes, and it frightened her. In a flash she suddenly re-membered why. That was exactly how Reggie had looked at her when first they met. As if he already possessed her, body and soul. That look had sucked her in, consumed her, and had eventually made her life a long purgatory of despair. Standing at her husband's graveside four years later, she had vowed she would never succumb to passion again.

Bathsheba stared into Dr. Blackmore's intense gaze a moment longer, then turned away.

Chapter 2

Lady Randolph was a finished piece of perfection, the most alluring John had ever encountered. Seated across from him at dinner, she ate with a dainty precision that utterly seduced him. From a distance, as he had seen her before in London, she was lovely—petite and lush, with gleaming coils of russet hair. But up close her beauty became a devastating weapon, one so powerful he had been knocked into speechless idiocy when Lady Dellworthy introduced them.

Even trapped in a labored conversation with Sir Philip, Lady Randolph sparkled with life. Her luminous green eyes shone with intelligence, presenting an enticing contrast to the pretty bow of her mouth. John had been tempted to lean down and taste that sweet, innocent-looking mouth when she stared up at him in the drawing room—Lady Dellworthy and her respectable guests be damned.

But then she had parted those soft lips and leveled him with a frosty insult. That had surprised him, given her initial response. She had certainly been affected by their meeting, unable to hide the evidence of her arousal. Her dilated pupils, the flush across her cheekbones, the hitch in her respiration, all told him she had responded in a visceral, sexual way. And, like a crowing fool, he'd been startled into giving her a triumphant smile that sent her running for the hills.

"What about you, Dr. Blackmore?" asked Sir Philip. "What do you think?"

He dragged his attention from Lady Randolph's entrancing face back to his host. "I beg your pardon, sir. I have been inattentive, which I can only blame on the excellence of the goose."

Sir Philip, seated at the head of the table, gave a congenial laugh as he leaned over and jabbed him in the bicep. "Oh, aye, the goose! I saw you with your eye on the countess. Not that I blame you. I can hardly pay attention to my own dinner, what with such great beauty next to hand."

He waggled his graying eyebrows at Lady Randolph, who sat at his left. She stared back at him before lifting her lips in a decidedly vicious sneer. Sir Philip smiled and carried on, apparently oblivious to the gaze that would have struck terror into the soul of a more perceptive man.

"Dr. Blackmore," he said, leaning back as one of an endless number of footmen removed his plate and replaced it with another, "I asked you and her ladyship what you think of our little castle. My lady worked hand in glove with the architect, and to great effect, if I do say so. Of course, it's nothing to compare with the beauties of Compton Manor. But still, I flatter myself that our efforts were not quite wasted."

Lady Randolph's sneer turned lethal. "Very few houses in Yorkshire can compare to Compton Manor," she said in a cold voice. "It's a pity that so many people these days fail to understand the principles of good taste. I always think it a great mistake when amateurs take upon themselves the work of experts."

Sir Philip flushed the color of faded brick. She smiled and turned back to her plate, delicately spearing a single, perfect strawberry and raising it to her mouth. Despite his irritation at her rudeness, John couldn't help but notice the moist fullness of her lips as they closed around the red berry or the smooth column of her slender throat as she swallowed. An inconvenient erection began to swell against the placket of his trousers.

"Oh, Dellworthy," called his wife from the other end of the table. "Are you boasting about the house again?" She gave a hearty chuckle. "He loves to talk about our little manor and my small role in its creation. My dear Lady Randolph, I assure you I tell him that he mustn't."

John smothered a grin at the stunned look on Lady Randolph's face. Her narrowed eyes and flaring nostrils registered her distaste with Lady Dellworthy's slapdash manners. In London, one would never call down the dining room table, at least not in a formal gathering. He suspected Lady Randolph rarely attended informal ones.

As oblivious to danger as her husband had been a few minutes earlier, Lady Dellworthy carried on. "My dear countess, did my husband point out to you the vaulted ceiling?"

John winced. The lady's voice had a peculiar, carrying quality. Even her husband and some of the other guests looked embarrassed. Lady Randolph looked ready to spit nails.

Their hostess waved an arm at the ceiling, her numerous gold bracelets clinking with a cheery little jangle. "I wanted to create the effect of a Norman cathedral. A nave in miniature. From the outside of the house, the dining room resembles a chapel. Perhaps you noticed that when you arrived? I think it a great success."

Obediently, the guests directed their gazes to the ceiling. All except Lady Randolph.

Not wishing to appear rude, John also looked up at the ceiling, a mad jumble of Norman and Gothic styles, with moldings and arches and painted chevrons, and even a few mythic beasts writhing away in the corners of the room.

He lowered his gaze to Lady Randolph's face. Her eyes

flashed, her lips parted, and he jumped into the conversation to cut off what would surely be another devastating insult.

"The ceiling is quite splendid, my lady," he said. "Did you develop the design for the chevrons yourself, or did you model them after an existing pattern?"

Lady Dellworthy blushed like a maiden, but Lady Randolph glared at him with eyes narrowed to irritated slits. He gave her a bland smile, even though he had to bite the inside of his cheek to keep from laughing. The entire house was an exercise in overblown vulgarity, but that was no excuse for rudeness. The imperious little countess—clearly a snob—needed schooling in simple courtesy, and part of him wished he could be the man to take on the task.

His conversational dodge worked, as Lady Dellworthy prattled on in answer to his question. Several other guests chimed in with their opinions and the crisis passed. He let his gaze roam the table before returning it to the red-haired vixen. Lady Randolph eyed him resentfully, then suddenly looked down. He was amazed to see a faint blush cross her cheeks, the clear wash of pink and the downcast eyes riveting his attention.

A discreet throat-clearing on his right recalled him. Miss Elliott, seated next to him, gave him a faint smile.

"A question, if I may, Dr. Blackmore," she said. "I understand that in addition to having a successful practice in Mayfair, you are also a member of the staff at St. Bartholomew's Hospital. Dr. Littleton says you hope to set up a lying-in ward at the hospital. Are there not already several such institutions in the city? Why do you feel it necessary to establish another?"

He set down his fork and studied her clever, narrow face. Few people, particularly those of the upper orders, displayed the slightest interest in his work. If they did, it was to enquire about the most effective treatment for gallstones, or the best

way to wrap a gouty foot. But Miss Elliott actually seemed
to want an answer.

"You are correct. Several lying-in hospitals already exist
in the city," he replied. "But their role in caring for women
both before and after they give birth is limited."

The spinster nodded encouragement, so John launched
into a detailed description of his dream to establish a ward
at Bart's for impoverished pregnant women, including prostitutes. The staff would do more than just deliver their infants and then throw them back out into the street. They
would also teach new mothers how to care for themselves
and their newly born babies. Miss Elliott listened attentively,
interjecting occasionally with interest and a surprising
degree of knowledge.

Only when John had embarked on a graphic description
of the dangers of childbed fever did he notice all the guests
at the table had fallen silent. He looked around. Sir Philip
stared at him with bug-eyed horror, Lady Dellworthy had
turned a sickly shade of green, and Mrs. Spencer, the vicar's
wife, seemed ready to swoon.

As for Lady Randolph, with her elbow planted on the
table and her perfect chin resting in her palm, she looked . . .
bored. He met her emerald gaze. One delicate brow twitched
up, as if to signal her disdain.

"Well, John," said Dr. Littleton, breaking the uncomfortable hush. "We must remember that the ladies are unused to
such discussion." His old teacher's eyes laughed at him. "Especially at the dinner table."

"I disagree," Miss Elliott said in a lofty voice. "I have
found it most invigorating."

Lady Randolph rolled her eyes, and John had to fight the
overwhelming desire to reach across the table and shake her.

Instead, he directed an apologetic smile at his host.
"Forgive me, Sir Philip. I have a tendency to forget myself

when discussing my work. Dr. Littleton has often remarked upon it."

Sir Philip hemmed and hawed, extracting a large hand-kerchief from his pocket and wiping his perspiring brow. Fortunately, Miss Elliott came to the company's rescue again.

"Dr. Littleton," she said, "please tell me how Mrs. Mc-Cartney is faring. I mean to visit her this week, if you tell me the danger of infection has passed."

Littleton's expression turned grave. John knew his friend had spent much of the last week treating a family of poor villagers. Husband, wife, and all three children had fallen ill with a putrid infection. The smallest child—little more than an infant—had died.

"Mrs. McCartney is recovering from the fever, although I fear she will not soon recover from the loss of her baby."

John heard a small gasp from the other side of the table. He looked at Lady Randolph.

"This woman. Mrs. McCartney. She lost her child to a fever?" she asked Dr. Littleton.

"I'm sorry to say so, my lady. But yes. The child passed yesterday."

John frowned, puzzled by the sudden pallor of Lady Randolph's countenance. She blinked and, for a moment, he thought a mist of tears obscured her gaze.

"Oh, Dr. Littleton," interrupted Lady Dellworthy. "Please tell me there is no risk of contagion in the village. One hears such dreadful things these days. Disease and riot. Where will it end? I live in dread of gangs roaming the countryside. Why, just look at what happened in Pentrich. I vow! We shall all be murdered in our beds. That is if we don't all die of the typhus first."

"Oh, tut-tut, my dear," soothed Sir Philip. "Nothing of the sort. The Crown will see to it that the Pentrich mob gets its comeuppance. The ringleaders will swing by year's end. Hang the whole lot of them, I say. That'll teach them to challenge their betters."

He smiled reassuringly at his wife, and several others around the table nodded their satisfaction that the poor bastards who had led the uprising in Pentrich—decent men, by most accounts—would be executed for high treason.

John clenched a fist around the slender stem of his crystal goblet. Anger pulsed through his veins. Thousands of men and women had been laid low by famine and disease this past year alone, some of those men loyal soldiers who had returned from the war with no employment to support their wives and children. But still the aristocracy retreated behind their high walls and gated estates, enjoying their privileged lives in willful ignorance.

Safely ensconced on a tidy and prosperous estate in the country, John's own family was no better. How often had his mother nagged him to give up his work with the poor and concentrate only on building a lucrative medical practice to the ton?

He struggled to keep anger out of his voice. "Perhaps, Sir Philip, if those in power attempted to alleviate the poverty that has befallen so many of our countrymen, addressing the food shortages in particular, we would not find ourselves having to contend with uprisings."

"Oh, I say, I don't think—" Sir Philip began to protest.

John cut him off. "As a doctor, every day I see lives cut short by starvation and disease." Littleton shook his head in warning, but John ignored him, too caught up in the frustration always lurking below the calm exterior he struggled to maintain.

"Can you imagine the despair that plagues a man when he cannot feed his family, or afford a doctor for his sick child? How many women die in childbirth, shrieking in unbearable agony, for want of a doctor or a midwife they could not afford? Who can blame a man for fighting such intolerable injustice? You might as well hang me, for I would likely do the same if I could see no other recourse."

He let his gaze sweep the table, not bothering to hide his

disgust. The Dellworthys and their guests averted their eyes. Only Lady Randolph, her face pale and composed, looked at him. Her hand, now resting on the table, slid a few inches across the starched linen before she jerked it back into her lap.

He frowned, his anger diverted as he noticed her nails were ragged and filed to the quick. No lady of the ton that he knew had such unkempt fingernails. Hers might have belonged to a child, one who compulsively bit them from nervous habit.

"Really, Blackmore!" Sir Philip's furious voice boomed out, bringing John back to the discussion. "It's treasonous to speak of such things. This is England, man, not France. We must crush these uprisings. Look at what happened to the Prince Regent just this past January. He was almost shot dead on his way to Parliament."

Lady Dellworthy gave a faint shriek. "Oh, do not remind me, husband. I didn't sleep for weeks after that horrific event. To imagine the Prince murdered . . . it doesn't bear thinking about!"

A charged silence fell over the room. His host glared at him and Littleton shook his head again, but John couldn't bring himself to apologize. He could forgive many things, including the Dellworthys' cheerful vulgarity and boastful displays of wealth, but not their callous lack of charity.

"Nothing about the Royal Family bears thinking about." Lady Randolph's voice, as dry as the expensive champagne they drank, sliced through the tension. "A more useless lot has never walked the earth, and the Prince Regent is the worst of them. I, for one, thought it a great tragedy that the marksman missed his shot."

Lady Dellworthy gasped with outrage. Out of the corner of his eye, John saw Miss Elliott grow rigid with indignation. But Littleton was having trouble repressing a laugh, and Lord Randolph, having been frozen into submission some time ago by one of Lady Randolph's killing glares, merely looked useless.

Lady Randolph carefully dissected a poached pear, seemingly oblivious to the salvo she had fired into the room. She glanced at him, and he caught a flash of mischief and of, what? Defiance in her bright eyes? As her gaze lanced through him, his anger drained away.

"Why, Lady Randolph, are you a radical?" His voice came out on a husky, deeper note, but he didn't care.

Her imperious eyebrows rose with elegant disdain. "Hardly, but I detest vulgarity. No one is more vulgar than the Prince Regent. He should be hanged for that offense, if no other."

Sir Philip tried to stifle a groan and failed. He stared pointedly at his wife, social panic stretching his face into a grim mask.

Lady Dellworthy leapt into the breach. "Well, ladies," she cried, lurching to her feet. "Shall we leave the men to their brandy and cigars?"

She scurried from the dining room before the men could stand, Miss Elliott and the other female guests trailing in her wake. Lady Randolph patted her pink mouth with a spotless napkin, rose in a leisurely, graceful movement, and nodded to the men. They came to their feet as one, staring at her like a group of idiotic schoolboys.

He couldn't help but smile. Her ladyship had the tongue of a viper, but she was nothing short of magnificent.

As she drifted from the room, her soft green skirts whispering against a body made for pleasure, he felt every muscle tighten with an overwhelming sexual intent. It had been months since he'd taken a woman to his bed. If he had his way, that was about to change.

Bathsheba's migraine thudded inside her skull like the beat of a kettledrum. She supposed she could ask Lady Dellworthy for some headache powders, but her hostess would more likely give her arsenic. She almost couldn't blame her.

Blast.

What had possessed her to come to Blackmore's defense? The man had stated his case admirably. Not that she necessarily agreed with everything he said, but she loathed prattling fools, and both the Dellworthys fell into that category.

And the discussion about Mrs. McCartney and her baby had unnerved her. Bathsheba had also sat vigil by a child's sickbed, long years ago. She had watched helplessly as fever brought her sister to the brink of death, and then robbed her of any semblance of normal life. When Lady Dellworthy had brushed aside Mrs. McCartney's tragedy, she felt the old pain clawing at her heart. She should be grateful Blackmore had taken their hosts to task and saved her the trouble.

But then why had she jumped into the fray, except to respond to some elusive emotion she had glimpsed in his extraordinary gray eyes? She couldn't seem to attach a name to that emotion, and she didn't think she wanted to.

Miss Elliott cleared her throat, glowering at her from across the tea table, as did Mrs. Spencer and two other women whose names she couldn't remember. They must think they harbored a seditious traitor in their midst, although Bathsheba couldn't think of one person in London who didn't hold Prinny in complete contempt. But that kind of opinion would never do in the country, especially amongst the womenfolk.

"More tea, countess?" Lady Dellworthy regarded her as one might a rabid dog.

"Yes, thank you," she replied, handing over her cup with a smile. Her hostess took it and snatched her arm away, as if she expected Bathsheba to take a bite out of her flesh. She refilled it, then gingerly slid it back across the table.

Bathsheba repressed a sigh. Perhaps she should fall to the floor and begin foaming at the mouth. They likely wouldn't be a bit surprised.

Tomorrow—and her return to London—couldn't come soon enough.

The conversation picked up again, but the other women pointedly ignored her. As she sipped her tea—an excellent and very expensive Lapsang souchong, of course—Bathsheba tried to amuse herself by wondering when respectable women had begun to hate her so much. It had happened so gradually that at first she had barely noticed, or had written it off to envy. But even before Reggie's death the slights had become obvious, thanks in large part to the rumors of her adulterous affairs. Rumors started by her insanely jealous husband. It didn't used to bother her, but now she wished she could talk as other women talked, about the things women talked about. But she had lost the knack for domestic conversation long ago.

The doors of the blood-red drawing room swung open and the men came in. Matthew threw a nervous glance around the room, as if half expecting that Bathsheba would have knifed the ladies while the men sipped brandy and discussed politics. In a reversal of the natural order, the other men avoided her as well, taking empty seats away from the tea table or squeezing onto the sofas and love seats with the other ladies.

All except the annoying Dr. Blackmore, who fixed on her like a hound on a scent. He strode straight across the room, hooked his arm around a chair, and pulled it right up next to her. She edged as far away from him as she could, disconcerted by the flush of heat that raced over her skin. Moisture began to mist her face and she had to resist the temptation to blot it away.

As Lady Dellworthy prepared his teacup—treating him as if he belonged in a kennel with the other mad dog—Bathsheba dared to give him a quick inspection.

Oh, Lord.

The man was handsome. Long and lean, but muscular. Broad-shouldered. And obviously easy in his own skin. Just sitting next to him made her pulse pound almost as hard as her throbbing head. She felt hot and jumpy, and wished she could call for her carriage, drag Matthew out by the ear, and flee to the uncertain safety of Compton Manor.

Even more alarming than his handsome face and big, masculine body was the way he had watched her all throughout dinner—with a predatory gaze all too familiar, since that was the way Reggie had studied her, too. The foolish girl inside still responded to that male intensity, preening with delight, even though the woman she had become knew how utterly dangerous a man in the grip of such a dark passion could become. Bathsheba had promised never to fall victim to that twisted emotion again—no matter how compelling the man who felt it might be. And the man sitting next to her was so much more compelling than her husband had ever been.

As Lady Dellworthy gave Blackmore his tea, her hand shook and the tea washed out of the cup and into the saucer.

"Oh," she gasped. "Do forgive me, Dr. Blackmore. I don't know why I should be so clumsy."

The doctor gave her a rueful smile. "You were no doubt unsettled by my foolishly heated arguments over dinner. Please forgive me, my lady. I can only hope you will excuse the poor manners of a man of science who ventures little into polite company."

Lady Dellworthy relaxed under the easy warmth of his apology, rewarding him with a girlish giggle. In a trice, she seemed to have forgotten the whole episode, chattering on to him about a visit she planned to make to London.

Bathsheba swallowed an unladylike snort. Obviously the good doctor knew exactly how to behave in polite company, and wrap said company—especially the female variety—around his little finger. She suspected that ten thousand apologies on her part wouldn't make a whit of difference to Lady Dellworthy, or any other woman in the room, for that matter. But they all appeared to have quickly forgiven him, since they were now hanging on his every word with breathless anticipation.

She took a gulp of tea and burned her tongue. Cursing silently, she banged her cup and saucer onto the tea table, attracting both Blackmore's and Lady Dellworthy's attention.

"Is everything well, Lady Randolph?" the doctor enquired in a mild voice.

"Yes, thank you. Please continue with your conversation."

Her hostess began to flutter nervously. Again. "If you'll excuse me, I'll just go see if Lord Randolph wants another piece of plum cake." As Lady Dellworthy scuttled away, Blackmore switched his unnerving quicksilver gaze back to Bathsheba.

"Lord Randolph says you rarely visit Ripon, preferring to live in the city. Why is that?" he asked.

Blast the man. Why wouldn't he leave her alone?

"I should think the answer is obvious," she replied in a nasty voice. "Because I hate the country." Perhaps if she were rude, he would go away.

No such luck. Instead, he began to query her about friends, seeking to discover if they had any mutual acquaintances. He settled into his chair, long limbs relaxed, his manner casual, but she wasn't fooled. She saw the sharp gleam in his eyes and the hungry way he studied her mouth. Perspiration dampened the inside of her thighs and the back of her knees, and she had to call on all her discipline not to squirm in her seat.

After several minutes of conversation—stilted on her part, completely at ease on his—Bathsheba saw Miss Elliott make her determined way toward them. No doubt she thought to save the doctor from her infamous coils. Unfortunately the pursed-lip spinster didn't realize she was the one who needed rescuing.

Miss Elliott planted herself in Lady Dellworthy's vacant chair, looking down her thin nose at them from her self-righteous heights. "Sir, Dr. Littleton tells me that you originally hail from the country. The Lake District, I believe?"

"That is true, Miss Elliott. I was born and raised in a village near Keswick."

She bestowed a beneficent smile upon him while doing a fine job of ignoring Bathsheba. "So lovely, the Lake District. You must miss it. And you must be glad to escape the grime and heat of London in the summer to enjoy the quiet beauties of Ripon and the glories of the surrounding dales."

Perhaps her headache was to blame, but Bathsheba could no longer tolerate more social inanities—or being treated like a pariah. "Good God, Miss Elliott. What are you talking about? The only thing worse than Yorkshire in the summer is Yorkshire in the winter. No person of intellect would want to spend any amount of time here. It's the most boring place on earth."

Too late, she remembered the spinster considered herself a person of intellect. She sighed, inwardly correcting herself. The only thing more boring than Yorkshire in the summer was a bluestocking in a fit of pique.

Miss Elliott's firm mouth thinned into an outraged line. If the woman had a pistol, there was little doubt she would aim the damn thing at Bathsheba's head and pull the trigger.

At least that would get rid of this headache.

She choked back a laugh as the spinster excused herself and stalked across the room to join Matthew.

"Why do you do that?" Blackmore asked, looking irritated.

"I don't know," she mumbled, suddenly tired of fighting. "Perhaps it's my headache. I believe someone is firing cannons inside my skull."

He reached out a big hand and took her wrist in a light but firm grasp. She tried to jerk it away.

"What are you doing?" she spluttered.

"Feeling your pulse. Sit still," he ordered.

She tugged, but his grip was unbreakable. Hard, warm fingers on the fragile skin of her wrist sent a shuddering wave of excitement through her veins all the way to her heart.

"Tumultuous," he pronounced. "I'll send over a powder tonight and stop by Compton Manor tomorrow."

"Don't bother," she said, finally able to snatch her hand back. Clearly, he had let her do so. "I'm returning to London tomorrow. I'll be fine once I'm away from the quiet beauties of Ripon," she finished sarcastically.

He regarded her with a cool arrogance. "I wouldn't advise that, Lady Randolph. You need rest, not travel."

"Thank you for your advice, Doctor. Shall I pay you now, or will you send me a bill for your services?"

As he studied her, the flinty look in his eyes gradually softened. "It's obvious something troubles you, my lady. Tell me what it is. Perhaps I can help."

She gasped, and he unleashed an engaging grin. Her heart fluttered madly in her chest.

"Doctors are all professional busybodies, Lady Randolph. We're trained to notice small things—signs of trouble. Your nails, for instance. You bite them, don't you?"

Her throat closed around the pain that lodged there. She couldn't move or speak. But she must. She must get away. Blackmore was the most dangerous man she had ever met.

He gazed down into her face, waiting confidently for her to break. She dredged up every ounce of willpower, calling on years of discipline, hard-fought and won in the face of her husband's tormenting ways.

Forcing herself to rise gracefully from her chair, she signaled with a nod to Matthew that she wished to go home. She turned and glanced down at the doctor. He looked anything but pleased.

"You flatter yourself, Doctor," she said coldly. "I have no troubles. And if I did, you would be the last man on earth I would go to for help."

Chapter 3

Matthew stared at Bathsheba, his irritation obvious even in the dim light of the coach lamps. Despite the shadows obscuring his face, she couldn't mistake that look. Sadly, they had at least another twenty minutes to Compton Manor. Plenty of time for a lecture from her aggrieved cousin.

"Good God, Sheba. Must you always play the harridan when you come to Ripon? For once, you might think about how your behavior reflects on me."

She rounded her eyes, feigning confusion. Then she fluttered her lashes, just for good measure.

"Stow it, cousin," Matthew growled, his basset face unusually fierce.

She grimaced and braced herself as the carriage jostled through another craterlike hole.

"I'm sorry, dear," she said, trying to sound apologetic. Matthew so rarely got angry she felt compelled to make amends. "I was joking, you know. I don't really think Prinny should be hanged. Not really. Well, maybe just a little."

He ignored her halfhearted apology as he went on to catalogue all the offenses she'd committed over the course of the evening. She didn't try to defend herself, since she was guilty as charged. Her friends and acquaintances in London had grown used to her sharp tongue—they expected and even looked forward to when she unleashed her vitriol on some hapless fool. She'd grown tired of the act some time ago, but it seemed like a second skin she couldn't shed.

Matthew finally wound down, subsiding into a grumpy silence. She dredged up a contrite smile, hoping it didn't look as rusty as it felt.

"I'm truly sorry, Matthew. If we ever have dinner with the Dellworthys again, I shall attempt to be on my best behavior."

He snorted. "Don't count on any more invitations. Lady Dellworthy looked ready to bolt out the front door into the night."

"Oh, no, dear. She would never do that. Not with all those evil gangs roaming the countryside, lying in wait to snatch up such a tasty morsel as Miranda Dellworthy."

That won her a grudging laugh, but he still appeared troubled.

She sighed. "You can blame it on my dreadful headache. That part, at least, is the truth."

Her head still throbbed to the sickening tempo of the migraine, one of her worst in months. Now that she thought about it, it had been foolish to refuse Blackmore's offer to send powders. These days the only thing that stopped the pain was laudanum, but she loathed the mental fog that came with it. Perhaps the doctor had some new potion in his bag of tricks that could provide her with some relief. But when he had gazed at her with that arrogant, all-knowing expression on his face, she had reacted instinctively, pushing back as hard as she could.

Bathsheba gave a little shiver as she recalled the feel of Blackmore's strong hand on her wrist. For those few seconds, while his long fingers probed for her pulse, she had forgotten her headache, the blood-red drawing room, and even Lady Dellworthy. She had been all sensation, the blood pounding through her veins as heat flushed her skin.

She shifted on the velvet squabs, irritated by the tightening in her belly and the growing softness between her thighs.

"Really, Matthew," she groused, trying to divert her wayward imagination, "you can hardly blame me for losing my temper. Sir Philip and his wife are such parvenus. And that house. Ridiculous!"

"They're not my first choice for an evening's entertainment, either, but I won't excuse your behavior. However, I must say I found the rest of the company quite pleasant, didn't you?"

She rolled her eyes. Pleasant? Fearfully dull was more like it, with their supposedly happy marriages and their respectable lives, hiding any number of nasty secrets behind a facade of gentility. There were always secrets. Always nasty secrets. Bathsheba hated them for pretending otherwise.

Peering out the carriage window into the fading summer evening, she wanted nothing more than to brood in silence, alone with her gloomy thoughts. But those thoughts made her squirm even more, because once Matthew stopped his yammering all she could think about was Blackmore. The blasted doctor with his beautiful but merciless eyes had breached her defenses, trying to pull her own terrible secrets into the glaring light of day. Just thinking about the consequences of that revelation stole the breath from her lungs.

She fought back another shiver and huddled deeper into her silk cloak. With a little luck, she'd be back in London in a few days and would completely forget Blackmore.

Matthew cleared his throat and tapped his walking stick on the carriage floor. She met his gaze.

"Yes, Matthew?"

"What did you think of Miss Elliott? A most intelligent woman, wouldn't you say?"

The hesitant but eager note in his voice made her sit up straight. She studied his face, startled to see him looking so shy. Even in the dim light of the lamps, she could see him blush.

"Yes," she answered cautiously. "Miss Elliott does appear to be a very intelligent woman."

He grinned, reminding her of a happy dog that had just been tossed a hefty soup bone.

"Isn't she? And she's a wonder around the village. Reverend Spencer says he wouldn't know what to do without her. She's always full of schemes to help everyone, and does so much for the deserving poor."

It took an effort, but she managed to hold back an acid retort on behalf of the undeserving poor. Do-gooders—especially bluestocking do-gooders—made her break out in a rash.

"Is that right?" she replied in a mild voice.

He nodded enthusiastically. "And do you know what else?"

"I can't imagine."

"She loves antiquarian books almost as much as I do. Why, she said my latest *Canterbury Tales* is finer than any she has ever seen! And she should know, since her brother teaches classics at Oxford."

He prattled away, happily recounting Miss Elliott's many virtues, as Bathsheba's headache swelled to epic proportions. Doom had just edged a bit closer.

Matthew had feelings for Miss Elliott, and the force of that realization hit her like a blow. She quickly replayed the events of the evening, trying to recall the interactions between her cousin and the starched-up spinster. In the drawing room, they had chattered away with all the comfort of old friends. And now that she thought about it, Miss Elliott had seemed quite taken with Matthew. Either she returned his affections or she had lately discovered a burning ambition to become the next Countess of Randolph.

Which would make Bathsheba the dowager countess, totally dependent on a man who could be swayed by any woman with a strong will. And Miss Elliott's will was strong, indeed, almost as strong as her dislike of Bathsheba.

As she leaned her aching head against the squabs, visions of life in Compton Manor's shabby old dower house flashed through her brain. She would be forced to leave London. Her widow's portion was minuscule, since her father had been desperate to have the bulk of her settlements at the time of her marriage. Only Matthew's generosity and her own ability to secure extravagant gifts from her lovers had allowed her to maintain an elegant lifestyle since Reggie's death.

She looked up to find Matthew eyeing her with a knowing arch to his eyebrows.

Oh, Lord. What else?

"You seemed quite cozy with Dr. Blackmore in your corner of the drawing room," he said with a sly grin.

Bathsheba's mouth dropped open when he winked at her.

"Don't try to deny it," he said with a waggle of his finger. "The man was clearly entranced with you. If you're looking for a husband, Sheba, you could certainly do worse."

Frustration and nerves bundled into a hard knot in the center of her chest.

"Don't be ridiculous, Matthew. Dr. Blackmore is an immensely irritating man. Besides," she said pettishly, "he's not nearly rich enough. And, he's also a physician. He must have to work all the time."

Matthew shook his head. "Blackmore's not just a self-made man. His family is good. Landed gentry somewhere up . . . now, where did Miss Elliott say he was from?"

"Keswick," she replied, unable to stop herself.

"Right. His family is quite wealthy, too. Own a very tidy estate, so Miss Elliott says. Unfortunately, Blackmore is a younger son, so he won't inherit. But he must get some income from his family and I know he has a thriving practice in Mayfair. With a little luck, he could be as successful as Dr. Knighton, or at least that's what—"

"Miss Elliott says." She finished his sentence in a waspish tone.

"I'm just saying you should keep him in mind," Matthew replied in an injured voice. "Everyone in the room saw he was very interested in you."

She scowled, annoyed by how much that pleased the foolish girl within. "Dr. Blackmore is the kind of man who flirts with any passably good-looking woman."

He began to splutter in protest but she held up her hand.

"No more. We're in deep trouble, Matthew, and Dr. Blackmore is certainly not the answer. Our finances require a great deal more than he could provide. I'll return to London tomorrow, and I'm sure I can find myself a rich husband before the Season starts in October. The ground is rather thin in town these days, but I'll manage."

He eyed her doubtfully but held his tongue.

"I don't even like Dr. Blackmore," she snapped, unable to keep her mouth shut. "He can keep his pulse-taking and his advice to himself."

Matthew's eyebrows shot up. She clamped her teeth shut, furious that she had revealed so much. Even with the blasted fellow miles away, Blackmore could make her blurt out the most foolish things.

Fortunately, the carriage had already turned into the long drive leading up to the manor and was now coming to a gentle halt by the south front door. Matthew helped her alight and she swept past him and into the hallway.

Sewell, the butler, gave a deep bow. "My lady."

She continued past him, heading to the stairs. If she didn't take something for this migraine immediately, her head would explode.

"My lady." Sewell's voice held a note of urgency.

She swallowed a groan and turned around, keeping one hand on the banister.

"Yes, Sewell?"

"An express came for you this evening, madam. From Thirsk."

Alarm shot along her already jangling nerves. Her sister resided in Thirsk, with the Wilsons. They would never send an express unless something was very wrong.

She stood paralyzed on the bottom step, overwhelmed

with dread, unable to face yet another addition to her enormous mountain of problems.

Matthew took the missive from Sewell and came to her side.

"Come, my dear." He gently steered her into the library. "We'll read it together."

She dropped wearily into the old leather armchair, praying that time would slow down—even reverse itself—as he brought her a large brandy.

"Do you want me to read it?" he asked.

She nodded, taking a gulp from the crystal tumbler. The liquor poured a welcome heat into her stomach and through her cold limbs.

Matthew scanned the short note, his brows drawing together in a heavy frown. Bathsheba's heart took a sickening dive to her feet.

"Rachel is ill," he said. "Very ill. A putrid infection of the lungs that came on quickly." He looked up, his droopy eyes full of sympathy. "The doctor is doing all he can, but . . ."

"Oh, God," she whispered, fighting back a hollow, ringing despair.

She wanted to crawl away and hide. Someplace deep and dark, where she didn't have to think or be responsible for one more person. The thought of sitting next to Rachel again, watching the life drain out of her, was almost more than she could bear. Bathsheba knew how deadly these fevers could be, the havoc they could wreak. And, coward that she was, part of her feared that if she went to nurse her sister she would fall ill, too. She might end up like Rachel, her mind and body all but destroyed.

"You don't have to go," Matthew blurted out, divining her thoughts. "The Wilsons will do all that needs to be done."

For a moment, she gave in to the fear that seemed to reside permanently in her heart. As much as she loved Rachel, she had gradually come to loathe her sister's physical weakness.

But Bathsheba was the weak one now, and she loathed herself for it.

She pushed herself out of the chair. "No. I must leave immediately. If you would see to the carriage, I would be grateful. It will only take me a few minutes to pack."

"You can't leave now," he exclaimed. "It's after nine o'clock."

She moved toward the door, barely pausing to glance back. "It's not full dark yet, and the night promises to be fine. The moon's almost full and my coachman is used to driving at night."

"But it's not safe," he protested. "What if you encounter a highwayman?"

"My grooms carry pistols, Matthew."

He made a choking noise. She finally took pity on him, turning around to meet his worried gaze.

"In case you were wondering," she said, "I carry one, too." And given the mood she was in, any highwayman who crossed her path might very well come to regret it.

Her cousin blinked rapidly. "You're a good girl, Sheba."

"No, I'm not. You said it yourself—I'm a harridan." She gave him a bitter smile and left the room.

"We've arrived back at Compton Manor, my lady."

Boland's Yorkshire burr penetrated the exhaustion that crushed Bathsheba into a listless daze. She blinked, forcing her bleary vision to focus on the comforting features of her longtime friend and abigail. The older woman sat bolt upright on the other seat of the carriage, looking as prim and self-contained as she had when they first set out from Thirsk several hours ago.

"Just a few more minutes, Lady Randolph, and I'll have you in a nice hot bath," Boland added. "You can eat your supper in bed."

Steel-framed spectacles obscured Boland's eyes, but

Bathsheba could feel her perusing her carefully, as she had done for years—ever since she was a little girl on her father's estate and Boland was her mother's nurse.

"And, your ladyship, we won't be leaving for London tomorrow, either. No, don't bother arguing with me. I won't have it." The older woman glared at her, the rigid posture of her slight figure signaling her willingness to fight.

Actually, it hadn't even occurred to Bathsheba to object. Time grew pressing, but she couldn't bear the thought of days on the road, jostling through the heat and the dust, only to return to her empty town house and all the problems she must face. Five days by Rachel's bedside had left her worn to the bone and feeling as substantial as a wisp of steam from a teapot.

They came to a halt in front of Compton Manor. The steps to the coach were quickly let down, and her groom handed her with tender care to the gravel of the drive. She staggered, feeling woozy as she stepped into the glare of the hot summer day. Her stomach cramped with nausea and she had to close her eyes and grab hold of the carriage door.

A slim but strong arm came around her waist. "I knew this would affect you." Boland's voice was grim. "You do too much, my lady. There was no need for you to sit up last night—"

"Hush," snapped Bathsheba, mindful of the servants clustered about them. "Don't fuss, Boland. I just need rest."

She shrugged off Boland's arm and headed to the door of the manor, which stood open in the fine weather. Her body ached with a weariness unlike any she had ever felt. Each step toward the house seemed to take her farther away, as if fatigue distorted the space before her. Even the air seemed to vibrate with a strange hum, a hum that dulled her senses and weighted down her limbs, making her wonder how she would ever manage to climb the stairs to her room.

"Sheba!"

Matthew rushed out the front door. He skidded to a halt

in front of her, spraying gravel over the top of her half-boots before enveloping her in a fierce hug. She gave a gasp and stumbled against him, stunned by the searing pain that ripped through the muscles of her neck and back.

"My lord!" Boland's sharp voice cut into the haze of pain. "Her ladyship should not be kept standing out here in the heat. Nor does she need you mauling her."

Matthew quickly released her and stepped back, unnerved as always by Boland's imperious manner. Bathsheba choked out a laugh that turned into a burning cough. She gasped, finally catching her breath.

"You forget yourself, Boland," she managed.

Her abigail stared back defiantly, and Bathsheba relented. "Go to my room and prepare a bath. I'll be up in a few minutes."

"See that you are," Boland muttered in a low voice as she stalked into the house.

"Honestly, Sheba, that woman is a menace," said Matthew.

"Forgive her, Cousin," she replied, taking his arm and steering him into the house. "It's been a long five days, and we're both very tired."

If every muscle in her body didn't ache so much, Bathsheba was certain she could have fallen asleep standing upright.

"Is everything all right?" Matthew peered at her anxiously as he helped her up the front steps and into the cool dark of the entrance hall. "Is . . ."

"Yes. All is well, thank goodness." She glanced around. The servants were busy unloading her luggage and hauling it up the stairs to her chambers.

She leaned in close to Matthew. "Rachel's fever broke yesterday morning. The doctor expects her to make a full recovery."

Relief washed over his face. "Thank God. Was it very bad?"

She rubbed her eyes, which suddenly felt dry as dust and

stung like the devil. "Yes. Those first few days I thought we would lose her. But Rachel is strong, despite her physical ailments."

Matthew smiled at her. "And she did all the better for having you there, I'm sure."

She nodded wearily. Her heart ached when she recalled the way her sister had clung to her. Rachel couldn't talk, but she'd had no difficulty communicating that she wanted Bathsheba—and only Bathsheba—by her bedside. Boland and Mrs. Wilson had spelled her whenever Rachel slept, but that wasn't often as the fever drove her sister to a restless agony that had subsided only yesterday.

She smothered a gaping yawn behind her gloved hand. No wonder she felt ready to drop. She hadn't slept more than a few hours at a time in five days.

"What a beast I am to keep you here talking, as if you don't need your rest," exclaimed Matthew. "Go up to bed, Sheba. You can tell me all about it later."

She started toward the stairs but came to a halt when her stomach seemed to do a slow revolution into her chest. Black threads began to drift before her eyes. Another step and the floor undulated beneath her feet, at once closer and yet somehow farther away. She stumbled, reaching for the newel post on the banister.

"Bathsheba!" Matthew's face loomed close through the tangle of black threads now obscuring her vision.

"I'm sorry, dear." A stranger's voice came out of her mouth—that of a weak and sickly girl. "I might need your help getting up the stairs."

But before he could grab her, she tumbled forward, sinking into a cold mist that rushed up from the floor.

John cursed, ducking low over his horse's neck as he narrowly avoided a branch hanging in his path. He had decided to save time by taking a shortcut through the home woods of

Compton Manor—clearly a mistake. The forest seemed to be in no better shape than the rest of the estate, and he doubted that any groundskeeper or woodsman had passed this way in a long time.

He steered the big roan around some broken tree limbs, guiding him through the creeping underbrush that narrowed the trail to little better than a goat track. Impatience and some other elusive emotion scraped along his nerves as he held the horse back to a walk.

There was little reason to believe Lady Randolph suffered from anything more than a minor complaint, and God knew the spoiled ladies of the ton loved to call for the doctor at the slightest sign of a cough. Still, the missive from Lord Randolph contained a genuine sense of urgency and more than a hint of fear.

John had been surprised when the Randolph footman brought word the countess was ill, as he'd assumed she'd left for London days ago. But after reading the note, he'd thrown down his napkin and abandoned his tea. Taking the stairs up to his room two at time, he had retrieved his medical bag, grabbed his hat, and rushed off to the stables.

Now, as the horse picked its way through the woods, he wondered again why he felt the need to dance attendance on a woman who wanted nothing to do with him. An intelligent man would have waited for Littleton to return from Sunday services and sent him to Compton Manor in his stead. An intelligent man would give the viperish little countess as wide a berth as possible. Obviously, John was not that man.

The trees began to thin and the horse finally broke out into an open field. He urged the animal into a canter, heading toward a low hedge on the other side of the gravel drive that led to the house. They cleared the hedge and a few minutes later he was dismounting from the roan. A waiting footman hurried to take the reins.

John strode through the front door, expecting the butler, but almost colliding with the earl instead.

"Dr. Blackmore. Thank God!"

Randolph looked frantic, his eyes bugging out of his sockets as he grabbed his arm and pulled him toward the large staircase. A butler materialized beside them, bleating plaintively as he tried to take John's hat.

"Oh, hang it, Sewell. There's no time for that," Randolph blustered.

John halted at the bottom of the stairs and gently pried the earl's clutching hand from his sleeve.

"Calm yourself, my lord. You will not assist her ladyship by working yourself into a frenzy," he said in a soothing voice.

The earl practically danced in front of him, his frustration and fear so palpable John could almost taste it.

"Just breathe, my lord, slow and steady." He kept his voice reassuring, waiting patiently for the earl to regain his control. The other man took a few deep breaths and the color returned to his face.

"Very good, Lord Randolph. Now, why don't you tell me about her ladyship's symptoms as we walk to her room?"

He nodded encouragement as the earl attempted to explain what had happened to the countess. His confused and anxious ramblings shed little light on the situation, but one thing was clear—Lady Randolph had likely contracted a dangerous illness from someone, although who that someone was seemed rather vague.

They stopped at the end of a long gallery and Randolph knocked softly on a door.

"Her abigail is taking care of her," he said in a loud stage whisper. "A real termagant, but an excellent woman. Been with my cousin since she was a girl."

John sighed. He'd dealt with any number of possessive and ignorant lady's maids in his time, and they almost always made the situation worse.

The door opened and they stepped inside.

"Here's Dr. Blackmore, Miss Boland. I'm sure he'll make everything as right as rain."

A thin, tidily dressed older woman wearing spectacles gave him a quick inspection and then dropped into a brief curtsy. Unlike the earl, she was the picture of self-possession.

"How is your mistress?" John inquired as he crossed to a huge canopied bed set against the wall. The room was shuttered and dim, lit only by one small lamp, and he blinked several times as he struggled to see.

"Very hot, sir, and yet to recover from her faint. She talks a bit, but makes no sense."

He could barely make out the slight figure in the bed.

"Miss Boland, would you open the drapes, please?" He tugged at his cravat. "And the window, as well. It's much too close in here."

She came to stand on the other side of the bed. One hand reached out to touch Lady Randolph's arm.

"The light seems to bother her eyes, sir. And I've always been told it's best to keep windows shut and the room warm when there's fever present." She sounded firm, but not belligerent or hostile.

"While that is often accepted as common wisdom, I've found that a little fresh air can make the patient more comfortable. Besides," he said, giving her a friendly smile, "I can't see Lady Randolph well enough to assess her condition."

For long seconds she stared at him with a wary gaze, and he wondered if he'd have an ally or an enemy in this particular battle. Then she nodded and moved to the window.

Ally.

She pulled the curtain back and sunlight flooded the room. The woman on the bed flinched and gave a pathetic whimper. He looked down at her and blinked again, his vision once more adapting to the change in light. As her features came into focus, he suppressed an exclamation of surprise.

Stripped of her finery and her carefully applied paints,

Lady Randolph looked a good deal younger. Pale and sweaty, her thick hair plastered to her skull, she seemed intensely vulnerable and innocent. And even in the grip of what was clearly a high fever, still lovely.

"How is she, Doctor?" called Lord Randolph from across the room.

John gave himself a swift mental kick, cursing his lack of self-control. He couldn't help her if he thought like a man. Pushing away all emotion, he retreated to the part of his mind that allowed him to become a scientist and nothing more. In the beginning, he'd found it difficult to distance himself from his patients, but since Becky's death six years ago it had become a simple and welcome exercise.

Lady Randolph stirred, murmuring unintelligibly as she thrashed her head on the damp pillow. He smoothed a hand across her cheeks and forehead, feeling a faint stirring of unease at the degree of heat. After checking her pulse—rapid and thready—he gently pried open one eyelid to check her pupil.

With a harsh intake of breath, she opened both eyes, staring at him with a blank gaze. He brushed back the tangled hair from her brow and gave her a reassuring smile.

"My lady, I'm here to help you. Can you tell me if your chest aches?"

She peered vaguely at him, then her mouth tilted into a childlike smile.

"Are you an angel?" Her voice rasped across strained vocal cords. "You're so handsome. You must be an angel, even though your hair is so dark. But your eyes are bright—just like silver."

He frowned, alarmed by how quickly she had fallen into a delirium. According to Lord Randolph, it had been less than two hours since she had been taken ill, and already the fever had affected her mind.

Obviously mistaking his grim expression, she shrank back against the pillows. Tears filled her beautiful, fever-glazed eyes.

"You're not an angel," she whispered. "I know who you are. It's because of all the bad things I've done, isn't it? You've come to take me to hell."

Chapter 4

"Lady Randolph, you needn't be afraid," John soothed. "I'm here to help you."

The countess threw aside the bed linens and scrambled back to huddle against the carved headboard, driven by whatever images tormented her fevered brain. Her voice rose to a thin wail of hysteria.

"No! You want to hurt me. Why won't you leave me alone?"

He reached for her but she shrank away, curling into a tight ball of fear on the rumpled coverlet. His heart ached with pity as he watched her struggle to pull in a breath, as fragile as a pink rose wilting in the summer heat. Her chemise slipped from one shoulder to reveal smooth skin flushed with fever.

"Sarah," she cried, bursting into tears. "Where are you? I'm frightened."

Miss Boland rushed from the window, glaring at John as she gathered Lady Randolph into a protective hug.

"There, there, lovey, don't cry," she crooned. "It's just the doctor, come to take care of you. You remember Dr. Blackmore, Miss Bathsheba. You met him at the Dellworthy dinner party."

Not wanting to frighten the countess, John sat on the edge of the bed, keeping some distance between them. He struggled to ignore a foolish impulse to snatch her from Miss Boland and pull her securely into his arms.

"You wound me to the quick, Lady Randolph," he said, adopting a conversational tone. "I was sure you would remember me. I must have made a poor impression for you to have forgotten me so quickly." He smiled and kept his body relaxed, as if they were just having a friendly chat—not about to begin a pitched battle to save her life.

She stared at him from the safety of her servant's embrace. Her breathing slowed as a glimmer of comprehension brightened her dull gaze.

"Dr. Blackmore?"

He nodded, holding his tongue while she studied him.

"I thought I got rid of you," she said in a sullen voice.

He laughed, relieved out of all proportion that she had regained some of her senses. "You certainly tried, but I'm like mud on an old boot. I tend to stick."

He rose and moved to the headboard. She frowned, obviously suspicious, but didn't retreat.

"My lady, I need to listen to your chest. Will you allow me to touch you?"

She glanced at Boland, who gave an encouraging nod.

"If you must," she grumbled. "Please be quick about it."

Lord Randolph cleared his throat loudly. "I'll wait in the corridor, Dr. Blackmore."

Boland rose and closed the door after the earl, allowing John to take her place on the bed. He gently pried Bathsheba's hands from their death grip on the sheets and slipped the crumpled linens out from under her body.

"Why don't you tuck back into bed, my lady? I don't want you getting a chill."

John needed her as warm and relaxed as possible so she would tolerate his examination. And as he glanced at her slender legs—exposed under the rucked-up hem of her chemise—he realized he had to get those lovely limbs tucked out of sight if he hoped to concentrate on his work. Doctoring the beautiful countess presented a greater challenge than he had anticipated.

She mumbled something under her breath as he helped her ease between the crisp sheets.

"I beg your pardon, my lady?"

"I said, it's a little late, isn't it? I've already caught the damn chill."

He smiled. Her refusal to be anything less than her sharp-tongued self was oddly endearing.

With Boland's help, he propped the countess up on a stack of pillows. As gently as he could, he unlaced the top of her chemise, exposing the creamy whiteness of her chest. His fingers lost a touch of their normal steadiness as he pushed the delicate fabric to her shoulders.

Bloody hell. What was the matter with him?

He glanced at her face and paused, caught by the hectic flush spreading across her cheekbones. She cast down her gaze, just as she had done at the Dellworthys' dinner party when he stared at her.

"Doctor! What are you doing?" Boland's sharp voice broke the tension. She moved to the other side of the bed, taking her mistress's hand in a firm grasp.

"I need to listen for congestion in Lady Randolph's chest," he replied. "It will help me diagnose her ailment."

He gave the countess a reassuring smile. "Try to relax, my lady. Just breathe normally."

Extracting a small, hollow wooden tube from his medical bag, John sat next to Lady Randolph on the bed. He angled his head over her chest, pressing an ear to one end of the tube and resting the other end on the top of her breast. Even with the few inches of wood between them, the heat from her skin washed over him.

"What is that thing?" she gasped in a panicky voice.

"It helps me to listen, my lady. Just try to relax."

As her breathing slowed, he began to hear scratches and raling sounds in her lungs. Pulling back slightly, he brought his hands to her chest and gave her several firm taps around the breastbone and over the lungs. The answering sound was muted and dull.

He sat up, concealing his growing unease. Where in God's name had she caught so severe an infection?

"Why did you do that?" she grumbled, rubbing the marks he had left on her white skin. "It hurt."

He gently brushed her hands aside. "I'm sorry, my lady. Just one more listen," he said, bending over her chest again. "Please take a deep breath."

This time, he tried it without the tube. The swell of her creamy flesh pressed against his ear as she struggled to take in a breath. At any other time he would have been entranced by the luscious sensation, but right now all he felt was alarm.

He straightened, meeting Boland's eyes. She blinked. The look on his face must have confirmed her fears.

Damn. His discipline must be slipping. He made a point of never showing strong emotions in the sickroom.

Schooling his features into a pleasant expression, he looked down at Lady Randolph. Her emerald eyes had begun to take on an unnatural sheen—delirium taking hold once more. He laid his hand against her damp cheek, hoping his touch would keep her with them. When she didn't respond he leaned down to stare directly into her eyes.

"Lady Randolph. Can you hear me? You must rest now. I'll return in a few minutes to give you something to ease your fever and help you breathe."

Her gaze wandered and she began muttering again, paying him no heed. Boland voiced a quiet moan, fear finally breaking through her icy calm. He inclined his head to indicate that she follow him to the door.

"I'm going to send for additional supplies from Dr. Littleton," he said. "Lady Randolph is suffering from a highly infectious complaint. It would be best if no one came into this room except you and me. She needs careful nursing, as her fever may well grow worse before it breaks."

Boland gripped the front of her skirts. "It will break, won't it?"

John studied her. She obviously adored her mistress and was shaken to the core. He didn't want to frighten her, but he would need her help if they had any chance of saving the countess.

"I hope so. I will do everything in my power to help."

"Will you stay, Doctor?"

"Yes. I'll send for my kit and extra clothing. I promise you I won't leave Compton Manor until her ladyship is out of danger."

She grabbed his hand and pressed it to her cheek. "God bless you, sir."

Before he could pull his hand away, she dropped it and hurried back to the bed. He shook himself free from his momentary paralysis and stepped out into the hallway.

The earl waited for him there, pale and anxious. John swiftly apprised him of the situation, scrawling down instructions in his pocket notebook as he talked.

"Dr. Blackmore," the earl interrupted, "would you like me to send for Miss Elliott? She's a levelheaded woman with a great deal of experience in the sickroom."

John turned a startled exclamation into a cough. If Lady Randolph came to her senses and saw Miss Elliott looming over her, she'd likely go into a fatal spasm.

"No, my lord. Her illness is highly contagious. I don't want anyone entering the room except Miss Boland and myself. Is that clear?"

The earl bobbed his head like a demented quail. A very frightened demented quail. Like Boland, he clearly had a great deal of affection for his cousin. John hadn't thought Lady Randolph the kind of woman to inspire such loyalty.

He handed the earl his instructions for Dr. Littleton and stepped back into the room. Boland sat quietly by the bed watching her mistress who had fallen into an uneasy slumber.

"Miss Boland."

"Yes, sir?"

"I need to know how and where Lady Randolph contracted this fever, so I might effect a better treatment."

She suddenly looked wary, her newfound trust vanishing in an instant.

"I don't know, sir." She set her jaw in mutinous defiance, and he knew with certainty she lied.

"She could not have caught it at Compton Manor or in town," he replied. "A few villagers were sick several days ago, but she would not have been exposed to them."

Boland clamped her mouth shut.

"I'll ask the earl if you won't tell me."

She glared at him.

"I only wish to help her ladyship," he said gently. "I will keep anything you tell me in the strictest confidence. You have my word as a physician and a gentleman."

She studied him. Sunlight glinted off her spectacles, hiding the expression in her eyes.

"In Thirsk," she finally replied. "She was visiting . . . distant relations."

That was closer to the truth, but she still held something back.

"And?"

"One of them, a young lady, fell ill with this same fever."

He frowned. "Why didn't Lady Randolph return immediately to Ripon?"

Boland's jaw worked. "Because she insisted on staying to nurse the lady."

John couldn't hold back his surprise. "Lady Randolph? Nursing a sick relative? I find that rather hard to believe."

Contempt flared in her eyes, obvious even behind the spectacles.

"Only because you don't know her! No one does. You

all think the worst, but my lady is the best woman in the world. If only you could see her as I do."

As her voice rang with barely repressed fury, Lady Randolph jerked in her sleep, reacting to the emotions that swirled around her. Boland gasped and turned her head, fighting to regain control.

"You're right," John said. "I don't know her, and I have no right to judge. Please forgive my impertinence."

She gave a grudging nod but refused to look at him. He had lost ground with her, and would have to make it up.

"Miss Boland, did her ladyship's relative survive the illness?"

"Yes, although it was not initially thought she would."

"Then it's best to assume the countess will, as well. She's obviously a strong woman. In fact," he mused, "it surprises me that she succumbed so quickly. I would not have thought it possible given how healthy she was a few days ago."

After a fraught silence, Boland said, "My lady has had many troubles lately. She is worn to the bone."

He studied the beautiful, frail woman in the bed, her pale brow furrowed in pain, her limbs twitching restlessly beneath the sheets.

"Yes, I thought as much," he said, almost to himself. "I wanted to help her, but she rebuffed me."

Boland's voice, heavy with despair, fell like a leaden weight on him.

"No one can help her, Dr. Blackmore. Not even you."

John came awake with a start, struggling to remember where he was and why his back ached like the devil.

Ah, yes.

He had fallen asleep in the ladder-back chair by Lady Randolph's bed, a piece of furniture that seemed designed by Torquemada himself. Not that any other piece of furniture in the room promised greater comfort. Every chair either sagged into decrepitude or had survived the passage of time simply because the wood was so hard nothing short of a raging bonfire could destroy it.

All was not well on Lord Randolph's estate, beginning with the sick woman huddled in the bed.

The countess was babbling again. That must be what had awakened him.

John hauled himself up, ignoring the protesting ache of his muscles. He and Boland had spent the last three days nursing Lady Randolph, battling the fever as it edged higher and refused to break. They had tried everything in his usual arsenal of medicinals, and several that were not. They had applied mustard plasters to clear her lungs and linseed oil poultices to ease her pain. John had poured ipecac syrup down her throat, dosed her with laudanum, and tried several combinations of powders sent over by the village apothecary. Boland had forced her to drink willow bark tea, nourishing broths, and barley water. They had managed to keep her alive, but for how much longer?

He leaned over her, fighting despair over her gray pallor and the dusky blue of her lips. Her eyes had become swollen slits, a slash of green barely visible under heavy lids.

She was awake—if one could call her delirium that—and she was babbling about her husband again. After three days listening to her terrified ramblings, John wished the bastard was still alive so he could beat him into a bloody pulp for all the pain he must have inflicted on his wife.

He wrung out a cloth in the basin of cold water Boland had left by the bedside. Washing Lady Randolph—trying to bring her fever down—had been torturous. At one point, the fever had spiked so severely that he and Boland had been forced to immerse her in a cool bath. She had wept, shaking in Boland's arms as he swiped a wet cloth over her slender, beautiful back. His heart had twisted with anger and pity that he was forced to expose her body to his gaze—a body that should have been flushed with the heat of passion, not with the infection that was killing her.

John tenderly wiped her face and neck, then rested his hand against her overheated cheek. If the fever didn't break soon, her chances of survival were slim. And that left him feeling despondent and furious. Almost as furious as when Becky died in childbirth.

But Becky was his sister, and he barely knew Lady Randolph.

He regretted the loss of any patient, but this was different. In the dark watches of these past few nights, he had gradually accepted a sense of responsibility for the countess. He hated that, but he hated even more the feeling that her death would leave a gaping hole in his heart, a heart he had been careful to shield from distracting emotions—especially when it came to women.

But this woman—infuriating, prickly, and oh-so-vulnerable—had blown his defenses to smithereens.

She stirred, nuzzling her cheek into the palm of his hand.

"My lady," he said. "Can you hear me?"

Her eyes flew open, and for one painfully joyous moment he thought she recognized him. But the dull glaze sheeting the normally bright green told him otherwise.

"Reggie, is that you? Why did you come back? I told you I didn't want to see you!"

John gritted his teeth. He didn't know if he could stand another minute of her tortured ravings about her husband.

He stroked her wet forehead. "No, my lady. It's Dr. Blackmore. There's nothing here to frighten you."

Her eyes widened, her mind still trapped in a past he now understood had been one of lonely anguish. Her ramblings had rarely made sense but one thing had been perfectly clear—her husband had been a paranoid monster who suspected her of every kind of licentious behavior. One who took a sick pleasure in punishing his wife.

"Reggie, no!" she wailed.

"Shh. You're safe," he murmured, smoothing back her hair.

She flinched, as if someone had slapped her. "Stay away from me."

She struggled against him, strong in her delirium as she tried to leap from the bed. It killed him to do it, but he grabbed her and held her down as she thrashed underneath him. Finally, she subsided, weeping quietly. Lifting her head, he held a glass to her lips and gave her a sip of cool water. She spluttered, still weeping a bit. A few minutes later she slipped into a heavy doze, and he laid her back down on the pillows.

He stood, gripped his hands behind his back and pulled down on his arms, stretching as he studied the figure huddled under the covers. A thousand times he had ransacked every bit of knowledge in his brain for a way to save her. He had tried everything. Now it seemed her life was in God's hands.

Unfortunately, God seemed remarkably callous toward those who most needed His help.

The door opened, and Boland bustled in with another tray in an endless line of trays. This one held a pitcher of barley water and a desiccated loaf of bread.

"What in hell is that?" he asked.

"Good Friday bread, sir."

John raised an eyebrow. Boland was a woman of few words. When he wanted information, he usually had to pry it out of her mouth.

"Well?" he prompted.

"It's baked on Good Friday," she explained, "and then hung to be preserved. Tradition says it has the ability to heal the sick."

He gave a snort and she sighed. "I know, Doctor. Cook found a loaf in the back of the pantry. She had forgotten it was there. She felt certain it would cure her ladyship, and almost every servant in the house agrees. It didn't seem right to insult them."

John tapped the loaf. It made a hollow, drumlike sound.

He looked at Boland's suspiciously rigid features and let out a rough laugh. Her mouth eased into a reluctant smile. He welcomed it. God knew they had few reasons to smile.

He watched her bustle about the room, folding towels and making things tidy. A comfortable silence—born of their shared burden—fell between them. He loathed breaking it, but compulsion forced him to.

"Boland."

"Yes, sir?"

"Did Lady Randolph's husband beat her?"

She gave him a startled glance. "Why would you ask me such a question?"

He gazed steadily at her and her face flushed. They had both heard Lady Randolph's mutterings, even though Boland had done her best to hush and soothe her mistress into silence.

He waited her out.

She reluctantly parted her lips. "I never saw any evidence that his lordship laid a hand on her in that way."

There was more. He knew it, and had to confirm it.

"Go on," he said, injecting a note of command in his voice. Boland had come to trust him and his commands, and he hoped she would respond to him now.

She drifted over to the bed, gazing down at her mistress. Her hands clutched the starched white towel she had tied around her waist.

"I never saw a mark on her, Dr. Blackmore, and she never said a word that he ever lifted a hand to her."

She looked up and met his gaze. "But Lord Randolph was a cruel man . . . a villain," she spat. "My lady suffered, worse than you can imagine. I may burn in hell for it, but I thanked our Creator the day the man broke his neck in a carriage race."

She gasped and clapped her hand over her mouth. "I . . . I beg your pardon—"

He cut her off. "Boland, you may always say whatever you wish to me. You have my complete trust and confidence."

She flushed and ducked her head.

"Why don't you bring something for her ladyship to eat—beside the, er, bread," he said, taking pity on her. "Broth might do more good than our mystical loaf."

"Yes, sir."

Once she left the room, he allowed the fury he had been tamping down to flood through him. Randolph might not have beaten his wife, but he had abused her nonetheless—in ways he suspected would mark Bathsheba Compton's soul forever.

"Dr. Blackmore."

The rasp of her voice jerked him around, and he strode to her bedside. She stared up at him, awake and obviously in her right senses.

He felt her cheek and forehead.

Still hot.

"It's good to see you again, Lady Randolph."

He slid an arm around her shoulders and lifted her up, bringing the glass of barley water to her lips. She drank a few sips before she gasped and weakly turned her head.

He didn't lay her back down, instead cradling her against his chest. Hardly professional behavior on his part, but he couldn't resist the impulse to hold her. She nestled into his embrace with a whimper of what sounded like relief.

"How do you feel?"

She didn't answer.

"Lady Randolph?"

"I'm going to die, aren't I?" The hopeless finality of the question wrenched his heart.

"No, dear lady. You are not going to die. I won't let you."

She made a soft, mocking sound and stirred in his arms. He tightened them, fighting an irrational fear that she might try to escape.

"You can't know that. You're not God."

"No, but I'm the next best thing. I'm a doctor. Now stop talking and rest."

She laughed weakly and huddled against him, turning her face into his chest. For a few minutes she rested, and he was more than content to hold her sweet body in his arms.

"Sometimes . . ."

He had to bend his head to hear her soft voice. "Yes?"

"Sometimes I think it would be much easier to just let go."

An ill-defined but scorching emotion blazed in the vicinity of his heart.

"Don't talk such nonsense. It doesn't become you." He sounded harsh, but he couldn't allow her to give up—to stop fighting. She lay poised on the knife's edge as it was.

"But I'm so tired. And few would miss me. Matthew and Boland, perhaps Ra—" She bit off whatever she had been about to say.

He shifted her around. Tapping her chin up, he forced her to look into his face.

"Matthew and Boland would be lost without you," he said. She started to speak, but he laid a finger across her lips. "And I, too, would miss you, more than I care to admit. You mustn't think of leaving us. I won't have it."

Her eyes grew round and tears gathered on her spiky lashes, little diamonds enhancing her emerald gaze.

He brushed away one drop that fell to her cheek. "I know you are troubled. I know you feel sick to your very soul. But you must trust me, Bathsheba. I will help you—whatever it is, I will help. And I will not allow you to die."

She stared at him, then burst into great racking sobs that shook her small frame. He let her cry, rocking her in his arms until she started to cough. Then he shushed her, rubbing her back until her breathing eased. She eventually quieted and he laid her back down on the bed.

"Sleep now, sweetheart," he said, stroking her brow. "All will be well. I promise."

She gave one sad little sniffle and closed her eyes, hiccupping a few times before she drifted off.

After a half hour's vigil, he realized she had fallen into a natural sleep, her breathing steady and even. She slept for hours without stirring, deep in a slumber that for once seemed untroubled by nightmares.

Later that evening her fever finally broke. John slumped in the chair beside her, overcome with weary relief and a tangle of unfamiliar, conflicting emotions. As he gazed at the sleeping beauty slumbering so peacefully in her rumpled bed, he wondered how the hell he was going to convince her that life was worth living.

And if he did manage to save the bewitching Lady Randolph from herself, what, exactly, would that mean for him?

Chapter 5

Bathsheba tilted her head back to capture the delightful warmth of the sun on her face. She stretched, sighing as she snuggled into the plump cushions of the chaise the servants had carried onto the terrace. Boland had created a peaceful outdoor retreat for her, complete with a small table and set of chairs, a stack of books, and some needlework.

Just off the library and partially shaded by a welter of creeping ivy and an old oak, the terrace looked east over a broad lawn and the Compton home woods. The foliage was sadly overgrown, but everything was gloriously green and fragrant, the serenity of the morning interrupted only by the call of the lark and the hum of the worker bee. Bathsheba had forgotten the verdant beauty of Compton Manor on a midsummer day.

She cast off her chip bonnet, eager to absorb the sunshine. It would surely bring out her dreaded red freckles, but for once she didn't care. It felt so wonderful to loll about in the welcoming heat, like the estate's barn cat that rolled around on the stones of the garden path a few feet away. Boland would no doubt scold, fearing she would return to London as brown and freckled as any country miss, but Bathsheba could always resort to her Denmark Lotion and cosmetics to restore her complexion.

Besides, Blackmore had ordered her to sit in the sun at least an hour a day. Who was she to argue with the man who had helped her cheat death?

At the thought of her handsome savior, she gave a little shiver, and not one generated by the horrendous fever that had plagued her for three long days. The memory of his powerful arms lifting her, his strong hands moving over her body as he tended to her, still left her breathless. Not even the shame of knowing how vulnerable she had been could take away her unexpected longing to feel his touch once more.

"My lady!"

Boland's sharp voice made her jump in her seat.

"Good God. You half frightened me out of my wits," Bathsheba grumbled. "Why must you sneak up on me like that?"

"Because that's the only way I can find out if you're following the doctor's orders," her abigail retorted.

"I am following doctor's orders. He told me to spend at least an hour a day in the sun. What does it look like I'm doing?"

The other woman bustled up to the chaise, her arms loaded down with extra pillows and some woven throws. Ever since Bathsheba had been allowed to leave the sickroom, her companion had fussed like an old hen, barely leaving her alone for an instant. As much she found comfort in Boland's unstinting devotion and care, she was beginning to find it a tad stifling.

Boland glared down at her. "You took off your bonnet. And you need another wrap." She threw a voluminous Norwich shawl over Bathsheba's shoulders. "The doctor said you had to keep warm."

"I am warm, Boland. It's August. It's in fact bloody hot out here, which is why I took off my bonnet. And you know very well that Dr. Blackmore doesn't believe in overheating a patient. He would laugh to see me bundled up like an old spinster."

Boland refused to back down. "You're barely well, Miss Bathsheba. And he may be the doctor, but I've been taking care of you since you were a girl. I think I know what you need and what you don't."

Bathsheba sighed. Boland had objected to Blackmore's direction that she take the sun and fresh air, and their disagreement had threatened to turn into a full-blown argument. She had been forced to intervene, speaking more sharply to her abigail than she intended. But she was tired of being smothered, and sick to death of feeling like an invalid.

"I know, Boland. But I'm fine now. You must stop making a fuss."

The other woman looked at her, and Bathsheba was stunned to see tears in her eyes.

"You almost died, my lady," she said, her voice hoarse with emotion. "I almost lost you."

Something clutched in Bathsheba's throat, and she had to struggle to swallow. She had spent the last few days trying to forget that terrifying fact. Hearing Boland say it made the nightmare come rushing back.

She sat up and tossed aside the blanket draped over her legs.

"Well, I didn't die, and I have no intention of doing so any time soon," she replied in a cool voice. "What time is it? It must be close to lunch. I'm famished."

She wasn't, but she didn't want to talk about her illness any longer. Ever again, if she could help it.

Boland stiffened and put on her best offended servant's face. "Luncheon will not be served for another hour, my lady. I'll bring you some tea and biscuits. If that wouldn't be making too much of a fuss," she finished, sarcastically.

As guilt shafted through her, Bathsheba caught the other woman's calloused hand. "I'm sorry, Boland. It's a wonder you've put up with me all these years. I don't know how you do it."

Boland clucked disapprovingly, but her cheeks pinked with pleasure. "Never you mind, my lady. You're just tired, that's all. I'll be back with your tea in a trice."

She turned to go, and then stopped. "Oh, and Dr. Blackmore arrived a few minutes ago. He's looking at the burn on Cook's hand, then he'll be out to see you. Would you like me to set a place for him at lunch?"

The butterflies in Bathsheba's stomach took flight, as they always did when someone mentioned his name. Forcing herself to smile, she prayed Boland would mistake the blush on her cheeks for color brought out by the sun.

"I'm sure Lord Randolph would be pleased to have the doctor stay for lunch."

Boland disappeared into the shadows of the library as Bathsheba wobbled to her feet.

Blast!

She still felt weak as a kitten, but she'd be damned if Blackmore found her lying on the chaise like a sickly old widow. Taking a deep breath to steady herself, she smoothed her hands over the bodice and skirts of her cream-colored gown of French muslin. She knew how ridiculous it was for a woman of her age to wear so girlish a color, but she loved the simplicity of it—the way it set off her auburn hair and drew attention to the curves of her figure instead of to the gown itself.

A firm step sounded on the squeaky floorboards of the library, then Blackmore emerged from the house into the glare of the afternoon sunlight. He paused, blinking to adjust his vision. She eagerly grasped those few seconds to study him.

He didn't dress like a doctor, at least not like any doctor she had ever seen. He dressed like a Corinthian, his tall, lean form set off to advantage by buckskin breeches and shiny black topboots—all that leather enhancing the muscled beauty of his legs. His broad shoulders strained through the expensive fabric of his dark green coat, and his gray waistcoat did nothing to obscure his powerful chest.

She knew the solidity and strength of that body. God, how could she ever forget it, after he had held her in his arms that night she had sobbed out her fears? She flushed again, discomforted by the reminder of that moment when he had stripped her emotions bare. But something else lurked underneath that humiliating memory—a growing desire to feel those powerful arms about her once again.

He stepped forward and smiled, making her a respectful bow.

"Lady Randolph, it is a great pleasure to see you up and about. I hope, however, that you are not overexerting yourself."

Bathsheba stiffened, the answering smile fading from her lips. Apparently, they would be observing all the formalities today.

Stung by the social barrier he had unexpectedly erected, she gave him a distant nod in return.

"Doctor," she said in a chilly voice.

He grinned, suddenly looking as wicked as any rake she had ever met. His eyes gleamed as he swiftly ran an appreciative gaze over her body. Her heart leapt in response, stuttering with a funny little beat she was beginning to recognize.

"Don't starch up, my lady," he said. Those amazing silver eyes laughed at her. "I didn't mean to sound like a stuffy old matron, but you surprised me. I haven't seen you in two days, and you look as pretty as a girl just out of the schoolroom. No one would ever suspect you were so ill just a short time ago."

As far as compliments went, she had heard better—much better. But she still blushed, at once ridiculously pleased by his attention and irritated that he could read her so easily.

"Won't you sit down?" she asked, trying to reclaim some dignity.

He moved, looming over her. His eyes half closed as he lowered his head close to her hair.

"Wh-what are you doing?" She couldn't keep a little quaver out of her voice.

"Mmm, you smell delicious." The husky note in his voice made her limbs weaken and tremble. "Like sunshine and rosewater."

"Don't be—"

His eyes gleamed at her from under heavy, sensual lids. "Foolish. I know. But you wore a different perfume the first time I met you. It was very lush. Beautiful, but heavy. I like this better."

She had to put some distance between them before her heart pounded out of her chest. Backing up awkwardly, she half sat, half fell onto the chaise.

"I can't wear it anymore. Not since I've begun to recover. It's too strong. I tried to put some on this morning and it made me cough." She sounded like a babbling fool, but she couldn't help it.

He instantly came alert, looking every inch the doctor. She blinked at the sudden transformation.

Sitting next to her on one of the chairs, he took her wrist, feeling for her pulse. She submitted, knowing it was useless to struggle.

"Your lungs are still sensitive," he said. "Perhaps in a few weeks you'll be able to wear it again."

She shook her head. "It doesn't matter. I'm not very fond of it, anyway." And it was deuced expensive. Unless she found that rich husband of hers very soon, she wouldn't be wearing French perfume.

He nodded absently as he brought a cool hand to her cheek and forehead, then extracted the ever-present wooden cylinder out of his pocket and listened to her chest. She stared up at the branches of the oak tree, trying not to look at the silky dark head so close to her breast.

He straightened. "Your lungs sound clear, but your heart-beat is a trifle accelerated. We don't want you succumbing to a relapse. This afternoon, you're to take a long nap. I don't want you leaving your room until dinner."

Just like a baby, she thought pettishly. "I'm fine. Stop fussing. You're as bad as Boland."

He grunted, running his eyes over her again. But this time, there was only the assessing, dispassionate gaze of a physician. She found it immensely annoying. How could he distance himself so easily, when her nerves—her awareness of his potent masculinity—were stretched as tight as the strings on a violin? One look from him and her knees turned to jelly, while he seemed unaffected by any emotion—sexual or otherwise.

Well, perhaps she would see about that.

Curling her legs up on the chaise, she draped one arm suggestively over the back of the bolster. The movement thrust her breasts up, straining over the top of her gown.

"Perhaps I am feeling a trifle agitated," she said, giving him a seductive smile. "But there's a reason for it. Would you like to know what it is?" She allowed one hand to drift down the front of her bodice to rest in her lap.

He sat bolt upright.

Finally. She slid a hand over to touch his sleeve.

"Stop that," he ordered.

She jerked her hand back. "Stop what?"

"That. Playing the wanton. It's unbecoming, and you don't need to do that with me."

Her mouth dried up, as did any words she might have thought to respond with. Only by sheer willpower did she stop herself from gaping at him.

His smoke-gray eyes were cool, even remote, as he studied her. Even though her throat and face prickled with heat, she refused to drop her gaze. How dared he reprimand her?

She was a countess, while he was . . . the man who had saved her life.

"I know who you are. At least I think I do," he mused, his voice now reflective rather than angry. She didn't know which was worse.

"You play the jaded aristocrat, but it's not your true nature. You're not the woman the gossips say you are. You're not a bitch and you're not a wanton."

She gasped at his brutal choice of words, but he was unrelenting.

"Why do you allow the world to believe those things about you? What purpose does it serve?"

She stared at him, unable to even blink. He sat quietly in his chair, one leg crossed over the other, totally at ease. His eyes studied her intently but objectively, as a scientist might study an exotic insect or animal.

Anger flared deep in her gut, even as she acknowledged the truth of his words. She wasn't a wanton. She was something worse—a coward, too afraid to let herself feel love or passion, or to allow any man to hold sway over her again. Since Reggie's death she had taken lovers, but only when her financial situation forced her to. She had tried to be discriminating but need often trumped desire. Only her last lover, the Earl of Trask, had stirred her to passion. Even then, she had never loved him.

She glared at Blackmore, dying to strike that calmly questioning look from his face. She had done what she must to save herself and her family, and perhaps her dignity had suffered for it. But the alternative was surely worse than having a bad reputation or a man she didn't particularly like in her bed. If the world thought her little better than a courtesan, so be it. She absolutely refused to spend the rest of her life in genteel poverty—or endanger Rachel's security, for that matter—and she'd be damned if she'd apologize for that or explain it away.

"You forget yourself, Doctor," she said, investing as much

scorn in her voice as she could. "I'm grateful for your care, but my gratitude does not allow you the right to pass judgment on my life or my actions. If you cannot behave appropriately in the company of your betters, then I suggest you take your leave."

He didn't stiffen or pull away as she expected him to. Instead, he leisurely uncrossed his legs, leaned over, and took one of her hands in his. She yanked, but he refused to let go. His big hand swallowed hers in a gentle but unyielding clasp.

"When you were feverish, you rambled quite a bit about your husband. About what he did to you."

Bathsheba flinched, feeling his worlds like a blow. Blackmore began to stroke the inside of her wrist, as if to soothe her. It didn't help. She didn't want to think about Reggie or remember the nightmare visions that had tormented her during those fevered hours. And she felt sick with shame for babbling it all out . . . like a stupid, weak child.

He studied her, his expression both kind and grave. It made her want to scream.

"Did your husband beat you?"

She blinked. "Of course not. Reggie would never be so vulgar. He found other ways to punish me." She was so unnerved by his question, she blurted out exactly what she was thinking.

"Jealous, was he?"

She almost laughed at the inadequacy of that description. Jealousy was the least of Reggie's crimes, but Bathsheba would cut her tongue out before she would reveal the ugliness of her married life.

Blackmore's eyes had taken on the color of slate, his mouth compressed into a hard line. "I remember hearing rumors after your husband died. Your affairs supposedly drove him to ruin. No one who knows you as I do would believe that, Lady Randolph."

She sat with her head bowed, trying not to pant even though pain squeezed her chest in an unforgiving grip. She had tried to forget—tried to ignore the whispers and rumors, hoping they would fade. But Reggie had done such a good job tarring her reputation that they never did.

They sat in silence, as if they were two people enjoying a pleasant afternoon in the sunshine. He gently stroked her wrist as she struggled to breathe. When her racing heart began to slow, he released her hand, placing it back in her lap.

"Why did you never defend yourself against his accusations?"

She shook her head, miserably aware of her inability to hide her mistakes from him. He already seemed to know everything about her—or at least about Reggie.

"It was my fault as much as his. I could never find a way to reassure him—to make him believe I loved him. Eventually, I didn't want to anymore." She looked down, unable to meet his eyes when she told him what made her seem almost as vile as her husband. "I wanted to punish him for . . . well, for what he did to me. That was the best way I knew how. Besides," she added bitterly, turning her head away, "no one would have believed me."

He grasped her chin in his long fingers and gently forced her to meet his gaze. She saw nothing in his eyes but sympathy, and the pain in her chest began to ease.

"I suspect there was nothing you could have done to reassure him," he said. "In my experience, that kind of jealous obsession is impervious to reason. You must not brood about the past—and your marriage—any longer. It serves no purpose but to depress your spirits. I speak as your physician, my lady, as well as your friend. It's time to let go of the past. Leave your husband in the grave where he belongs."

Bathsheba wanted so much to believe him. She had struggled for so many years to accept that Reggie's perverse passion wasn't her fault. The understanding and kindness she saw in his eyes almost made her think she could.

He briefly cupped her cheek, then leaned back, putting distance between them. She closed her eyes, fighting the overwhelming desire to crawl into his arms and seek the same comfort he had given her when she was ill. But now she wasn't, and her senses had returned days ago. To still feel that craving for his touch frightened her almost as much as the pain of remembering those years as Reggie's wife.

"Now that you are almost recuperated, Lady Randolph, when do you mean to return to London?"

She opened her eyes, surprised by his quick return to neutral ground. Surprised the terrace looked as it always did, and that the day was still sunny and beautiful. None of it seemed possible given what had just happened between them.

He lounged in his chair, an easy, friendly smile playing around the corners of his mouth. She could almost pretend he had never probed into the darkest corners of her soul.

She scrambled to rearrange her scattered wits, pathetically grateful he'd decided to sound a retreat.

"Sometime next week," she replied. "After the feast of St. Wilfrid. The procession is this Saturday, and there's to be a carnival in the village afterward."

A wicked flash of silver gleamed in his eyes. "You astonish me. Lady Randolph attending the village fair with all the local bumpkins. I would not have thought it possible given your hatred of the country."

She cast him a rueful smile. "It's not the country I can't stand. It's the people."

He laughed. "Then why go? You could plead illness. I could vouch for you, if you ask me nicely."

The husky sound of his laughter sweetly touched some lonely chord in her heart, and she had to fight the impulse to sigh.

"I promised Matthew. He says it's expected. Everyone would be offended if I didn't come, though I can't imagine why." She wrinkled her nose. "But I suppose I've trod on enough toes already, and it's the least I can do to repay my cousin for all his kindness."

He nodded with mock solemnity. "I wish I could be here to see it."

A pang of dismay shafted through her. It hadn't occurred to her that he would leave Ripon so soon.

"You're returning to London?"

"Yes. On the morrow. I came today to check on you, and to bid you farewell."

"Oh." She cleared her throat. "I shall be sorry to see you go."

"And I will be sorry to go, but I have left my work unattended for weeks. If I remain away much longer, I might not have any patients to return to."

She fixed a smile on her face, hoping he didn't sense her disappointment.

Silence fell between them again, and she couldn't think what to say to break it. He cleared his throat and shifted in his seat. "Lady Randolph, I wondered if you would allow me to call on you—when you return to London, that is."

As quickly as dismay had filled her, happiness took its place. She tamped it down, loath for him to read schoolgirl emotions on her face.

"I should be happy to see you, Doctor."

"Thank you," he said, exhaling a tight breath. Did he really think she would have refused him?

"I have another favor to beg of you," he continued.

Her mouth went dry. She felt breathless with a foolish excitement. "What is it?"

"I would like you to consider taking a place on the Board of Governors of St. Bartholomew's Hospital. You know a little of the work I do there and what I hope to accomplish. I'm convinced that a woman of your standing and intellect could do much good for the institution."

Her heart gave a hollow thump in her chest. "You want me to work at your hospital?"

"Well, on the board. Yes."

All her excitement drained away, leaving her muscles slack and weak.

"Let's be clear, then, Doctor. You want me to use my social connections to raise money for the hospital, don't you?"

He frowned, no doubt alerted by the flat tone of her voice.

"Yes, of course. In part. But I also want you to do this for your own sake. I believe you suffer from a lack of purpose that causes you to dwell too much on the troubles in your life. You are much too intelligent to lead such an idle existence."

Amazement, then anger, left her speechless for a moment until she composed herself.

"I didn't realize I was so useless. Such a burden on society."

His head jerked back a fraction. "I did not say you were useless. Of course you're not. Your life is little different from many women of the ton, and that's the problem. As far as I can ascertain, you're bored and restless. A woman of your intellect needs mental stimulation. A purpose in life."

When she opened her mouth to object, he cut her off.

"You're not some dainty piece of fluff, Lady Randolph. You're better than that. There is so much good you could do in the world, if only you would see to it."

Anger hummed through her body, restoring her strength. Ever since Reggie's death she had fought to create a life of her own—one where she made her own decisions, and not had them forced upon her. Her marriage had almost destroyed her. Reggie and his friends in the ton had almost destroyed her. How much more was she expected to sacrifice?

And how dared he tell her how to live her life? She had had enough of that to last an eternity.

She rose quickly to her feet, forcing him to do the same.

"You flatter me, Doctor, but you're quite mistaken. You'll have to look elsewhere for your lady patroness. I'm perfectly satisfied with my life, and have no desire to change it."

The warmth in his eyes disappeared, and the day felt suddenly chill.

"I find that hard to believe," he said.

"Believe what you will. I would no sooner set foot in your hospital than I would shave my head. Illness bores me, and I've had quite enough of that these last few weeks. Now, if you'll excuse me, I'll take my leave."

She tried to brush past, but he stepped in front of her, blocking her path.

"How dare you," she gasped after she pitched headlong into his chest.

She caught her balance and glared up into his face. His features were hard, his expression so icy she shivered.

"Why are you acting so foolishly?" he asked. "This isn't who you are—I know it."

"You know nothing of me, you stupid man," she snapped. "This is exactly who I am." Rage dug in its spurs, and she flung the next words into his face. "And as for being bored, you know I'm more than capable of finding all the stimulation I want, and I know just where to look for it. As soon as I return to London I have every intention of finding exactly what I need."

She stood panting in front of him, vibrating with fury. He, however, might as well have been carved from stone. But his eyes spoke volumes, freezing her, driving out the last remnants of warmth from her bones.

After a few charged moments he stepped back.

"I regret that I misjudged you, my lady. Please accept my apologies. I won't trouble you with my presence any longer."

He gave her a brusque nod and turned on his heel.

Bathsheba suddenly felt sick with guilt. To treat him, of all people, in such a contemptuous manner. The man who had fought for her. The man who had pulled her back from the brink of death.

"Dr. Blackmore! Please wait." She hurried after him.

He stopped but didn't turn to face her. She rushed around to stand before him, forcing herself to meet his gaze. Anger flashed in his eyes, perhaps even disdain. Tears prickled behind her eyelids, and she had to blink several times to clear her vision.

"You are shocked by my behavior, but no more than I," she said. "I am indeed ungrateful to speak to you so unkindly, after all your care for me."

The anger began to fade from his gaze, but his features remained cold as marble. She forced herself to continue.

"I . . . I do not want to part this way," she said. She hated the catch in her voice. Blast the man for making her feel so horrid and shy! "You have been so kind to me, Dr. Blackmore, and I shall always be grateful. I offer you my hand in friendship, and hope you will not reject it."

She swallowed hard and held out her hand, knowing all too well he would be a fool not to walk away. Her heart pounded and the blood rushed in her ears. One lone dove called out to his mate, and then all was silence.

Suddenly he grabbed her shoulders in a crushing grip. He uttered a truly nasty curse before yanking her into his arms and taking her mouth in a ruthless, devouring kiss.

Chapter 6

Bathsheba gasped and opened her lips to the onslaught of Blackmore's ravening mouth. Heat swamped her, softening her limbs and sending a luxurious pulse to the deepest parts of her body. She sagged against him as one of his arms lashed around her waist, pulling her flush with his muscular torso.

His tongue surged past her teeth, caressing her mouth with a coffee-flavored sweep. She moaned, so completely taken by the hot power of the kiss that she could do nothing but open to him, answering his need with a matching hunger. His taste, the wet glide of his mouth slanting across hers, sang deep in her veins, blasting away exhaustion from illness, and pain from anger and grief. Amazement blossomed within her as she recognized the pull of desire—the sweet ache of sensual yearning she hadn't felt in such a long time.

He answered her moan with a rumble deep in his throat, a low animal sound that triggered a soft release of dampness between her thighs. She clutched the front of his coat, digging her fingers into the expensive fabric, holding on as if her life depended on it.

As if responding to her desperation, he captured her in an unyielding embrace. One arm circled her waist and the other went round her shoulders, pulling her firmly against his chest. His careful physician's touch had fled, replaced by the hard grip of a conquering male.

Bathsheba whimpered and he deepened the kiss. He claimed her, exploring her mouth with a passion so brutally possessive and yet so erotic she melted against him. Her legs began to tremble, and the breath seized in her throat. She pushed weakly at his chest, struggling to pull in some air.

John relaxed his grip and released her from the kiss. She gasped, pulling in huge gulps of air as she stared into his face. The hot look that gleamed in his eyes—the ferocity of his lust—quickly turned those small shivers running down her legs into quaking tremors. Part of her, the most feminine part, responded to his desire to dominate her. But she had seen that look before on other men's faces, and it sent a chill snaking up her spine.

He must have sensed her anxiety, because he seemed to wage a short battle for control. He eased her back, gentling his touch, but did not let her out of the circle of his arms. She couldn't utter a word, only able to stare at his hard, sensual mouth, still damp from their kiss.

He closed his eyes and drew in a harsh breath, his chest shuddering with the strain. When he opened them again, some of the wildness had faded. But the very air around them shimmered with an insidious, seductive heat.

"Damn it all, woman." His voice sounded strangled in his throat. "I must be losing my mind. What are you doing to me?"

He rested his forehead against hers for a moment before straightening. With a gentle hand, he brushed a few stray curls back from her forehead.

"Um," she stuttered, trying to clear the woolly feeling from her brain. "I believe I was asking you to accept my apology. And I think you just did."

He gave a harsh crack of laughter. "Is that what it was? How foolish of me not to have realized."

She settled more comfortably into his arms, staring into his lean, handsome face. He didn't seem inclined to let her go and, just for a minute, she allowed herself to feel completely besotted with him. That smoldering, smoky look returned to his eyes and she couldn't hold back a little sigh of satisfaction.

"You're playing a dangerous game, my sweet," he murmured, ducking his head so he could nuzzle his mouth against her cheek.

She tilted her head, giving him better access. "I know. But it's so much fun."

He trailed a string of damp kisses along her jaw, and a throbbing hum of desire rolled through her veins.

"I'm such a fool," he groaned. The words vibrated against the sensitive flesh of her neck. She shivered.

"The last thing I should be doing is kissing my patient out here in broad daylight. On the terrace, where anyone could see us."

"I know." She giggled. She *never* giggled.

He gave another one of those delicious growls and she squirmed against the erection that now lay hard and heavy against her pelvis. It felt so wonderful—better than anything she could remember in a long, long time. Lord, she'd missed that feeling, even though the intensity of his passion made her brain raise a warning flag.

It was a warning she decided to ignore.

She reached up and tangled her fingers in his thick hair, bringing their faces, their mouths, just a breath of air apart.

"You are a fool," she whispered. "But don't stop. Not yet."

He groaned, and this time his kiss was impossibly tender, sweeter than she could have imagined. He took his time, playing with her, slanting his lips across her mouth in a slow, moist slide. She snuggled against him as he held her in a gentle but all-encompassing embrace.

The kiss went on forever. Slow, wet, and so hot she thought she would melt. Then it grew more urgent. His hands moved up to her face, holding her still as he deepened the connection between them. Long fingers traced the curve of her jaw, drifted down to caress her neck. She squirmed against him, seeking to ease the ache between her thighs. One of his hands wandered down and curled around her bottom. He lifted her enough to slide his leg between her thighs.

She gasped, arching back as the muscles deep in her core spasmed in a fast, tight contraction. Her heart slammed with a hard jerk, and she instinctively pushed down.

A moment later he cursed and broke away, holding her at arm's length. She blinked up at him, dappled sunlight obscuring her vision while a hazy sensuality clouded her brain.

"What's wrong?" she whispered.

His jaw dropped open. "What's wrong? I'm one minute away from dragging you back to that chaise and getting you flat on your back. That's what's wrong. We can't do this, Bathsheba. Not here. Not now."

She couldn't break free of the sensual daze that gripped her. "We could go up to my room. I'll tell Matthew I'm not feeling well. That you want to give me an examination. No one has to know."

His lips peeled back over strong white teeth and he growled—actually growled—at her. She felt the luscious sound of it deep in her womb.

"That's a very bad idea, my lady," he said. "Because once I get you on your back, you're not moving from that position for a very long time. And once I've had you that way, I can think of at least a dozen other ways to take you, as well. So unless you're ready for all that, I suggest it would be wise for you to let me go."

The crudity of his suggestion slapped her like a driving gust of sleet. She stepped hastily away from him, stumbling over one of the broken stones on the terrace. His hand shot out to steady her.

"Easy," he said. "You're not ready for this."

Bathsheba swallowed, suddenly feeling nervous and vulnerable. He was right. She wasn't ready. She might never be ready and, in any event, he was the wrong man. She didn't need a lover, especially one who looked at her with such unfettered desire, such hot lust. One who threatened to consume her with passion and make her as dependent on him as she had once been on Reggie.

The thought of her husband made her suck in a fearful breath.

Blackmore muttered something and took her arm in a gentle clasp. "Come, my lady." He steered her back to the chaise. "You need rest, not a great brute like me pawing away at you. I should be taken out behind the barn and shot."

She sank gratefully onto the cushions. He hunkered down beside her, carefully inspecting her face. One hand reached out to brush her cheek.

"Better now?" he asked in a soothing voice.

Blackmore was nothing like Reggie. Nothing like any other man she had ever known. The hell of it was, he might be exactly what she wanted—at least for now—but he wasn't what she needed. She needed a rich husband, and preferably a boring and safe one. Blackmore wasn't safe, and he never would be. He was the most dangerous man she'd ever met. She'd lose herself in him if she wasn't careful.

"My lady?" he prompted.

"Yes?" she said, forgetting what he had asked her.

He smiled and brushed a feather-light kiss across her lips. Desire rustled again, hot and dark in her belly. He was so dangerous. And he certainly wasn't what she needed. But still . . .

"Are you sure you have to go?" she asked in a dreamy voice. "Why don't you stay for the festival? No one will pay any attention to us, not later, anyway. When night falls—"

A flash of something hot and fierce flared in his eyes. Then it vanished. He rose to his feet and took one step back, but the distance seemed much greater.

"I've already stayed away from London for far too long.

I can no longer afford to neglect my patients or my work at the hospital. Please forgive me."

She started to flinch, stung by his rejection, but forced herself to hold still. But Blackmore, damn him, must have seen the small movement.

He cast a rueful smile and took her hand. "Believe me when I tell you I would much rather remain in Ripon."

She tugged her hand away and gave him a tight smile. "Well, I'm sure you're needed a great deal more in London than here. Have a safe journey, Doctor, and thank you for all your help. I'll make your good-byes to Lord Randolph."

She reached for her bonnet and made a show of putting it on, determined not to let him see how much he had wounded her. It was all for the best, she silently argued. She did not need another stupid affair with a man who could give her nothing. Nothing but passion, which never led to anything but pain.

He stared down at her but she refused to meet his gaze. After a few moments he gave a quick bow, turned on his heel, and strode away, disappearing through the library doors.

Bathsheba sat quietly with her face tilted to the sunlight, listening to the sounds of the day and waiting for the ache in her heart to subside. When that didn't happen, she slowly rose from the chaise and made her way into the shadowed coolness of the house.

Chapter 7

"I say, old girl!"

Matthew jabbed Bathsheba in the ribs with his elbow. She winced, then stood on tiptoe, straining to hear him over the noise of the boisterous crowd that milled about Ripon's old market square. He pointed in the general direction of the procession moving slowly toward them.

"Look at that float passing the confectionary shop," he shouted. "Can you make out what the theme is?"

She craned her neck to see over the shoulders of the people in front of them.

"I can't see," she yelled back.

Matthew's eyes twinkled with mischief. "The theme of the float is money is the root of all evil. Guess we could tell them a few things about that, eh?"

They both snickered behind their hands. Money might be the root of all evil, but Bathsheba was more than willing to indulge in a little wickedness if it pulled them free of their quicksand of debt.

Miss Elliott turned from inspecting the pageant floats to give them a disapproving frown. "It is a worthy sentiment, as I'm sure you will agree."

Matthew's eyes grew round and he nodded vigorously. Bathsheba smiled politely, determined to stick to her vow not to irritate the stern bluestocking any more than she already had.

When Matthew told her over dinner last night that Miss Elliott would be joining them for the festival, Bathsheba had almost spit a mouthful of onion broth into her soup bowl.

"You must be joking," she had spluttered when she could finally catch her breath.

He'd had the grace to look guilty, but tried to justify it by claiming Miss Elliott had a superior knowledge of the local customs.

"She'll be able to tell you all about the St. Wilfrid's procession, Sheba. I was sure you'd find it interesting."

"No, I wouldn't, and you know it," she had retorted. "You just wanted an excuse to ask Miss Elliott to come with us."

He had grinned sheepishly at her, and she lacked the heart to chastise him any further. After all, who was she to throw stones? She had practically begged Dr. Blackmore to come to the festival with her, and she barely knew the man. Surely Matthew could be excused for wanting to spend the day with the woman he loved, even if that woman made the hair stand up on the nape of Bathsheba's neck.

So here they were, crammed like sheep in a pen at the edge of the market square, watching the most boring parade she had ever had the misfortune to witness.

She sighed, listening with one ear as Miss Elliott explained the theme of yet another pageant float to Matthew. Not that it wasn't obvious. After all, it was a depiction of Wellington's victory at Waterloo, but Matthew hung on the woman's every word, looking utterly foolish. He would do anything to remain in Miss Elliott's good graces, including listening to her pedantic lectures.

Lucky her, she thought sourly. Miss Elliott had her swain sitting in her pocket, whereas Bathsheba, standing in the midst of a large crowd, might as well have been in the middle of a desert for all that anyone paid attention to her.

Anyone like Dr. Blackmore, she grumbled under her

breath, growing more irritated by the second. Blast the man for kissing her like that—awakening all sorts of dormant feelings—and then turning on his heel and walking away. These last few days she had thought of little else but of his hard mouth sliding over her soft lips. It was driving her mad—mad with heat and longing. If she didn't get back to London soon, she would leap into the River Ure just to stop thinking about him.

Someone in the crowd jostled her, almost knocking her to the ground. She clutched Matthew's arm to steady herself.

He jerked around in alarm, ready concern springing into his eyes. "Are you all right, Sheba? Do you want to go back to the inn to rest? Or would you rather I take you home?"

She shook her head. "No. I'm fine." She wasn't, but she didn't want him to worry. Her feet hurt, her head ached, and it seemed they had been watching this damned procession for hours. When in God's name would it come to an end?

She leaned across Matthew and touched Miss Elliott's sleeve. "Miss Elliott, when does St. Wilfrid come by? I believe he is the last member of the procession, is he not?"

"Yes, Lady Randolph. But I'm afraid we have at least an hour to wait." Miss Elliott looked grumpy. "The saint," and she invested the word with a great deal of sarcasm, "and his retinue stop by every tavern they pass and drink a pint of beer. It takes forever, and by the time they reach the end of the procession . . . well, I'm sure you can imagine."

"Oh, no," groaned Bathsheba. "That's terrible."

"Indeed it is, your ladyship," replied the other woman, unbending a little. "I'm pleased you share my dismay at such an unfortunate tradition."

Bathsheba's only dismay was the thought of standing on the hard cobblestones for another hour. She couldn't blame St. Wilfrid—or the man posing as St. Wilfrid—for relieving the tedium of the procession. She would have been happy to slip into a nearby pub and do the same, but Miss Elliott would surely fall into an apoplectic fit.

"Tell me, Miss Elliott," beamed Matthew, "why does the good saint stop at every pub along the way? Hard to imagine how such a tradition came about."

"Indeed. But the superstitious locals believe it is unlucky for St. Wilfrid to pass by any tavern without stopping for a pint. Hence, we must all wait here in the hot sun, while half the participants in the parade become fuddled. Hardly proper behavior for a religious festival, if you ask me."

Matthew looked surprised. "Well, we can't expect an Englishman not to have a good time, especially during a festival. Nothing wrong with having a beer now and again, is there, Miss Elliott?"

Dismay registered on the spinster's pinched countenance and she began to lecture Matthew on the evils of excess. The look of apologetic consternation on her cousin's face tempted Bathsheba to laugh, then she remembered that Matthew was likely to get himself leg-shackled to Miss Elliott and the impulse died.

Impatiently, she retrieved her kerchief from her reticule and wiped away a trickle of sweat dripping down her neck. She *had* to get back to London in the next few days and start looking for a husband, or she was done for.

"Yoo-hoo, Lord Randolph!"

Lady Dellworthy's shrill voice rose over the crowd, a remarkable feat given the noise in the square. But the cacophony of hundreds of spectators and several musical bands couldn't match her ladyship's lung capacity.

They turned to see her waving madly as she plowed her way through the bystanders. Her husband trailed behind her, as did . . . Dr. Blackmore. Bathsheba's head began to buzz as all the blood drained south to her feet. She staggered, tightening her hold on Matthew's arm.

"Steady on, old girl," he cried. "Don't want to take a header in this mob. You'll get trampled to death."

"I'm . . . I'm fine," she stammered. She raised her eyes to look at Blackmore, still several feet away. He must have seen her stumble, for he frowned as he brushed past the Dellworthys to reach her side.

"Look who we found wandering around the square," crowed Lady Dellworthy. "I was absolutely astonished, I tell you. Why, Dr. Littleton himself told me that Dr. Blackmore was to return to London two days ago."

The others expressed the appropriate amount of surprise and delight, all talking at once. Blackmore ignored them as he slipped a strong hand under Bathsheba's elbow.

"My lady, do you feel faint?" His mouth was close to her ear, and his warm breath puffed across her neck. A delicious shiver tickled down her spine. She did feel wobbly, but it wasn't the heat or the crowds that made her legs tremble.

"No. I'm well," she said. Incredibly, she felt shy and tongue-tied. She hadn't been expecting to see him again. That must explain her foolish reaction.

Well, that and the fact he was the most enticing man she had ever met. Out here in the square, surrounded by so many people, the impact of his tall, masculine figure and his lean grace was strangely magnified.

His amazing eyes still inspected her with concern, drawing the attention of the other members of their party. Matthew cast Bathsheba a swift, astute look, and then stepped forward to offer his hand to Blackmore.

"A pleasure to see you again, Doctor. Sheba told me you'd be long gone by now."

"Oh, indeed," trilled Lady Dellworthy. "But the doctor just couldn't bring himself to leave—not yet. He said he had heard so much about the St. Wilfrid's procession that he couldn't think of departing until he had seen it. Isn't that right, Doctor?"

"Exactly right, Lady Dellworthy," he answered with a charming smile.

Bathsheba looked up to meet his gaze. His silver eyes laughed back at her, daring her to say a word. She blushed hotly, cursing her lack of discipline. But he would stand *right there*, his big body pushed up against hers by the crowd, his legs pressing into her skirts. She might faint just from the sheer pleasure of being close to him once more.

He finally took pity on her, edging away to give her some room. She drew in a shaky breath of relief, intensely aware that the others still stared at them.

Blackmore shifted so that he faced Miss Elliott and Lady Dellworthy.

"Miss Elliott, perhaps you would be kind enough to explain the origins of this festival to me. All I know is that Ripon has been celebrating the procession for centuries. Lady Dellworthy assured me that you would have all the facts and history."

"Oh, yes, Miss Elliott," chimed in Matthew. "Please do. I was telling Bathsheba last night how knowledgeable you are about the local customs."

The spinster beamed, almost pretty under the warmth of all that male attention. She launched into a detailed and tedious history of Ripon's honored festival. For once, Bathsheba didn't mind her pedantry. It diverted attention away from her idiotic reaction to the doctor.

Blackmore gradually moved behind her, using his large body to shield her from the jostling crowd. She loved that he was such a strapping man, with broad shoulders and a muscular chest. A demented impulse to cuddle against him swept over her, so overwhelming that she had to stand as straight and stiff as a pike to avoid doing just that.

Suddenly, a man carrying a frothing cup of ale bumped into her, spilling some liquid onto her skirts.

"Yoiks! Sorry about that, miss. Didn't see you there. You bein' such a little thing and all."

The young, handsome lad, perhaps an apprentice or a day laborer, gave her a good-natured, rueful grin. She shook out her skirts and returned his smile, about to answer when Sir Philip jumped in.

"That's enough of that, boy. That's Lady Randolph you're

addressing, and you'll keep a respectful tongue in your head when you speak to your betters. Now, be on your way or I'll call the constable."

The young man blanched under his tan.

"It's quite all right," Bathsheba said. "My gown is barely wet. There's no harm done at all." She nodded reassuringly at the lad, who ducked his head gratefully and melted into the crowd.

"Well done, my lady," murmured Blackmore in her ear. She flushed with pleasure at his simple words of praise.

"He was just a boy," she said.

"A boy who doesn't know his place," growled Sir Philip. "The whole country is going to wrack and ruin, starting with the lower classes. Don't remember their proper place in the world, and that young jackanapes was the perfect example."

"I must agree with you," said Miss Elliott. "Insubordination and lack of respect for one's superiors have become the distinguishing characteristics of our age."

Matthew shifted uncomfortably as he glanced around. Bathsheba, too, saw the scowls on some of the nearby faces. The music and cheerful shouts of the crowd hadn't been loud enough to drown out Miss Elliott's or Sir Philip's comments.

"Surely you exaggerate, Miss Elliott," Blackmore said. "In my experience, the average working man labors long and hard, with little recompense for his work. I cannot blame him for seizing a little respite from all his cares."

"By drinking himself into the gutter, you mean," retorted the spinster. "I cannot agree. Not when that man's respite takes food from the mouths of his wife and children. That, sir, is any man's first responsibility—not pleasure."

Blackmore inclined his head. "You're right, of course. But for too many Englishmen, the burdens of life are harsh and the anxieties of it weigh down their souls. I cannot be surprised when such men seek occasional solace with a pint of ale or a dram of blue ruin."

Miss Elliott's thin mouth grew thinner. *God help Matthew,* Bathsheba thought.

"Dr. Blackmore, you approve of such licentious behavior?" demanded Miss Elliott.

"No. But I can understand, and try to forgive."

Bathsheba waited for the explosion, but it didn't come. Instead, the spinster eyed Blackmore thoughtfully before giving a quiet harrumph.

"I don't agree with you, Doctor, but I suppose I understand your point of view. You must see much to disturb you in your line of work."

Lady Dellworthy's hands flew dramatically up to her expansive and beruffled bosom. "Well, I don't understand it at all. Really, Doctor! How you can bring yourself to mix with the lower classes so frequently is something I can never begin to fathom. Why, Sir Philip practically had to drag me to the festival today. So many low characters wandering about—cut-purses and thieves surround us this very minute, I'm sure. One doesn't feel safe even in broad daylight!" She waggled a hand loaded down with expensive rings at her husband. "But, naturally, my lord and master insisted we come."

Sir Philip smiled indulgently at his wife. "It's expected, my dear. Can't be too high in the instep, now can we? No need to stay any longer than necessary, though. After the service in the cathedral, we'll return home in a trice. You have my word on it."

"Well, thank the good Lord for that," Lady Dellworthy exclaimed. She leaned past her husband, clutched Bathsheba's arm, and spoke in a stage whisper that could likely be heard on the other side of the square. "I would advise you do the same, Lady Randolph. You won't believe what goes on after the procession has ended. Why, just look at all the loose young women parading up and down."

Bathsheba glanced around, seeing only happy families and the usual assortment of young folk—chattering couples sauntering about the square, gaily dressed misses laughing and flirting with their adoring beaus. As tame a scene as a Thursday evening at Almack's.

She shrugged her shoulders.

"Exactly," the older woman said, nodding wisely. "Licentiousness is all around us. The girls expose themselves in the most reprehensible manner, seeking to attract male attention. And then the men latch onto them and carry them off to dancing rooms." Her watery blue eyes bugged out with a horrified excitement. "And after that, we can only imagine what happens. I absolutely forbade any of my maids to leave the house today because I will not tolerate such immoral behavior."

Words failed Bathsheba. Behind her, she could feel Blackmore shaking with silent mirth. She gulped, biting the inside of her cheek to keep from giving in to her own laughter.

Miss Elliott leveled a suspicious gaze on them, then returned her attention to the other woman. "Very wise, Lady Dellworthy. As you say, one can only imagine."

Bathsheba had a hard time believing the spinster could, in fact, visualize what might happen between those imaginary couples. She swallowed even harder, desperate to keep down the mad giggles swelling in her throat. Blackmore squeezed her elbow—in warning or commiseration, she wasn't sure. But the fact that he shared her amusement only made it worse.

"Oh, look," exclaimed Matthew, sounding relieved. "There's St. Wilfrid. About bloody time, I must say."

"Lord Randolph!" Miss Elliott's shocked rejoinder necessitated another round of profuse apologies from Matthew.

An imposing St. Wilfrid clopped by on his white steed, followed by his retinue of monks. All looked exceedingly cheerful, and only slightly worse for wear. The crowd began to break up, some moving to the food and craft booths scattered around the square, and others following behind the procession toward the cathedral.

Miss Elliott took Matthew's arm in a firm grip. "Shall we proceed to the service?"

Bathsheba peeked at Blackmore, who was making his farewells to Sir Philip and Lady Dellworthy. Obviously, he had no intention of going to the service. Gritting her teeth, she turned to follow her cousin and Miss Elliott. It killed her to have to spend the afternoon cooped up in the cathedral—where it would surely be hot and stuffy—but she couldn't abandon her party no matter how much she longed to stay with Blackmore. The local gossips would have a field day with that, and she didn't have the heart to cause any more scandals during the rest of her stay.

Blackmore's hand reached out and grasped her wrist, bringing her to a gentle halt. Startled, she gazed up at him. His expression was grave, but he had the devil in his eyes.

"Lord Randolph, a moment, please," he said to her cousin.

Matthew stopped abruptly, causing Miss Elliott to collide with a stout matron walking behind her. While the spinster made her apologies to the scolding woman, Matthew gave Blackmore an enquiring look.

"I would prefer Lady Randolph not spend the afternoon in a crowded and stuffy church," said the doctor. "She needs to eat and drink, and perhaps to stroll by the river for some fresh air."

He glanced down at her, a gently mocking smile playing around the corners of his mouth. "Wouldn't you agree, my lady? Or would you prefer to attend the service?"

Her mouth went dry, which certainly bolstered his claim that she needed something to drink.

"Oh! Of course, I shall be sorry to miss the service," she said in a plaintive voice. "But my throat is parched, and I do feel quite overcome with the heat. A stroll by the river sounds most refreshing." She finished with a pathetic cough.

Miss Elliott finally managed to disentangle herself from the irate matron and righted her poke bonnet. She stared at them through narrowed eyes. "I'm sure her ladyship will benefit from sitting quietly at the service, out of the sun."

"I don't agree, Miss Elliott," Blackmore replied. "And, as her doctor, I insist on having the last word."

He gave the bristling spinster a charming smile, then took Bathsheba's hand and placed it in the crook of his arm. His subtly possessive manner sent heat coursing low in her belly.

"Well, it's all settled, then," exclaimed Matthew. "Sheba, we'll meet you back at the Unicorn after the service. And if you get tired, ask for the carriage and John Coachman will take you home. I'm sure I could beg the Dellworthys to give me a ride. Just a few miles out of the way, wouldn't you say, Sir Philip?"

Before Sir Philip could reply, the crowd surged around them and carried Matthew and his party along toward the cathedral. Blackmore drew Bathsheba close, shielding her as he edged them in the opposite direction. Matthew, swept along with Miss Elliott, gave a cheerful wave before being swallowed up in the mass of people.

"That was easier than I thought," Blackmore said as he steered her toward a cluster of tables set up by the food booths. "For a moment, I thought Miss Elliott would take you by force to the cathedral." He grinned at her. "For your own good, of course."

She burst out laughing, unable to hold it in any longer. Several passersby turned to stare, but they all smiled back, seeming to enjoy her merriment.

"Thank you," she finally gasped. "The thought of spending another minute with Miss Elliott and the Dellworthys was truly more than I could bear. I've been good, but I couldn't vouch for my behavior much longer, even if we were in a cathedral."

"Even taking into consideration your seditious remarks at the Dellworthys' dinner party—and I was possibly more outrageous than you were—why has Miss Elliott taken such a dislike to you? Even Lady Dellworthy has forgiven you."

She smiled up at him as they sauntered through the crowd. For the first time in a long time, Bathsheba felt free. Free to relax, free to laugh . . . free to enjoy the company of a handsome man without needing anything from him in return.

"She sees me as a corrupting influence. As far as I can tell, our Miss Elliott has taken quite a liking to you. She's convinced I'll try to debauch you."

His eyes went sultry and dark, and she felt an answering throb in her belly.

"I can only hope Miss Elliott's fears will be realized," he murmured.

She flushed, and the wobbly feeling came rushing back. In a second, Blackmore's expression returned to that of a doctor instead of an ardent suitor.

"When was the last time you had something to eat?"

"Breakfast." And she'd only picked at her food, too gloomy to eat. But now she was famished.

He shook his head, his disapproval clear, and steered her toward a table partially occupied by a boisterous family with three children. They obligingly made room, and the husband promised to look after Bathsheba while Blackmore went in search of refreshments.

"Not to worry, sir. I'll keep the young bucks away from your little wife. They won't touch a hair on her pretty head."

Bathsheba frowned at the man's presumption, but Blackmore just laughed, winking at her before moving off to join the long lines in front of the food booths. After a moment's hesitation, she decided it wasn't worth making a fuss about. Besides, she needed a few quiet moments to think about why Blackmore had stayed in Ripon. The answer seemed clear, and her heart pounded with excitement knowing he had deliberately sought her out.

But what could that really mean for her? On Monday she must still return to London, to her search for a husband. Blackmore could be nothing more than a temporary diversion, even if he did awaken feelings and sensations she had thought dead and buried.

Bathsheba took a calming breath and watched him weave his way back through the crowd. Catching her gaze, he smiled—a smile full of sensual intent. So full it almost felt like a threat. A cloud passed over the sun, throwing the square into shadow, and she shivered. A sudden anxiety washed through her. If she hadn't been wearing gloves, she would probably have given into her weakness and bit one of her fingernails down to the quick.

"Here, missus." The pleasant voice of the young wife at their table made Bathsheba start.

The woman gave her a friendly smile. "Slide in a bit so your husband will have room to sit beside you."

Blackmore strode up to the table, holding a cup and a tankard in one big hand and two plates crammed full of cakes and pastries in the other. When she didn't slide down the bench, he gave her a questioning look. She hesitated, then moved over to give him room. His thigh, sheathed in buckskin, brushed against her. It seemed absurd, but the heat of his body practically scorched her.

She blushed, silently cursing her apparent return to her days as a painfully shy schoolroom miss.

He handed her the cup. "Drink this."

She sniffed before taking a cautious sip. Lemonade, and quite good lemonade at that. He moved one of the plates in front of her and gave her a fork.

"Now eat," he said, his deep voice a rumbling purr.

"Yes, Doctor," she replied obediently, and he laughed.

As she tried to make a dent in the ridiculous amount of food he had fetched for her, Blackmore fell into easy conversation with the young family whose table they shared. In between pulls on his tankard of ale, he discussed local politics with the father and complimented the mother on the beauty and health of her children.

Bathsheba found the banality of the conversation strangely

soothing, and her tension started to drain away. She allowed herself to relax against the hard, male body sitting so close to her on the bench, but jumped when he casually reached back and slipped an arm around her waist. After a few moments of silent panic, she decided it would make more of a fuss to draw away or insist he remove it. Besides, in the crush of the tables and the crowd, no one would probably notice anyway.

While Blackmore drank his ale and demolished his plate of food, Bathsheba made a funny face at the toddler nestled in her father's arms on the other side of the table. The little girl's blue eyes widened and she grinned back, playing peek-a-boo from between her chubby fingers. Bathsheba laughed, mostly at the silly game but also at herself. The fever must have damaged some portion of her brain, since she actually seemed to be enjoying an afternoon spent eating cakes and playing with dirt-smudged infants. And pretending to be the wife of a man she barely knew.

Blackmore removed his arm from her waist and stood. "Well, my dear," he said, obviously enjoying the charade as much as she was, "shall we take that stroll down by the river?"

He extended his hand as he gazed at her with a sensual, heavy-lidded intent. One part of her—the woman who had been Reggie's wife—whispered a warning. But another part of her, the one he had called forth with his kisses, couldn't resist that look. She murmured her good-byes to the young family and took Blackmore's hand, letting him pull her to her feet.

He rewarded her with a smile and tucked her hand firmly in the crook of his arm. He didn't rush her through the square, but his pace was steady and determined, as if he had more in mind than just a leisurely stroll by the river. Energy crackled between them, and she felt the stirrings of desire in the most intimate parts of her body.

They turned into a quiet side street that led to the river. Bathsheba studied the neat row of classical-style town houses, interested in her surroundings despite the distraction of the large man prowling next to her. She hadn't been into Ripon proper in years. On the few occasions when she came north to Compton Manor, she rarely left the Randolph estate. But Ripon really was a lovely town, especially on a beautiful summer's day. As they strolled along, she could almost pretend she didn't have a care in the world, and that Blackmore actually meant something to her.

"Did you have enough to eat?" His husky voice broke into her thoughts.

"You gave me enough to feed a small army. Apparently, Doctor, you think I have the appetite of a farm laborer." She lifted an eyebrow. "I'm not quite sure what to think of that. Perhaps I should be offended."

"Someone has to take care of you," he said reasonably. "No one else is doing it."

Her feeling of contentment withered away, replaced by a dull ache somewhere in the vicinity of her heart.

"I'm perfectly capable of taking care of myself, thank you. I don't need anyone to do it for me."

"But I think you do," he replied in that same reasonable, aggravating tone.

She tried to pull her hand out from his arm, but he kept a steady grip on it.

"Come," he said. "There's a little ruin just on the other side of the Hewick Bridge where you'll be able to sit and rest. You're obviously feeling agitated and out of sorts."

"If I'm out of sorts, it's because of you," she snapped.

He gave her that superior doctor's smile, but held his tongue. Silence fell between them. She was too annoyed to break it. Unfortunately, he didn't seem the least uncomfortable, while she could have sworn that ants had crawled underneath her stays.

After several minutes of deafening silence, her nerves shredded into pieces. If she hadn't been agitated before, she certainly was now. And blast him for being so cool and collected. What the devil did he intend by her, anyway?

"Why did you stay in Ripon?" she finally blurted out.

He gave her a hooded glance, his eyes watchful as he led her onto the stone bridge crossing the River Ure.

"Not here," he said. "Wait till we get to the ruins. Then I'll tell you."

She grumbled under her breath, his only response a smile that barely lifted the edges of his lips. Strangely, he now seemed as tense as her, the muscles of his arm as hard as iron under her fingers.

"Well, where are these famous ruins?" she demanded.

"There." He pointed to a tumble of walls barely visible through a stand of oak trees, half hidden by creepers and a riot of tangled rosebushes.

Taking her hand, he towed her down an overgrown path to the back of an old chapel that had crumbled into picturesque decay. The roof had fallen in ages ago, and massive granite stones lay scattered on the ground. The sounds from the festival and the town had faded away, and she could hear only the flow of water from the river and the trilling of a songbird.

Blackmore led her to one particularly impressive stone in the shadow of the tumble-down church walls. He let go her hand, grabbed her waist, and plopped her gently down on the stone, which was covered in a dense and springy moss. She squeaked in surprise, reaching for his shoulders to keep her balance. He moved closer, slowly pushing her knees apart to stand between them. She sat high on her rustic seat, their faces on the same level.

"I . . . I don't want to sit," she protested. She hated feeling this vulnerable.

"You need to rest," he said, stroking his long fingers down the side of her neck. She fought back a tremor, furious with her lack of self-control. An hour ago, she had wanted this . . . wanted him. She still wanted him, but not all the complications that would come with it.

Scowling, she crossed her arms across her breasts.

"Well, we're alone now. Nobody can overhear us, so answer my question. Why did you decide to stay?"

The smoldering fire in his eyes sucked the air right out of her lungs. His fingers slid up her throat to capture her face in a tender but unbreakable grip. Moving in, he took her mouth in a hard kiss—raw, punishing, and glorious. She whimpered under the onslaught and he pulled back, still holding her face between his big hands.

"This, Bathsheba," he growled. "I stayed for this."

Chapter 8

Bathsheba stared at him—flushed, beautiful, and seemingly as stunned by his kisses as any untried maiden. Her eyes were round and dazed, and the moist fullness of her parted lips made the heat burn through John's veins and race down to his groin. His body grew hard and hungry, and the need to taste her again drove him back to her mouth.

He pulled her into his arms and her lush breasts strained against his torso. She gasped, a sweet inhalation of air that opened her mouth to his plundering kiss. He devoured it, exploring her damp softness, stroking in and out before gently sucking her tongue between his lips. She surrendered, wrapping her arms around his neck with a voluptuous sigh.

John slid one hand between their bodies to capture her breast. Beneath the fabric of her muslin gown and her stays, her nipple peaked into a hard bud. He rubbed, tempted beyond reason by the pearled tip of flesh obscured beneath the layers of her clothing. She whimpered and pushed against his fingers, and her eagerness seared his self-restraint. He had to slow down before he ripped the clothes from her body and fell on her like a primitive brute.

With a last nuzzle of her lips, John eased her firmly back on her seat. Her eyes had been closed but now they sprang open, looking as soft and green as the moss that dappled the rock underneath her bottom. She blinked several times, as if trying to bring her gaze into focus.

"What's wrong?" she whispered. Her voice held a wrenching note of uncertainty.

He stroked the smooth velvet of her cheek. "I want you too much, my sweet. If I don't restrain myself, you'll be flat on your back in thirty seconds with my rod deep inside you. I think we both want more than that."

"Oh," she said, her big eyes growing even bigger.

Bathsheba looked shocked—even nervous. In fact, if he didn't already know who and what she was, John could have sworn his arrogant little aristocrat had just been released from the schoolroom to begin her first Season. That's how young and innocent she seemed, perched on that rock with her kiss-stained mouth and huge eyes conveying an unexpected vulnerability.

Time slowed, and John could do nothing but drink in the glorious sight of her. She had surprised him again. Instead of a sophisticated and sexually experienced widow, his sensual onslaught had revealed a lovely girl not quite sure of her own feminine powers. Part of him wanted to laugh with the delight of that discovery, but his chest—no, his heart—ached to see her so defenseless, so in need of his protection. He had meant what he said back on the bridge. She needed someone to take care of her.

That someone was going to be him.

The unexpected realization clawed him in the gut. *Take care of her?* What the hell was he thinking? They might travel in the same circles, but their worlds could not be more different.

"Dr. Blackmore?"

Now she sounded more annoyed than anxious. He kissed her again, slow and deep, to keep her from asking any questions, and to give him time to think.

He played with her mouth for a few minutes, their kisses

moist and hot. Her mouth was silky . . . sweet as hell and as addictive as opium.

Their tongues danced in a tangle of heat. Her small fingers clutched the lapels of his coat, and she wriggled to the edge of the stone to nestle against him. Without a thought, he lashed his arms around her, holding her close. As if she already belonged to him.

God, what a fool I am.

He had allowed his heart to become involved—he could feel it. As surely as he could name every organ in her lush body, his emotions were entangled, despite all his vows to keep them firmly detached. The only entanglement he sought was that of arms and legs as they enjoyed each other. Anything else was unacceptable, would surely lead to disaster. His heart was for pumping blood, and nothing more. He couldn't afford to fall in love, especially with a woman like Bathsheba Compton.

She yanked hard on his ear.

"Ouch!" He jerked back and stared at her. "What was that for?"

She looked decidedly put-out and totally adorable. "You weren't paying attention, Doctor. If I'm boring you, perhaps you would be so kind as to help me off this rock and escort me back to town."

He smiled. "I think not, my lady. We're just getting started." He dropped his voice to a husky note. "And I think it's time you called me by my given name—John."

She swallowed hard, looking shy again. But then something shifted in her gaze. That bruised, vulnerable look faded away, and his wicked countess—sultry and knowing—stared back at him.

He laughed softly. "There you are."

She tilted her head and everything changed again. Her eyes grew soft as something elusive and shadowed chased the wickedness away. He looked deep into her secret gaze and knew he was lost. There was no going back, and no possibility that his heart could remain untouched. Desire swamped him, driven by a need to possess—a need he could no longer deny.

"John." Her voice, soft as swan's down, drifted over his senses. She reached up and knocked his hat from his head, sending it toppling to the ground. Her fingers busied themselves in his cravat. He allowed it, using those few seconds to throttle his hunger back under a precarious control.

The cravat followed the hat to the ground, but when she started on the buttons of his waistcoat, he stopped her.

"Enough—for now," he said, taking one of her small gloved hands in his. She lifted an eyebrow, but didn't object.

He unbuttoned the glove and slowly removed it. Bringing her hand to his lips, he slowly licked the tip of each finger before tasting the plump swell of her palm and the fragile turn of her wrist.

She shuddered. With great care, he repeated the action on her other hand. Her breathing grew unsteady, the fullness of her breasts rising and falling in a luscious, quivering rhythm. Lust dug in its spurs, urging him to spread her thighs and taste the hidden cove of her body. But he held back. This was the first, precious time he would have her. He would not rush it—for both their sakes.

After tossing her gloves on the rock, he untied the ribbons of her ridiculously high-crowned bonnet. She sighed in relief as he removed it. A sheen of perspiration misted along her hairline and down the edge of her cheek. He leaned over and licked her temple, savoring the salty taste of her perfect skin. She reached for him, but he stepped away before she could touch him.

"Now what?" she moaned. "Why must you take so long?"

"You're a mystery to me, Bathsheba," he replied, dropping to one knee to remove her kid half-boots. "I'm a man of science, and scientists like to peel away the mystery. One layer at a time."

She crossed her arms under her breasts, pushing them up to swell over the lace trim of her bodice.

Soon, he promised the prowling beast within. Soon he would lick and suck those luscious mounds to his heart's content.

"You make me sound like an onion," she grumbled.

He chuckled hoarsely. "A sweet onion, with a bite to it."

He slid his hand under her skirt, letting it drift up a slender calf to the firm swell of her thigh. His fingers brushed against the curls between her legs, barely touching the plump flesh hidden by the soft thatch. She bit her lip, showing her little white teeth. A shaft of heat bolted through him, and his cock grew harder against his buckskins.

He stood and reached behind her. His fingers shook for a moment, then steadied as he went to work on the buttons at the back of her gown. He tried to ease the full, heavily trimmed sleeves of the dress from her arms, but they were buttoned tightly at the wrist.

"Christ," he muttered, as he struggled with the tiny buttons. "No wonder you always feel faint. Why must you wear something this heavy on a warm day like today?"

She tried to help him but he brushed her hands away.

"I don't always feel faint. And you can't expect me to go around dressed like a peasant girl," she said, letting him have his way.

He moved to the other sleeve. "I think you'd make a damn fetching peasant girl. And at least you'd be dressed more appropriately for the heat. Of course, your neckline is certainly cut low enough to give you some relief."

It was, too, and he leaned over to kiss the tender white flesh that strained over the top of her bodice. The skin there tasted a bit salty, too, and of warm, sultry woman. He pushed his tongue under the lace to find the fragile edge of rosy-colored flesh surrounding her nipple. She moaned, and her hands fluttered up to rest on his shoulders.

He straightened and gave her a lascivious grin, one that

brought a little pant to her lips. She looked like a pagan goddess, flushed and half wild, with her dress sagging to reveal the creamy glow of her shoulders and breasts.

"I'm feeling rather hot myself," he said. He stripped off his coat, but didn't drop it to the ground.

"Here." He slid one arm under her bottom and lifted, then slipped the coat underneath her. "I don't want you to get dirty."

"Of course not," she said in a breathy voice. "That would never do."

He nodded, satisfied that his coat and the thick layer of moss would shield her body from the hard stone. With impatient fingers, he unbuttoned his waistcoat and dropped it on the ground beside his hat. He unlaced the strings of his shirt, but didn't bother to remove it.

She watched him all the while, her eyes glittering with unfettered desire under half-closed lids.

"Let's get rid of that dress," he murmured.

He eased down the sleeves, and helped her as she wriggled it down past her waist and hips. Next, he quickly unlaced and removed her stays. She perched demurely on the stone seat, clad only in her linen chemise and stockings, somehow managing to look every inch the countess and yet also appear on the verge of sexual abandon.

He stood back to enjoy the picture. A few rays of sunlight penetrated the thick cover of the oaks, catching the red fire in her hair and heating her ivory complexion to a golden sheen. She looked like an outrageously expensive and polished confection in this rustic setting, and he couldn't wait to devour every bit of her.

"Let's get that off you," he said, reaching for the chemise.

"Let me." She took the hem and with a teasing slowness pulled it up, revealing one creamy inch of flesh at a time. Over her soft rounded thighs, past the silky nest of dusky red curls—already glistening with moisture—over the curve of her belly, and finally to her breasts.

He clenched his teeth as the linen drifted over the round

globes, catching on her nipples. Then the chemise was off, tossed to the side, and he could see her breasts. They were perfect—full and white, with rosy areolas surrounding the erect pink nipples. He salivated just at the sight of them—at all of her—and couldn't wait a second longer.

She smiled at him, wanton and wicked, and shifted on his coat, parting her legs just a bit. It was pink down there, too. He could see the soft, feminine flesh peeking out from behind the pretty tangle of curls.

"What's next, my dear doctor?" she purred.

He dropped to his knees in front of her and pushed her legs wide.

"This," he said, and buried his mouth in her liquid heat.

Bathsheba let out a strangled cry as John parted her thighs, his mouth fastening with a luscious suck on the cleft between her legs. Sensation bolted through her—electric and hot—and her bottom jerked up of its own accord as she strained against him.

It was too much. Too fast. She was too exposed. His broad shoulders pushed her legs wide, opening every part of her to his ministrations. For God's sake. He could see *everything*.

She tried to wriggle back, torn between the thrill of his tongue and the embarrassment of her undignified position. Since she began to take lovers after Reggie's death, she had always made sure to control the circumstances of her lovemaking—the time and place and, most particularly, how she looked. And she always made sure she looked perfect. Her lovers expected nothing less.

Now, she was splayed on a rock like some bizarre pagan sacrifice. She was hot and sweaty, and her thighs looked enormous mashed up against John's shoulders.

The flat of his tongue dragged across the already quivering peak of her sex, and she felt a mortifying amount of slick moisture dampen her curls. He licked her, thrusting his tongue into her cleft, murmuring with evident satisfaction as he tasted her body's release.

"John, stop," she gasped, trying to wriggle away.

His big hands wrapped even tighter around her thighs, holding her in place. He lifted his head, stared at her with a hot, smoky gaze, then slowly licked his lips.

She almost fainted.

"Don't you like it?" His voice was a deep rumble.

"I . . . I . . ." She did, but that hardly seemed the point. And she couldn't really explain that she wanted him to stop because she was sweaty and her thighs looked fat.

His hands slid underneath her bottom. "That's what I thought. Come here." He pulled her back to his mouth. "Just lie back and enjoy it, Bathsheba. Doctor's orders."

His mouth descended once more to her heated flesh, and all thoughts of looking dignified—or at least not sweaty— fled her brain.

She groaned, leaning back on her elbows. Her head bobbed heavily on her neck, making her want to sink back onto his coat and the mossy rock as he had his way with her. But, wickedly, she wanted to watch as he feasted—and *feasted* was the only appropriate word—swirling and flicking his tongue across her throbbing sex.

Shifting a bit, she settled on her forearms and elbows, giving in to an impulse to spread her legs wide. He growled his approval, kneading the globes of her bottom as he tilted her hips up to delve more deeply into her body. He sucked, his lips closing around the rigid nub of her sex, and a series of small, intense contractions began to pulse through her sheath.

She gazed down over her breasts, full and white, the nipples stiffly erect, and longed to feel his mouth on them, too. Her smooth belly quivered under his onslaught, and she suddenly realized that she loved seeing herself like this—spread wide, naked and completely open to the attentions of this handsome and powerful, almost fully dressed man. It was wicked—a dark, erotic fantasy come to life.

A hard spasm contracted her womb, drawing a long moan from her throat. He drew back for a moment and looked at her, his eyes fierce and possessive as he let his gaze roam over her body to finally rest on her face.

"God, Bathsheba," he groaned. "I want to devour every inch of you. You taste so damn good—like hot honey."

She wriggled her bottom. "Don't stop."

He made a remarkably feral noise in his throat as he pushed her legs even wider. She finally collapsed onto the rock, gazing up through the dense trees but seeing nothing, feeling only the hot suck of his lips, the wet lave of his tongue thrusting into her. She began to lift her hips against his mouth, pushing hard, straining to find the climax that throbbed so close.

"John, please," she begged, shocked by the desperation in her voice but too far gone to care.

He knew what she wanted. Without taking his mouth from her drenched flesh, he carefully inserted one, then two fingers into her sheath. Pleasure arced through her body with a pulsing heat. From a distance, she heard a woman's voice, pleading and sobbing, and realized it was her own.

But John was merciless, keeping up the tantalizingly slow pump of his fingers, all the while as he sucked her tender flesh.

Bathsheba couldn't take any more. She draped her legs over his shoulders and pushed down against his mouth. He responded by reaching farther inside her, pressing and massaging with a sustained rhythm. Deep within her womb the shudders began, rippling outward. He gave a hard suck and she detonated, her voice lifting to a high, keening wail. Spasms pushed her into a rapturous, quivering release until she fell back against the cushion of his coat, limp and spent.

She lay there, panting and staring at the rustling leaves above her, her heart still hammering in her chest. John planted a last kiss on her thigh and came to his feet. Although his hands drifted over her legs in a soft caress, he said nothing. The moment stretched, and as her body settled, the pleasure fading to a dim glow, a vague sense of unease began to overtake her.

"Are you going to stare up at the trees all day, or do you think you could bring yourself to look at me?" he asked.

Blast him, now he sounded amused.

She pushed herself up on her elbows and glared. Sure enough, he started to laugh.

"You, my lady, are remarkably hard to please. Here, let me help you up."

He took her hands and gently pulled her into a sitting position. She looked down at herself, flushed, damp, naked, and . . . and . . .

"I look a wreck. God only knows how I'll put myself back together," she grumbled, pushing back the hair from her face. Although she couldn't see it, her coiffure had certainly been demolished.

He shook his head. His silver eyes glittered with mischief, and he looked so handsome that her heart flopped over in her chest.

"You're daft," he said. "You're the most beautiful thing I've ever seen in my life."

He bent and nipped her shoulder. She gasped, the painful little bite sending a thrill right down to her core. That's all it took for her to want him again. Which, of course, was out of the question.

"John, I really don't think—"

"Stop thinking," he purred, swooping in to take her breast as masterfully as he had taken the flesh between her thighs. His lips fastened to her nipple and he sucked hard. She moaned as her womb contracted, and grabbed his head with both hands, holding him to her chest.

He groaned, the vibration of it rippling across her skin. Reaching up to her other breast, he gently tweaked the rigid nipple. A maddening pressure built once more in the juncture of her thighs, and she thrust her hips against his lean, hard torso as the wildness returned.

That thrust brought her against the length of his erection, huge and hard on her damp flesh. She grew softer and wetter, aching for the feel of him inside her.

Although Bathsheba loved the sensation of his tongue sucking her and his teeth scraping over her tight nipple, she wanted—needed—more.

"John," she moaned, tugging on the silky ends of his short hair.

He murmured something, but refused to release her breast from the hot pull of his mouth. For a moment she just watched him, his masculine body thrusting between her naked thighs, watched as he devoured her, his eyes closed but his face drawn and intent with sexual hunger. One hand cupped her other breast, his fingers pulling the nipple into a stiff, burning peak.

She grabbed his head and yanked it up. He was so far gone in the throes of lust that it took a moment for him to focus on her face.

"Now," she commanded.

His lips peeled back in a smile that looked more like a snarl, and he freed himself from his breeches. His erection sprang free, jutting huge and heavy between her thighs.

Before she could react, he grasped her hips and pulled her to the edge of the rock. With one sharp thrust he penetrated her, filling her completely and driving the breath from her lungs. He was so big, so hot, so perfect that she could do nothing but wrap her legs and arms around him and hold on for dear life.

"Oh, God," he moaned, dropping his head onto her shoulder. "You're perfect, Bathsheba. So hot and wet. So tight."

He began to move then, thrusting in a slow, controlled rhythm. Little spasms rippled along her sheath. Her heart began to beat erratically, and she knew her climax was almost upon her. She tightened her legs around him, digging her heels into his thighs.

Somehow he knew. "Not so fast, sweetheart. I'm not ready for you to come yet."

He gently pulled her arms from around his neck and eased her down, laying her flat on her back. With a soft murmur, he urged her to relax the grip of her legs from around his thighs. Once more, she lay spread before him. But this time his cock pushed deep inside her, stretching her with a delicious, almost painful, ache.

He wrapped his hands around her hips and began to pump again, never taking his eyes from her face. She gazed back at him and felt herself tumble into the endless silver pool of his eyes. Sex had never been like this before, not even in that first year with Reggie, when she had been so mad for him. Her husband had manipulated her, always playing games—sometimes dark and perverse games that had been exciting, but afterward left her with a terrible sense of shame.

But here in this ruined little church—long since empty of its worshipers—everything was right. Bathsheba felt wild, free and somehow innocent, as if making love with John in the sun and open air had cleansed her of her sins.

He watched her behind heavy lids, his handsome face bronzed with passion. Leaning over, he entwined her hands in his and raised her arms over her head. The next thrust brought his body in hard contact with the peak of her sex, and she cried out his name from the sheer joy of it.

"Bathsheba," he groaned before taking her mouth in an urgent kiss. His pace increased, and the delicious fire between her legs spiraled high.

She broke free of the kiss and thrust up against him, loving the wild sound it brought to his lips. Their eyes met, and her heart took a leap at what she saw in his gaze. She saw no sick obsession in those smoky depths—only passion and, miracle of miracles, genuine tenderness. This man would never hurt her. With him, she was safe. To be herself. To cry out, to be messy, to not care who she was or how she looked.

The need was upon him now, she could tell. He pumped hard, his thick staff rubbing against her with delicious friction. The contractions began deep inside her sheath, milking him, sending them both in the final climb. She arched, silently urging him to the finish.

He understood. With a last demanding thrust he rocked her hips, sending her into climax. She cried out.

He shuddered, spilling himself into her. And with pounding hearts and fractured breath, they fell together into the sweet rushing tide of release.

Chapter 9

John was a big, powerful man, and right now he was doing a marvelous job of squishing Bathsheba into the rock. Even through his coat and the cushion of moss, every unforgiving jut of the uneven surface pressed into her body. As they sprawled in a heap, sweaty and panting, every muscle in her back shrieked in protest.

Even so, she couldn't bring herself to push at him to get off. It was heaven to be wrapped in his embrace, his erection still hard and thick within her. No sex had ever been so good, or so deliciously forbidden.

She wriggled, trying to dislodge a pebble beneath her spine. Sensing her discomfort, John withdrew with a reluctant groan and pushed himself up. She gave a sigh, one that mingled regret and relief.

"My poor sweetheart," he murmured as he quickly buttoned up the fall of his breeches. He gazed down at her with seductive eyes, looking far from sated. "Let's get you down before I'm tempted to take you again."

She groaned as he slipped his arms around her and helped her sit up. "Not today, I think, Doctor. I may possibly be crippled for life."

He frowned and began to rub her back, smoothing his strong fingers along her spine.

"Did I hurt you, Bathsheba?"

His husky growl had been replaced by a quick note of concern and, perhaps, a touch of guilt. She loved that about him, loved that he was so aware of her, caring more for her well-being than he did for his own.

She smiled, resting her head against the rumpled linen shirt that covered his broad chest.

"No. It was delightful," she said. "But I'm not sure I want to repeat the experience of making love on a rock pile."

He gave a soft laugh, the huff of his breath stirring her messy coiffure. "I told you I was a brute. But it's your fault. I can't seem to keep my hands from you."

Then he swept her off the mossy stone—coat and all—and into his arms. He lowered himself onto the ground and leaned back against the rock, cradling her carefully as he sank down. With a few quick movements, he had her arranged and resting comfortably in his lap.

"Better, my lady?"

"Mmm. Much better," she purred, snuggling into his arms. They tightened around her, and his mouth pushed through the tangled curls of her hair to nuzzle the top of her head.

They sat peacefully as the quiet of the late afternoon and the deepening shadows settled around them. A drowsing hush fell over the small ruin and the sheltering trees. Even the swallows had lost their voices, and only the rustling wind through the leaves and the buzz of the cicadas broke the heated silence of the summer day.

Bathsheba decided to ignore the little voice in her head that urged her to scramble from his lap and get dressed. They had to return to town, preferably before the others made their way back to the Unicorn. But her energy had been drained away by their fierce lovemaking, and John didn't seem inclined to release her from his embrace. In any event, the bells announcing the end of the church service had yet to ring. With luck, Miss Elliott would buttonhole the rector and drone on about some problem or other, perhaps the evils of strong drink or all those loose women wandering about Ripon.

Besides, it was so comfortable sitting in John's lap, and she felt certain she needed a rest after such vigorous physical activity. After all, she was still recuperating.

She was drifting off to sleep when the bells of the cathedral began to toll, jerking her awake. And just like that—as if someone had smacked her in the head—Bathsheba realized how much trouble she was in. Sitting on the ground, naked, a few hundred feet from the road, having just made love to absolutely the wrong man. If someone crossing the Hewick Bridge decided to wander out to visit the ruins, and discovered her like this . . .

The scandal would be so enormous that she'd have no choice but to marry John.

A vague panic began to coalesce, curling its way up from her stomach into her throat. She was about to climb out of John's lap when he suddenly covered her belly with a large hand, his fingers spreading from hipbone to hipbone.

"What are you doing?" she squeaked. She winced at her shrill tone, but they just couldn't make love again. She had to get dressed and away from here before the villagers who lived on this side of the river began returning home.

"I'm measuring the width of your pelvis," he said, carefully positioning his hand.

Despite her spiking anxiety, her stomach quivered to feel the calloused warmth of his fingers on her sensitive skin.

"Why?" she asked, momentarily diverted.

"For such a small woman, you have a nicely roomy pelvis."

She scowled, anxiety quickly transforming into irritation. No man had ever complained about her hips before, especially after making love to her. Quite the opposite, in fact.

"Are you calling me fat?"

He snorted, then nuzzled the side of her face.

"No. Your hips are perfect. I'm simply relieved to know

you should have no difficulty bearing children. Small women often do, you know."

She shivered as a cool breeze rustled through their little glade, chasing tiny goose bumps over her flesh. His arms tightened about her.

"Well," she ground out, "since I never became pregnant after four years of marriage, I don't expect I ever will."

He tilted her chin up, forcing her to look at him. His lean, strongly etched features grew watchful as he perused her countenance.

"That may have been your husband's fault, Bathsheba."

"It hardly matters." She shrugged off his embrace and clumsily scrambled up, using his shoulders for balance. He tried to help her, but she wouldn't take his hands.

"What's wrong?" he said, rising to his feet. "You seem . . . anxious."

A hysterical little laugh bubbled up from her throat as she swiped her chemise from the rock and pulled it over her head.

"What could I possibly have to be anxious about?" she said as her head emerged from the wrinkled linen.

He stood in front of her, hands braced on his hips, a big, dominating man preparing to be difficult. She knew the signs, and she knew exactly what she had to do about it.

"Bathsheba—"

"It would be best if you not get in the habit of calling me by my first name, regardless of what just happened between us. I would hate for you to slip and use it in public."

That shut him up for the ten seconds it took to retrieve her stays and slip them around her body.

"As you wish, my lady," he responded dryly.

A sharp little stab caught her in the chest. She hated treating him like this, but what else was she to do?

"I'm sorry to ask you to play lady's maid, but I need your help," she said, trying to sound both pleasant and unconcerned, as if he'd just examined her tongue and taken her pulse, not made her explode into a thousand little pieces of heart-wrenching joy. She blinked back a few self-pitying tears.

Without a word, he began to deftly lace up the stays. After finishing, he trailed his fingers over her shoulders with a gentle caress.

Move, she thought, but she seemed frozen in place by his touch.

"My sweet, please tell me what troubles you." His deep voice was as soothing as his hands on her body.

She had to clench her teeth against the sob that fought its way up from her chest. "Nothing is wrong," she rasped.

His skillful physician's fingers moved up to her neck, massaging away the knot she didn't even know was there until he touched it.

"That's odd, because I could swear you're displaying the symptoms of a woman suffering from a full-blown case of regret."

She forced out a laugh as she moved away from his too-seductive touch.

"Goodness, I make a point of never regretting anything in life, including my mistakes."

She heard the slow hiss of an angry exhalation, could feel the change in the air between them. Still, she refused to look at him, knowing it would probably kill her to see— well, what would most likely be an expression of contempt on his face.

"Help me with my dress, won't you?" She grabbed her gown from the rock and shook it out. Thankfully, it didn't look too crumpled. With luck, no one would know how they'd spent the afternoon.

She slipped the muslin over her head and turned her back to him, her heart thumping as he began to fasten the buttons. His fingers moved slowly, torturing her as they drifted up her back.

"Do you call this—what happened between us—a mistake?" Hurt, not anger, colored his voice, hurt she had inflicted on him when all he had ever done was take care of her. A small, cold ache of misery lodged behind her breastbone.

"No," she whispered, unable to lie. "I could never regret this."

He turned her around and took one of her wrists in his hands, going to work on the tiny buttons on her sleeves. Taking a deep breath, she forced herself to look at his face.

His fingers stilled on her cuff as his gaze lifted. The silver in his eyes had lost some of its luster, but his handsome features remained etched with determination. She had an inkling why he looked so serious, and it filled her with nervous dread.

"Bathsheba, we must talk," he said in a gentle voice, as if he didn't want to frighten her. "It's true that what happened between us was unexpected. My behavior has been nothing short of outrageous, and for that I must apologize. But, like you, I regret nothing. Just the opposite, in fact."

He finished with her cuff and moved to the other wrist, his eyes firmly trained on the task of securing a dozen little pearl buttons.

"There seem to be many differences between us," he continued in a suspiciously neutral voice, "but I believe our similarities outweigh those differences. I am a gentleman, from a well-established and prosperous family. My prospects are excellent, and I can offer you—"

"What are you talking about?" she demanded. She sounded like a fishwife, but she was surprised she could even hear herself over the mad thumping of her heart.

He sighed and engulfed her cold hand in both of his. "I'm trying to tell you, if you'd stop interrupting me. Do you think you could do that?"

She gave a jerky nod. He answered with a tight smile, and for the first time she noticed the tension around his eyes and the slight flush glazing his cheekbones. Her alarm spiked even higher.

"My feelings for you have grown quite strong," he continued, looking more stubborn by the second. "While it's true we didn't plan for this—for what happened here today—I want to explore it. I want to see what the future holds for us, and hope you will agree."

"Explore it," she said, feeling blank.

He gave an annoyed sigh. "I want to court you," he said in a slow voice, as if she were an idiot. But his gaze fastened warily on her face, gauging her reaction.

A sharp pang of regret sliced through her, and she had to choke back the sob rattling in the back of her throat. Exhaustion and something else tempted her to just give in to him—to say yes—but that was impossible. John's prospects might be good, but they weren't good enough. Not for what she needed.

She pushed back the useless, stifling emotion, taking refuge in the cynical persona she had created during the bitter years of her marriage.

"You must be joking, Dr. Blackmore," she said, tugging her hand away. Reluctantly, he let her go.

"Your gallantry is charming, but completely unnecessary." She grabbed her bonnet and shoved it onto her head, avoiding his eyes as she tied the ribbons in a large bow under her chin. "As I mentioned to you a few minutes ago, I'm incapable of getting pregnant, so there is no need for you to feel any concern."

"You can't know that," he said harshly.

"I assure you I can. You needn't give what happened between us another thought." She moved to brush past but his hand shot out and grabbed her wrist. Finally, she looked at him and the breath seized in her throat.

He was furious, as furious as any man she had ever seen. His eyes blazed with it, as deadly as a lightning strike in a summer storm. Something awful closed like a fist around her heart, and suddenly she saw her husband's face. He used to look at her that way, just before he lost his temper.

"Let me go," she rasped, struggling to escape him.

John released her and she stumbled back a few steps. With a visible effort, he wrestled his emotions under control.

"Hell and damnation. Forgive me, Bathsheba. I didn't mean to frighten you. You know I would never hurt you."

She fought to calm the pounding of her heart, then gave him a stiff nod. Of course he would never hurt her. He wasn't Reggie. But John posed a threat to her with his foolish desire to marry. He wouldn't give up unless she forced him.

"Apology accepted, Doctor," she said as she drew on her gloves. "But I suggest we return to town, before our charming interlude descends into farce."

"A charming interlude," he repeated in a flat voice.

She steeled herself, then lifted an eyebrow with disdain. "What else would it be?"

His eyes, no longer blazing, grew as hard as the stone that had served as their bed.

"I expected it would mean more than an opportunity for you to bed the nearest available man."

She gasped. "How dare you?"

"Forgive me, your ladyship, but I think it a little late to fall back upon your honor. Either you're lying to me for some reason, or I have misread you. I hope it is the former, because I would hate to think you really are the shallow jade the rest of the world believes you to be. But since you refuse to talk to me, I'm forced to draw my own conclusions."

Her gut clenched as if he had kicked her there. It was anger, she told herself as she swallowed the ice-cold pain that threatened to swamp her. Not despair. She was done with that emotion—a long time ago. Now it was time to be done with *him*.

"Really, Dr. Blackmore," she said in a brittle voice. "Whatever were you thinking? I'm the Countess of Randolph, not some innocent maiden yearning to be swept off her feet. Can you really imagine me as a physician's wife?"

His eyes narrowed to silver slits. "Until I actually ask you to marry me, no," he said in a hard, dismissive voice.

Shock fused with humiliation, and heat flooded her cheeks. Misery froze her into immobility as he shrugged into his waistcoat. His movements were clumsy and stiff, nothing like his usual, graceful self.

Bathsheba summoned up all her willpower, forcing herself to move.

"You'll forgive me, but I must return to the Unicorn to meet my cousin. He'll be expecting me. Shall I wait for your escort, or would you prefer we part company here?"

He paused, tailcoat in hand, regarding her with a baffled, furious gaze. She waited for a reply, but he remained silent.

She managed a twisted smile. "Then I'll bid you good day, my dear sir. Thank you for a most enjoyable afternoon."

Turning her back on him, she headed for the path out of the glade. She flinched when he uttered a truly foul curse, but she didn't look back. As she hurried through the trees, she strained to hear his footsteps behind her—praying he would follow, and praying just as hard he wouldn't. When she emerged from the wooded path onto the road, she turned back to look. But the path remained empty.

Bathsheba drew in a shuddering breath, shook out her skirts, and settled her bonnet more firmly on her head. Then she paced up the street toward the market square.

Alone, as always.

Chapter 10

Bathsheba knew she looked her best—stunning, in fact, in jade green silk—but that didn't prevent her from feeling as skittish as a debutante at her first ball. According to Sarah Ormond, the first whispers of rumors were beginning to circulate that Bathsheba's pockets were growing thin. If those rumors grew, her chances of landing a rich husband might evaporate in a matter of days.

"Come along, my dear," murmured Sarah. "We can't stand around in Lady Fancote's hallway all evening, can we? Even if it is the most luxurious hallway in London."

Her best friend smiled at her and gave her hand a reassuring squeeze. Bathsheba managed a weak smile in return, then forced herself to release Sarah's hand. Things were bad, but she needn't act like a frightened child longing for her mother.

Sarah glanced around the ornately marbled entrance hall. "Now, where is that husband of mine? Oh, naturally," she said sardonically. "Where else would he be?"

Richard Ormond had barely escorted them through the front doors of Fancote House before abandoning them to buttonhole one of the more important members of Liverpool's cabinet. Sarah's husband, a relatively new MP, was brilliant, principled, and addicted to politics. And although he adored his wife, eager to grant her every wish, he never missed an opportunity to cozy up to a potential political ally.

Sarah rolled her eyes. "Typical. I can't tell you how many times he's deserted me before we even step foot in the ballroom."

She sounded exasperated, but the love that shone from her big blue eyes told a very different story. And Richard clearly felt the same about his wife. He glanced across the room, obviously noting the wry expression on Sarah's face. Although he didn't break from his conversation, the heat in his gaze as he let it drift over his wife's delicate face and her trim, graceful figure practically scorched the air between them.

Bathsheba clenched her teeth, hating how jealous she felt. Sarah was her dearest friend, standing loyally by her side through the worst years of her marriage, always defending her against Reggie's vicious gossip. Aside from Boland, only Sarah knew the ugly truth of her relationship with her husband. After all, Reggie had done his best to get Sarah into his bed, even after she married Richard. In fact, the bastard had wanted Sarah and Bathsheba in his bed together, driven by a sick passion to have two of the most beautiful women of the ton in his sexual thrall.

That had been the moment when she realized once and for all what a cruel jest her marriage had become.

Sarah, of course, had wanted to tell Richard, but Bathsheba wouldn't let her. They had argued long and hard, but Bathsheba finally prevailed. Richard would have challenged her husband to a duel, and Reggie was a crack shot. Even if Richard had survived, word of the duel would have leaked out and the scandal would have destroyed his political career before it began. Bathsheba refused to have his demise— physical or political—on her conscience. Reggie had made her life a misery for refusing to help lure Sarah into his bed, but she had survived it, as she had survived everything else.

She sighed and pulled her soft kid gloves firmly up past

her elbows. Sarah's gaze switched back from mooning over her husband to settle on Bathsheba's face. A ready sympathy filled her eyes.

"I know, darling," she said in a low voice. "I wish you could find a man who would truly make you happy. Goodness knows you deserve it."

Bathsheba shrugged and gave her a rueful smile. "Perhaps I already have, and I let him get away." The image of John's hurt, angry face on that last day in Ripon swam into her mind, and she blinked away a sharp sting of tears.

"Nonsense. I refuse to believe that." Sarah reached her arm around Bathsheba's waist and ushered her to the gracefully curving staircase that led up to the Fancotes' ballroom. "The very man you seek may be here tonight. And you look so ravishing, he just might propose to you before the ball is over."

Bathsheba laughed. "Oh, Sarah, how can you be so absurd?" But she felt lighter, the other woman's affectionate concern easing the melancholy ache that refused to release its hold on her.

As they climbed the staircase with the rest of the guests, quite a respectable number given the time of year, she leaned in close to murmur in Sarah's ear.

"You're sure no one beside Lady Devoning and Mrs. Marpleson said anything about the state of my finances?" Despite her friend's earlier insistence that the rumors were little more than vague whispers, she still couldn't help but worry. In fact, just thinking about all the terrible ramifications if the truth emerged almost made Bathsheba want to flee back to the safety of Matthew's ramshackle estate.

Almost.

Sarah shook her head so vigorously that the crystal beads entwined in her golden hair clattered against each other.

"You mustn't worry so much. Lady Devoning was simply repeating gossip started by her dressmaker, who is also your dressmaker."

"Not for long," muttered Bathsheba.

"As I was saying," continued her friend with a quelling glance, "Lady Devoning then passed it on to Mrs. Marpleson. We did our best to scotch the rumor. Pretty effectively, I think. Richard told her that one would have to be delusional to think the Randolph fortune could be anything less than substantial. You know what he can be like when he puts on his MP voice. Thank God he happened to be at home yesterday when those two old biddies came to call. But, darling, you do realize better than anyone that it's almost impossible to squash that kind of gossip—at least not completely."

Bathsheba met her friend's sympathetic gaze and gave a tight nod. For years she had danced around the rumors, always putting on a good show, able to control the situation as long as Matthew stayed away from London. But time was quickly running out—almost as fast as her money. Faster, if Matthew was foolish enough to marry Miss Elliott.

They reached the top of the stairs and waited in the receiving line to greet Lord and Lady Fancote. A few minutes later, they strolled arm in arm into the magnificent ballroom. Bathsheba had always loved this room with its huge chandeliers, ormolu and rosewood side tables, and French-inspired chimneypiece and gilt doors. It was elegant, luxurious, and expensive—just the way she liked it. Her evening gown was a few shades darker than the color of the satin wallpaper, which was why she wore it. The colors set off the flame of her auburn hair to perfection.

Immediately, the two women were surrounded by a swarm of men, all begging for the favor of a dance. Sarah laughed and rolled her eyes at Bathsheba before allowing a very young and newly minted marquess to lead her into the next set.

For a few minutes, Bathsheba narrowed her eyes at her friend's dance partner, doing a swift appraisal of his potential as marriage material. He was handsome enough and rich, she knew, but he looked to be all of twenty-two. Not completely out of the question, and his youth might even be an advantage, making him easier to control.

But as she watched the young man lead Sarah through the figures, her hands grew damp within her gloves as she once again saw John's handsome, utterly masculine face in her mind's eye. She almost staggered as the dancers suddenly rippled and swam before her vision.

She pressed the tips of her gloved fingers to her temples, fighting despair. How was she ever to do what she must if all she could think about was a man she could never have?

"I say there, Lady Randolph. Looking a bit green around the gills, if you ask me. You might want to have a sit-down before you swoon right here in the middle of the ballroom."

She jerked around, startled to see Mr. Nigel Dash inspecting her with wary concern. Her small bevy of admirers had wandered away to pursue other game, seemingly put off by her lack of attention.

Bathsheba and Nigel stared at each other for long seconds, the silence between them growing awkward. He was a close friend to Simon, the Earl of Trask, the man Bathsheba had tried to blackmail into marriage. It was a testament to Nigel's impeccable manners that he not only noticed her lapse, but actually offered to help her.

She gave him a warm smile, genuinely touched by his consideration. "Thank you, Mr. Dash. I am rather feeling the heat. If you would be so kind as to escort me to a chair, I would be in your debt."

He looked surprised, but then his jovial social mask slipped back into place. She wasn't fooled. Nigel Dash dressed like a fop and acted like a rattle, but she had always suspected him of having more brains than most members of the ton gave him credit for.

"My honor, your ladyship." He offered her an arm and politely steered a path through the crowd, leading her to a small but comfortably padded chair set by a tall window wreathed in gold velvet swags.

"There," he said as she sank down gratefully onto the seat, "it's a bit cooler here." He peered at her. "Not that you look flushed, if you don't mind my saying so. Pale, more than anything else. Sure you ain't coming down with something?"

She stifled a bitter sigh. If only he knew how bad things really were. He would probably laugh, as would all her enemies, thinking that justice would finally be meted out to the Countess of Randolph.

"I must admit to feeling rather parched," she said. "Perhaps I might prevail on you to fetch me a glass of punch."

He frowned, looking confused. "Punch."

"Yes, please," Bathsheba replied, feeling confused herself. "Not champagne?"

Ah. No wonder he was puzzled. Everyone knew she never drank anything but champagne at parties. But since recovering from her illness, she seemed to have lost the taste for it.

Before he could answer, a tall, broad-shouldered man emerged from the crowd to loom in front of them.

"Nigel, you old dog. Leave it to you to hide away in the corner with the most beautiful woman in the room."

She looked up and opened her eyes wide with surprise. The most handsome man she had seen in ages except for John, of course—stood before her, his sapphire blue eyes fixed on her with great interest. Dressed in regimentals, he was obviously an officer of some rank. Bathsheba felt a pang of regret. He was handsome and didn't look stupid, but military men rarely possessed the kind of fortune that would serve her purposes.

"Stanton," cried Nigel, "didn't know you were back in London. Thought you were still abroad on some diplomatic business or other."

A Stanton.

Bathsheba perked up, interested now both in the man's parentage and the expression that flashed across his face.

For a moment, the hard angles of his sculpted features reflected a combination of cynicism and resentment.

But only for a moment, and then an easy, quite devastating smile took its place.

"No, I'm back," he said. "I'll be cashing out in a few weeks and joining the rest of you poor sods in a life of unending pleasure."

He turned his magnetic blue gaze back to Bathsheba.

"Speaking of pleasure, Dash, why don't you introduce me to your lovely companion?"

Nigel looked uneasy, but he could hardly refuse. "Lady Randolph, may I present Major Lucas Stanton, nephew to General and Lady Stanton, and just lately returned from the Continent." Bathsheba couldn't fail to miss the warning note in his voice.

"I'm delighted to meet you, Major," she responded with a seductive purr. "I have, of course, heard of your military exploits, even though I've not had the honor of meeting you until now."

Nigel turned as stiff as a hitching post beside her, and she could practically hear him repressing a groan. Not that she could really blame him. After all, to Nigel she was the dastardly vixen who had nearly destroyed Sophie Stanton's reputation, and now he had accidentally thrown another Stanton into her spider's web.

The major was most certainly not the average, impecunious officer. He was a wealthy viscount's heir, and all the gossips swore the current holder of the title was not long for the world. That, no doubt, was the reason Major Stanton was selling his commission. His aunt and uncle, General and Lady Stanton, would surely object to him falling into her clutches, but he hardly seemed the kind of man who worried about what his relations might think.

She flashed another quick gaze over his face and physique. Handsome and clearly rich and, judging by the way he was looking at her, unattached.

In a word, perfect.

He gazed down at her, his blue eyes heating with amusement and interest. She smiled back, leaving no doubt about her intentions.

"Dash, old man," the major said, turning his attention briefly to Nigel, "I'm sure her ladyship could do with a drink. Why don't you run along and find her something suitable."

Nigel opened his mouth, ready to object, when Bathsheba jumped in.

"Mr. Dash had just offered to fetch me a punch before you came up, Major." She fanned herself languidly. "It's so close in here, don't you think? I would be so grateful to have something cool to drink."

She watched Nigel stand there, his innate politeness warring with his reluctance to leave his friend in her nefarious clutches. The look of dismay on his face almost made her laugh out loud.

"Capital," exclaimed Major Stanton, clapping his friend on the shoulder. Nigel staggered slightly under the blow. "Run along now, Dash. I assure you, I'll take good care of her ladyship."

He gave her an outrageous wink and, for the first time in days, Bathsheba began to enjoy herself.

Nigel hesitated, then gave his usual faultless bow but couldn't help muttering to himself as he moved off through the crowd. Major Stanton lifted his eyebrows and he and Bathsheba broke into laughter. He settled with easy grace onto the chair next to her.

"Never saw Dash act like that before," he said. "I honestly thought he was going to refuse. Must have wanted to keep you all to himself."

"Something like that," she murmured.

They spent the next several minutes engaged in an amusing and lighthearted conversation. He quizzed her about life in London—claiming ignorance after so many years spent abroad in the army—and paid her any number of ridiculously entertaining compliments. The man was a hardened flirt, but she didn't think she'd mistaken the genuine interest in his gaze when it traveled over her.

A cautious hope dawned in her breast. It hardly seemed possible, but this just might be the man who could make her forget John Blackmore and solve her money problems at the same time.

When the orchestra struck up a waltz, Major Stanton broke off in the middle of an amusing tale about the latest antics of the royal princes. "Well, there's a piece of good luck. The first waltz of the evening and I just happen to be sitting next to the most beautiful woman in England. My dear lady, tell me that my luck will hold out and that no one else has engaged you to dance. I would hate to have to break the poor fool's head who tried to take you away from me."

He was outrageous, but she laughed anyway. "I'm all yours, Major. If you want me."

Something flickered in the cool blue gaze he leveled on her and, suddenly, what had been a light flirtation transformed into something much more serious.

"Oh, yes, Lady Randolph," he answered in a low rumble. "I definitely want you."

The moisture in her mouth evaporated, and she suddenly felt uneasy. But that was ridiculous, so she pinned a bright smile on her face and took his hand. After all, she could hardly afford to ignore the glorious opportunity that had just fallen into her lap.

"Lead on, Major," she said.

He swept her onto the crowded floor. As he swung her into the first turn, his torso brushed against her, sending an unexpected and unwelcome flash of heat right down to her toes. He was big and hard, both graceful and unyielding in the way he held her just an inch too close to his chest. She looked up into his face and the polite words she had been about to speak froze on her tongue.

His gaze held both ruthless calculation and hot lust, a

combination that startled her and set her nerves jangling once more. For the first time in a long time, Bathsheba felt trapped in a web not of her own making. She shivered, even though the room was hot and he held her fast in his arms. Something bad was happening, something she couldn't seem to control.

She dropped her eyes to his waistcoat, taking slow, even breaths—not an easy task with such an active dance partner. As she tried to focus on the steps, she silently berated herself for acting like a naïve fool. Flirtation and seduction were second nature to her, the most effective tools she possessed. This was what she wanted. No, needed. And she'd be damned if John Blackmore or any other man, including the one she was dancing with right now, would prevent her from reaching her goal.

"Lady Randolph?"

She looked up. He must have sensed her emotion, for he inspected her face with concern.

"Yes, Major?"

"Is something wrong?"

He seemed genuinely worried, and her nerves began to settle.

"I'm just a little overheated. I fell ill a few weeks ago, and I don't think I've recovered all my strength."

"I'm sorry to hear that," he said. He slowed his steps as he eased her toward the edge of the dance floor. With a few graceful turns they were out of the crowd and standing in a window alcove.

"Blast Nigel," he muttered as he scanned the room. "Where is he with that damned punch?"

A little spurt of laughter escaped her lips. "Really, Major, I'm fine. Please don't beat Mr. Dash when he comes back. I'm sure he thought I'd abandoned him. The fault is mine."

He gave her a lopsided, apologetic grin, and the last bit of her anxiety died away. Major Stanton really was a very nice man, and exactly what she needed right now. Perhaps God had forgiven her all her sins, after all.

Someone cleared his throat loudly behind them. Bathsheba turned, and her heart sank when she encountered Robert Stanton's stony gaze. Grandson to General Stanton and brother to Sophie Stanton—now the Countess of Trask—young Robert had as much cause to hate her as anyone.

"Robert," said Major Stanton. "What are you doing lurking about and making the ladies jump out of their skin? Where's your wife?"

"Annabel is sitting with Grandmama," he replied. Then he turned from his cousin and gave Bathsheba an exquisitely correct bow.

"Good evening, Lady Randolph," he said. "My wife tells me that you were recently ill. I'm very sorry to hear that."

As Bathsheba murmured a polite reply, she had to acknowledge that none of the Stantons—or Simon, for that matter—had ever publicly snubbed her. They might hate her, but only the most astute observer would ever guess how they felt. Their conduct baffled her and left her feeling vaguely resentful.

As the three of them chatted about nothing, she couldn't help thinking what a fine young man Robert Stanton had turned into. She wished she could tell him she wasn't the ogre his family thought she was. That she would do anything to take back what she had done to his sister. But that was a lie, really. Bathsheba had been an ogre that autumn in Bath two years ago and, given the same situation, she didn't know if she'd act any differently now. To pretend otherwise would be cowardly and foolish.

Depression took up its familiar lodgings in her chest, and she couldn't completely stifle a sigh. The two men paused in their conversation and Major Stanton lifted an aristocratic brow. Now that she thought about it, he looked alarmingly like his uncle, General Stanton. Only much younger and better looking, of course.

After a quick glance at Bathsheba, Robert turned to the major.

"Sir, I hate to interrupt your conversation with Lady Randolph, but Grandmama sent me to fetch you. She says you haven't said a word to her all evening, and she insists you not neglect her a moment longer."

Bathsheba's depression turned into an absolute fog of gloom. That was why Robert had butted in. His grandmother had sent him to rescue the unsuspecting major from the claws of the family's enemy.

So much for God's forgiveness.

Major Stanton looked exasperated. "Robert, I'll be along shortly. But I have no intention of deserting Lady Randolph."

"Of course not, dear fellow," Robert spluttered. "I'd never suggest such a thing. I had every intention of escorting Lady Randolph down to supper myself."

He turned to her with a brave smile, rather like the ones she imagined the Christian martyrs gave each other before they were thrown to the lions. Well, the Stantons could all go to perdition before she allowed herself to be an object of contempt—or pity.

"Indeed, that won't be necessary, Mr. Stanton. I'm sure your wife is already missing you," she said, fixing a generous smile on her lips. "Major, of course you must see to your aunt. Family always comes first, you know. I'm a firm believer in that philosophy. I'm having supper with Mr. and Mrs. Ormond, so you needn't have a care about me. No, no," she said as the major started to object. "I insist."

"Well, my lady," Major Stanton said with obvious reluctance, "if you insist. But I hope you will remember we didn't finish our waltz. Don't be surprised if I come to claim another."

"I shall look forward to it," she said with genuine warmth.

Robert made a quick bow, obviously relieved to have escaped from the lion's den, and practically dragged his protesting cousin away. Bathsheba watched them make their way to Lady Stanton's side before easing her way through the crowd to join the small knot of people who had clustered around Sarah.

"Darling," cried her friend as she pulled her into the middle of the circle. "Isn't this a sad crush? Especially for August! It's a wonder we haven't all swooned away from the heat. And who was that ravishing officer you were dancing with?"

Bathsheba answered her questions absently, letting the conversation ebb and flow around her. All her attention was focused on Major Stanton and Lady Stanton, now deep in conversation on the other side of the room. Once, his head jerked up, as if he was startled, and his gaze searched for and then found her. He watched her for a few moments, and even across the length of the ballroom she could feel the change in his demeanor, could see his countenance grow hard. Then he turned back to his aunt and didn't look her way again.

The ache in Bathsheba's chest grew into an icy block, spreading its chill through every inch of her body. There would be no more waltzes with Major Stanton.

Chapter 11

Bathsheba would have snorted with derision if anyone had predicted she would find herself stalking the dirt paths of Green Park at ten o'clock on a Friday morning. The only other people up and about so early were nursemaids and their young aristocratic charges, duly trotted over for a bit of fresh air from the nearby streets of Mayfair. No fashionable person would be seen walking at this time of day, and if her friends saw her now they would likely think her touched in the head.

She'd awakened again at the crack of dawn—hot, restless, and sick of London in summer. That had never happened before, since she much preferred the city at any time of year to rusticating at Compton Manor, or just about anywhere in the countryside. If she could have afforded it, she would have decamped to Brighton with the Regent and the rest of his crowd. Not that it would likely make any difference. Bathsheba suspected she would be just as bored and restless in Brighton as in London.

She veered off the Broad Walk and headed in the direction of the ornamental dairy, her footman trailing discreetly behind her. Perhaps when her bad temper subsided she would stroll up to Hatchards. The search for a husband was providing precious little entertainment, but a new book might give her a bit of relief from the cares that pressed in on every side.

As if to remind her of the swift passage of time, a church bell tolled out the half hour. She had returned from Ripon two weeks ago and was no closer to finding a husband. Not that men didn't flock to her side. But what most of them wanted was something she could no longer afford to give. And, if she were honest with herself, she had to admit that her heart wasn't in the hunt. Every time she tried to develop an interest in a man—even on the most basic, physical level—all she could think of was John, and how much she missed him.

She scowled as she stomped along the path. The fact that she still ached for him made her want to scream. The blasted man was ruining her life, and if she were to ever see him again she might be sorely tempted to hit him over the head with the nearest heavy object.

Compounding the situation was the absolute dearth of interesting men in London, especially at this time of year. With the exception of Major Stanton, she had yet to meet one man who made her feel anything but depressed. If something didn't happen soon, she just might get desperate enough to have a go at Nigel Dash, even if he did loathe the very sight of her.

She sighed, slowing to a halt in front of the foolish but pretty little dairy that was the park's main attraction. The sting of humiliation still burned as she recalled that night at Lady Fancote's, and the way Major Stanton and his aunt had turned their identically cool, disapproving gazes on her. Even worse, whenever she encountered the major at a ball or a party, she had to resist the urge to blurt out an apology for the harm she had done his family. But she couldn't do that. Her actions had been taken to protect *her* family, and she could never be sorry for that.

She gave herself a shake and headed back to Piccadilly Street. Enough moping about. Her time would be much better spent in running through the potential list of candidates she had compiled in her mind.

As she strode up the path, she reviewed her options. Mr. Portnoy had an attractively large fortune, so large that Bathsheba could almost forget it had been acquired in trade. But Mr. Portnoy was almost as big as his bank account and, shallow creature that she was, she quailed at the thought of spending the rest of her life with a man who wore a corset.

Perhaps Lord Brompton might do. He was titled, rich, and not bad looking. But then she remembered his mother—a veritable dragon who barely let him out of her sight and, rumor had it, managed his finances.

That left only one man—Sir David Roston, a cultured, polished, and very wealthy baronet. He had shown her quite a lot of flattering attention over the last several months. Bathsheba had never considered him because his attentions had been more those of a friend than an aspiring lover. Because he was a good fifteen years older than her, it simply hadn't occurred to her that Sir David would be on the lookout for a wife. But now that she thought about it, lately, he had made a point of searching her out at every party they both happened to be attending. True, he had a very dreary sister who lived with him, but that could hardly be considered an obstacle. Sisters could always be taken care of, especially when their brothers were as rich as Sir David.

She halted in her tracks, ignoring her grumbling footman, who apparently grew tired of her stops and starts. The answer had been staring her in the face for days, but she'd been too dull-witted to see it. Sir David, who, fortuitously, would be at Sarah's dinner party this very evening. When Bathsheba returned home, she would send her friend a note asking her to make sure she and Sir David were seated next to each other. With a little luck, she could leg-shackle the man before the rest of the ton returned to London for the Little Season.

With a self-satisfied nod, she resumed her brisk pace up

the walk. Sir David might not be the most exciting man in the world, but he would give her exactly what she needed.

As she made her way toward the gates leading onto Piccadilly, she happened to glance to her right. A young and very pregnant woman was leaning heavily on another woman as they slowly made their way to a shaded bench.

Bathsheba paused. The pregnant woman appeared distressed, and the girl accompanying her—a servant, from the looks of her attire—seemed on the verge of tears.

She frowned, glancing around, but no one else was anywhere close to the two women. Grumbling under her breath, she abandoned the path and cut across the lawn toward the bench. Her visit to Hatchards would have to wait.

As she moved closer and finally got a good look at the pregnant woman, Bathsheba had to stifle a groan. It was Meredith, Marchioness of Silverton, niece by marriage to General and Lady Stanton, and sister to Annabel Stanton, Robert's wife.

Oh, joy. More opportunities to be snubbed by a Stanton. Bathsheba cast another quick glance around, but she and her footman seemed to be the only people in this corner of the park. Lady Silverton had obviously not brought her own footman, and her maid looked ready to launch into a fit.

Bathsheba hurried over to Lady Silverton just as she sank down on to the bench.

"Oh, Lady Silverton," exclaimed the maid in a quavering voice. "His lordship will have my head if anything happens to you. I knew we shouldn't have left the carriage." She ended on a high note of hysteria.

"Hush, now, Grace," gasped Lady Silverton. "I'll be fine. I just need to rest for a minute."

Fixing a smile on her face, Bathsheba stepped up to the bench. "Lady Silverton, forgive my impertinence, but I couldn't help noticing that you seemed unwell. Might I be of assistance?"

Lady Silverton looked up, her face pale and her skin

damp with perspiration. Any reluctance Bathsheba might have felt died as alarm took its place. The woman really did look sick.

Lady Silverton's weary gray eyes flashed with recognition and, Bathsheba thought, relief.

"Oh! Lady Randolph," she said, trying to smile but failing miserably. "How do you do? I feel so foolish, but I can't seem to catch my breath. My carriage is waiting outside the park, but for some reason I don't have the strength to walk back to it. I wanted to send Grace to fetch one of the footmen, but she wouldn't leave me."

Grace hovered over her mistress, wringing her hands. "Oh, I couldn't leave you, my lady. Lord Silverton would—"

"Have your head," Bathsheba interjected dryly. "Yes, we heard you. I suspect everyone in the park heard you."

The maid jerked back, as if Bathsheba had just given her a bracing slap. Good. The last thing Lady Silverton needed was for her maid to succumb to the vapors.

Grace started to bristle but Bathsheba ignored her, turning back to the marchioness.

"Lady Silverton, where exactly is your carriage?"

"At the other end of the walk," she answered, pointing in the direction of Piccadilly. She took a deep breath and rested her hands on top of her huge belly, as if to protect the precious cargo she carried inside.

Bathsheba glanced at the maid. "You, er, Grace, is it? Go find her ladyship's carriage and have the coachman bring it to the top of the walk. My footman and I will escort your mistress out of the park as soon as she has rested a bit."

Grace looked offended, but Lady Silverton gave her a weak smile and a nod. The maid spun on her heel and marched up the walk.

Bathsheba inspected Lady Silverton's pale, beautiful face. Little rivulets of sweat were trickling down from under her bonnet, plastering her thick black hair to her neck. She seemed to be focused inward, her eyes half-closed as she took small, gasping breaths.

As Bathsheba sat down next to the marchioness, she pulled a handkerchief out of her reticule, fighting a rising irritation. What in God's name was the silly woman doing out in this heat, especially in her condition?

"Forgive me, your ladyship," she said, "but I think we should take off your bonnet."

Lady Silverton's eyes snapped open as Bathsheba began to untie the silk ribbons of her fashionable, high-crowned hat.

"Oh, no," she protested weakly. "I'm sure I'll be better in a few minutes. I just can't seem to catch my breath."

"You're overheated," Bathsheba replied as she gently removed the bonnet and placed it on the bench.

Lady Silverton sighed with relief and gratefully took the offered handkerchief, dabbing her sweat-dampened temples and forehead.

"You must think me a complete idiot, Lady Randolph. I'm absolutely mortified that you had to see me in so humiliating a situation. For a countrywoman to succumb to the heat this way is disgraceful."

Bathsheba relaxed a bit. It appeared that this Stanton, at least, was not going to bite her head off. Of course, Lady Silverton hadn't been born into the aristocracy, and was barely tolerated by some members of the ton even though she had married one of the most powerful men in the land. By all accounts, she had none of the arrogant attitude so often displayed by her in-laws.

"Well, I did wonder what you were doing out here. You look quite . . ." Bathsheba delicately let her voice trail off.

Lady Silverton grimaced. "Enormous?"

Bathsheba laughed. "I was about to say somewhat pale and sickly, but I suppose enormous is a better description."

Humor flashed through the marchioness's eyes. They really were extraordinary, now that she got a closer look.

Huge and gray, with thick black lashes, and full of curiosity as she turned her gaze on Bathsheba.

"Ridiculous, isn't it? I'm not due for another month, yet I look bigger than the Prince Regent. It's a wonder my husband can stand the sight of me."

Bathsheba grinned. "Nonsense. All pregnant women are beautiful. And I've noticed how your husband looks at you. It's obvious to the whole world he worships at your feet."

Lady Silverton blushed, and it brought some color back into her cheeks. "It's sweet of you to say so, but it's been weeks since I've been able to see my feet."

She took a deep inhalation, breathing more easily. Her skin, which a few minutes ago had been dead white, now kept its faint, pink tinge as she seemed more comfortable.

"Do you think you might be able to walk back to your carriage now? Thomas and I will help you."

Lady Silverton nodded. Bathsheba replaced her bonnet on her head, leaving the ribbons untied.

"Thomas," she murmured. The footman stepped forward and they each took one of Lady Silverton's arms, helping her carefully to her feet. Not an easy task, given both her considerable height and her bulging belly.

The marchioness staggered a bit as she came to her feet. Bathsheba steadied her, even though the woman must be a good seven inches taller than her.

Lady Silverton huffed in exasperation. "You wouldn't think such a long meg as I am would have so much trouble carrying a babe."

"Lord Silverton is very tall, as well. Your baby probably takes after the both of you."

They slowly made their way up the path toward Piccadilly, Thomas on one side of the marchioness, Bathsheba on the other.

"So you're saying that my baby is probably a giant?" said Lady Silverton, a faint laugh in her voice.

"I think it quite likely. My lady, please don't be afraid to lean on me. I may be small but I'm strong. And Thomas, as you can see, is a very sturdy fellow."

As they approached the edge of the park, Bathsheba looked ahead. To her surprise, she encountered the astonished gazes of Lady Stiles and her freckly-faced daughter, standing not ten feet away. What were they doing in Green Park at this hour of the day?

"Oh, no," groaned Lady Silverton under her breath.

Bathsheba gave her hand an encouraging squeeze, but remained silent. No one had to tell her that Lady Stiles and her daughter were incurable and malicious gossips.

As the two parties reached each other, Bathsheba tried to guide Lady Silverton past, but Lady Stiles planted herself directly in their path.

"Goodness!" she exclaimed. "I would never in a thousand years have expected to run into Lady Silverton and Lady Randolph rambling in Green Park together. It was worth dragging myself out of bed so early to see it. As you can imagine, I rarely go about at this time of day, but my darling Maria and I are on our way to the dairy to meet some of her friends. Quite a refreshing thing to do on such a hot day, don't you think?"

Bathsheba murmured a polite reply and once more tried to steer Lady Silverton toward the gate. Lady Stiles shifted to intercept them. Her small, pale blue eyes glittered with malice.

"Lady Silverton, I heard that you and the marquess had recently returned from the country. I'm astonished you would even think to wander about in your condition. Whatever would Lord Silverton say—and your mama-in-law? She will be astounded, I have no doubt."

Her daughter smirked at her mother and gave a nasty little titter.

Bathsheba felt a slight tremor pass through Lady Silverton's limbs. Everyone knew Silverton's mother had objected to her son's marriage to the commonly born Meredith Burnley—quite vocally, by all accounts.

"Lady Stiles," answered Bathsheba, injecting just the right note of boredom into her voice. "Don't let us keep you. After all, your daughter shouldn't be kept standing out here in the sun. Her complexion is quite ruined already. So many freckles. She obviously takes after you. I would suggest Denmark Lotion and crushed strawberries, but I suspect not even that will suffice. Such a pity."

Lady Stiles and her daughter froze into twin pillars of outrage, glaring at Bathsheba as she and Thomas moved Lady Silverton up the path.

"Just a few more feet, Lady Silverton," Bathsheba soothed, worried to feel the trembling in the other woman's body. "Then you'll be able to rest."

"No," the marchioness replied in a quavering voice. "I'm about to go into whoops." And then she burst into laughter.

Bathsheba grinned as relief flowed through her veins. She found herself liking the marchioness a great deal.

"Oh, Lady Randolph, I wish I had your wit," she wheezed as she began to recover. "I loathe that woman, but my tongue always ties into knots whenever I encounter her."

"That's because you don't possess the killing instinct," Bathsheba answered. "Fortunately, I have it in abundance."

Lady Silverton gave her a startled glance but held her tongue. For that, Bathsheba was grateful. What had possessed her to blurt out such a remark in the first place—especially to a Stanton?

They reached the carriage, and Lady Silverton's servants rushed to attend to them. The steps were let down, and the marchioness was carefully hoisted inside. She smiled gratefully at Bathsheba and offered her hand.

"Thank you so much for taking care of me. I don't know what I would have done without you."

Bathsheba brushed her hand aside and climbed up the

steps into the carriage. Lady Silverton gaped at her as she settled onto the opposite seat.

"Lady Silverton, you must be mad if you think I'm leaving you. I won't be easy until I see you safely bestowed in your own house, and the doctor called to attend you."

She ignored the other woman's protest, leaning out the door to speak to her footman.

"Thomas, you may take my carriage and return to Compton House. I'll be along later. And tell Lady Silverton's coachman to drive on."

The carriage moved smoothly away from the park. Bathsheba looked at Lady Silverton, who was staring at her with a bemused expression on her lovely face.

Bathsheba lifted an eyebrow. "I know what you're thinking—the dreaded enemy helping a Stanton. But sometimes even a Randolph can rise to the occasion."

Silence fell over the carriage during the short ride to Grosvenor Square but, oddly, Bathsheba didn't feel uncomfortable. Lady Silverton had stared at her thoughtfully, but didn't seem inclined to judge. And she radiated a sweet serenity, even in her physical discomfort, that felt neither cloying nor artificial. No wonder the Marquess of Silverton had been so intent on making her his wife.

After a few minutes, the marchioness stirred.

"Lady Randolph, I can't thank you enough for your help. My husband will be so grateful to you."

Bathsheba very much doubted that, but held her fire. "It was nothing, my lady. I'm simply glad I was there to assist you."

Lady Silverton seemed to hesitate, then gave her a rueful smile. "You must wonder what I was doing wandering around the park with only a maid to attend me."

"A bit, yes."

"I was raised in the country, where I much prefer to spend my time. But Lord Silverton insisted we return to London for my lying-in. My doctor is here, you see." She grimaced. "I hate being so confined. I'm used to walking every day. My husband prefers that I take my walks in Grosvenor Square, but I can't bear the thought of all my neighbors watching me lumber about. I thought going to Green Park first thing in the morning would be more private, and a bit more like being home in the country."

Bathsheba could certainly sympathize with her desire for privacy. "Does your husband know you went to Green Park this morning?"

Lady Silverton looked guilty. "No. I suspect he'll be quite annoyed with me."

Bathsheba smiled. "Well, then I best come into the house with you. He can be annoyed with me, instead."

"I would like that very much," said Lady Silverton with enthusiasm.

Bathsheba laughed.

They drew to a halt in front of Silverton House, an imposing, three-story mansion on the northeast side of the square. Bathsheba had been there a few times with Reggie in the first years of her marriage, and she had always been struck by its expensive elegance.

Two footmen sprang into action as soon as the steps were let down. Along with Grace, they carefully helped Lady Silverton into the house. Bathsheba trailed behind as a calm-faced butler bowed her through the door.

Lady Silverton removed her bonnet and gloves with a sigh, handing them to her maid.

"Hammond," she said to the butler, "Lady Randolph is joining me for tea. Would you please bring it to the morning room?"

Servants scurried off in several directions and, minutes later, Bathsheba found herself ensconced in a very pretty and comfortable sitting room at the back of the house. The butler and a footman set up the tea service, then withdrew.

"Would you mind pouring?" asked the marchioness. "This blasted stomach of mine gets in the way of everything."

Bathsheba fixed her a cup and put a few delicate sandwiches and cakes on a plate for her.

"You should eat, Lady Silverton," she said. "It will make you feel more like yourself."

The marchioness accepted the plate with a sigh. "I've forgotten what it feels like to be myself. You mustn't think I'm not happy to be having a baby—I'm delighted. But my pregnancy has been difficult. I haven't felt well in months."

"What does your doctor say?"

Lady Silverton frowned. "Not much of anything, really. He takes my pulse, and he's a great advocate of bloodletting. Each time he bled me I felt worse, so I finally refused to allow him to do it anymore. Since then, whenever I complain of discomfort he tells me that it's natural for women to suffer in pregnancy. Apparently, as daughters of Eve, it's our lot in life," she finished dryly.

Bathsheba nearly choked on her tea. "He sounds like an ass! Who is he?"

"Dr. Steele. Supposedly the best accoucheur in London."

Bathsheba had met Steele at several social occasions. He had always struck her as an ambitious and arrogant man.

"You're frowning," said Lady Silverton. "Do you know him?"

"Slightly."

"What do you think of him?"

Bathsheba paused, but the marchioness looked at her intently, seeming to want a truthful answer.

"I really do think he's an ass."

"So do I," said Lady Silverton, looking unhappy, "but I don't know what to do about it."

"Have you discussed this with Lord Silverton?"

"Yes. He's concerned, but everyone swears Dr. Steele is the best. And I don't want my husband to worry any more than he already is."

Bathsheba started to reply, then fell silent. What right had she to interfere? Besides, it would be dangerous beyond all imagining if she were to—

"Lady Randolph, what are you thinking?"

She looked up to meet Lady Silverton's smoky silver gaze, the color so similar to John's that she could almost believe she was staring into his eyes. Only a fool would do this, but the anxious vulnerability on the other woman's face touched a reluctant chord of sympathy in Bathsheba's heart. Or at least that's what she told herself.

"I know of another physician in London—an accoucheur—who is very accomplished. He's younger than Dr. Steele, and from what I understand he has trained at the best schools, both in Scotland and on the Continent. Perhaps he might be persuaded to consult with you."

"Do you think you could speak to him for me?" Lady Silverton asked eagerly. "I realize he might be reluctant to offend Dr. Steele, but . . ."

Bathsheba smiled, trying and failing to hold back a tangled surge of emotions—excitement, anxiety, and, oddly, relief. She would surely hate herself later, but the prospect of seeing John again made her spirits soar.

"I'll be happy to speak to him on your behalf, my lady. If he agrees, I'll ask him to call on you at your earliest convenience."

The marchioness closed her eyes for a moment. When she opened them, Bathsheba was surprised to see tears glimmering in the gray depths.

"Thank you. That would greatly relieve my mind. And please," she said rather shyly, "call me Meredith. It seems foolish to use titles after today."

"I would be delighted. And you must call me Bathsheba."

Meredith gave her a dazzling grin, and Bathsheba couldn't help feeling touched. It had been years since she made a new friend, especially one who seemed unaffected by the cynical sophistication that characterized so many inhabitants of their social circles.

"You're nothing like I imagined," Meredith blurted out. "You always frightened me a bit. You seemed so . . ."

"Hard?" Bathsheba finished the sentence for her.

"I hope I haven't offended you."

She sighed. "No. It's the truth. I wasn't always like that, but the years in London have changed me."

Meredith looked curious now, leaning back in her soft, overstuffed armchair, her slender hands resting protectively on her belly.

"You didn't grow up in London?"

"No. I am from Yorkshire. My father didn't like city ways, and my mother was often too ill to travel. I had only one Season when I was nineteen, and I didn't take."

Meredith's jaw dropped. "How is that possible?"

Bathsheba shrugged. "No dowry. My father was an impecunious viscount."

"But you married an earl."

"I met him a year later, in Yorkshire. Lord Randolph didn't care about money. He wanted something else," she finished, trying to keep the bitterness out of her voice.

"Did you find it difficult—leaving the country behind?" Meredith sounded wistful.

"Yes, at first. Then I got used to it. You will, too."

"I don't think so. You were born into the nobility, so the ton accepts you as one of their own. That has not been the case with me. I don't think I'll ever fit in."

She broke off and wrinkled her nose. "That sounds horrible, doesn't it? As if I'm a spoiled child. I have a husband and family who love me, and I live in luxury. What could I possibly have to complain about?"

Bathsheba repressed an irksome flash of envy. "One also wishes to be accepted," she said. "To feel that one belongs."

Meredith nodded. "Yes. That's why I prefer the country. I do feel I belong there. In London . . ."

Bathsheba gave a sympathetic little snort. "Lady Stiles and her ilk."

"Exactly. No one has the nerve to snub me in front of my husband, or General and Lady Stanton. But, as you saw today, it does still happen. I never mention it to Silverton, though. It makes him furious."

"Lady Stiles is a bitch, as are her friends," Bathsheba replied, raising her Sèvres teacup to take a delicate sip. "You should ignore her."

Meredith stared at her in shock, then a grin lit up her elegant features. "Oh, I do like you, despite what—" She clamped her lips shut, looking suddenly uncomfortable.

"It's all right," Bathsheba said. "You've been very kind, when I don't deserve it at all. Believe me when I tell you that I would take it all back, if I could."

The other woman's brows drew together in a puzzled frown. "Why did you try to ruin Sophie's reputation?"

Bathsheba took a deep breath, reluctant to disturb the painful memories that never failed to flood her with shame.

"Desperation," she finally admitted.

Meredith nodded, as if something had been confirmed.

"I won't pry any further," she said, "but if you ever wish to tell me, I promise I will listen without making judgments."

Bathsheba felt her mouth curl into a wry smile. "Perhaps someday I will."

"I—" Meredith broke off at the sound of a firm tread out in the hallway. Her face lit up with a joyous smile. "That would be my husband. I'm so glad you're still here to see him."

I'm not, thought Bathsheba.

A moment later the door swung open and the Marquess of Silverton, dressed in riding clothes, strode into the room. Like his cousin, Major Stanton, he was a tall, gorgeous man, with piercing blue eyes. And, like his cousin, those eyes looked at her with suspicion and disapproval.

"Silverton." Meredith's affectionate voice held a hint of warning.

The marquess immediately switched his attention to his wife. The hard angles of his handsome face softened as he crossed the room to stand by Meredith's chair.

"I'm very cross with you," he said in a husky voice that would melt any sane woman into a pool of butter. "I understand you went to Green Park this morning."

Obviously not immune to his charm, his wife took his hand and held it briefly to her cheek. Still, she managed to look guilty.

"Whatever am I to do with you, Meredith," he said, clearly exasperated. "I leave the house and you're out the door like a shot."

"I'm fine," she said emphatically. "I simply became overheated. Fortunately, Lady Randolph was also taking the air, and she and her footman helped me back to the carriage. She insisted on coming home with me, just to make sure I suffered no ill effects."

She offered Bathsheba an appreciative smile, then shot her husband a surprisingly stern look. "I'm very grateful to her, Silverton. I was in no danger, but I did feel quite uncomfortable."

The marquess stared down at his wife for a moment, then turned and bowed to Bathsheba.

"Then I am also in your debt, Lady Randolph. Please accept my heartfelt thanks." He sounded like he actually meant it, although his expression was still guarded and wary.

"I was happy to be of assistance," Bathsheba replied.

"And you, my love," he said, refocusing on his wife, "are to rest for the remainder of the day. I'll send a note around to Dr. Steele, asking him to call."

Meredith's gaze shifted to Bathsheba for a few seconds before returning to her husband. "That won't be necessary."

"I insist, Meredith." His voice remained soft, but no one would mistake the note of command.

Meredith's jaw set mutinously as her eyes narrowed on

her husband. Propping his hands on his lean hips, he glared right back at her.

Time to go.

Bathsheba rose to her feet. "Lady Silverton, I must be off. No, don't get up," she said, waving at her to remain seated.

The marchioness made a wry face. "You'd be long gone before I actually managed it. Please accept my heartfelt thanks, once again. I look forward to hearing from you very soon."

The women exchanged a knowing look. Silverton's gaze filled with suspicion as he studied their faces.

"I won't forget," Bathsheba promised.

Meredith smiled, her relief evident. "You are always welcome at Silverton House, my dear lady. And remember, please call me Meredith."

Eyes opening wide as he stared at his wife, Silverton now looked like a man who had just been punched in the gut.

Repressing an evil grin, Bathsheba gave him a perfect curtsy and let herself out of the room.

Chapter 12

Bathsheba groped in her reticule and extracted a woefully inadequate lace handkerchief, slapping it over her mouth and nose as she tried not gag. The smell of hundreds of trapped animals permeated her carriage as it inched through the Smithfield Market toward the hospital entrance. The noise was deafening, the bellowing of the cattle drowning out every other sound, including the rattle of carriage wheels and the cries of the farm workers who drove the unhappy beasts to market.

After an eternity, her carriage finally rolled to a halt in front of the imposing North Gate of St. Bartholomew's Hospital. The steps were let down and one of her dust-covered footmen handed her to the pavement.

"Best have a care, my lady," he shouted above the din. "It's as dirty here as you can imagine."

"Thank you, Arthur," she replied faintly. He shook his head, obviously unable to hear over the noise.

She lifted her skirts and picked her way through the dirt, avoiding piles of manure and other debris from the market that didn't bear looking at. What in God's name had prompted her to wear a cream-colored Parisian walking dress to a hospital in the East End—especially one directly across from a cattle market?

A laugh tinged with hysteria escaped her lips, but she clamped her mouth shut at the foul taste of dust in the air. The answer to her question was Dr. John Blackmore. Her lovely new gown gave all the appearance of modesty, but the superb drape of the material displayed her figure to advantage, especially her breasts. Knowing she would see John again—and her stomach flip-flopped at the very thought—she wanted desperately to look her best. After all, who knew how he would react to her unexpected and probably unwelcome visit?

Coming to a halt in front of the richly ornate North Gate, topped by its statue of Henry VIII, Bathsheba wished she could take a deep breath to steady her nerves. Only her promise to Lady Silverton yesterday had kept her from losing courage at the last moment. Now that she was here, she could finally admit she had dressed so carefully to bolster her confidence rather than to deflect John's anger.

But more than his anger, she feared his contempt. For most of last night, she had tossed and turned in her bed, convinced he must surely be grateful she had walked away.

She swallowed, unable to take those last few steps through the carved arch into the hospital despite the noise and stench of the market behind her. Casting her eyes up to the statue of the Tudor king, she tried to scold her feverish nerves into submission. Henry, one fist resting on his marbled hip, glowered down at her as if issuing some kind of challenge.

As she stared back at the dead monarch, irritation finally overcame anxiety. The hell with John Blackmore, anyway. What did it matter if he didn't want to see her? Bathsheba had given her word to a woman who should have treated her as an enemy and had, instead, extended a hand in friendship. She'd be damned if John's contempt, her nerves, or anything else would make her break that promise to Lady Silverton.

Hitching her shoulders, she marched under the gateway, through the passage and on past the small parish church dwarfed by the hospital's extensive grounds. Just ahead, she saw a large, four-story building with tall windows and an arched door set under a marble porch. She went inside and found herself in a spacious entrance hall. A clerk sat behind a desk, out of the flow of traffic coming through the door.

"Excuse me," she said. "I wonder if you could tell me where I might find Dr. Blackmore."

The man's balding head jerked up. Watery blue eyes grew round as his gaze traveled from the crown of her feathered, high-poke bonnet all the way to her absurdly dainty and no longer white kid slippers.

"Argh . . ." he gurgled, obviously flummoxed by the sight of a fashionable lady in the hallowed halls of Bart's.

"Dr. Blackmore?" she prompted, giving him an imperious lift of an eyebrow.

He scrambled to his feet. "Yes, my . . . who should I say is calling?"

"The Countess of Randolph."

"One moment, your ladyship." He waved frantically to a young man passing through the hallway. "Mr. Simmons is Dr. Blackmore's medical student, Lady Randolph. I'm sure he'll be able to hunt him down."

The burly young man, who looked more like a prize-fighter than a doctor, changed course and hurried to the desk. As the clerk whispered in his ear, a startled expression flashed across his blunt features. He cast Bathsheba a quick, knowing glance and then nodded to the clerk.

"Lady Randolph." He gave a respectful bow, but studied her with open curiosity. "Dr. Blackmore is in the admissions room. If you will be so good as to wait here, I'll fetch him immediately."

He strode away and the clerk sank down behind his desk, warily observing her as if he expected her to cause some kind of commotion. She had a wayward impulse to allay his fears. After all, she'd already done the most insane thing possible just by coming here.

In an effort to distract herself from the sensation that her stomach was climbing into her throat, she wandered over to the beautiful oak staircase in one corner of the hall. Set high up above the wainscoting were two massive pictures, each painted in a lush, highly allegorical style. She moved to the base of the steps to study them.

A depiction of Christ healing the sick loomed over her, the giant figures too vivid for comfort. One especially caught her eye—a young girl, looking frail and emaciated, and disturbingly like her sister Rachel during her illness last month.

Bathsheba's mouth went dry as frightening memories of her own battle against the deadly infection came flooding into her mind. She shuddered, repelled by the sense of desperation bleeding out from the figures on the rococo-framed canvas, and yet she couldn't look away. The images were too compelling—too real. It was almost as if the artist had walked the halls of this very hospital, stamping in his memory all the images of sickness and despair to be later transferred to his painting.

Feeling light-headed, she forced herself to turn away and focus on the other picture. Slowly, her pounding heart began to settle, and she was able to examine the elaborate painting.

It also appeared to be a biblical allegory. A vague recollection stirred, but she couldn't quite place the story. One man, dressed only in a winding cloth, lay on the ground. Hurt or sick, she couldn't tell which. Another man, having just dismounted from his horse, was helping him.

"It's the parable of the Good Samaritan," rumbled a deep voice behind her.

She gasped and lurched around, bumping her elbow into the unforgiving wooden balustrade of the staircase. John stood a few feet away, his eyes flat discs of gray that revealed nothing.

"I'm sorry I startled you," he said. "Did you hurt yourself?"

She gaped at him. "What?"

As he glanced down, she realized she was rubbing her elbow.

"Oh. No, I was just looking at the pictures. They're quite . . . large," she finished lamely. God, she sounded like a complete idiot.

John's mouth, stretched into a hard line, actually twitched, and the tension in her stomach eased a notch. She had forgotten how beautiful his mouth was.

"They're Hogarth's," he said. "He donated them to the hospital. Supposedly, he modeled the figures on actual patients at Bart's."

"I can believe it." Not that she wanted to think anymore about Hogarth or his gruesome pictures. All she wanted to do was gaze into John's handsome face, greedily absorbing everything she had missed about him these last three weeks.

She'd forgotten how tall he was, and how his height and broad shoulders made her feel so . . . ridiculously feminine. Soberly clad in a dark, high-buttoned coat and black trousers, he seemed every inch the physician, and a somber one at that.

Bathsheba frowned, disturbed that he looked so grim. His eyes held so much weariness. Deep lines scored the sides of his mouth, as if he had spent the time apart from her clenching his teeth. Her heart wrenched with guilt, even though she couldn't help rejoicing that he seemed as miserable without her as she was without him.

His gaze flicked over her breasts and then back to her face. He didn't move, but a barely contained impatience vibrated in the air between them.

"How can I help you, Lady Randolph? It must be of some import to bring you to this part of the city."

She winced at the sarcastic tone of voice. Not that she could blame him. It was a miracle he hadn't thrown her out into the street as soon as he laid eyes on her.

"Dr. Blackmore." Her voice quavered and she dropped her gaze to his polished boots. She blew out an exasperated breath. Having survived four years of marriage to Reggie, she could certainly survive an apology to a man who more than deserved it.

Tilting her chin up, she stared directly into his eyes. "You can help me by accepting my apology. My behavior that last day in Ripon was beyond the pale, and nothing I can do will ever make up for it. But you must believe me when I say that I didn't want to insult you. I simply couldn't . . ."

God, she had rehearsed the words most of the night, and still she couldn't spit them out.

"Yes?" His voice, gentler now, encouraged her.

"I was unsettled by what I felt," she finished, giving a helpless shrug.

A sudden heat flared in his eyes. She shivered, like the first time he had looked at her that way. Longing transformed the hard lines of his face, and she saw once again the passionate man who had made love to her in the blazing sunlight of a summer's day.

Then the flat gray look in his eyes returned.

"You came all the way to Smithfield just to apologize to me?"

She hesitated. "No. There is something else I must ask you, if you have a few moments to spare. I promise I won't take up any more of your time then is necessary."

She could sense his disappointed retreat, but he recovered quickly. "Of course, my lady Why don't we go upstairs to the Great Hall? It's slightly more private than the front entrance. We can sit in one of the window alcoves."

Taking her arm in a light grip, he guided her up the staircase. She studiously avoided looking at the Hogarth paintings— the gruesome one, anyway.

"How are you feeling?" he asked. "Have you seen a physician since you've returned to London?"

"It hasn't been necessary."

He snorted, making his disapproval clear. Her spirits began to lift ever so slightly.

"Truly," she said, "I feel perfectly well."

He shook his head and muttered something under his breath, tightening his hand just a fraction around her arm. She repressed a triumphant smile. Perhaps he didn't trust her, but he obviously still worried about her.

They entered the Great Hall. Bathsheba paused, surprised by the elegant and spacious beauty of the room. She had never imagined a hospital would look like this—all polished wood and carved oak friezes, and a fretwork ceiling that wouldn't be out of place in the mansions of the ton. But the men and women who passed through the hall were nothing like the inhabitants of Mayfair. Plainly dressed, they moved with purpose, serious people intent on serious business.

With a gentle nudge, John steered her to an out-of-the-way alcove that held a few square-backed chairs. He handed her into one before sitting down beside her.

"What can I do for you, my lady?"

"For one, you can stop referring to me as 'my lady.'"

His silver eyes grew cold as a lake frozen by the first blasts of winter. "Correct me if I'm wrong, but the last time we spoke, you instructed me to only address you by your title."

She blushed. How could she have forgotten that?

"Oh. Perhaps that would be better," she said, wishing she could disappear in a puff of smoke.

He folded his arms across his chest and sighed. "Whatever am I to do with you?" He sounded more resigned than exasperated.

Tears prickled behind her eyelids, catching her off guard. She blinked them away, praying he wouldn't notice.

"I realize this is awkward," she blurted out, "but—"

He reached over and engulfed her tightly gloved fingers in the warmth of his big hand. His thumb caressed the inside of her palm, sending tingles of heat through the fabric to her skin. The words she had been about to utter died on her lips.

"Hush, Bathsheba," he murmured. "This isn't the time or

place." He glanced around. "Hospitals are hotbeds of gossip—like the ballrooms of Mayfair."

Her heart thrummed in her chest. Did he mean there would be another time and place? An opportunity to discuss how everything between them had gone wrong—how *she* had made them go wrong? She stared into his handsome face, knowing she must appear little better than an infatuated simpleton.

He gave a soft, disbelieving laugh, then released her hand.

"Why don't you tell me the other reason you came here," he said. "Before I forget myself and do something we both might regret."

She sucked in a shaky breath, trying to calm the pounding of her heart. If she wasn't careful she would forget, too—forget why she couldn't have him. Bathsheba had told herself that her visit was not about her, or about John, for that matter. Lady Silverton needed help. That was the reason she had come to Bart's. Not to engage in an impossible love affair, no matter how much she desired it, but to secure assistance for her newly found friend.

"I need your help as a physician," she said.

He frowned, looking worried again.

She shook her head. "Not for me. For a friend."

As she explained her request, the sexual heat in his eyes died away. He frowned and his expression grew distant, as if he contemplated some thorny problem. Bathsheba talked on, explaining in a low voice her encounter with Lady Silverton, and relating the marchioness's concerns about Dr. Steele.

When she finished, John rested his forearms on his powerful thighs and stared absently at the floor. A faint pulse of unease stirred in her chest. If he refused to help, she had the feeling Lady Silverton would be devastated.

"Lady Silverton tried not to show it, but I could tell she

was frightened. She doesn't trust Dr. Steele. Frankly, neither do I," she ended on a challenging note.

He shot her a startled glance and sat up straight.

"How does the marquess feel about this situation?"

"He didn't reveal his thoughts to me," Bathsheba responded dryly. "But he seems to share the general opinion that Dr. Steele is one of the best accoucheurs in London."

"He does indeed have that reputation."

She heard a doubt in his tone that belied his words.

"You don't agree?" she asked.

His mouth pulled into a disapproving line. "No, but it would hardly be politic for me to say so, especially around here. Steele is very popular amongst the aristocracy. That makes him powerful in the medical establishment. But he is old-fashioned and arrogant, and he allows his patients to suffer needlessly."

"He told the marchioness that pain and suffering was the lot of those descended from Eve."

He shook his head in disgust. "What an ass."

She grinned, feeling inordinately pleased. "That's exactly what I said."

They exchanged looks. He didn't smile, but he didn't have to—the amused, appraising gleam in his silvery gaze told her everything she needed to know. A slow, syrupy pleasure welled forth somewhere in the vicinity of her heart.

"Well, my dear lady, be that as it may, you have put me in a bit of a fix." He looked suddenly very intent, almost stern. "As I understand it, neither Lady Silverton nor her husband has relayed to Dr. Steele that his services are no longer required. If I were to call on her ladyship without Steele's permission, I would surely offend him. He won't take that lightly, I assure you."

She stiffened. "Are you afraid of him?"

He gave her a long-suffering look, and she relaxed.

"No. But there could be consequences, for Lady Silverton as well as myself. After speaking to me, she might decide she prefers to remain with Steele. If he were to discover she had consulted with me, he might refuse to treat her. Nor do I wish to cause a breach between a wife and her husband."

Bathsheba gave her head a very positive shake. "You couldn't possibly do that. Lord Silverton is devoted to her. As for wishing to remain with Dr. Steele, I can assure you that she doesn't. She thoroughly dislikes him and does everything she can to avoid seeing him."

As he contemplated the floor again, a new, very unpleasant thought struck her. If she hadn't been wearing her gloves, she would have been tempted to chew on a nail.

"Will you get in trouble with your colleagues—with the hospital—if you see Lady Silverton?"

She studied him anxiously, knowing how much his position at St. Bartholomew's meant to him. If taking Lady Silverton on as a patient was to risk his position . . .

He shrugged, a graceful movement of hard muscle sliding under the light wool of his coat.

"Perhaps. Steele is an old friend of Dr. Abernethy, my superior here at the hospital. But that wouldn't stop me from doing it, if that is what Lady Silverton desires."

The slow stream of syrup in her chest turned into a torrent, sweeping her over some internal cliff. John Blackmore was like no man she had ever known. His courage, his willingness to champion those who needed his help—even at the risk to his career—overwhelmed her carefully wrought defenses and tumbled her dangerously close to adoration. But the very qualities that made him so attractive also made her uneasy. That a man would be willing to risk his professional reputation—the means by which he supported himself—was something she couldn't fathom. Try as she might, she would never be brave enough to risk her own security and social standing.

With a start, she realized he was studying her with a slightly bemused expression on his face. She flushed, knowing she must look like an absolute bird-wit. But her little moment of revelation had shaken her down to the soles of her shoes.

Don't think about it now. Think about Meredith.

"So, you'll call on the marchioness, Doctor?"

He hesitated, as if some unresolved scruple held him back. She glanced around. No one seemed to be looking their way, so she dared to rest a hand on his sleeve.

"John, I have no right to ask this of you, but please do it for me."

He gave her a fierce scowl, but she thought she detected a mocking gleam in his eye.

"Lady Randolph, I do believe you are attempting to manipulate me."

She smiled. "Perhaps." Tilting her head, she studied him from under her lashes. *Definitely mocking.*

"Is it working?" she asked, letting her voice go husky.

He gave a grudging laugh. "All right, Bathsheba. I'll send a note to Lady Silverton this afternoon."

Equal measures of delight and relief bubbled up within her. "Thank you! I'm so grateful. I can't begin to tell you."

He stared at her, his eyes suddenly sleepy-looking and seductive. "I wonder how grateful? Perhaps I should ask you to demonstrate."

His chair creaked under his weight as he leaned into her, just slightly. No one looking at them would notice he had moved closer. But she noticed—her entire body noticed, responding to the crackle of sexual energy that leapt between them. His gaze turned dark and smoky as it drifted to her chest, lingering there for a few moments before returning to her face. She felt her cheeks flush, and a hot pulse of desire throbbed low between her thighs.

"Ah . . ." she stuttered.

He pulled back, a wicked grin on his face. "Lady Randolph, do you recall I once asked you to consider becoming a board member of this hospital?"

She blinked. "What?"

He rose from his chair, a study in masculine grace. She sat, gaping at him, feeling flat-footed and awkward.

"The hospital. Remember?" he prompted. "I promised to give you a tour."

She frowned. "I don't remember any such thing." Why would she agree to that? She hated anything to do with sickness, especially sick people.

"Wouldn't you like to see what it is that I do?" he asked, and now she heard the subtle note of uncertainty in his voice.

She gazed straight into his eyes, and her heart squeezed with a sweet ache. For a strong, confident man, John looked surprisingly vulnerable as he waited for her answer. She wanted so much to say yes, to give in to him, even if it meant following him around a disease-ridden and very public hospital. But it would be a colossal mistake to stay in his presence one moment longer. She had to leave, and she had to do it now.

"Yes," she heard herself say. "I would like that very much."

Chapter 13

John clenched his jaw, feeling the grind of his molars as they caught against each other. He'd developed the habit over the last few weeks, and the woman by his side was the cause. Most likely, also the cure.

Christ.

He must be losing his mind to allow Bathsheba Compton to pull him back into her web of sensual deceit. Despite the open invitation in her eyes, she didn't know what she really wanted from him. Hell, *he* didn't know what he wanted from *her*. Aside from the obvious, of course—get her prone as soon as possible.

Bathsheba drifted by his side through the Great Hall, a perfect little package of seductive beauty. The head of every man in the room turned as she passed, and one or two smiled boldly at her. Not that she would ever acknowledge them, but he hated that they eyed her like a common trollop.

When he'd first seen her a few minutes ago, contemplating the paintings over the staircase, weeks of repressed anger had welled up to the surface, competing with an equally unwelcome tug in his groin. She had dressed with the intent to distract, and it had worked. It had taken all his discipline to keep his eyes on her face and his emotions in check. But then she had apologized, appearing genuinely remorseful as she stared at him with emerald eyes full of longing and regret.

That had stunned him. After the stupidly tragic scene in Ripon, he'd done his best to forget her by telling himself his instincts about her had been wrong. That she was as shallow and wanton as the world believed. For a month now, he had battled to drive her from his mind and even from his dreams. But her image—the feel of her velvet skin, the honeyed taste of her—had stuck to him like a plaster, and the surprising wound she had inflicted had stubbornly refused to heal.

Bathsheba murmured her thanks as he opened the door into the corridor that led to the wards. Her fluttering skirts whispered across the front of his trousers as she brushed past him, and his arousal went from a coiling ache to a full-blown erection.

With an inward groan, John flexed his hands and forced himself to keep them by his side. One more encouraging look from her and he would throw every last vestige of caution to the winds, yanking her into the nearest closet and pushing that virginal white dress up around her waist. Just thinking about her supple, moist flesh cinching around his—

"Dr. Blackmore?" Bathsheba's voice, holding a faint note of curiosity, pulled him from the brink of career suicide. Hauling a rich countess into a closet for a fast, hard rutting would hardly endear him to Abernethy or the Board of Governors.

Or, for that matter, to said countess herself.

He cleared his throat. "Yes, my lady?"

Her lips curved into a dimpled smile and she looked genuinely happy. She hadn't when she'd first launched into her stuttering apology. Instead, she'd looked wan, and the dark smudges under her eyes told him something had disturbed her sleep. He was a petty bastard, he supposed, but some part of him rejoiced in her suffering and hoped that he was the cause.

"Pardon me," she said with a teasing lilt to her voice. "I

didn't mean to break into whatever deep thoughts you seemed to be having, but . . ."

The little minx actually had the nerve to grin at him. From the gleam in those big green eyes, he could tell she knew exactly what he was thinking. And she seemed thoroughly pleased about it, too.

He responded with mock solemnity.

"You are pardoned, Lady Randolph. What is your question?" he asked as he led her down the stairs to the South Wing.

"What, exactly, will you be showing me on this tour?"

The smile still curved her lips in the most charming fashion, but her voice held a faint note of apprehension.

Damn. It hadn't occurred to him until this moment that her recent illness might have made her skittish about hospitals and sick people. The tour had mostly been an excuse to keep her by his side as long as possible.

He laid a hand on her arm and drew her to a halt.

"I'm sorry, Bathsheba. Apparently, I'm a fool. The last thing you need right now is to spend your time wandering around a hospital. Come. I'll escort you back to your carriage."

Her expressive eyes filled with dismay. "Please don't. I want to see the hospital. Truly, I do. It just that I'm rather . . ." She trailed off, her pale cheeks flushing with embarrassment.

"Squeamish?"

"I can't help it," she grumbled, looking adorably defensive.

"Don't worry, my lady. The surgical theater is not part of the tour—at least not today. Besides, we don't have any amputations currently scheduled, so it's not really worth the effort."

She choked back a gasp, eyes widening with alarm.

He laughed. "Bathsheba, you really are a very easy mark."

The stunned look on her face quickly transmuted into a scowl. "And you, Dr. Blackmore, are an absolute beast. If we weren't in a public place, I would be tempted to inflict a very severe punishment on you."

Oh, he would know just what to do if she tried something like that. "And what might that punishment be, my lady? I do hope it involves something that goes on behind closed doors—preferably while both parties are naked."

She shot him a startled look, then gave a grudging laugh. "A lady generally keeps those kinds of thoughts to herself, sir. Especially in public, and especially when an esteemed medical doctor is about to give her a tour of a hospital."

"Fair enough," he said, escorting her through the entrance of the South Wing. "But I reserve the right to return to the subject of my punishment at your hands another time."

She obviously didn't know whether to look offended or interested, so she compromised by sweeping by him, sticking her pretty nose up in the air. Hurrying into the entrance hall of the South Wing, she made sure to keep several feet ahead of him.

John prowled behind her, enjoying the sway of her luscious backside as a surge of purely masculine satisfaction hummed beneath his skin. Yes, she was well and truly caught—of that he felt certain. The sexual heat practically shimmered in the air between them. She might fool herself into thinking she had come only to request help for a friend, but she sensed the pull between them as strongly as he did, although she might not be ready to acknowledge it. For now he would push her no further.

He lengthened his stride to catch up with her.

"I thought we might start in the women's ward," he said, slipping back into his professional demeanor.

She cast him an uncertain glance, then squared her shoulders and nodded. "I'm ready."

Poor darling, steeling herself for the worst.

John bit back a smile, both flattered and moved by her tenuous courage. She expected God only knew what, but it wouldn't stop her. Even better, he knew she did it for him.

He threw open the door to the women's ward and she froze on the threshold. But with a gentle nudge and a light hand on her waist, he guided her into the room.

Bathsheba moved slowly toward the center of the ward, her pink lips dropping open in a sweet oval. He watched with pride as she gazed around the spacious, light-filled room. The tiled floors had been sanded and swept clean, and the faint smell of limewater attested to the recent whitewashing of the walls. The sisters, neatly dressed and starched to perfection, attended to their patients under the careful supervision of the ward sister.

"I had no idea it would be like this," Bathsheba murmured.

She turned in a slow circle, her astonished eyes taking in everything—the quaint wooden bedsteads framed by their blue Lindsey curtains, the cupboards for the patients' belongings, the tables holding the various potions sent up from the apothecary's room.

"It's so much . . ."

"Cleaner and better organized than you expected?"

She ducked her head, looking vaguely ashamed. "It's just that one hears such terrible stories about hospitals."

"And many of them are true, particularly when it comes to the lying-in hospitals. The rate of infection and death in those institutions is particularly high. But the governors of Bart's pride themselves on a well-run ship. We have our faults, but dirt and disorganization are not amongst them."

She began to look interested. "Is that why you want to establish a wing for pregnant women here at St. Bartholomew's? Because of the conditions at the lying-in hospitals?"

"Yes. Those who are fortunate enough to gain admittance here receive the best care in London. I'd like to extend that to any woman in her time of need, whether she can afford to pay for it or not."

She frowned. "Why doesn't St. Bartholomew's already have a lying-in ward?"

John searched her beautiful face, looking for signs of polite disinterest. But she actually seemed genuinely curious.

"Because there are many physicians and surgeons who believe the practice of midwifery is inferior to other branches of medicine."

She looked quizzically at him. "But *you* don't. And men like Dr. Steele are very well regarded in the community."

He grimaced, feeling the usual frustration when he thought of the obstacles in his way. "You are correct, my lady. But Steele and his colleagues confine their practices to women of the upper orders. My goal is to establish a ward that will never differentiate between a respectable woman and one who is not. Those who live in the rookeries—the prostitutes and the very poor—need the most help. It is they who end up suffering the most in childbirth. I'd like to change that, and I'll do whatever I must to make it happen."

She studied him, her gaze sharply perceptive. He suddenly felt exposed, almost vulnerable. If only he had held his tongue.

"So," she said, "you're willing to risk your standing at the hospital to fight for something the other doctors don't want. That makes me curious, Dr. Blackmore. Why does it mean so much to you?"

He shrugged, mentally backing away. "It's what I do. I'm a physician. I help people who need me."

Her mouth twisted in a wry, disbelieving smile. Those pink lips opened again—obviously to ask another uncomfortably probing question—but he'd had enough.

"Come," he interjected before she could say anything more. "Let me show you around the ward."

She looked startled and a bit annoyed, but allowed him to tuck her hand into his elbow.

Relieved when she let the subject drop, he slowly led her around the room, explaining the workings of the ward as they strolled. He pointed out a few of the patients, explaining their ailments, but was careful to keep any distressing details to himself. Most of the women bobbed their heads and smiled. Bathsheba even managed to return their greetings with a tentative one of her own.

When they reached the end of the room, the supervising sister, ensconced behind her desk, gave Bathsheba a curious glance. But after a slight shrug and a respectful nod to John, she returned to her work. The other sisters ignored them, too busy dispensing medicines and folding linens to pay them any heed.

"I thought it would be much more crowded," Bathsheba said when they returned to the head of the room. "It's quite airy in here. I didn't realize the windows would be so large, or that there would be so much space between the beds."

"The large windows promote the circulation of fresh air. And the beds are kept at least six feet apart in order to diminish the risk of fever and contagion."

Her hand jerked on his arm. He glanced at her, concerned to see the roses fading from her cheeks. Her features suddenly looked pinched.

"Bathsheba, you needn't be concerned," he said in a quiet voice. "There are no fever patients in this ward. Every woman in here is a surgical patient." He tapped a finger under her chin, forcing her to meet his gaze. "I would never put you at risk."

She glanced sideways at him and gave a tight smile that failed to reach her eyes. Drawing her hand from his arm, she put a few inches between them. It an instant, her trust seemed to have bled away and a barrier of fear stood in its place. He could sense the ugly emotion draining the vitality from their connection, and it caught him completely by surprise.

"I'm sorry," she said in a flat voice. "You must think me a complete coward."

"You were very ill. Your reaction is perfectly understandable."

She nodded and turned away, hiding her face behind the

rim of her bonnet. Recognizing the signs, he had to swallow a groan. She had gone into full retreat.

"If you don't mind, Dr. Blackmore," she said in a distant voice, "I should like to go now."

Frustration took hold—sharp as the cut of a scalpel and just as painful. How could he have been so foolish as to believe she would be interested in his work? Or in him, for any other purpose than a sexual dalliance? If he needed proof of the gap that separated them, this seemingly innocuous episode had provided it.

"As you wish, Lady Randolph."

He ushered her back to the hallway and led her to the stairs that would take them out to the central courtyard. His anger was matched by the return of his black mood. Despite his long-held determination that he would never allow a woman to affect him like this, he knew it would take a very long time to forget her. She had ripped the wound open again. It would take much work and self-discipline to stanch the bleeding.

A familiar voice called out from behind them. "Blackmore! Hold up, man."

Hell!

It was Wardrop, a fellow physician at the hospital and one of his oldest friends. On any other day John would have been glad to see him, but the last thing he wanted to do was explain Bathsheba's presence. Wardrop fancied himself a ladies' man, and he could never resist a beautiful woman— even one ready to bolt out the front door. If his friend showed the slightest inclination to flirt, John had little doubt he would be forced to knock him senseless.

Wardrop hurried up to them, a wide grin splitting his face as he barely managed not to ogle Bathsheba. She didn't respond with her usual flirtatious charm, but instead moved closer to John and slipped her gloved hand around his bicep. Astonished, he tucked her against his side.

"Blackmore, you old devil," cried Wardrop. "Haven't

seen you in days. I was just about to ask where you'd been keeping yourself, but I think I know the answer to that question."

"Lady Randolph, may I present Dr. James Wardrop, a colleague of mine and a lecturer at Bart's. Wardrop, the Countess of Randolph."

Only an idiot would ignore the warning in his voice. Wardrop wasn't an idiot, but he clearly had no intention of allowing John to frighten him off.

Instead, he gave Bathsheba a deep, flourishing bow, looking the perfect idiot.

"Lady Randolph," Wardrop purred in what he mistakenly thought was a seductive voice, "to what do we poor souls owe the honor of your presence? I assure you that Bart's has never had its humble halls graced by a beauty as radiant as yours."

John snorted in disgust, but looked uneasily at Bathsheba. Surely she wouldn't fall for such drivel.

"Dr. Wardrop," she answered in a chilly, off-putting voice. "It's a pleasure to meet any colleague of Dr. Blackmore's."

When Wardrop tried to snatch up her free hand to bow over it, she evaded him, clamping her fingers around John's arm. The other man looked disconcerted, and John barely managed to hold back a laugh.

"I'm escorting Lady Randolph on a tour of the hospital," he said.

"That's a waste of an afternoon. Why the deuce would you want to do that? Begging her ladyship's pardon," Wardrop added hastily.

Bathsheba regally inclined her head. "Dr. Blackmore has asked me to consider serving on the Board of Governors. Naturally, I wanted to see the facility before taking on such a commitment."

Wardrop's mouth gaped open for a moment before he recovered. "Really? Have you, ah, mentioned this to Abernethy, Blackmore?"

"I intend to speak to him later today," John replied.

"Hate to inform you, old chap, but don't think that will be necessary. Have a look behind you."

John glanced over his shoulder. Abernethy strode down the hall, fixing them in his sights. As usual, he looked ready to pitch a fit.

"Just remembered something I must do," muttered Wardrop. "Lady Randolph, pleasure. Hope to see you again." And then he was gone, practically running out the front door in his haste to escape.

Bathsheba gazed after him, a puzzled frown on her face. "What an odd man."

"Just one of many here at Bart's, my lady. Prepare yourself to meet our head surgeon and chief oddity, Dr. John Abernethy."

She gave him a shrewd glance and then turned to meet the enemy in the trenches.

Abernethy steamed up to them. "Blackmore, what are you doing escorting ladies through the hospital in the middle of the day? Not at all proper. Very disrupting to our routine. I expect a full accounting from you immediately."

John raised a brow. "Would you prefer I escort them in the middle of the night, Dr. Abernethy?"

Bathsheba pinched his arm—hard.

"Dr. Abernethy, I am the Countess of Randolph," she said, exerting every ounce of her considerable aristocratic charm. "Dr. Blackmore has been kind enough to take me on a tour of your wonderful hospital. I can't tell you how impressed I am. Everything is so clean, so well organized. And your patients, I think, must receive the best care in London."

The old bastard stared at her, taken aback. He wasn't used to being interrupted in mid-tirade. "Er, thank you, my lady. We pride ourselves on a well-run institution. Nothing but the best for our patients."

Obviously thinking he'd paid her enough attention, he directed a scowl at John. "If I had known her ladyship was in the building, I would have been happy to escort her on a tour. It was remiss of you, Blackmore, very remiss, not to bring her to my office first."

"Lady Randolph is mulling over the idea of taking a seat on the Board of Governors," John said, ignoring Abernethy's complaint. The man cordially hated him, and nothing John ever said or did would change that.

"Yes," interjected Bathsheba. "I surprised Dr. Blackmore by stopping in unexpectedly. You may be sure, my dear Dr. Abernethy, that the next time I come to the hospital I will seek you out first thing."

She flashed him one of her dimples, and Abernethy could do nothing but clear his throat.

"Very good, my lady. I'll let you get on with your business. Blackmore," he said, directing another scowl his way. "When her ladyship has departed, I need to see you in my office."

He spun on his heel and marched back the way he came.

"I see what you mean," murmured Bathsheba. "That man is almost as rude as I am."

"My lady," John responded in a dry voice, "even you could never hope to compete with the great Abernethy. Why, he once banished the Duke of Wellington from his office. He told England's hero he had to wait his turn, like all the other patients."

Bathsheba burst into laughter—a full-throated, husky sound that sent a shot of warmth into his chest. The barrier between them collapsed into dust. He stood grinning at her like an idiot.

"You'd better not keep him waiting any longer than you have to," she said. "And I'm sure I've taken you away from your duties for much longer than I should have."

"Not at all. It was my pleasure," he murmured, studying her face. Her complexion was still too pale for his liking.

He skimmed the tips of his fingers over her cheek. *Ah!* Now that brought the color back.

"Bathsheba, I'm sorry if you found the ward distressing. I was a fool for taking you there."

Her eyes grew soft as moss. She reached out as if to touch his chest, then drew her hand back.

"No, John. I should apologize to you."

When he murmured a dissent, she shook her head vigorously.

"I'm a coward, you see. I hate anything to do with sickness. It terrifies me. I can't explain it, but something came over me back there in the ward." She flushed, looking ashamed. "I . . . I wanted to run. Just looking at those women made me . . ."

"No, don't," he said, his heart wrenching with guilt. "You don't owe me an explanation."

She carried on as if she hadn't heard him. "I've been like this since I was a child, perhaps because my mother was always sick. That's my first memory of her—in bed with some illness or other. I don't know what. My father never wanted to talk about it."

"How old were you when she died?"

A shadow crossed her face. "Fourteen. She died in Baden-Baden. My father had sent her to a spa, with Boland to nurse her, hoping it would make her well." She looked away and shrugged. "It didn't."

"I'm sorry," he said quietly.

Her mouth twisted, as if she had tasted something bitter. She finally looked up to meet his gaze.

"God, I detest being maudlin. You must think me a child." She spoke lightly, as if trying to make a joke of it.

He raised her gloved hand to his mouth and gave it a brief

kiss. "I suspect you know exactly how I think about you, and it has nothing to do with children."

She gave a delicate snort and shook her head. "You have a knack for saying just the right thing at the right time, my dear sir. Now, I mustn't keep you from Dr. Abernethy a moment longer. He seemed quite eager to speak with you."

John took her arm and escorted her into the central courtyard, heading across the packed dirt toward the North Gate.

"Since I'm sure whatever he has to say to me won't be pleasant," he said, "I'm more than happy to delay our meeting."

Her brow wrinkled with concern. "I hope my visit won't cause you any trouble."

"I'm sure it's something else entirely," he said, pleased that she worried about him.

They passed through the gate and out into the dusty street. A liveried footman, lounging against the side of an elegant town coach, sprang to attention as soon as he spotted them. He let the steps to Bathsheba's carriage down, and John took her slender hand to help her in. She hesitated before stepping up.

"I'm very happy we had the chance to speak." She gave him an enchanting half-smile, looking almost shy as she gazed up into his face.

"As am I," he answered. "I hope we have the opportunity to speak again very soon."

Her dimples came out to play, and John was lost. Any chance of staying clear of her had just evaporated.

She started up the steps and paused again, turning so she could look him directly in the eye.

"Do you like the opera, Doctor?"

"Yes, I'm quite fond of it," he replied, wondering about the point of her question.

"I'm going to Covent Garden tomorrow night with friends. Kitty Stephens will be singing. I'm sure you would enjoy her performance very much."

With that leading remark, she stepped into the coach and settled on the padded bench. He reluctantly relinquished her hand.

After he shut the door she leaned out the window, her face suddenly grown serious.

"And you will write to Lady Silverton, won't you?"

"Rest assured, my lady. I'll see to it."

She bestowed a joyous smile on him—one that struck him with the force of a Scottish gale—and the carriage moved off. He watched as it threaded its way through the busy marketplace before spinning on his heel and retreating to the relative quiet of the hospital courtyard.

As he strode into the North Wing he struggled to wipe the self-satisfied grin off his face. He took the steps to Abernethy's office two at a time, preparing himself for another boring reprimand. But there wasn't a thing his crusty old superior could say or do that would make a dent in his exultant mood.

Bathsheba had come back into his life—deliberately, it appeared. And this time, John had no intention of letting her escape.

Chapter 14

John leaped back to the pavement as an overburdened dray cut in front of him, barely an inch from the toes of his topboots. Silently castigating himself for being an idiot, he actually managed to look this time before crossing Piccadilly. Perhaps he should have taken a hackney to Silverton House after all, but he'd hoped the walk from his town house in Market Lane would help clear the sleep-deprived fog from his brain.

He'd been up all night, he and Roger, attending a relatively easy delivery of a first-time mother. The woman had shrieked all the way through it while her husband cowered in the corner of their bedroom, too terrified to offer one word or touch of comfort to his wife. The birthing was very painful—as most first labors were—but a large portion of the woman's distress had come from fear, and her husband had been useless consoling her. Every time John had tried to step away from the bed the woman clutched his arm, begging him in piteous tones not to leave.

Finally, she safely delivered a baby boy. When Roger presented the child to his father, the man fainted dead away on the floor. It had taken fifteen minutes to revive him, and then another half hour to convince him he wouldn't damage the infant just by holding it. They had only been able to leave near dawn, after Roger managed to rouse a female neighbor to assist the woefully unprepared new parents in their duties.

John turned into the relative quiet of Berkeley Square, slowing his pace as he focused on the task ahead. Taking Lady Silverton on as a patient was not without risk—certainly for her, but mostly for him, especially after his disturbing encounter with Abernethy yesterday afternoon after Bathsheba left the hospital. Expecting the usual dressing-down for what his superior called unorthodox practices, he had been stunned when Abernethy dropped a crudely written complaint on the surface of his enormous desk, one which charged John with deliberate neglect. It had been brought by O'Neill, the Irishman who had accused him of killing his wife and unborn child.

"I realize it's all a hum," Abernethy had thundered at him from behind his desk. "But the last thing this hospital needs is accusations from ignorant Irish peasants that we're trying to murder their women."

John had tried to explain the circumstances of the birth, but his superior had refused to listen and ordered him to stay out of the rookeries.

"The board won't have it, I tell you, and neither will I," barked Abernethy. "There are reasons why we don't treat these kinds of people, Blackmore, as you very well know. If they need help, they can find it at the poorhouse or at one of the public dispensaries. You bring disrepute onto yourself and to this institution by prowling around the stews at night, associating with criminals and prostitutes. You do it at your own peril. I would strongly advise you to give it up and focus your attention on your duties at Bart's, and on the clients who attend your practice."

There was no chance John would abandon his work in the East End, but he didn't need another reason for Abernethy to get rid of him. His position at the hospital provided him with the prestige he needed to build a successful practice in Mayfair, and without the money from his wealthy patients he wouldn't be able to help those who needed him most. Other physicians would be happy to replace him at Bart's, and Abernethy would be glad to oblige. He had tried before, but John had enough supporters on the board to stave him off—at least for now. But whatever the consequences, he wouldn't be bullied into abandoning those who needed him most, not even someone like O'Neill.

And he'd be damned if an old prig like Abernethy told him how to practice medicine.

Cutting through Charles Street, John arrived a few minutes later in Grosvenor Square. He skirted the park to the northeast side and to Silverton House. A footman led him through the entrance hall and up a marble staircase to a comfortable sitting room decorated in cheerful shades of light blue and yellow, with an assortment of chairs, footstools, and a velvet sofa set near the fireplace. A young woman reclined on it—obviously his prospective patient, given her advanced state of pregnancy. A tall, proud-looking man, dressed in the height of fashion, stood behind the sofa. He frowned as John advanced into the room, moving in front of the marchioness as if to shield her.

Bathsheba was right. The marquess was obviously both jealous and overprotective, and would likely cause John all manner of trouble.

He gave Lord Silverton a correct, if brief, bow. No point in being obsequious. The man would run right over him, given the chance.

"You are Dr. Blackmore?" Lord Silverton's voice was coldly correct.

"I am, my lord. I'm honored to be of service to you and her ladyship."

If anything, his high and mighty lordship looked even more imperious. He put his hands behind his back, holding his ground as if he had every intention of preventing John from approaching his wife.

"Silverton, do get out of the way," said a gentle but firm

voice from the sofa. "How do you expect Dr. Blackmore to examine me if you act like you're defending the castle keep?"

A reluctant smile crossed the marquess's face, and suddenly he seemed human. He turned and gazed down at his wife, his expression so full of affection that John had to squelch the impulse to excuse himself from the room.

"Now, Meredith, there's no need to get testy," her husband said in a soothing voice, as if he were speaking to a child.

"I'm not the one being testy. You are. Dr. Blackmore is hardly going to run away with me—not in my condition. Now, please step aside so I might actually have the opportunity to speak to him."

Silverton reluctantly took his place back behind the sofa, but not before giving John a stern warning look.

Message received, my lord.

Lady Silverton swung her feet down onto the floor. John moved forward to greet her, then came to a halt, stunned as she raised her pewter-gray eyes to his face.

Becky. She had the same eyes, the same coloring as his sister—an uncanny resemblance, especially at this late stage of pregnancy.

"Is there a problem, Dr. Blackmore?" The challenging tone of Lord Silverton's voice brought him back to his senses. That, and the puzzled look on Lady Silverton's face.

"No, my lord." He smiled and bowed low over the marchioness's hand. "My lady, it is a great pleasure to meet you. You and your husband must be sure to let me know exactly how I can help you."

She lit up with a warm, welcoming smile. Though her face was puffy and her body heavily rounded, she was a devastating beauty. But she looked ready to drop with exhaustion. No wonder the marquess acted like a feral dog ready to defend his mate.

She gestured for him to take a seat opposite her. "Thank you for coming, Doctor. I'm so grateful to you and Lady Randolph. She tells me that you're an excellent physician."

Lord Silverton made a scoffing noise, but after a quick glance his wife ignored him.

John frowned. He had expected some resistance from her husband, but not such hostility. He was missing something, and he didn't think it was simply loyalty on Steele's behalf.

"Lady Randolph is very kind," he replied in a neutral tone of voice.

"Isn't she, though?" Lord Silverton interjected dryly. "Before we go any further, Doctor, I'd like to know what your experience and qualifications are. You are on staff at St. Bartholomew's, I believe, and I understand you studied in Edinburgh. I would, however, be grateful if you would elaborate for me."

Lady Silverton rolled her eyes and looked ready to make a cutting remark. John intervened before she had the chance.

"Of course, my lord. I did study under some very fine doctors in Edinburgh. I also have two medical degrees—one from Oxford, and one from Gottingen University in Hanover." He swiftly outlined his experience, pleased to note that the arrogant marquess began to look reluctantly impressed. Halfway through his recital, Lady Silverton turned and beamed at her husband with smug satisfaction. John resisted the temptation to laugh.

"Now," he said after he had finished, "I need to know a little more about Lady Silverton's situation." He turned his gaze back on her. "Why don't you tell me what concerns you, my lady—what symptoms most trouble you."

In a soft but no-nonsense voice, Lady Silverton outlined the difficulties she had been experiencing throughout her pregnancy. Her morning sickness continued to be severe, and she suffered from extreme fatigue with the occasional shortness of breath. John ran a quick, assessing gaze over her body, surprised that so tall and sturdy a woman should be having so much difficulty.

"Do you generally suffer from poor health, my lady?" he asked.

"Never," she replied. "I've always been as strong as an ox."

Lord Silverton gave a soft chuckle and stroked her thick, black hair. "My wife is a countrywoman, Dr. Blackmore. You'll find she has a plain manner of speech."

"Then we shall deal extremely well together, since I also grew up in the country. In any event, plain speaking is always best in medical matters. Lady Silverton, you must never hesitate to tell me exactly what you think, or be afraid to share any of your concerns." John met the marquess's cool blue gaze. "And you, as well, my lord. You may say anything to me that you think necessary. It is impossible for you to offend me."

Lord Silverton gave him a narrow-eyed sizing up, then seemed to relax. "I'll hold you to that promise, Doctor."

The marchioness threw her husband a reproachful glance before giving John an apologetic smile. "You may have noticed that my husband is a trifle overprotective."

"Not at all, my lady. His behavior seems perfectly rational to me."

She laughed, and some of the tension left her body.

He ran his gaze over her figure again, noting the size of her belly. "Lady Silverton, how advanced is your pregnancy?"

"According to Dr. Steele, I am two weeks shy of eight months."

John blinked. She was extraordinarily large for a woman with six weeks before her labor.

She looked at her belly with amused chagrin. "I know. It doesn't seem possible, does it?" She sighed. "Or that I have another six to eight weeks of this."

Silverton gently stroked her cheek, and she leaned into him for comfort.

"I'd best have a closer look," John replied. He glanced up at the marquess. "My lord, I should like to give your wife a physical examination. It would be helpful if she were to change into a dressing gown, so that she might be more comfortable."

Lord Silverton suddenly looked suspicious. "Is that really necessary?"

His wife gave an exasperated huff of breath. "For pity's sake, Doctor, don't ask him. Ask me. I'm the one who has to put up with it."

"Of course, my lady," said John, "but for safety's sake, I thought I'd ask your husband first."

She cast her husband a wry glance. "Very wise. But you mustn't wonder why Lord Silverton is surprised you will conduct a physical examination. You see, Dr. Steele never does—except for feeling my pulse and looking at my tongue."

John clamped his teeth shut to hold back the retort that sprang to his lips. Of course Steele never examined her. That's why the bloody fool didn't have a clue what was wrong with her.

"Dr. Steele has a great familiarity with your case, my lady," he said instead. "But I will be able to render a more precise opinion after I examine you."

With her husband's assistance, Lady Silverton hauled herself to her feet and disappeared into her dressing room. Lord Silverton made no effort to break the silence, and John cordially returned him the favor. After a few uncomfortable but fortunately brief minutes, Lady Silverton returned, a gray satin dressing gown wrapped about her round figure. A maid accompanied her.

"What would you like me to do, Doctor?" she asked.

"Please lie down on the sofa, my lady," John replied, moving to her side. He helped her get comfortable, swinging her legs up on the soft cushions.

Lord Silverton's face looked set in stone as he glared at him. John had the distinct impression that if he laid a hand on his wife, mayhem might ensue. God only knew what the marquess would do when he put his hand up under the skirts of her dressing gown.

"Oh, Silverton, do please leave the room," groused her

ladyship, clearly at the end of her patience. "I won't have you scowling at me while the doctor is simply trying to help. Grace will stay with me, and I'll have her fetch you once the examination is completed."

John didn't know how he managed it, but the marquess looked both guilty and mortally offended.

"I wasn't scowling at you, my love," he said defensively to his wife.

"Well, the effect is equally unpleasant, even if you're not directing your ire at me. I would be most grateful if you would leave my room—now." Her voice was stern, but John detected the hint of a smile in her intelligent eyes.

Silverton sighed. "As you wish, my love. I'll wait in the library." He moved to the door and stopped, hand on the doorknob. "And I'll expect to hear from you, Doctor, very shortly."

Lady Silverton muttered, but John readily agreed. No point in irritating the man any further than he already was. "I'll send the maid to you as soon as I'm finished my examination, my lord."

"Please don't be offended, Dr. Blackmore," said Lady Silverton once the door had closed. "My husband is terribly worried. I try not to complain, but he knows how uncomfortable I am."

"Let's try to alleviate those worries, shall we? For both of you." He smiled at the maid. "You take care of her ladyship, do you, Grace?"

"Yes, sir," she replied, bobbing respectfully.

"Please sit behind your mistress on the sofa, so that she may lean back on you. That's right," he encouraged as he guided the two women into position.

John knelt beside the sofa. Now that her husband had left the room, the marchioness began to look anxious. As he took her pulse, he cast about for a way to draw her focus away from his actions.

"How long have you known Lady Randolph?" he asked, moving up from her wrist to check the pulse at her throat.

"I've seen her in company, of course, but I never really talked to her until the other day in Green Park."

"Ah. That surprises me. Will you open your mouth, my lady?"

She obediently stuck out her tongue, said *ah*, then sat quietly while he raised her eyelids for a look.

"Why does that surprise you?" she asked when he had finished.

"Lady Randolph was insistent that I see you," he said. "Given her level of concern, I assumed you were old friends."

She smiled. "She is a very determined woman. I tried to send her on her way once she assisted me to my carriage, but she climbed right in and wouldn't leave until she saw me safely home."

John could well imagine Bathsheba's high-handed techniques. "She does tend to get what she wants, it seems. My lady, I need to touch your stomach now. Do I have your permission?"

"Of course, Doctor," she replied, sounding nervous but trying to put a brave face on it.

He slid his hands across her abdomen, gently probing as he searched out the baby's position. She flushed, looking embarrassed, but withstood it well.

"How long have you known Lady Randolph?" she asked brightly. John had the sense she needed to distract herself from the liberties he was taking with her body. He was happy to oblige.

"I met her in Yorkshire some weeks ago while visiting one of my old professors. Lady Randolph was in residence at Compton Manor, the family estate."

Lady Silverton frowned. "Yes, I'd heard she spent some weeks in the country. Everyone seemed to think that quite odd, since she professes to hate leaving the city."

He nodded, sliding his hands around her belly, mystified by her enormous size.

"She fell ill with a fever. That delayed her return to London," he said absently.

He took his hands away and sat back on his heels, running through the possibilities in his head. When he raised his gaze to meet hers, she was studying him with lively curiosity. Something he had said about Bathsheba must have piqued her interest.

"Did you care for her while she was ill?" she asked in a suspiciously innocent tone.

"Yes," he said, suddenly wishing he had kept his mouth shut. The last thing he wanted to do was set off any gossip that might send Bathsheba running back to the hills.

Lady Silverton gave him a self-satisfied grin, looking as if she had discovered an amusing secret. "I like her. She's . . . different. More direct and honest than most women of the ton."

He gave a short laugh. "That's one way of describing her. Now, my lady, I'm going to rest a small wooden cylinder on your stomach. It won't hurt, but it will help me detect your baby's heartbeat."

"And if you can't?" she asked. Her smile vanished. Instantly, she looked so vulnerable, so much like Becky that his heart squeezed with the memory of it.

"You're not to worry. It's more common to not hear the heartbeat, especially depending on the position of the baby. I trust you feel movement, though—the babe kicking inside you?"

She scrunched her nose. "Sometimes it feels like a prize-fight going on in there. There's so much thumping and banging it wakes me up at night." Her round face softened with a sweet glow. "And sometimes my belly moves, as if his little arms and legs are pushing out."

"Hoping for a boy, are you?"

"A boy would be lovely, but so would a girl. I do, however,

have a strong feeling that my baby is a boy." She made a wry face. "He must be a boy to kick up such a fuss. No girl would dare be so misbehaved."

He repressed a grin. First-time mothers—especially aristocratic mothers—always thought they were having a boy.

"Grace," he said, glancing at the long-suffering maid, still propping up her mistress. "You can get up now. Lady Silverton, would you please lie flat on the sofa?"

The maid slid out from under her mistress, gently helping her to recline on the plump cushions of the velvet sofa. The marchioness still looked apprehensive, but there was little John could do about that except give her a reassuring smile and hope his suspicions were correct.

He extracted the cylinder from his medical bag and propped it on the tight drum of her belly. "Just breathe normally, my lady. This won't take long."

She nodded and blew out a quick breath, then settled. As he positioned his ear to the tube, a soft, almost sacred silence enveloped them. John let his surroundings, all outside distractions fade away, focusing his senses, his knowledge— even his intuition—on the quickening of life in her body. Time slowed to a snail's crawl. Her stomach growled, went quiet, and then . . . then he heard it. A heartbeat. Fast, steady, and strong.

He smiled and shifted over her, moving to the other side of her belly. Again, he listened, longer this time, straining to hear what he suspected was there. Lady Silverton shivered, and he murmured a soft word of comfort. He held his position, waiting for it.

Yes. There it was. Another heartbeat. Not as loud as the first, but beating out a regular, rapid pulse.

"Is everything well?" Lady Silverton's voice held a thin edge of fear.

John straightened up. "Everything is fine, my lady. Just

a little more unpleasantness and we'll be finished. Here, let me help you sit up."

Grace rushed to assist. When Lady Silverton was sitting up again, John quietly told her what he needed to do next. He explained every one of his actions as he gently reached under her robe and made a quick examination. She had turned a fiery red by the time he was finished, but she bore it with dignity, unlike Grace, who gaped at him, looking twice as shocked as her mistress.

"Thank you, my lady," he said, rising to his feet. "I apologize for the inconvenience."

She laughed unsteadily. "I don't know if inconvenience is really the right word, but I must admit that now I'm *very* glad Dr. Steele never examined me in such a fashion."

John grinned. He knew exactly what she meant. Steele was a pompous, overbearing ass, with a brusque manner. Any woman of sense would run in the opposite direction before allowing him to lay a hand on her body, and Lady Silverton clearly had a great deal of sense.

"My lady, allow me to wash up first, and then I'll be happy to explain the results of my examination to you and your husband."

"Of course. Grace, show the doctor to the bath, and fetch his lordship from the library."

After cleaning up in a very modern and luxurious bath, John returned to Lady Silverton's sitting room. He tapped on the door, and Lord Silverton's voice bade him enter.

The marquess sat beside his wife on the sofa, his arm wrapped protectively about her shoulders, talking softly in her ear. When John entered, they both looked up. Lady Silverton smiled, but her husband looked ready to kill. Obviously the marchioness had provided details of her examination.

Lord Silverton came to his feet, looking every inch the powerful aristocrat. John was tempted to laugh. It was little wonder Steele didn't lay a hand on Lady Silverton—her husband had probably terrified him.

"Well, Doctor. What are the results of your examination?" Lord Silverton's voice held a note of challenge, but John could also hear the anxiety in it.

"I'm happy to report that your wife is doing very well, under the circumstances."

His lordship's eyebrows snapped into a straight line. "What circumstances?"

"Oh, Stephen, for heaven's sake! Let the man speak," exclaimed Lady Silverton.

"It's quite all right, my lady," John replied. "By circumstances, I mean that you are pregnant with twins. All your symptoms—your fatigue and nausea, for instance—can be explained by that fact."

Lady Silverton's beautiful gray eyes popped wide. She fell back against the cushions. Her husband simply looked stunned.

"Twins?" she echoed in a faintly horrified voice. "How can you tell?"

"Aside from your size and your symptoms—which are common with twins—I heard two heartbeats."

The marquess stared at his wife with a wondering gaze. He sat down very carefully next to her. "Are you quite certain?" he asked, glancing at John.

"Yes, my lord. I heard both heartbeats distinctly. Lady Silverton, I assure you there is nothing wrong with you. Your last several weeks of pregnancy will not be comfortable, but there is no reason to believe you won't be safely delivered of your babies."

She gave a dazed laugh and leaned against her husband's shoulder. "Thank you, Doctor. I can't tell you how relieved I am."

Lord Silverton dropped a kiss on her head and hugged her close, but after a moment his brows drew together in a thoughtful frown. "Dr. Blackmore, why did this rather pertinent fact escape the notice of Dr. Steele? The man's been attending my wife for months."

It shouldn't have.

John bit back the quick retort. If Steele had done a thorough examination on Lady Silverton in the last few weeks, he likely would have got it right. But it was difficult to determine the presence of twins, as he had learned years ago with Becky. His sister had been pregnant with twins, and the local doctor had never guessed—not until it was too late.

"It is difficult to detect twins," he replied. "Most women and their doctors never know until the babies are actually born."

"You knew," replied Silverton. His voice was carefully neutral, but John had the distinct impression from his cold blue gaze that the man was angry. He was also willing to bet Steele was the source of that anger.

"Yes."

Lady Silverton nudged her husband in the ribs. "I told you Dr. Blackmore was a good doctor. Bathsheba said so."

"So you did, my love," said the marquess, wiping all traces of anger from his face. "As always, I should heed your opinion in all things. Dr. Blackmore, my wife and I would be exceedingly grateful if you would take her on as your patient. If you accept, I will inform Dr. Steele that his services are no longer required."

John felt an intense surge of relief that he didn't have to convince Lord Silverton to allow him to treat his wife. Steele was both arrogant and sometimes incompetent, and the thought of leaving a vulnerable woman—especially one who reminded him so forcibly of Becky—in his blundering hands made the skin crawl on the back of his neck.

"I should be honored to attend to her ladyship's needs. If you so desire, I am also ready to discuss the matter with Dr. Steele."

Lord Silverton gave him a grim smile. "That won't be necessary. I'll take care of it."

The marchioness sat up straight, her smooth brow wrinkling with concern. "Dr. Blackmore, I do hope this won't cause any problems for you. With Dr. Steele, I mean."

He gave her a reassuring smile. "I assure you, my lady, I am well able to deal with Dr. Steele. My only concern is your well-being."

"If you ever have any difficulties with Steele, you will let me know." Lord Silverton's tone of voice made it clear he was not making a request.

John nodded. "As you wish. Now, my lady," he said, smiling at his new patient. "You must take very good care of yourself from now on. No more walks in Green Park. If the weather is not too hot, you may take a stroll around Grosvenor Square, on your husband's arm. And I would suggest you curtail any socializing you might still be inclined to do. You may have a few friends visit you at Silverton House, but that is all."

She gave him a jaundiced look. "You're going to be a tyrant, aren't you?"

"Yes, I am."

"So be it," she said with a sigh, ignoring her grinning husband. "What else must I do?"

"You must rest and eat well. Your body is working twice as hard, and requires excellent nourishment and extra caution." He extracted a pocket book and began to make notes. "Please follow these instructions. I'll send over more detailed ones later, along with something to help you sleep."

"I will be all right, though, won't I? And my babies?" She rubbed a hand over her belly, suddenly looking like a very young, very green girl.

"You'll be fine, my lady. You must trust me." He smiled. "I'm good at what I do."

"I do trust you," she said. He could tell she meant it.

John detailed a few more instructions and made his farewells. As he cut through Grosvenor Square on the way back to his house, he thought about Steele's likely reaction to the news that he had lost one of his most prominent clients. The man would be furious, seeing John as an upstart rival who had stolen a patient. Without a doubt, he would complain to Abernethy, and that would make life at the hospital more difficult. But the marchioness needed him, and John wasn't about to say no.

He had said no once before, and Becky and her twins had died. He wouldn't make the same mistake twice.

Chapter 15

For the first time in her life, Bathsheba wished she were sitting in the pit at Covent Garden, along with the half-naked Cyprians, carousing tradesmen, and drunken bucks of the ton who all looked to be enjoying themselves a great deal more than she was. Instead, she was ensconced in Sir David Roston's private box, hemmed in on one side by the mild-mannered baronet and on the other by his sister, the most severely correct woman in London. For the last forty-five minutes, Miss Roston had engaged in a diatribe about the decline of modern manners, delivered in a flat monotone that stretched Bathsheba's nerves to the breaking point.

She had to give Miss Roston credit—the aging spinster had a nose for sin, homing in with unerring skill on any member of the ton whose behavior suggested even a mild flirtation with vulgarity or vice. Since that represented almost everyone in the theater, she didn't lack material to fuel her outrage.

Several times, Bathsheba had cast a long-suffering look Sir David's way, hoping he would rescue her from his sister's dreary homily. But he had simply given her vague, placating smiles and turned away, launching back into his endless philosophical discussions with Mr. Peters, Lord Torton, and any number of political men who drifted in and out of their box. She might as well have been sitting on a clump of gorse in Yorkshire for all the notice the baronet had shown her this evening. That baffled her, for his attentions in the last few weeks had been quite pointed. She could only hope he had already decided to marry her, and so no longer felt the need to engage in active pursuit.

With a sigh of gloomy resignation, she tried to ignore the twinges sparking at the back of her eyeballs, hoping they didn't develop into a full-blown headache. The caterwauling on stage didn't help. Kitty Stephens—she of the dulcet voice—had yet to appear, forcing the audience to endure a number of appalling musical interludes before the real talent appeared. Not that the hundreds of patrons stuffed all the way up to the pigeon holes seemed to mind. They came as much for the show in the boxes and in the pit as for the performance on the stage. Bathsheba usually did, too, often playing a part in the grand spectacle herself. But not one of her regular flirts had cared to subject himself to the utter boredom of Sir David and Miss Roston's company.

"Good gracious," droned the taffeta-clad gorgon sitting next to her, "is that Lord Burton sitting with Harriett Wilson? One wonders what Lady Burton would say if she could see her husband openly peering down the front of that creature's gown. One can hardly imagine."

Bathsheba pressed the throbbing point between her eyebrows, wishing she didn't have to answer. But she supposed she had to make some attempt at conversation with the woman who, horrible as the thought might be, could soon be her sister-in-law.

"Miss Roston, we might assume that Lord Burton would not be gazing down Miss Wilson's dress if Lady Burton were here with him. In any event, his lordship gazes down the front of every woman's dress, so I suspect Lady Burton is quite used to it."

Although now that Bathsheba thought about it, his lordship would probably make an exception in Miss Roston's case, since the woman had no bosom to speak of.

"It's the principle of the thing, Lady Randolph," intoned the other woman, sounding more priggish by the second. "One does expect one's husband to behave with a sense of propriety, doesn't one? Your late husband, for example, was by all accounts a most devoted and faithful spouse. If only all the men of the ton could display the fidelity and loyalty of a Lord Randolph. How devastating, how infinitely tragic that he was wrenched from your arms at so early an age. I pity you for his loss."

Bathsheba's temples exploded with lancing pain. She swallowed her fury, fighting back the impulse to pull the stupid woman's tightly woven, mouse-colored braids out by the roots. Miss Roston surely knew as well as anyone that she and Reggie had had a terrible marriage.

"My dear lady," she ground out, ignoring the sickening display of false sympathy, "if you despise the opera and theater so much, why do you come?"

The spinster lifted her evangelical gaze from the good-natured, lascivious romps going on below and fixed her cold eyes on Bathsheba's face.

"Why, I come at my brother's request, Lady Randolph. Could you imagine otherwise? As his hostess, I fancy I set a certain tone at all times—even in so depraved an environment as Covent Garden. You must know that Sir David's political career is very important to him. My presence discourages the vain and ill-mannered from pestering him, and I make sure to keep away those *women*," she invested the word with volumes of contempt, "who seek to take advantage of his open and gracious temperament."

Bathsheba frowned. "Your brother is an intelligent man, Miss Roston, well past the follies of youth. Surely he is capable of passing judgment on those who seek his friendship. After all, he is a politician."

"For a politician, my brother has a most unsuspecting and open nature. This is especially true in his dealings with the fair sex. He seems incapable of suspecting any woman not of the lower orders of any ill intent. While it does him great credit, you and I both know his fortune and standing in society make him very eligible. Over the years, many an unscrupulous woman has sought to prey on him only to better her own situation."

Bathsheba called up all her years of training to keep the panic from showing on her face. She suddenly understood what this demented conversation was all about. Miss Roston had always seemed like a footnote to her brother's life, fortunate enough to escape the sad existence of a poor relation but wielding no great influence on him one way or the other.

"Fortunately," the spinster continued relentlessly, "my brother understands that his too-tender heart can be a weakness. He relies on me to guide him in these matters. We are very close, perhaps because our parents died when we were so young. I am his only sibling, and his elder. He trusts my judgment completely."

At that moment, Sir David glanced away from his friends and gave Bathsheba an admiring smile. He was a rather colorless, self-contained man. But although she had always found his soft, hesitant manner of speaking rather irritating, she had never thought him weak. Not until this moment, when she saw him through his sister's eyes.

She managed to dredge up a weak smile, praying her dismay didn't show on her face. He appeared satisfied, for he returned to his conversation with a lifeless smile playing around his lips.

Bathsheba glanced at Miss Roston to find the woman studying her with a calculating assessment, her thin mouth folding in on itself. She allowed her contemptuous gaze to drop down and catch briefly on the low bodice of Bathsheba's burgundy silk gown.

"Lady Randolph," she said, not bothering to hide her

disdain, "I will not mince words, nor pretend to ignore what is happening between you and my brother. It is to be hoped that you appreciate your good fortune in attracting his attention. Although he and I have together led a useful and productive life—one which I have no desire to change—he feels a great deal of responsibility to our family name. For reasons which I must in all honesty say elude me, he has fixed his favor on you. Although you have many faults, you are not a stupid woman. I assume you realize he is considering asking you to be his wife."

Bathsheba felt the muscles in her jaw begin to slacken. It would seem that Miss Roston did everything for her brother, including reviewing prospective marital candidates. "Ah, well . . ." she stuttered, at a loss as to how to respond to the harridan's interrogation. She cast a wild look around the box, but Sir David and his friends remained deep in conversation.

Miss Roston waved an impatient hand. "I beg you. Do not insult my intelligence, Lady Randolph. We both know very well that you do, and that you welcome my brother's attentions. Given the kind of life you have led these last few years, I must wonder why you chose a man so unlike yourself. But my brother is quite captivated with you . . ."

She paused to give a hard swallow, as if someone had shoved something large and bitter down her throat. "I must—at least for now—respect his choice. I speak frankly so that you may fully understand how your behavior will reflect upon him. If you are to be his wife, you must realize you will be held to a very high standard indeed."

Bathsheba stared back, afraid even to blink as she silently commanded the panic in her chest to subside. Clearly, Miss Roston was her brother's keeper, and the only way for Bathsheba to reach her goal was to win the jealous sister's approval.

As she struggled to compose an appropriate answer, something deep inside fought its way to the surface, something she had once known and which cried out to be remembered. Whatever it was rebelled, urging her to stand up, leave the box, and refuse to be handed over again into another man's keeping. But this was nothing like her first marriage. It wouldn't be her father enacting the transaction, using her as coin to barter away his debt. This time, it was she who would sell herself. This time, love—and yes, she had loved Reggie when she first married him—had no bearing on the equation.

She blinked the hot sting of tears from her eyes, furious with her momentary weakness. This was her last chance to save Rachel, to save herself. If she had to toady to the likes of Miss Roston and marry a man she didn't care about, then so be it. At least Sir David would never be cruel, or make her life a misery. Everything she knew about him told her that he would honor any commitments he made to her. He was reserved and under his sister's thumb, but he had a reputation for keeping his word. She simply had to find a way past his sister and convince him—in bed, if necessary—that he was making the right decision by asking her to marry him.

"Have you gone deaf, Lady Randolph?" asked Miss Roston in a soft, malicious voice. "You are so rarely at a loss for words."

Bathsheba almost did gape at her this time, stunned that she could have ever mistaken the woman for merely a pale shadow of her brother. A vaguely formed thought crossed her mind that she would rather throw herself on the rigid but just mercies of Miss Elliott than place herself in thrall to Sir David's sister. Perhaps life as a dowager countess in Yorkshire wouldn't be so unpleasant, after all.

She thrust that surprisingly attractive image away and leveled her most placating smile at the viper sitting next to her.

"Miss Roston, I do indeed understand. Let me assure you that I have the keenest appreciation for your brother's generous attentions to me. I hesitate to appear forward, but it is my fondest wish to find approval in his eyes and, of course, in yours as well."

The other woman's gaze narrowed with suspicion. Bathsheba held steady, not challenging her, but refusing to be cowed. The seconds ticked by, the tension stretching between them, transmuting into a battle of wills no less fierce for being conducted in silence.

Suddenly, one of Sir David's companions laughed, and the chatter from the crowd around them seemed to swell. The second interval had begun and soon their box would crowd with visitors. Bathsheba kept a polite smile fixed on her face, resisting the urge to sag with relief into her seat.

Miss Roston made a scoffing noise. "Very well, Lady Randolph. I will take you at your word. But know that my brother's interests will always come first with me. If you toy with him, or I find that you are using him, rest assured I will turn him against you."

Bathsheba gave her a dignified nod, actually relieved that her enemy had so openly declared herself. If Miss Roston felt the need to do so, then surely Sir David's intentions must be very serious. With a little luck, they might even be married before the Season began.

As Sir David rose from his seat and moved to stand next to her, she tried to imagine spending the rest of her life as Lady Roston. The bright red and gold trim of the theater, illuminated by three rows of gigantic chandeliers, shimmered and swam before her vision. She suddenly felt light-headed and ridiculously close to fainting. When Sir David's fingers brushed her naked shoulder, she had to repress an intense shudder of revulsion.

"My dear Lady Randolph, are you well?" he asked. He sounded puzzled rather than concerned. "You look quite pale."

"Goodness, no," she said with a forced laugh. She took a deep breath, and her momentary dizziness passed. "I am well, although I do find it quite stuffy in here."

"Lady Randolph and I have been discussing your career, my dear brother," interjected Miss Roston. "I have been explaining how important your work is."

"I'm sure you must find that a dead bore," he replied with a gentle laugh. "Most women do. My sister, of course, is an exception."

"Not at all," Bathsheba protested. "I find it absolutely fascinating."

Actually, she found it dreadfully dull, but she refused to be compared to Miss Roston and found wanting.

His mild brown eyes warmed with approval. "I'm pleased you think so. Nonetheless, I do owe you an apology. I'm afraid I've been neglecting both you and my sister. But I assure you, my lady, you will now have my undivided attention for the rest of the evening. Not another word about politics shall pass my lips."

"Nonsense, brother," exclaimed Miss Roston. "Nothing is as important as your work. I understand that, as does Lady Randolph."

"Indeed I do, sir," Bathsheba said, gifting him with her brightest smile. "I wish you will tell me all about it."

Much to Miss Roston's evident annoyance, Sir David dragged his chair over and launched into a description of the new Irish Constabulary. Bathsheba did her best to follow him, making appropriate noises whenever he paused to allow her to do so. She had done it a thousand times before—flattering a man's vanity with careful little attentions. A seductive smile, a touch on the sleeve, an enthusiastic response to whatever idea he put forth—inane or not. And, as it had every time before, it worked. Sir David preened like a peacock, listening not so much to her but to the sound of his own voice. It was what he expected as his due, and she gave it in good measure. But doing it made her stomach turn, more strongly than ever before.

When Sir David paused to take a breath, his sister interrupted him. For once, Bathsheba was grateful to her. If she had to play the sycophant much longer, she'd be tempted to throw herself over the railing into the pit.

"Brother, Lady Randolph and I were speaking of a most interesting subject earlier in the evening."

Miss Roston gave her that now-familiar malicious smile, instantly turning Bathsheba's gratitude to alarm.

"Do you remember, my lady? We were speaking of Sir David's philanthropic work, especially in relation to the charity schools. Those schools are very important to him—to both of us."

Miss Roston paused to give her brother a treacly smile before returning her unforgiving gaze to Bathsheba. "My brother believes all women of good breeding have an obligation to spend much of their time engaging in works of charity. I know he would be most interested to hear what you do to contribute to the greater good of society."

Sir David gave her a happy, encouraging smile. "Indeed, Lady Randolph. Please do tell us which charities you find worthy of your attention."

She looked first at him, then at her adversary, grim resolve stiffening her spine. Miss Roston clearly hoped she would condemn herself out of her own mouth, forced to expose her frivolous, useless life to Sir David. It was time to show the mean-spirited old biddy exactly what she was up against.

"As it so happens," she drawled, "I am about to become a governor at St. Bartholomew's Hospital. I do believe that sitting on the board of London's finest hospital constitutes a most worthy cause."

Miss Roston's sparse brows inched up her tight forehead, speaking volumes of derision. "Really? My brother and I are very good friends with Dr. Abernethy, and I've heard him mention nothing of the sort. One simply doesn't waltz in and become a governor, you know, whatever you might choose to believe."

Sir David cast a doubtful glance between the two women, finally sensing the tensely charged atmosphere in the box.

"Nonetheless, it's true," Bathsheba retorted, unable to keep the sarcasm from her voice.

She winced at the look of surprise on Sir David's face. Miss Roston smiled, unable to contain her petty triumph.

Bathsheba cast a frustrated glance around the theater, cursing her temper and wondering how she had gotten herself into such a ridiculous mess. Even more importantly, how was she to get out of it?

Like the answer to a prayer, her gaze caught and held on a man in a box across the way. The man stared back. Well, glared back, if she wanted to be accurate.

John.

She couldn't repress a triumphant little smile of her own. "You might not believe me, Miss Roston, but I trust you will believe Dr. Blackmore. He's a physician on staff at St. Bartholomew's. Perhaps you've heard of him."

Miss Roston's face grew positively Medusa-like. Bathsheba wouldn't have been surprised if the braids in her hair starting writhing like snakes.

"I've met Dr. Blackmore," Sir David exclaimed. "He comes from a distinguished family. And he seems a most accomplished physician."

"Well, he's sitting right across the way," purred Bathsheba, enjoying how Miss Roston's forehead creased with baffled fury. "I met with him only yesterday to discuss the details. Perhaps the next time you speak to him, you might ask him about it."

"Excellent," enthused Sir David. "But why wait? There's no time like the present."

He nodded and waved at the other box, clearly indicating his desire that John join them.

Bathsheba stared at Sir David, stunned, dismayed, and infuriated by her own stupidity. How could she not have considered the possibility that he would invite John to their box? She had virtually challenged him to do so. But she had been in such a fury, wanting to spike Miss Roston's guns. Instead, she was pitching her erstwhile lover and her future fiancé into close contact, creating the most potentially catastrophic social situation she could think of.

She stifled a groan, lamenting her impulsive invitation of yesterday. After all, she hadn't really expected John to show. Never once had she seen him at the opera or the theater, simply assuming he hadn't the time for such frivolities. But clearly he had taken her at her word, more fool that she was.

Steeling herself, she gazed across at John's box. Thankfully, he no longer glared at her, but now studied her with a thoughtful air. As their eyes met, she felt an unwelcome pull between them, the inconvenient, bittersweet yearning that afflicted her whenever she saw him. It made her feel stupid things, reckless things—like wanting to be with him again, forgetting all her obligations. Even forgetting who she had to be.

John smiled, and the force of it reached all the way across the theater, stealing every bit of breath from her lungs. He rose to his feet, exchanging a few words with his companions before disappearing from the box.

She choked back a gasp. He was coming to her, as surely as if she had called out to him.

"Well, Lady Roston, it would appear that Dr. Blackmore will be here momentarily," said Sir David. "I look forward to hearing all about your plans to join the board."

He reached over and took her gloved hand. "It is a most worthy goal indeed. I can't tell you how pleased I am that you have chosen such an important cause for the devotion of your charitable energies."

Unbelievably, he raised her hand to his lips. Any satisfaction Bathsheba might have taken from the look of horror on Miss Roston's face died at the thought of John walking in on the baronet's clumsy attempts to flirt with her.

Tugging her hand away, she dredged up another weak

smile for her suitor. God, who would have ever thought she would become a ghastly imitation of a nervous miss?

Sir David gave her a look of mild reproach, but was too much a gentleman to protest her rebuff. Before she could think of a suitable remark to assuage his pride, the curtains at the back of the box parted. She twisted in her seat, both dreading and longing to see their visitor.

"Dr. Blackmore, do come in," Sir David said, rising to exchange bows. "Of course you know Lady Randolph."

Bathsheba gave John a brief nod, then ducked her head.

"And you have also met my sister, Miss Eugenia Roston," continued the baronet.

The proper greetings were made as Bathsheba kept her eyes firmly cast down.

Idiot. Why had she not prepared for this? Had she really thought their social paths would never cross?

With a welcoming gesture, Sir David indicated the seat vacated by Lord Torton. Out of the corner of her eye, Bathsheba watched John settle in comfortably, as if ready to spend the night. She sighed, wondering what other nightmares the evening would bring.

Miss Roston wasted no time going on the attack. "Dr. Blackmore," she said, making his name sound like a call to battle, "I understand from Lady Randolph that she is to be a governor at St. Bartholomew's Hospital. Is this true?"

John raised a brow at the impertinent tone of the question. He cast an amused glance in Bathsheba's direction before answering.

"I certainly hope so, Miss Roston. We spoke about it at some length. I know she would make an excellent addition to the board."

The other woman went from grim to positively foreboding. "I'm amazed to hear so. I spoke with Dr. Abernethy at Mrs. Podworth's dinner party just the other night. He mentioned nothing of the sort to me."

John gave the spinster a disarming smile. Even though it wasn't directed at her, its potent charm made Bathsheba's heart skip several beats.

"Lady Randolph only met Dr. Abernethy yesterday afternoon, Miss Roston. I can assure you, he is delighted that she is considering taking up the position."

"As am I, Dr. Blackmore," exclaimed Sir David. "Any project her ladyship takes on is of great interest to me."

He reached over and took her hand once again, gazing at her with possessive pride. Bathsheba almost fainted on the spot.

John's eyes narrowed into chips of ice. "And why is that, Sir David?"

For once, Miss Roston served a useful purpose. "Dr. Blackmore," she interjected, clearly annoyed by the direction of the conversation, "I'd like to ask you a question about the admissions policy at St. Bartholomew's. It seems to me there has been a great deal of laxity as of late. Or so I'm told by Dr. Abernethy."

John kept silent, his big body at ease as he lounged in his chair. But his gaze remained fastened on Bathsheba's hand, still captured in Sir David's grip. A hot flush crept up her neck. She tried to extract her fingers, and the baronet finally let her go. Only then did John turn his attention to Miss Roston.

As Bathsheba struggled to recapture her abused composure, Dr. Blackmore responded to the other woman's question. She apparently didn't like his answer, for her reply came back sharp and disagreeable. Bathsheba, however, didn't comprehend a word, too caught up in her struggle to appear calm in the face of impending disaster. If John were to give even the slightest hint of their past relationship—

His deep voice interrupted the downward spiral of her thoughts.

"Lady Randolph, are you quite well?"

She gasped and pressed a hand to her temple. Perspiration dampened her kid glove.

"I . . . I beg your pardon, Doctor. I seem to have developed a headache."

John frowned, and as she could have predicted, reached for her wrist. He felt for her pulse through the thin material of the glove. Bathsheba forced herself to keep still, even though the feel of his strong fingers made her want to jump out of her skin.

Miss Roston's face pinched with outrage. "Dr. Blackmore. Really! Is that appropriate?"

"Lady Randolph is only recently recovered from a severe infection, Miss Roston. She was under my care," he replied.

Sir David clucked his tongue. "Oh, dear. I didn't know that. She mentioned earlier that she found the air rather close." He peered at her, looking genuinely concerned.

John ignored him as he studied her face, keeping her wrist in a light clasp. Bathsheba's heart took up a hard, pounding rhythm as she met his steady gaze.

"Her pulse is tumultuous and her complexion is flushed. I think it best Lady Randolph cut short her evening and return home. It won't do for her to become overstimulated."

She blushed even harder, knowing exactly why she was overstimulated. And, she suspected, John knew it, too.

"Of course," exclaimed the baronet. "We will take her home immediately."

"Oh, no. Really, that won't be necessary," protested Bathsheba. "I feel fine."

"I don't think you are," John said in a soft but determined voice.

"Really, Doctor," spluttered Miss Roston, "if Lady Randolph doesn't think it necessary to leave, then why should we? And Miss Stephens is about to perform."

She cast Bathsheba an angry glance before turning to her

brother. "You know how much I enjoy hearing her sing. I would be devastated to miss her performance."

Her brother looked startled. "You would? I—"

John smoothly interrupted him. "There's no need for you to trouble yourself, Sir David. I will escort Lady Randolph home. It wouldn't do for her to suffer a relapse, as I'm sure you will agree."

"Oh, yes," Miss Roston enthusiastically agreed. "That would no doubt be the best course."

Sir David hesitated, looking like a whipped puppy as he gazed at his sister. It suddenly occurred to Bathsheba that she would like nothing better than to get as far away from the Rostons as she possibly could.

"Perhaps Dr. Blackmore is correct," she said, affecting a plaintive voice. "I *am* feeling rather light-headed. It might be best if I were to return home."

As Sir David embarked on a confused attempt to explain why he couldn't escort her, John helped her out of her chair and bundled her into her shawl. The baronet jumped to his feet, still apologizing, as Bathsheba murmured her farewells.

As John guided her toward the door, she glanced at Miss Roston's face. A malicious and knowing satisfaction glittered in the woman's eyes as she studied the protective arm John placed across the back of her waist. Bathsheba silently cursed. The brother might be naïve, but the sister was anything but.

A moment later they were out in the corridor and down the stairs into the Grecian-themed lobby. John took her arm in a firm grip, hurrying her along to the doors. She pulled, but he refused to let go.

"If you don't slow down, I might suffer a relapse," she snapped.

He finally came to a halt once they exited onto the street. Under the flare of the gas lamps lighting the imposing portico of the theater, she could clearly see the irritation marking his handsome features.

"Do forgive me, your ladyship," he said in a sarcastic tone, "but any fool could see you were begging to be rescued. Or did I mistake your little performance back there? Is it a doctor you truly need, or me?"

Chapter 16

Bathsheba took several deep breaths, willing her heartbeat to resume its normal rhythm. She managed a lethal glare back at John, doing her best to ignore her giddy response to his possessive, predictably masculine behavior.

Of course she had wanted to be rescued. Otherwise, she would never have allowed him to haul her from Sir David's box. And it wasn't just their dash from the theater that was making her heart race with a disconcerting combination of anxiety and excitement. It had been doing that since the moment he walked into the box. It happened every time he came near her, blast him—this easy breach of her defenses. It made her want things. Made her believe he could repair her life, much the same as he had repaired her body. This terrible wanting made her weak, when she had never been weak before.

He knew it, too, and threw the knowledge right back into her face.

"Dr. Blackmore," she finally replied in a frosty voice, "I am, of course, grateful for your assistance, but your assumption is both incorrect and offensive. I'm extremely disappointed that circumstances forced me to cut short my evening. I was having a perfectly lovely time with Sir David and his sister. And may I point out," she added with a haughty lift of her chin, "you were the one who insisted I return home. I was most reluctant to refuse, for fear you would make a public scene."

He gave an incredulous snort and waved his arm to summon a hackney. "You're quite the accomplished actress, aren't you, my lady? But I'm having none of it. You were bored out of your mind. You did everything but get down on your pretty knees and beg me to get you out of there. What the hell were you doing with the Rostons, anyway?"

She opened her mouth to snap back at him, but then she heard the smothered guffaws coming from a group of coachmen lounging around the carriages lined up on the street.

"Sir David is a very distinguished man, and most kind," she replied with a dignified air. "And his sister has an extremely well-informed mind."

John took her arm and steered her toward the hackney, now inching its way through the tangle of carriages in front of the theater.

"Sir David is a dead bore. And his sister is the worst kind of martinet. I repeat, what the hell were you doing with them?"

She paused with one foot on the step of the hackney, arrested by what she heard, or thought she heard in his voice. Faint, it barely colored the words with a thin wash of emotion, but it was still there. John Blackmore was jealous.

She glanced over her shoulder, taking in the hard set of his jaw and the grim line of his mouth. His eyes stared back at her, their silver depths shimmering with a barely concealed challenge. A quiver of illicit pleasure rippled through her, moving from her belly to settle deep between her thighs.

"Why, Doctor, you surprise me," she breathed, opening her eyes wide with faux innocence. "I would think Sir David and his sister were precisely the kind of people you would wish me to associate with. They're both so improving, don't you agree?"

His gaze grew diamond hard. "Get in," he growled.

She yelped as a large hand covered her bottom and

pushed her up into the cab. After issuing a terse direction to the driver, John followed close behind, hands on her hips to guide her as she collapsed in an undignified heap on the padded bench.

"How dare you?" she gasped as she struggled to sit upright. Her skirts had rucked up around her knees, and one of her shoes had dropped from her foot to hit the floor with a tiny thunk.

He came down on the bench beside her, his big body exuding enough heat to start a bonfire. She thought she had been warm in the theater, but the fierceness of his temper—and his hot masculine presence crowding so closely against her—brought the blood rushing to her cheeks and weakened all her limbs.

With a concerted effort, she yanked her skirts back down as she felt for the errant footwear. It was so dark inside the coach she could barely see anything, including him. But she could *feel* him, so muscular against her softer body, and that contrast set every nerve leaping in anticipation of sexual submission.

Which, naturally, would be a huge mistake.

"Really, Dr. Blackmore," she huffed, trying to reclaim her equilibrium. "I find your behavior completely unacceptable."

His only answer was a laugh that sounded more like a cat's purr—a feral cat. She felt the vibration of it along the length of her body, humming between them wherever they touched.

Repressing a mad urge to pull her skirts up around her waist and climb into his lap, she scraped her toes along the straw-covered floor of the cab, searching for her shoe. She gave a little groan when something thick and slimy dampened her silk stocking.

"Allow me, my lady," said John. His voice was edged with laughter—smoky, hot, and still holding the remnants of his anger.

Reaching down, he groped for a moment before finding her kid slipper. His long fingers closed around her ankle, stroking upward, then lingering to gently tickle the sensitive area behind her knee. She couldn't quite repress the whimper that fell from her lips.

"Is something wrong?" he asked as his hand dropped to slip her shoe back on her foot.

"Not a thing," she said in an airy, somewhat breathless voice.

But deep inside, all the nerves in her body jangled like wildly pealing bells. What was she doing here, alone in a dark carriage with the one man she couldn't have? Danger lurked on every side. With the slightest hint of scandal, she would lose Sir David's favor—his sister would see to that. Bathsheba could no longer afford the luxury of sensual indulgence, not if she wanted to save herself and her family. And indulgence was exactly what was happening in the velvet darkness of this hot little carriage.

She edged away, squishing her shoulders into the corner of the cab. With a desperate grab at the fraying ends of her common sense, she reminded herself of the last time she had let her emotions run riot. When she had blackmailed Simon. The results of that ill-conceived episode had been far-reaching and disastrous.

And at least with Simon there had been a compelling reason for her actions. But now she was behaving irrationally, against her own interests. John was not the answer to her problems, and he never would be.

He stirred, shifting to gently pin her against the wall of the cab. She clenched every muscle in an effort to resist the siren lure of his warmth and strength.

"What are you worried about, Bathsheba?" he asked. "I think I've proven to you that I can be trusted. That I have your best interests at heart. Tell me what's wrong."

His voice slid through her veins like heated brandy, tempting her to blurt out every sordid detail of her dreary, exhausting life. But her intellect recognized—even if her body did not—that he spoke with the voice of a doctor, not a lover, and the distinction made her skin crawl with shame.

After several fraught moments of silence, she managed a reply.

"As I've already told you, Dr. Blackmore, I find your unwelcome assumptions quite offensive. Please do me the courtesy of keeping your opinions to yourself. Unless I ask for them, of course." She punctuated her remarks with as much sarcasm as she could muster.

He muttered a curse—she had certainly heard worse— and retreated to the opposite corner of the cab. As the hackney inched its way along Piccadilly, bars of light from the occasional gas lamp slashed through the window, highlighting the clean, fierce lines of his aristocratic features. He stared straight ahead, his mouth pressed into an unhappy line.

Bathsheba sighed, feeling as unhappy as he looked. Why must he always force her to injure him? And why did an injury to him feel as though she had inflicted one upon herself?

As they bumped their way through the clogged street into Mayfair, she cast about for some innocuous comment to break the strained silence that hung between them.

She cleared her throat. "Dr. Blackmore, I was wondering if you had an opportunity to call on Lady Silverton."

He made a small, scoffing noise, accompanied by a slight shake of the head. "Yes, Lady Randolph. As I promised, I called on the marchioness this morning."

She felt her shoulders relax. His arctic tones lowered the temperature inside the cab several degrees, but at least he answered her.

"Can you help her?"

"I believe I can," he replied in a clipped voice.

Bathsheba breathed a silent prayer of thanks. Lady Silverton's kindness had touched her more than she cared to admit. It had been ages since she had met anyone possessed of such a warm and generous nature, and even longer since that kind of warmth had been offered so freely to her.

Except for John, of course, but that was different. He was a man, and men generally liked her. But women . . . well, Bathsheba supposed she had only herself to blame for the fact that most of the female members of the ton couldn't stand the sight of her.

She cast him a sidelong glance, wondering just how far she could pry. But with a growing sense of surprise, and more than a touch of consternation, she realized how much she wanted Lady Silverton to be safe from harm.

"Dr. Blackmore," she blurted out. "Do you think the marchioness will be safely delivered of her baby?"

He turned in his seat to examine her face. His dark brows dipped together over his nose, but he seemed puzzled rather than annoyed.

"The outcome is never certain, Lady Randolph, as I'm sure you realize."

He seemed reluctant to elaborate, which did little more than feed her sense of anxiety.

"Lady Silverton isn't ill, is she? She seemed so very tired the other day."

Even in the dim light of the cab she could see a smile tip up the corners of his mouth.

"She's fine. Her ladyship is carrying twins, which is the reason her pregnancy has been unusually difficult. But she's a strong and healthy young woman, so I have little doubt she'll do very well."

"Twins!" Bathsheba let out a relieved laugh. "That would certainly explain her enormous size."

His lips twitched into an easy grin, but only for a moment. Then he gazed down his nose at her, looking for all the world like a severe schoolmaster.

"You're not to breathe a word of this, Bathsheba—not to anyone. I had no business telling you. Not without Lady Silverton's permission. I only did so because—"

She stopped him by laying a hand on his arm.

"Thank you, John. I won't ask any more questions or say a thing to anyone. I promise. It was very kind of you to tell me."

He looked down at her hand, and her gaze followed his. Tightly encased in soft kid, her fingers looked small and strangely vulnerable against the coarser dark fabric of his coat.

"Bathsheba," he said in a gruff voice.

The carriage jerked to a halt, throwing her against him. His arms came round her, enveloping her with an alluring warmth. For a moment she allowed it to happen, but then she struggled, all too aware of the false sanctuary of his embrace.

"Let me go," she gasped. "We've reached Curzon Street."

He made a frustrated noise but loosened his hold. She scrambled for the door handle, fumbling in her panic—not because of what he might do, but because of what she would surely do if she stayed one second longer in this dark, unbearably intimate space.

He gently pushed away her hand and opened the door. After he helped her alight, he turned to pay off the driver. She stood on the pavement, staring at the Palladian facade of her house, taking slow, steady breaths in an effort to still her trembling limbs.

When John had finished with the driver and joined her by the steps leading to the front door, she lifted her head and gave him a bright smile.

"Thank you for taking me home, Dr. Blackmore. It was most kind of you."

She extended her hand but he ignored it, taking her by the shoulders and guiding her up the shallow steps.

"What are you doing?" she said, wriggling in a vain attempt to free herself.

"I'm coming in with you. I'm not convinced you're completely recovered from your illness."

She rolled her eyes. "Don't be ridiculous. I'm perfectly well and you know it."

He pounded on the knocker, still keeping a hand on her shoulder.

"And how many medical degrees do you have, Lady Randolph?" he asked sardonically. "I have two."

She was about to deliver a scathing retort when the door swung open.

"Good evening, your ladyship," said Buckles, the junior footman.

"Good—"

She choked off her reply as John's hand settled on the small of her back, just grazing the upper swell of her bottom. He gently pushed her over the threshold.

"Good evening," he said to Buckles as he handed over his hat. "I'm Dr. Blackmore. Her ladyship was taken ill while at the theater tonight."

The footman's eyes grew round with concern. "I'm sorry to hear that, my lady. Is there anything I can do?"

"I'm perfectly—"

"Lady Randolph could use a brandy," John interrupted. "Please bring it to her bedchamber immediately."

"Yes, sir. Right away."

To her immense irritation, Buckles scurried away without a second glance.

"How do you get them to do that?" she groused.

His hand pressed against her spine, urging her across the entrance hall and toward the iron-work staircase. For some demented reason, she couldn't seem to resist him.

"Do what?"

"How do you get absolutely everyone to do everything you want?"

He chuckled. "Because they know I'm right. Now up with you, and show me to your room. I'm not leaving until I'm satisfied you're not experiencing a relapse."

Bathsheba affected a long-suffering sigh, but his determination, as usual, wore down her resistance. Perhaps she did need a quick examination. After all, she was feeling a tad light-headed, and her heart continued to beat in a rapid and somewhat alarming fashion.

"Oh, very well," she capitulated. "But please be quick about it. This evening has already been irritating enough without you poking and prodding away at me."

"Why, Lady Randolph, I thought you were enjoying yourself. Could it be possible you were lying to me?"

She scowled back at his laughing face. He gave her another nudge, and she led him up the spiral staircase to her apartments.

As they entered her sitting room, he stopped and looked around.

"This is a beautiful room, Lady Randolph. I commend you on your excellent taste."

She frowned, confused by his cool tone of voice, and even more so by the carefully blank look on his face. What the devil was bothering him now?

Before she could puzzle out the answer to that question, Boland slipped through the connecting door from her bedroom. Concern leaped into her eyes, visible even behind her steel-framed spectacles.

"My lady! Dr Blackmore, is her ladyship unwell?"

"I'm fine, Boland. There's no need to make a fuss. I simply felt a little faint at the opera. Dr. Blackmore was kind enough to escort me home."

Her abigail rushed over, her sharp features marked with distress.

"I knew you shouldn't be gadding about," she scolded. "Dr. Blackmore, I told her that she was doing too much—especially in this heat."

Bathsheba frowned. "Don't be ridiculous, Boland. You always feel the heat worse than I do. In fact, I believe I told you to have Lucy wait up for me. I don't want you getting sick."

Truly, Boland looked exhausted and pale. How could the woman have been so foolish as to disobey her orders?

"Go to bed. Now, Boland," snapped Bathsheba, anxiety making her voice sharper than she intended.

The older woman immediately starched up, looking mutinous and ready to argue.

"You needn't worry, Boland," John interjected. "I'll see to her ladyship."

Boland looked suspiciously between the two of them, and opened her mouth as if to voice an objection.

Bathsheba cut her off with a sharp stab of the hand. "Go to bed, Boland, before I lose my temper with you."

John looked startled, then annoyed, but held his tongue.

"As you wish, my lady," said Boland. She made a stiff curtsy, directed a final glowering look at Bathsheba, and left the room.

"Why are you angry with her?" John said in a quiet voice after the door had closed.

Bathsheba cast her shawl over the striped silk divan and began to unbutton her gloves.

"I'm not. I'm angry with you."

"Ah," he murmured, as if that explained everything.

A tap sounded on the door. John opened it and, over Buckle's objections, took the tray holding the brandy and a glass before closing the door in the footman's face.

Bathsheba sniffed. "You're very high-handed with my servants, Dr. Blackmore."

"Not as high-handed as you," he said, handing her a glass of brandy. "Now take your shoes off and sit down and drink this."

She thought about saying something cutting, but she was tired and sick of arguing—with everyone, it seemed.

"Oh, very well," she grumbled. "I suppose you'll just nag at me until I do."

He smiled, but didn't answer as he followed her over to the divan. With a grateful sigh, she kicked off her shoes and tucked herself against the cushioned bolster. He stood over her, his eyes intent, his gaze smouldering in most undoctorlike fashion.

The air seemed to thicken in her lungs. She took a large gulp of brandy, welcoming the distraction as it seared down her throat.

Looking up at him, she met his heavy-lidded gaze with a defiant one of her own.

"I thought you were going to conduct an examination, sir. That *is* why I let you come up here."

He laughed. The husky, baritone rumble vibrated through her like a silent caress.

Oh, Lord. Bathsheba's toes actually curled at the sound of it.

"Scoot over, my lady, and take your gloves off."

The command brought a hot flush to her cheeks—whether from irritation or pleasure, she couldn't tell—but she did as he instructed. Tucking her legs up under the soft skirts of her evening dress, she began removing her gloves. He watched with an amused, appreciative gleam in his eyes, clearly enjoying her discomfort.

Now *that* was annoying. Bathsheba would throw all her jewels out into the street before she acted like a simpering miss in front of any man—even John. *Especially John.*

She slowly unbuttoned her gloves and seductively drew them off, letting the delicate fabric whisper over her skin with a lazy slide. She felt rather than saw the change in him. Felt it in the way the muscles of his powerful arms flexed. Felt it in the silence that suddenly throbbed with a sense of darkness and danger.

She took an unsteady breath, refusing to meet his gaze, trying to heed the warning voice in her head. Why in God's name was she trying to tempt him? Had she truly gone mad?

"Give me your wrist."

She looked up, startled by the faint note of bitterness shading his voice. Obediently, she gave him her hand, as she had done so many times before.

Eyes half closed, he bent his head, focusing his attention on the place where his fingers touched her wrist. Yearning slipped through and filtered along her veins to her pulse, coalescing like a small, aching wound under his touch. So simple an act, and yet it conveyed a world of meaning. It had become an expression of his devotion and of her need, the only expression she could ever allow between them.

She squeezed her eyes shut, willing herself not to do something irretrievably stupid. Casting about in her mind for something—anything—to distract her from his touch, she blurted out the first thing that came into her head.

"Why were you glaring at me so fiercely in the theater tonight?"

He glanced up, looking surprised by the question. "You were flirting with another man."

The direct admission caused her heart to miss a few beats. He frowned, obviously feeling the stuttering rhythm under his fingertips.

She affected a casual shrug. "It's what I do, Dr. Blackmore. You do realize that, don't you?"

"You won't anymore," he replied.

She gasped. "How dare—"

"Not if you want to leg-shackle Roston, which is what I assume your little performance at the opera was all about."

She fumed, longing to give him a set-down. But how could she? After all, blast him, he was correct.

His deep-set eyes studied her. They were unreadable, but she had the uncomfortable notion that he knew exactly what she was thinking.

"I need to listen to your heart," he said abruptly. "Your pulse is too fast."

"If my pulse is too fast then it's your fault," she retorted. "You've spent most of the evening insulting me, which I don't find amusing at all. I think it's time, Dr. Blackmore, for you to take your leave."

"Soon," he replied in a soothing voice. "Just lie back against the bolsters. I promise I won't insult you anymore."

She grumbled, but warily sank into the padded cushions propped at her back.

When he leaned over her chest, resting his ear on the swell of her bosom, she gave a start. The sight of his head nestling there, his mouth so close to her silken-clad breast, set off a sudden clenching of desire in the cove of her thighs.

Oh, God! Bathsheba could feel her nipple budding into a hard point. It was mere inches away from his mouth, begging for the wetness of his tongue.

"Why aren't you using your wooden tube?" She winced at the shrill tone of her voice.

He moved his head slightly, and his raven curls tickled the sensitive flesh plumping out over the top of her bodice. She bit her lip, forcing back a moan.

"I rarely take my medical instruments to the opera with me." The laughter was back in his voice.

She stared up at the frescoed ceiling, praying for the strength to resist him.

"Perhaps you should," she said, trying to sound as nasty as she could. She simply had to put an end to this, before what little self-restraint she had evaporated. "Who knows when you'll feel compelled to rescue some hapless theater patron?"

He sat up and she gasped—both from relief and from the loss of the delicious heat of his body.

But clearly he wasn't finished. Before she could take another breath, he brushed her tiny sleeves off her shoulders, sending the edge of her bodice slithering down to the top of her nipples. In fact, she could see the dusky areolas peeking out from under the Belgian lace trim.

"What are you doing?" she demanded.

"Examining you," he murmured, his voice deep and deceptively soft. "And I'm happy to say that you're in excellent health. These, for instance—"

He yanked her bodice and chemise down to expose her breasts.

"—are very fine specimens, indeed. But I think I should examine them more closely, just to make certain."

She grabbed his shoulders and pushed, even as a savage weakness invaded her limbs and robbed her of any strength.

"How . . . how dare you?" Her voice ended on a squeaky high note as his calloused thumb flicked over one already painfully aroused nipple.

His lips curled back in a predatory smile as he lifted his gaze to meet hers. She shivered weakly at the raw passion that ignited his eyes with a midnight fire.

"Ah, Bathsheba," he murmured as he closed the distance between them. "You were the one who dared me. And you must know by now that I can never resist a challenge."

Chapter 17

Bathsheba was a vixen, a hellion who repulsed any attempt at domination. Her very nature demanded she resist his—or any man's—efforts to mold her to his desires.

John knew all that, but the knowing made it no more tolerable. She had been fighting him at every turn, driving him insane with her mercurial shifts in temperament. One moment she could melt like wax under his hands. The next, she pushed him away, straining with every bit of her formidable will to deny the sexual hunger consuming them both.

But she wasn't fighting anymore. Those little hands, fisted against his shoulders, suddenly opened and her fingertips clutched into the fabric of his coat as she pulled him closer. Her breasts, so creamy white and full, pushed against him, and he was suddenly mad to feel her naked body clinging to his own.

He leaned over, using his weight to push her into the firm bolsters of the sofa. Her lips parted, and she sucked his tongue deep into the brandied heat of her mouth. The taste of her, the wet slide of her sweet tongue as she tangled with him, drove a rush of blood to his aching groin.

She wriggled, settling her shoulders as he stretched out on top of her. With one leg, he gently nudged her knees apart so he could cradle his erection low against her belly and soft mound. A husky little murmur of appreciation rippled up from her throat, whispering from her lips into his mouth—a sound of quiet submission. A fierce joy took hold, stoking his sexual need. He ravished her mouth, using his lips, his tongue—even his teeth—to consume her, drugging himself on the nectar of her response.

But her mouth, as delicious as it was, could only be a foretaste of things to come. She lay sprawled beneath him, her naked breasts pushing into the satin of his waistcoat. Even through the layers of fabric, he could feel her nipples, hard little points thrusting into his chest. As much as he loved the moist slide of their lips and tongues, he needed more—to feel the arch of her body, straining up to him as he sucked those tight beads of flesh into his mouth.

With a reluctant nuzzle of her lips, he ended the kiss. Bathsheba's eyelids fluttered open, and her eyes, soft and green as newly grown moss, stared up at him. Her hands slipped up his arms to clasp the back of his neck.

"Don't stop," she whispered, her voice both a purr and a plea. "I've been dreaming about kissing you for weeks."

The admission drove another pounding rush of blood to his groin.

"Later," he rasped. His voice sounded harsh, revealing how close he was to the limits of his control. "At the moment, there are other things I need to taste besides your mouth."

Her kiss-swollen lips curved into a smile rich with anticipation. "Don't let me stop you."

He wanted to laugh, but even her voice aroused him. It was all he could do not to rip her dainty silk and linen garments to shreds and drive his hot, aching length into her yielding flesh.

Instead, he pressed kisses into the soft column of her throat, forcing himself to slow down, to savor all he had been longing for these last endless weeks. The swell of her white bosom rose from her tattered chemise, which he *had* managed to rip in his haste to bare the treasures her garments so selfishly concealed. He was too impatient to undress her further, so he finished the job, ripping the soft linen and shoving it down to her waist. Bathsheba gasped, then gave a nervous giggle, which, perversely, fed his own sexual hunger.

For a moment, he simply gazed at her. At her beautiful, expressive face, her lush mouth and slim white throat, and then down to the full, round globes that quivered so prettily with the rise and fall of her breath. Her breasts—so soft, with their pink, flushed tips—were the picture of feminine vulnerability. All evening they had tempted him—*she* had tempted him. Teasing him with her attentions to other men. Making him feel like a savage, obsessed with the need to carry her off for a very thorough and possessive ravishing.

He swooped, fastening his mouth over her right nipple in a hard suck. Bathsheba gave a choked gasp and arched her back. She clutched his head, weaving her fingers tightly into his hair and holding him against her breast.

John was happy to oblige. He suckled and licked her, relishing her moans, feeling how the little tip grew even harder under the flick of his tongue. He brought his hand into play, kneading her other breast, gently tweaking and pulling the nipple into a rigid peak. All the while Bathsheba squirmed and moaned beneath him, apparently driven as mad by their mutual passion as he.

As he gave a particularly deep suck, drawing the white flesh of her breast into his mouth, she bucked against him. The sudden movement almost dislodged him, sending them both teetering to the edge of the sofa. Only by slapping his hand down on the carpet was he able to keep them from tumbling to the floor.

With an unsteady laugh, he lifted his head while keeping them braced against the back of the narrow piece of furniture.

"My sweet, if we're not careful, we're likely to end up in a heap on the floor. The last thing I want to do is play doctor because one of us gets hurt."

Her eyes, drowsy with passion, sparked with amusement. "Yes, I think we've played doctor quite enough for one evening, don't you?"

He smiled, loving that she could make him laugh, even in the midst of such heated passion.

"Bathsheba, the first time I took you was on a rock in the woods. I would be exceedingly grateful if this time at least, we could make love in a bed. Like civilized people. Although," he said in a mocking tone, "if you prefer the floor I'm sure I can be persuaded to accommodate you."

She laughed. "That won't be necessary, Dr. Blackmore, although I appreciate the offer. The bedroom will do just fine."

He heaved himself up, wincing at the straining erection pressed against the fall of his trousers. With an apologetic smile, he straightened himself. She rolled her eyes but forbore to tease him, and he spared a moment to appreciate the joys of lovemaking with an experienced woman. He could be himself—as earthy as he chose, and she wouldn't be offended.

"Up with you, my lady."

He pulled her to her feet, steadying her between his hands as she staggered a bit. Her dress and chemise sagged around her waist, tattered pieces of fabric that only served to obscure the rest of her beauty. He pushed them down past her hips, letting them slide to her feet.

She stepped gracefully from the crumpled heap of clothing, stretching her slender arms up to reach around his neck. With one quick movement, he swept her up in his arms and headed for the bedroom, relishing the feel of her generous, naked curves. Her fingers danced across the back of his neck, sending a prickle of lust racing down his spine.

He shouldered his way through the door and into her bedroom, pausing for a moment as his eyes adjusted to the flickering light cast by a few branches of candles.

The large room was dominated by a massive bed, set

slightly back into an alcove. It was richly upholstered and hung with elegant silk drapes. The rest of the furnishings seemed to be in the French style, in rich tones of yellow and green, matching the swags and curtains now drawn over the windows. It was elegant, lush, and expensive, just like the lady herself.

John paused on the threshold, as he had done when he first entered her apartments, brought to a sharp awareness of the differences in their stations. By no means would anyone consider him a poor man, and the blood that ran through his veins came from a family as old and distinguished as hers. But Bathsheba was a countess, and a rich one at that. Their lives—how they viewed the world—had almost nothing in common, save for the fact that their social circles occasionally overlapped.

Bathsheba stirred in his arms. "What's wrong?"

He shook his head, casting away the doubts that bedeviled him. For tonight, at least, he would let nothing stand between them. He would claim her, making her his and his alone.

John dipped his head and gave her a playful, nibbling kiss. "Nothing is wrong, my sweet. What could be, when I've captured such a tempting prize?"

She squirmed in his arms. "Then get on with it, before I lose interest."

He laughed at the imperious note in her voice.

"As my lady desires."

He dropped her lightly on the bed. She gave another of those un-Bathsheba-like giggles and scrambled back to rest on the ridiculously large mound of pillows piled up against the headboard. Her limbs fell into a graceful, naturally seductive pose. Slender legs, still covered by sheer silk stockings, slightly parted to allow him a glimpse of her intimate flesh. She looked like a cherished concubine in the harem of an Egyptian prince.

One slender, dark brow rose with an arrogant tilt.

"Well?" she asked. "What are you waiting for? You best do something soon, or I just might decide to find alternative entertainment for the evening. After all, Doctor, you know how prone I am to boredom."

She was a demon to tease him, and even though he knew that's all it was, he still couldn't hold back a dark surge of jealousy. The thought of Bathsheba with any man but him, her body responding to another's touch . . .

He shrugged out of his coat and waistcoat, tossing them in the general direction of an armchair. Slowly untying his cravat, he let his gaze wander up her body as he loomed over her. Her cheeks flushed pink and she bit her lower lip as she boldly eyed him.

He grasped the cravat between his hands, holding the length of material taut like a rope.

"Perhaps I'll tie you to the bed, my lady. Then you won't be able to escape, and I'll have you at my mercy."

She stilled. Her features suddenly went blank, as if a hand had wiped clean a slate. All traces of her confident sensuality disappeared as she sat up, stiff and straight against the pillows.

"I'm sorry, John, but I don't want to play any silly games with you," she said in a brittle voice.

He sat on the edge of the bed, careful not to touch her. Even so, ever so slightly, she moved away from him.

"Sweetheart, it was only a jest," he soothed. "You must know I would never do anything to hurt you."

She glanced at his hands—at the cravat—then looked away.

"I know," she replied, sounding weary. "Don't mind me. I'm just being an idiot."

Puzzled, he gazed down at the piece of fabric in his hands. Why had his foolish jest disturbed her so deeply? The answer came to him in a flash, and he crumpled the linen and threw it on the floor.

"This is about your husband, isn't it?" he asked as gently as he could. Every muscle in his body twitched with the need to pull her into his arms, but he forced himself to hold back.

She stared grimly at some point on the opposite wall, her lips firmly sealed. He patiently waited her out. After several long moments, she gave a jerky nod of her head.

"Bathsheba, did he tie you up?"

Her arms went across her breasts, covering as much of herself as she could. Another tight nod.

Fury surged through his body in a cold, splintering wave. It was a good thing Randolph was dead, because at that moment John would have gladly pounded the bastard into a pulp.

"Did he hurt you?" he managed to ask through clenched teeth.

Her startled gaze flew to his, and he saw something in the sea-green depths that stunned him.

Shame.

His face must have shown his reaction because this time she turned her head away, refusing to look at him.

Carefully, John reached out and brushed aside a tumbled lock of hair falling over her eyes. "He didn't hurt you, did he?"

She hunched her shoulders, but didn't jerk away.

"You can tell me," he urged. "Nothing you say will shock me."

When she didn't answer, he took her chin and gently forced her to look at him. "And nothing you say will change my feelings for you, or my desire to be with you."

Her gaze fastened onto his, her expression both wounded and vulnerable. For a moment, she reminded him of an innocent girl. Then the cynical countess returned, looking as bitter as he had ever seen her.

"Reggie never hurt me that way," she said in a hard voice. "In fact, I liked what he did. At least in the beginning, when I thought he loved me. I found it exciting . . . the games we used to play. I did everything he asked me to do, no matter how outrageous or ridiculous."

That last bit was flung at him, but he simply returned her defiant look with a steady one of his own. Some of the starch went out of her, and she slumped onto the pillows.

"What kind of decent woman enjoys things like that?" she asked softly. "But then, I suppose we've already established that I'm not a decent woman."

John took her cold hands between his. "My sweet, you've done nothing wrong. Nothing is forbidden between loving couples, as long as one doesn't seek to degrade the other. You loved your husband and you wanted to please him. He was a fool not to realize what a treasure you had bestowed upon him."

Bathsheba clutched at his hands, gripping so fiercely he suspected her bluntly cut nails would score his skin.

"You don't understand," she blurted out. "There were other things. Things he did that I hated. Things I should have—"

She broke off, too upset to continue. His heart wrenched to see her pride so thoroughly stripped away.

With a quiet murmur, he urged her to move over, giving him room to join her on the bed. He wrapped his arms around her rigid body, pulling her against his chest.

"Then why don't you tell me, so I can understand," he suggested quietly. "And it might do you good to talk about it. I find that sharing problems can sometimes ease the burden."

Bathsheba cast him a doubtful look, but then gave a cautious nod. After taking a deep, shuddering breath, she launched into a halting narrative, describing her husband's growing taste for depravity and her attempts to assuage it.

"But, eventually, nothing I did could satisfy him," she said. Her voice was steady, but it held a lifetime of heartache. "He grew angry, accusing me of not loving him. He began to ask for things I could not, would not do. Ugly things. Soon, any affection he had for me withered. Reggie turned to other pleasures to satisfy his needs. It was terrible what he did, but I couldn't stop him."

A light mist of perspiration broke out over her skin, and she began to shiver. He tightened his arms around her.

"Go on, sweetheart. What did he do that you hated so much?"

She swallowed noisily. "He wanted young girls. Very young girls. He would bring them home late at night, after all the servants were in bed. Only his valet knew. I think he helped Reggie procure the girls. Where he found them, I don't know. Perhaps a brothel, but I never knew for sure."

John fought not to show his revulsion. "How did you learn about this?"

"He wanted me to join them in his bed. When I refused, he decided to punish me."

"How?"

She nodded to a door on the other side of the large marble fireplace. "We had connecting bedrooms. He forced me to leave the door open, to hear everything."

His stomach clenched with useless rage, but he pushed the emotion away. This was about her feelings, not his. Bathsheba had been abused and abandoned by the very man whose duty was to protect her. John couldn't—and wouldn't—fail her now.

"But that wasn't the worst part," she continued. "Of course I hated him for humiliating me like that. But I hated him more for the girls, for what he did to them."

Her strangely flat tone raised the hairs on the nape of his neck. He steeled himself for the worst.

"Most of them were prostitutes," she said. "But . . . some

were virgins, I think. He would threaten them, so they never dared to make much noise, but still I would hear them weeping. Afterward, he would give them money. If he really liked the girl, he would give her a piece of my jewelry. Obviously it was enough to keep them quiet. His valet would take them away, and that would be the end of it."

"How long did this go on?"

"Not long. Perhaps a month or two. Until one night, when it was late and I had already fallen asleep. I woke up to screams from the other room. I ran in and saw him on top of a terrified child. She couldn't have been more than nine or ten."

She pulled in a rasping breath. As he murmured comfort, his gut roiled with a combination of sorrow and fury.

"I threw myself on top of Reggie, trying to drag him off," she said in a voice taut with emotion. "But he was like a madman, completely out of control. It was . . . awful. For a moment, I thought he would kill me, but at least I stopped him from doing any more harm to that child."

Bathsheba clamped her lips shut, as if she had to hold something back. Clearly, she was leaving out details of that horrific night—whether to spare him or her, he couldn't be sure.

After collecting herself, she continued. "Eventually, Reggie came to his senses. Boland and I did what we could to help the child, but my husband insisted on sending her away that night. He told me that if I said anything—well, let's just say he knew how to make good on his threats to keep me quiet. Even so, he worried that he had gone too far. That was the last time he brought a girl back to the house."

She sat up and pushed herself out of his arms. John let her go, understanding her need to put some distance between them.

"Even though it was too late to help those other girls, I couldn't stand it any longer," she said. "And Reggie was a little afraid of me now, because of that night—of what he had done to me, and to that child. So I started to punish him, using the only weapon I had at my disposal—myself."

Bathsheba finally turned to look at him, and the blazing hatred in her gaze scorched the air between them.

"You see, Reggie didn't love me, but I was his most prized possession. He was very jealous when other men paid attention to me. Earlier in our marriage, when he first accused me of infidelity, I denied it. But then I realized I could use his suspicions to strike back. I no longer denied that I was having affairs, but let him draw whatever conclusions he wanted to make."

She paused, a cold smile lifting the corners of her mouth. But the bleakness in her gaze tore at John's heart.

"I didn't dare challenge him openly, of course," she continued. "But, then again, I didn't have to. A flirtation or two, playing the strumpet now and again, and he assumed the worst. It drove him mad with jealousy. Finally, when he could no longer control himself, he challenged a man he presumed was my lover to a carriage race. Reggie was drunk, of course. He overturned his curricle and broke his neck."

She paused, as if waiting for him to respond, but what could he possibly say that would give her comfort? All he could do was listen with sympathy and understanding.

After a moment, she shrugged and carried on.

"When I heard the news, I laughed. I was in a room full of people, and I laughed. No doubt I will burn in hell for it, but it was the happiest day of my life. I will never apologize for that."

He nodded. "No sane person could expect otherwise."

She looked taken aback, as if she had expected another response. He drew her resisting body into a comforting embrace.

"Bathsheba, did you ever tell anyone about what he did to you? To those girls?"

She scoffed at him. "Who would have believed me? I was a nobody from Yorkshire—the daughter of an impecunious viscount. I had no family in London, no influence to speak of. Most of the people I knew were Reggie's friends. And he was the Earl of Randolph, so handsome and charming, so popular. So wealthy. As far as the ton was concerned, it was a miracle he noticed me in the first place."

Suddenly, her voice broke, and she sagged against him as she started to sob. "But I should have tried harder. Been stronger for those poor girls. I should have done something."

She wept, bitterly and for a long time, while John cradled her in the circle of his arms. He tried to absorb her grief with his own body, wishing he could pull it away from her and take it into himself. Not since Becky had died had he felt so helpless and so enraged.

After a time she quieted. The candles had burned low, casting the room in a thick, warm darkness. Only the occasional hiccup from the soft bundle of misery in his arms broke the silence.

When she was calm enough to listen, he made her sit up and face him.

"Bathsheba, listen to me. Your husband was a monster, and there was nothing you could have done to make him change. Sadly, you were also right to think that no one would have taken your word over his. It's loathsome, but that is the way of the world when it comes to men of wealth and power. And he would have punished you for making the attempt."

She dropped her gaze, refusing to meet his eyes. He gave her a slight shake.

"You must stop blaming yourself. It was no fault of yours, and you only torture yourself with useless recriminations."

"I deserve to be tortured," she whispered.

"You've already been doing that for years," he said in a firm voice. "It's time to let go of the past."

She sniffed like a sad little waif and gave him a wavering smile, trying to look brave. But when he smiled back she flushed and looked down at her hands. His gaze followed, catching on her ragged fingernails. Now he understood.

"I don't know how you can stand to look at me," she said in a low voice.

He gave an exasperated snort. "I'll tell you what I see when I look at you," he said, taking a hand and kissing her fingertips. "I see a brave, intelligent woman who should be cherished and protected—even though she doesn't need that protection. I see a woman who endured humiliation and abuse, and yet refused to bend under the burden of her troubles. I see a woman so worth having that any man in his right mind would walk over hot coals to be with her."

She kept her head down, but the edges of her lips twitched up just a bit.

"I would walk over those flaming coals to be with you," he said, nuzzling her ear. "And I would laugh while I did it. That's how much I want you."

She gave a watery giggle. "Then you're an even bigger fool than I took you for, John Blackmore."

He gently turned her in his arms and settled his lips over hers, tasting the sorrow and the grief, and the need to be loved. She didn't push him away, but she didn't put her arms around him either.

"Do you want me to stop?" he whispered. It would probably cripple him, but he couldn't stand to take advantage of her vulnerable state.

She closed her eyes and sighed. "No."

The sadness in her voice almost cleaved his heart in two. He pressed another soft kiss to her lips, then drew back.

"Won't you look at me, Bathsheba?"

She shook her head. "Not yet."

He slid his arms around her and lowered her onto the mountain of pillows.

"Then keep your eyes closed. Keep them closed and just let yourself feel. Because I'm going to make love to you, sweetheart, the way you truly deserve."

Chapter 18

Bathsheba stifled another hiccupping sob, squeezing her eyes shut as John eased her onto the pile of cushions jammed against the headboard. She couldn't look at him—not yet, anyway. It was just too mortifying. Except for Boland—and Sarah, of course—no one knew anything about the nightmare of her marriage. Even Sarah didn't realize the extent of Reggie's perversities. For years Bathsheba had kept the knowledge buried in the darkest corners of her soul, too ashamed to tell anyone.

But John had found a way to breach her secrets, and he had done it so quietly and so skillfully that she could hardly explain how it happened. And for the first time in a long time, she no longer felt alone.

The mattress moved, springing up as John rose from her side. For a panicked moment she thought he was leaving, finally unable to contain his disgust at her cowardly behavior. Then she heard the whisper of clothing being removed and a few moments later the mattress dipped as his long, lean body came down next to her. His muscular arms pulled her against his chest, the dusting of curly hair tickling her cheek as she instinctively snuggled into the security of his embrace. He murmured soft nonsense words, kissing the top of her head as he brushed the hair away from her face.

By some undeserved miracle, he hadn't rejected her. Even now, he lavished her with tender caresses, his questing mouth moving over her cheeks, along her jaw and chin to finally capture her lips in a sweetly scorching kiss. She moaned and opened for his tongue, tangling with him in a heated exchange that weakened all her limbs and brought a hot rush of moisture between her thighs. It seemed impossible she could respond so effortlessly given the emotional torment she had felt only moments ago. He possessed a kind of magic. She could hear it in the deceptively gentle voice and feel it in the wandering, sensual touch that drove her to the edge of abandon.

As he delved into her mouth, tasting her with a deepening pressure, his hands continued their bone-melting exploration, stroking from her throat to her shoulders, lightly massaging, as if to draw away any lingering grief or sorrow.

Bathsheba murmured her approval into his mouth as her body surrendered to pleasure. She arched her back, silently begging him to touch her breasts. Her nipples, tight with need, tingled with anticipation as his skillful fingers danced across her skin. The velvet darkness behind her eyelids seemed to accentuate every sensation as shivers raced down to her belly and below, teasing her innermost flesh with a luscious, tormenting ache.

Moaning, she broke the kiss and turned toward him, insinuating one leg between his, savoring the feel of his muscular thighs and calves, and the coarse hair that tickled her smoother skin. Her mound pressed against his torso, sending a spasm of pleasure deep into her pelvis. His erection, heavy against her belly, seemed to twitch in response.

God, she loved this. Loved the feel of his body—so hot and hard—loved how she grew soft and wet, and ready for the taking. Because with him, she knew she was safe.

"Christ, Bathsheba," John groaned. "You're driving me mad. I can't wait much longer."

She smiled in the sweet, self-imposed darkness, pressing

her lips to his chest, tasting the salty tang of his damp skin. The agony of revelation—of sharing those terrible, shameful secrets—seemed to fade to nothing, replaced by a bright, blazing desire.

Bathsheba tipped her head back, arching her spine as she thrust her breasts into the wall of his chest. With a tempting wriggle, she rubbed her throbbing nipples against the dense, rock-hard muscles. He growled and his hands moved down to capture her bottom in a convulsive grip. Lifting, he positioned himself, nudging the head of his thick staff just between the folds of her sex.

With a gasp, she jerked against him. She had to bite her lip—hard—to keep the delicious spasms from swamping her. It was too soon. She wanted him to take her slowly, to feel her pleasure-swollen nub throb on the edge of orgasm again, and again. Pulling back until she was finally ready for a release, one so strong it would shatter all the bitter memories and ugly self-loathing that had plagued her for so many years.

"Bathsheba." John's voice was so rough she barely recognized it.

"Yes?" Hers was groggy, sated with pleasure, though they had barely begun.

"Open your eyes. I want you to look at me."

A pulse of anxiety shot through her. She shook her head, still too afraid of what she might see in his eyes. No man had ever looked at her the way John did. The desire she understood and welcomed. But beneath that lurked other things— compassion, understanding. And perhaps something more. Something she wasn't yet ready to face.

He growled his frustration but, as if he couldn't help himself, gave another slow pump of the hips. Bathsheba's anxiety faded and the pleasure returned. By succumbing to his sexual needs, John gave her back a measure of control. She knew he would channel that need into giving her the shattering release she craved with all her soul.

She slipped a hand down between their bodies and gently

squeezed the hard, satiny column that pressed into her mound. With a muttered curse, he pushed her on her back. Before she had time to protest, he settled between her thighs, slipping his erection once more between the lips of her wet flesh. She drew her knees up, deepening the contact, rubbing against him to increase the friction on her throbbing bud.

"Do you approve, my lady?" he murmured in a dark, wicked voice. He moved, teasing her with an agonizingly slow penetration.

She moaned, clutching his buttocks, trying to bring him even closer. "Don't stop. Just keep doing it like that."

He gave a hoarse laugh. She felt the breath of it whisper across her nipple, making it tighten with an almost unbearable intensity. The urge to open her eyes—to watch him making love to her, to watch her own body and its response to him—grew stronger by the second. But she refused to yield, too enthralled now by a darkness that heightened all sensation and focused all feeling on the touch of their bodies and the heady musk of their arousal.

A second later his mouth fastened on her nipple. Heat swirled from the point of contact and another hard spasm took her in the vee between her thighs. She gasped, sucking in the muscles of her belly as she tried to hold back the cresting tide.

"Ah. Now I have you," he murmured, giving her nipple a slow, rasping lick.

He brought his hands into play, holding her breast, kneading it as he sucked and nipped. She fought to pull the breath into her lungs. He played with the other nipple, pulling and tweaking it into a rigid, exquisitely tormented point.

A growing awareness pulsed in a thick beat through her veins. No man had ever aroused her so—to the edge of all restraint, awakening a storm of emotions she had never experienced. Yearning, fear, desire, all rode along the knife edge between pain and pleasure. She had to move. Had to push back against her impulse to submit, or else she might lose herself in the raw power of his sexual hunger.

He stilled. John's mouth left her breast, leaving it cold and tingling.

Bathsheba opened her eyelids to see him looking straight down at her, his silver eyes glowing with heat, transfixing her with the force of his desire. She stared back into his sternly beautiful face, held captive by the ferocity of her own mystifying needs.

The hard planes of his features softened. "Bathsheba," he whispered.

She pushed hard against his chest, toppling him to his back. In a flash, she straddled him and slapped her palms onto his shoulders, pinning him to the bed. It was laughable, of course. He would only stay there if he wanted to, but she hoped with all her heart he would.

A sly grin lifted the corners of his mouth. "What is your wish, Lady Randolph?"

She frowned, trying to look severe. "My wish is that you keep your hands and mouth to yourself, my dear doctor. It's my turn now."

His body grew taut beneath her as erotic tension shimmered in the air. He gave a jerky nod. She rewarded him a lascivious smile, delighted by the way his hands clutched the sheets.

With a soft laugh, she slithered down between his legs. She bent her head, letting her hair swing over her shoulders to brush across his groin and the swollen head of his erection. He groaned and closed his eyes.

"You're killing me," he muttered.

"Not yet, my darling. But soon."

And then she dipped and took him between her lips, taking as much of the hard length into her mouth as she could. His hips bucked, but she refused to relinquish her hold. Now *she* controlled *him*, and that power, combined with the hot beauty of the act, brought another surge of moisture to dampen her thighs.

For several minutes he surrendered, groaning as she caressed his rock-hard length with her mouth. Every muscle in his body flexed and strained, clearly fighting the need to prevail in this unexpected, entrancing battle for dominance.

Taking a deep breath, she lifted her head to study him. The head of his erection was flushed—smooth and slick from the attentions of her mouth. She gently rubbed her thumb through the moisture, letting her fingers drift down the thick column of flesh.

John groaned, arching his muscular torso as she pleasured him. Just looking at him made every nerve in her body throb with lust. And made her heart ache with an unfamiliar tenderness. Tonight, at least, she could have her fill, and make him as crazed for her as she was for him.

Twice she brought him to the brink of orgasm and twice he fought to hold himself back. No matter how skillfully she used her hands, her mouth, her tongue, he resisted all her efforts. It had become a wicked game, but one played in deadly earnest. And he was clearly as determined to win as she was.

But John was only a man, and eventually he broke.

"Enough," he finally growled.

He reached out, taking her by the shoulders and forcing her to withdraw. He flopped onto the pillows, gasping for breath. Humming with satisfaction, Bathsheba sat back on her knees.

John pushed himself up on his elbows to study her, and the game changed again. The civilized doctor had disappeared. With his heavy-lidded eyes and thick, dishevelled hair, he reminded her of a buccaneer, one who had just boarded her ship, determined to claim his treasure.

Bathsheba panted with excitement. She felt vaguely alarmed, but couldn't deny the thrill of knowing she had pushed him to the edge of his limits.

Eyes full of smoky intent, he returned her taunting smile with one of his own. In that moment, she realized the game was lost—by her. Her alarm spiked as she sat frozen on her knees, waiting like a silly little rabbit for a predator to strike.

He lifted a hand and crooked a finger at her.

"Come here."

The deep, growling command made her pulse trip and flutter. She tried to tell herself she had no choice. But she did. And the choice she made was to surrender, knowing with an instinctive flash of wisdom that he would keep her safe.

She crawled up his long body until she straddled his hips, presenting her breasts to his mouth as a gift. He closed his eyes and sucked. First one nipple, then the other. She moaned, just about to sink down on his rigid length when he pulled away.

"Come up higher, Bathsheba," he said in a lazy voice. "I want to taste you."

She hesitated for a second but then complied, inching up and planting her knees on either side of his shoulders. His low murmur of satisfaction as he brushed his calloused hands on the inside of her thighs made her shiver.

"Take hold of the headboard," he ordered. Then his big hands grasped her bottom, and he guided her down to his mouth.

She jolted as his tongue delved deep between her sensitive folds. He parted her with his fingers, spreading her wide as he sucked and played. Desperately, she clutched at the headboard. Her legs quivered as he ravished her with his mouth.

He spread her tender flesh, fingers stroking as his tongue darted in and out. She swayed against him, using her hips to urge him to move his mouth, and that wicked tongue, onto the throbbing bud of her sex. Never had she felt so hot, so wet—a burning tightness that begged for the relief only he could provide.

"John," she pleaded, her voice rising to a broken wail.

He teased her with his tongue until she started to sob with frustration. She knew she would do anything for him, be anything for him, if only he would give her what her body so urgently craved.

Finally, his mouth moved, closing the tiny, crucial gap. He fastened on the aching peak and sucked, and her insides detonated with luxurious spasms.

As wave after wave rolled through her, he pulled her down to his hips. With one hard thrust he surged into her, impaling himself in her wet sheath. She pressed down on his groin, her fingers clutching his shoulders as he stretched her with his thick erection. He pumped, grinding her hips against his pelvis, and another wave of violent shudders racked her limbs.

John bit out a strangled oath as his climax gripped him. She could feel her inner muscles clenching around his staff, drawing him even deeper—to her very core—as he poured his seed into her body.

Then the slow, delicious collapse. Trembling, she slid down, still straddling him as she curled against his chest. His arms wrapped about her, holding her in a fierce embrace. As exhausted as she was, she smiled to feel the muscles of his brawny arms twitch.

They lay like that, panting and sweaty, until her knees finally started to protest. With a wince, she lifted herself and clumsily swung her leg over his stomach. He reached to help, guiding her down to the mattress.

"Did I hurt you, sweetheart?" His voice held a sharp note of concern, as it always did when he worried about her.

She smiled, planting a sloppy kiss on his chest before settling against him.

"Well, I suspect some heretofore undiscovered muscles might be a bit sore in the morning. But I'm confident I'll survive."

He sighed, pulling her close. "It's your fault, you know. If you weren't such a seductive little minx I wouldn't have lost control like that."

"You lost control? I hadn't noticed."

He made a scoffing noise, one that told her he thought she was being silly. Somehow, it seemed absolutely right.

Her eyelids began to droop as a feeling of drowsy contentment stole through her body. It would be careless to fall asleep, but she couldn't remember the last time she had felt so happy—or so safe. As if being in John's arms was exactly where she was meant to be, now and forever.

On that thought her eyes flew open and her gaze coasted over their naked, entangled bodies. Far from being safe, she was smack in the middle of making one of the costliest mistakes of her life.

Chapter 19

Bathsheba jerked fully awake. John dozed beside her, obviously unaware that disaster could strike at any moment.

Taking a deep breath, she tried to calm her racing heart. What time was it? How long had he been in her chambers? The last thing she needed was for rumors to circulate through the ton that John was her lover. Bathsheba paid her servants well to ensure their loyalty, but even so . . .

She tried to sit up, but John's arms clamped around her in a viselike grip.

"Where are you going?"

"John," she whispered, struggling to get free, "it's late. You must leave."

"Why are you whispering? You were anything but quiet a few minutes ago."

Blast him, he was right. The whole house had probably heard her shrieking in ecstasy.

She subsided against him with a groan. Like a besotted fool, she had allowed her emotions to run free, and look where she landed—in the middle of a potentially fatal scandal. Miss Roston had already shown herself to be uncommonly suspicious of her friendship with John. If the old harpy heard even the slightest hint of gossip, she would happily pour poison in her brother's ear.

John stirred, giving her bottom a soothing pat. "Don't fret, sweetheart. It's late. Past two o'clock, I should think. I'm sure most of your servants have long been asleep."

"Past two o'clock!" This time she most certainly shrieked. "Truly, John. You must go. If anyone were to see you leaving the house at this hour of the morning, I don't know what they would think."

She wriggled out from under his arm. Scrambling down off the high mattress, she grabbed a silk dressing gown that was draped over a chair and threw it around her shoulders.

John sat up, shoving the mound of pillows into a pile so he could lean comfortably against them. He gave her a lazy smile, looking more than ready to settle in for a long chat.

Swallowing a curse, Bathsheba darted around the room collecting the scattered pieces of his clothing. John folded his arms across his naked chest, watching her with a mild curiosity.

"Bathsheba, come back to bed before you catch a chill."

She paused. With the beginnings of a night beard shadowing his hard jaw, he looked both roguish and unbearably handsome. As her gaze traveled over his solidly muscled frame, a trembling weakness began to invade her limbs. Her foolish heart—and her still-hungry body—urged her to yield to temptation.

No. She had to resist. Passion had ruined her life once before, and she wouldn't allow it to happen again.

She strode to the bed and dropped his clothes on the rumpled coverlet.

"I'm sorry, John. You must get dressed. I won't pretend that I didn't want this to happen, because I did." She took a deep breath, fighting to get the words past the sudden lump in her throat. "But you must not assume I can give you anything more. And whatever my actions might have led you to believe, I don't want to have an affair with you."

Reclining on the pillows as if he hadn't a care in the world, John didn't stir. But his body underwent a subtle change, as did his face. His eyes narrowed ever so slightly, and his sensual mouth looked carved from stone.

Oh, God. He was furious. And wounded. She could see it in his eyes. Beneath the flare of anger, a pained surprise that she was rejecting him again.

The lump in her throat turned into a boulder. She simply couldn't bring herself to lie to him again, to let him think she really was the harlot the rest of the world believed her to be.

"It's not that I don't want to be with you," she blurted out. "I do. But it's just not possible. I'm sorry if I misled you, but there's . . ." She trailed off, suddenly feeling like a stupid schoolgirl as he gave an exasperated shake of the head.

He threw the covers off and his feet hit the floor. Panic prickled along her nerves, and she thought of fleeing to her dressing room and locking the door behind her.

Before she could act on that thought, he was there. His big hands wrapped around her waist, lifted her up, and plopped her down on the mattress.

"Bathsheba," he said, fisting his hands on his hips as he glared down at her, "you don't really think I'm going to let you marry Roston, do you? Or anyone else, for that matter."

She scowled as she yanked the slippery fabric of her robe out from where it had bunched up under her bottom.

"May I remind you, Dr. Blackmore, that it's none of your concern who I do or do not marry. As I told you earlier, you may keep your impertinent remarks to yourself."

He bent down, bringing them nose to nose. "Perhaps you should have thought of that before you lured me back into your bed. I told you once before that I was not to be trifled with."

She gasped, outraged by the accusation. "I'm not trifling with you. And, by the way, if memory serves, it was *you* who lured *me* tonight! Not the other way around."

"And what about yesterday? When you came to the hospital. Were you just trifling with me then, as well? Was Madame Countess bored and in need of diversion?"

Anger squeezed her chest. "Of course not! How can you

even think that? I came to the hospital because I wanted to see you."

Satisfaction flared in his knowing gaze. She bit her lip, suddenly understanding he had deliberately provoked her into blurting out an admission.

With a weary grumble, she let her shoulders slump. "Damn you, John. What do you want from me?"

He knelt in front of her and took her hands. "You already know the answer to that, my love. The question is what do *you* want?"

She gazed miserably into his kind, patient face. "I don't know."

"Bathsheba, what are you afraid of? Why do you keep resisting what's happening between us?"

She fought to keep a childish sob from welling up into her throat. How could she even begin to explain without revealing every ugly secret she had guarded all these years? But sure as the sun rose in the morning, John would wait her out with that relentless patience that always managed to breach her defenses. And she could never seem to resist it.

"I'm poor," she finally said. The hot shame of her admission brought the blood to her checks.

He sat back on his heels, stunned. "I don't understand. You're one of the wealthiest widows of the ton."

She shook her head. "That's what Matthew and I have led everyone to believe, but it's not true. The Compton estate is in terrible condition—which I'm sure you must have noticed when you came to the manor house."

Comprehension slowly dawned on his features.

"Yes, well," she grimly continued, "I don't even have my widow's portion anymore. Not that there was much to begin with. But now there's nothing—nothing except debt. Unless there's a miracle, our estate manager predicts we will be bankrupt in only a few months, if not sooner."

He slowly got to his feet and joined her on the bed. One

arm slipped around her waist. She leaned into him, grateful for at least the illusion of protection.

"Bathsheba, how did this happen?"

"In addition to his other sins," she explained bitterly, "Reggie was also a spendthrift and a wastrel. I didn't realize the full extent of his profligacy until he died, when I got my hands on the estate accounts."

She went on to explain her failed attempts to rescue the family fortune, and to stave off the rumors that would bring disaster crashing down once and for all. He held her tightly but mostly kept silent, murmuring only a few words of comfort during the long, sorry recital.

"I've sold most of my jewelry," she finished up. "Not the estate pieces, but anything I had that Reggie gave me, or that I bought for myself. But there's nothing left to sell. If something doesn't happen soon, we're lost."

"And why is it your problem to solve, and not the current earl's?"

She gave him an irritated look.

A humorless smile twisted his mouth. "Ah, yes. I'm guessing the earl doesn't have a head for business."

"Not to put too fine a point on it," she responded dryly.

"But surely that doesn't require you to sacrifice yourself in a loveless marriage, does it? Which I presume is your plan. After all, once the earl weds Miss Elliott—and from what I hear, Miss Elliott will see that he does, even if your cousin doesn't yet realize it—that should solve most of your problems. Since Lord Randolph never comes to London, he can rent this house out and you will be free of that financial burden, at least."

Frustrated, she shook her head. "You don't understand. That won't be nearly enough to cover our debts and maintain the estate in Yorkshire."

"Perhaps not. But Miss Elliott's fortune will be more than enough to maintain Compton Manor, and then some."

Bathsheba frowned. "What are you talking about? Miss

Elliott doesn't have any fortune. Her brother's a professor at Oxford."

John looked at her as if she were an idiot. "And her mother was the daughter of an extremely wealthy viscount. She left Miss Elliott very well-endowed. Two thousand pounds a year, if Dr. Littleton is to be believed, which I'm sure he is. And, as you must have noticed, Miss Elliott is quite a capable manager. She'll have Compton Manor whipped into shape in no time."

Bathsheba gaped at him. "Really?" she asked faintly.

He gave her chin a gentle tap. "My love, the next time you visit the country, I suggest you make a better effort to listen to the local gossip. You might just learn something."

Bathsheba wanted to scold him for teasing her, but her brain felt too scrambled to find the words. All these months, debt had squeezed her in its unforgiving iron jaws. She had struggled to find a way out of the trap, burdened by responsibilities that only she had the strength to shoulder. And now, like a puff of smoke, they were dissolving into thin air.

"I . . . I don't know what to say," she stuttered.

"Well, you could say you'll marry me. I know you likely never thought about it, but I wish you would," John announced casually.

Shock slammed through her.

"What?" she yelped.

He winced. "I thought you didn't want to wake the servants."

Her mind whirled, a riot of conflicting emotions. For a few mad seconds his outrageous proposal seemed possible. After all, she did have feelings for him—very strong feelings. Nothing like the girlish love she had felt for Reggie. Something very different and so much deeper. Something she couldn't yet put a name to. But more importantly, she knew John would cherish and protect her, and treat her with the utmost respect.

She cautiously met his gaze, some part of her convinced he must be making a cruel jest. But the heat in his eyes and the firm set of his mouth told her this was no joke. And it struck her, with the force of a blow, just how much she wanted this. Wanted him.

And then she remembered why she couldn't, and burgeoning hope withered.

Desperate for him not to see the tears welling into her eyes, she slid down off the mattress and wandered over to the marble mantelpiece.

"I . . . can't marry you, John," she said, surreptitiously rubbing one eye. "You can't ask this of me. Please let's not talk about it anymore."

She heard him pad across the floor. Taking her shoulders in a gentle grip, he turned her around.

"Bathsheba—"

"You really should put some clothes on," she groused, annoyed by how much his naked body tempted her.

He ignored her complaint. "What are you afraid of?" His voice turned cool. "Do you not think me worthy of you?"

Stung, she jerked her head back to meet his eyes. "Of course I think you're worthy. Don't be absurd."

"Then what is it? Our feelings for each other are not in doubt. Do you fear that I won't be able to provide for you? Such is not the case, I assure you."

She sighed with resignation. He would never give up until she told him the rest of it.

"I have a sister," she said, all in a rush. "Her name is Rachel. I'm all she has, and I simply can't abandon her. Not for you. Not for any man."

For a second time that night, he look stunned. But his astonishment soon turned to concern, then pity as she described Rachel's illness, and how her father had insisted she be forever hidden away in the countryside.

"But why did you maintain the fiction after your father died? You were a countess. No one would have questioned you. Certainly, you wouldn't be the first member of a noble family to have a feeble-minded relation. Your sister's condition is the result of fever—not a taint in your family's blood."

She pressed her hands against her stomach, sick with self-loathing.

"I tried to explain that to Reggie, but he wouldn't listen. He agreed with my father's belief that any knowledge of Rachel's existence would reflect poorly on me. Besides, everyone thought she had been dead for years. Can you imagine the scandal when it was revealed she was not? No. Reggie agreed to pay the bills for her upkeep, but that was all."

John frowned thoughtfully, his hands absently stroking over her shoulders and arms. After several moments of silent contemplation, he nodded.

"That's how he controlled you, wasn't it? He used your sister against you."

She met his gaze. "Yes. Whenever I refused to obey him, he would threaten to remove her from the only home she remembers—one where she is loved—and put her in an asylum for the insane."

John's eyes turned hard as flint. "What a shame Lord Randolph didn't meet with his fatal carriage accident before he met you."

She shrugged. "I don't know if he would ever have done that to Rachel, but I couldn't take the risk. And," she added, with another surge of self-loathing, "after a while I talked myself into agreeing with him. I dreaded the scandal almost as much as he did."

His hands dropped from her arms. What else could she expect? After all, when it came to this she was little better than her monster of a husband.

"Still want to marry me?" she asked cynically.

He huffed out an impatient breath and drew her back across the room to the bed.

"I don't know why I have to keep repeating myself, Bathsheba, but none of this is your fault. Your father and your husband were to blame, not you. You were simply trying to survive, and take care of your sister as best you could. And yes. Of course I still want to marry you."

Her vision blurred, but she sternly blinked the tears away.

"That's very kind of you, John. But no."

He tilted his head, looking puzzled. "Why not? Do you have other family members hidden away that you haven't told me about?"

She glared. "Of course not!"

"Then what the devil is the matter now?"

"Haven't you been listening? I'm responsible for Rachel's care, and it's not exactly cheap. And," she said defiantly, "I don't want to be poor. You may laugh at me all you like, but my father was the definition of impecunious gentility, which was why he was so happy when Reggie offered to marry me. No one else would—I had no dowry. Call me whatever names you want, but I refuse to spend the rest of my days outrunning the constable. I've had quite enough of that to last me a lifetime."

John rubbed his forehead as if he had a headache. "Bathsheba, don't be such a goose. I'm not poor."

"Well, you're not rich," she retorted.

"No, but I will be. My practice is growing, and I've made a number of investments that will eventually yield a considerable profit. And may I remind you, my arrogant countess, that I come from as good a family as you. My relations may be country gentry, but they're exceedingly well-off. In addition," he said, looking very haughty, "my mother's paternal grandfather is an earl. I believe that gives me a pedigree every bit as elevated as yours."

Bathsheba couldn't help it. She burst into laughter, suddenly realizing how ridiculous it was to be comparing family pedigrees, naked in the middle of the night.

"I beg your forgiveness, dear sir. It was not my intention to insult your family."

His lips twitched, and he gave her a reluctant grin.

"So, does that mean you'll marry me?"

She sighed. "I don't know. My head is spinning, and I'm too exhausted to make any decisions tonight."

"Will you at least consider it?"

"Y-yes, I'll consider it. But under one condition."

"And that is?"

"That we keep our relationship a secret."

He started to protest, but she held up a hand to silence him.

"I'm not saying that we can't be seen together in public, but you mustn't give any indication that anything exists between us but friendship. What we do in private is another matter, but I will not countenance rumors or speculation that you're courting me."

He gave her a sardonic smile. "Hedging your bets, are we?"

She winced, but didn't bother to deny it. There was simply too much at stake to push caution aside, especially for the sake of passion. If there was something else between them . . . well, she wasn't ready yet to acknowledge that.

He sighed. "Never mind. I don't expect you to change overnight. Trust takes time to develop, and I'm willing to give you that time. But I insist you agree to a condition of mine in return."

"What is it?" she asked suspiciously.

"That you keep Roston and any other man who wants to court you at a respectable distance. I won't be held accountable for my actions if you play the flirt."

That made her smile. "John, surely you can't be jealous of so mild a creature as Sir David."

He walked her backward and tipped her onto the bed, pinning her to the mattress with his long legs. His eyes smoldered as he gazed down at her.

"I'm jealous of anyone who could take you away from me, as you may well find out."

Her heart melted into a gooey puddle. "Then I will take care to ensure you have no reason to doubt me," she whispered as she wrapped her arms around his neck.

He gently scissored her legs open and settled between her thighs.

"Bathsheba, I'm going to make love to you again," he said, "whether you like it or not. And this time, I will not be rushed."

"Why, my dear sir," she murmured, shivering with pleasure as he began to nuzzle the tender skin of her neck, "you know I always follow doctor's orders."

Chapter 20

John glanced up at the speaker behind the high podium, then transferred his gaze to Bathsheba. Seated next to him on the bench, she was still looking vaguely queasy. That didn't surprise him, given the subject matter of Dr. Taverner's lecture to the Royal Society. For the most part, the talk had been unexceptional, consisting of observations on the treatment of consumptive diseases in pregnant women.

Much to John's surprise, Bathsheba had seemed almost as interested in the lecture as he was. Throughout the talk, he had stolen glances her way, distracted as much by her entrancing face as by her unflagging attention to a weighty scientific presentation. And he would have noticed if she had grown bored. After spending so much time with her these last two weeks, John had become highly attuned to her feelings. As each day passed, the emotional connection between them grew ever stronger.

He applauded absently as the lecture came to an end, still keeping one eye on Bathsheba. Sure enough, after a wary glance to see if anyone was watching, she removed a handkerchief from her reticule and dabbed at her perspiring forehead.

Not that he could blame her. The last bit of Taverner's lecture had been gruesome, even by John's standards.

Now that the presentation was over, most of the audience

came to their feet. A cheerful din arose as both scientists and amateurs launched into vociferous arguments, exchanged greetings and gossip, or simply made their noisy way to the staircase leading down to the vestibule of Somerset House.

Bathsheba, however, remained seated, as if not yet ready to test out her legs.

"Too much for you, my lady?" John asked sympathetically, peering under the brim of her high-poke bonnet to get a better look at her face.

She gave a weak smile. "It was fine until the end, but that last bit was ghastly. If I had known what was coming, I would have chosen the exhibit at the Royal Academy."

Sarah Ormond, seated on the other side of Bathsheba, broke off her conversation with James Wardrop.

"Well, Dr. Blackmore," Sarah said. "If this is what you and Dr. Wardrop consider an afternoon's entertainment, I'll have to succumb to a migraine the next time Bathsheba asks me to accompany her."

Bathsheba huffed at her friend. "Sarah! How can you have the nerve to blame Dr. Blackmore? It was you who suggested a lecture at the Royal Society when I asked for your opinion on what to do this afternoon."

"Well," Sarah replied archly, "*you* were very anxious to find a diversion that Dr. Blackmore would enjoy, and this seemed just the ticket. Or at least Mr. Ormond thought so when I asked for his advice. Don't blame me if it's all gone tragically awry."

Bathsheba flushed and looked annoyed, but before she could raise any objections Wardrop chimed in.

"Certainly not, Mrs. Ormond. A lady of your delicate sensibilities and refined nature couldn't help but be shocked by Dr. Taverner's lecture," he intoned soulfully.

John almost groaned. His colleague, an accomplished flirt, had jumped at the invitation to spend the afternoon with two of London's most famous beauties—even if it was at a scientific lecture. But at least the group outing gave

John the excuse to spend time with Bathsheba—outside the bedroom, that is.

"Never thought Taverner had it in him," Wardrop continued, warming to the topic. "To describe something so monstrous in front of ladies . . . not done. Really, Blackmore. You should have known better." He widened his eyes in mock horror, even though he was clearly trying not to laugh.

After giving his friend a warning frown, John returned his attention to Bathsheba.

"I'm sorry if you found the subject matter disturbing, my lady, but it's not often one has the opportunity to hear accounts of such dramatic mistakes in the natural order of things. Dr. Taverner is exceedingly fortunate to have a correspondent in India who can bring such unusual cases to his attention. He should have given some warning, however, before reading out the letter from the Reverend Clarke. It was clearly not part of his regular lecture."

"Yes, he should have," cried Sarah. "I couldn't believe the description, and Dr. Taverner read it out so calmly. A baby born with two heads, four arms and four legs, and—"

"Please, Sarah," groaned Bathsheba, "once was quite enough, thank you."

"Of course it was, Lady Randolph," soothed Wardrop. "Consider the matter closed." With an elegant flourish, he helped Sarah to her feet.

Bathsheba remained seated, ignoring the other couple. "I can't help thinking about the poor mother," she murmured. "Can you imagine her terror when she first saw her own child? How full of guilt she must have felt?"

John drew her to her feet, touched, as always, by the tender heart she hid beneath her polished exterior. "One can only feel sympathy for the poor woman."

She sighed. "You must think me very foolish for letting it affect me so greatly."

"No one would ever call you foolish, my lady."

He gave her elbow a gentle squeeze as he steered her to

the aisle. As usual, he was caught off guard by his urgent need to protect her, and frustrated by his inability to do so in public. He didn't know how much longer he would be able to maintain the charade of casual friendship she insisted was necessary.

"Blackmore." Wardop spoke over his shoulder. "I suggest we leave our scientific endeavors behind and repair to Gunter's for refreshment. I don't know about the rest of you, but I'm parched."

Sarah didn't answer, lifting an enquiring eyebrow as she waited for Bathsheba's approval.

"That is, of course," said Wardrop, obviously noting the silent exchange, "if the beautiful ladies can lower themselves to tolerate the company of two feckless and impecunious physicians."

Sarah gave a ladylike snort. "Impecunious, indeed! What a tease you are, Dr. Wardrop. I have it on good authority that Sir William Knighton, for instance, makes at least ten thousand pounds a year."

John had to bite back a laugh as Bathsheba's mouth dropped open. Apparently, she hadn't yet realized how rich some of his colleagues actually were.

They weaved their way through the knot of people at the top of the staircase. The going was slow, but a few minutes later they were strolling through the imposing vestibule of Somerset House toward the entrance leading out to the Strand.

Before they could exit, they were forced to pause behind a cluster of chattering matrons who had just emerged from a meeting of the Antiquarian Society. They jostled Bathsheba against him and her soft, full bosom pressed into his arm. Desire curved through him from the point of contact, and he had to push back the overwhelming urge to drag her behind one of the huge marble columns and take her sweet mouth in a ravishing kiss.

He clenched his jaw to hold back the hot rush of lust. He

would go mad if he had to play this secret game much longer. A few dinners at the Ormonds', the occasional waltz at a ball—even the late nights spent in delicious lovemaking at her town house on Curzon Street—it no longer satisfied. In fact, it had the opposite effect. It stoked the flames and fired every possessive impulse in his body.

John no longer doubted he wanted to marry her. Very few really knew the woman she was, and he took savage pride in realizing only he had seen past all her feints—her troubled past and present fears—to claim the prize within. Yes, she possessed a keen intellect and wit. More importantly, she had bone-deep integrity, and was the most loyal woman he had ever met. Add to that her lush beauty and sensual nature and any man would have to be insane not to want her as his wife. God knew she had her faults, but so did he.

Bathsheba glanced up at him, looking puzzled and slightly anxious. He suddenly realized the crowd had cleared away and Wardrop and Sarah had already passed through the doors of Somerset House out to the Strand. Yet John stood nailed to the spot, staring down at Bathsheba with an intensity that would surely rouse the curiosity of anyone who happened to look their way.

He cleared his throat. "Forgive me, Lady Randolph. I seem to be woolgathering. I was just reviewing a few of Dr. Taverner's points in my mind."

The tension on her features eased into a grateful smile. It usually pleased him to comfort her, but right now he couldn't help feeling annoyed she so obviously feared public exposure of their relationship.

"I'm not surprised," she responded eagerly. "I, too, found the lecture fascinating. Did you hear anything today that will benefit your own patients?"

He smiled reluctantly, struck once again by her unexpected interest in his work.

"Certainly. Dr. Taverner's techniques can be applied to any pregnant woman, but they are critical to the care of those who suffer from malnourishment and disease. I can only guess how many women could be saved if they had a nourishing diet and received good doctoring instead of being shunted off to crowded lying-in hospitals or left to die in the squalor of the stews."

A hostile voice interrupted them from behind.

"Spouting your radical views again, are you, Blackmore? I should be careful if I were you. Taverner isn't popular, what with all his talk about doctors inflicting suffering on women. Not to mention his ridiculous notion that man is just another species of animal. I'm surprised you had the gall to pollute Lady Randolph's ears with that kind of blasphemy."

Repressing a curse, John turned to face his nemesis.

"Dr. Steele," he said blandly. "I didn't realize you had attended the lecture. Forgive me for neglecting to notice you. Obviously you already know Lady Randolph, so I won't bother to formally introduce you."

Steele was a tall man, fit and handsome for his age, with a ruddy complexion. Right now he was turning red as a brick, furious at John's slight. But he managed to curb his spleen, instead diverting his attention to Bathsheba.

He gave a deep bow. "Lady Randolph, it is an honor to see you. I do hope you weren't offended by Taverner's disgusting lecture. It is beyond me why the fellows of the Royal Society allowed him to give it in the first place."

John gave him a humorless smile. "Perhaps because they are interested in the advancement of science?"

Steele glared back, looking like an overheated beaker on the verge of exploding. Bathsheba smoothly intervened.

"On the contrary, Dr. Steele," she said. "I found the lecture quite fascinating. I won't pretend to understand everything I heard, but Dr. Taverner struck me as a most thoughtful man. He clearly has the best interests of his patients at heart. Now, if you will excuse us, sir, our friends are waiting outside."

She gave Steele a slight inclination of the head, superbly

calculated to signal exactly what she thought of the old bastard, and slipped her hand in the crook of John's arm.

"Are you ready, Dr. Blackmore? We've kept Sarah and Dr. Wardrop waiting long enough."

A snakelike breath hissed out from between Steele's teeth. Even with his best efforts, John couldn't hold back a smile as he and Bathsheba moved away.

"I know what you did, Blackmore."

The sheer hatred in Steele's voice brought John up short. Reluctantly, he turned back to confront the other man. He had hoped to avoid this type of encounter in public, especially in front of Bathsheba.

Steele was beyond furious. John braced himself, belatedly realizing how seriously he had underestimated the man's reaction to losing one of his patients to another physician.

"I understand you have taken over Lady Silverton's treatment," Steele barked. "Is that correct?"

Bathsheba's hand, still tucked into John's elbow, jerked convulsively. He gave it a slight squeeze before letting it go as he moved to stand in front of her.

"If you have anything to say to me, Dr. Steele, I suggest you allow me to call on you later today. We needn't subject Lady Randolph to any unpleasantries, especially in so public a venue."

Steele glowered back at him, his mottled features distorted with hatred. Obviously, he was too far gone to care about making a fool of himself.

"You stole Lady Silverton from me," he spat out, "and impugned my good name to the marquess. How dare you suggest I don't know how to care for my patients? I who was practicing medicine before you were out of short pants."

Behind him, Bathsheba made a soft noise of distress and John's heart sank. She would be mortified to be caught in the middle of so ugly a scene, especially one that would attract so much attention from the gossips.

And attracting attention was exactly what was happening.

Steele's blustering fury had caught the notice of several men who still lingered in the vaulted space of the vestibule. A few of them were doctors from Bart's and had clearly recognized both him and Steele. Not only would Bathsheba be subjected to a humiliating scene, it was almost certain that word of the altercation would reach Abernethy's ears in short order. John throttled back his frustration as he tried not to imagine his superior's reaction to the damaging gossip.

"Dr. Steele," he said calmly, "Lady Silverton ultimately made the decision to request my services. I assure you I did not solicit the case."

Steele flicked a venomous glance at Bathsheba. "Yes, I know who to thank for that. You should know better, Blackmore, than to leave these decisions in the hands of women. They are incapable of making rational choices in scientific or medical matters. Even more so when the woman is pregnant."

Behind him, Bathsheba muttered something nasty.

"I'm sure your patients would be thrilled to know your opinion of their judgment," John replied dryly. "I must decline, however, to argue the point. Or discuss my patients in public. As I said, I'm happy to call on you this afternoon, and explain exactly how—"

Steele cut him off. "You can keep your explanations, Blackmore. I have nothing but contempt for a doctor who undermines his own colleagues, especially one who engages in dangerous medical practices."

John was stunned by the accusation. "Dangerous medical practices? What the hell are you talking about, Steele?"

Bathsheba's fingers gripped his arm, breaking his focus from the madman in front of him. Her gaze flitted around the vestibule. John glanced around, cursing silently at the cluster of bystanders avidly listening to their every word. Wardrop and Sarah had also returned to the hall, and now stood with Bathsheba.

"Blackmore, we're keeping the ladies waiting," said Wardrop, making the warning clear.

John nodded. "Forgive me."

He gave Steele a brief bow and took Bathsheba's arm, ready to follow Sarah and Wardrop out to the Strand.

"I know what you did, Blackmore," growled Steele. "I know what you did to that Irishman's wife."

John froze, astounded the man could be that much of an idiot.

Wardrop gave a resigned sigh. He took Bathsheba by the arm and pulled her back to stand with Sarah.

Steele pulled his lips back in a self-satisfied smile. "You think you got away with what you did to that woman and her baby, but you didn't. I know all about it, and I'll see that you suffer for it, Blackmore. If it's the last thing I do, I'll run you out of Bart's—and straight out of London, if I have to."

John felt a sudden rush of feminine fury come up by his side.

"How dare you threaten him, you horrible man," stormed Bathsheba, jabbing her finger right up to Steele's face. "Dr. Blackmore has the full support of Lord and Lady Silverton, and mine as well."

Steele's smile widened into a taunting smirk. John clenched his fist as he prepared to wipe the gloat from the bastard's face.

"Blackmore!" Wardrop bit out the warning.

John could barely hold himself back. But Steele wasn't finished. Like some foul predator, he veered onto another track.

"Is Lady Randolph aware of your habit of visiting the stews?" he asked. "You spend so much time amongst the whores and thieves of St. Giles it's a wonder you find the time to attend to your paying clients."

Bathsheba took a hasty step forward, but John held her back.

"He's not worth it, my lady," he murmured. "Please come away."

He grasped her hand and drew her after Wardrop, who had already started to lead Sarah from the building.

"Best watch your step, Blackmore," Steele called out. "Who knows what other tales might begin to spread about you. Then we'll find out who your friends really are."

Fury roiled in John's gut, but concern for Bathsheba quickly replaced it. Her hand trembled as he tucked it into his elbow. Even worse, she had turned as pale as milk. If she suffered any ill effects from this afternoon, he would hunt Steele down in the street and beat him senseless.

They broke from the shadowed interior of Somerset House into the sunny, bustling atmosphere of the Strand. John took a deep, calming breath. After the poisonous exchange with Steele, he welcomed the ordinary tumult of the city street.

He bent his head to murmur in Bathsheba's ear. "I'm going to fetch a hackney and take you home. I think it best if we forgo the visit to Gunter's. After this, I'm sure you must be in need of a rest."

She stopped, dragging him to a halt in the middle of the pavement. Pedestrians hurried by, jostling them on every side, but she ignored them.

"Are you mad?" she snapped, glaring up at him. "I don't need a rest. I need to go back and strangle that pig for the things he said to you. When I'm done with him, I swear there won't be a person of any consequence in this town who will have anything to do with him."

John felt his mouth drop open, but was too surprised to do anything about it. He was certain she would be mortified by what had just happened—and angry with him for not shielding her from it.

Something deep inside—a subtle tightness—began to ease. Not until that moment had he realized how unsure he'd been of her, or how it had pulled constantly at the edges of his consciousness. The scene with Steele should have sent her into full retreat. Instead, she had ripped up at the man, defending John as fiercely as a lioness defending her cubs.

He stared at her beautiful scowling face, her eyes glittering like emeralds in a perfect setting, and began to laugh. Happiness rustled up from his belly, and filled his chest with a sweet ache.

She crossed her arms beneath her chest. "Now what?" she huffed. "Really, John. Sometimes you can be the most irritating man."

"Never mind. I'll explain later. It looks like Wardrop is hailing a carriage. Are you sure you don't want to go home?"

"Positive. What I'd like to do is walk. If I don't do something, I just might go back inside and give Dr. Steele another piece of my mind."

He laughed again. "Well, we can't have that, as much as I'd enjoy seeing it."

They joined Wardrop and Sarah, who waited patiently by a hackney.

Sarah gave Bathsheba a smothering hug. "Darling, are you all right?"

"Of course I'm all right," Bathsheba grumbled, extracting herself from her friend's embrace. "Why does everyone keep asking me that?"

"Mrs. Ormond has expressed a wish to go home," Wardrop said to John in a low voice. "I'm going to escort her."

He cast a quick glance at the two women as they exchanged outraged and surprisingly salty comments about Steele. "And I suspect you and Lady Randolph might have a few things to discuss."

John sighed. "It's that obvious, is it?"

Wardrop's eyes glinted with amusement, but he managed to look grave. "Blackmore, I haven't a clue what you're talking about."

John grunted, but gave his friend's shoulder an appreciative squeeze.

Wardrop went to hand Sarah into the carriage, but hesitated. "John, be careful of Steele. He has his enemies, but he has friends in powerful places, as well."

"As do I. Don't worry, I'll take care of Steele."

Wardrop looked morose. "Abernethy will be sure to get wind of this. He'll be bound to think I'm mixed up in it, too."

"I'll assure him you were an innocent bystander. By the time I'm finished describing what happened, Abernethy will know Steele is a complete ass."

Wardrop snorted, obviously convinced that neither of them believed that. "And I'm the Princess of Cleves," he retorted. "Yes, yes, Mrs. Ormond. I'm coming. Lady Randolph, it's been a pleasure, as always."

With a wave, Wardrop followed Sarah into the hackney and they were off.

John turned to Bathsheba, who stood pensively watching the hackney disappear into the stream of carriages and drays clogging the Strand.

"Lady Randolph? Shall we go?"

She started. "Oh, yes. Let's be away, before that dreadful man comes out. I won't be answerable for my actions if I see him again."

He took her arm and they made their way along the pavement toward Charing Cross. For several minutes, John was content not to speak, keeping her close by his side in the bustle of harried shoppers and rushing pedestrians. The life of the city flowed around them, but he and Bathsheba might as well have been strolling down a country lane for all he cared. He had eyes only for her. He studied her clean profile, offset by the frilly trim of her bonnet, and felt her small hand on his arm and the warmth of her body against his side. In that moment they belonged only to each other. The world didn't own them, and they had no responsibilities to anyone but themselves.

In a rare moment of contentment, John knew exactly where he was meant to be.

Bathsheba made no effort to break the silence between them, clearly taken up with her own ruminations. She looked solemn—even grave—and every now and again she worried her lower lip as if she were trying to solve a puzzle.

As they skirted the chaos of Charing Cross, she finally lifted her gaze to meet his. The tiny frown that had creased her brow had disappeared, and she looked as if she had reached some kind of decision.

"John, may I ask you a question?"

"Anything you want, Bathsheba. I have no secrets from you."

"What was Dr. Steele talking about when he accused you of using dangerous medical practices? Something about an Irishman?"

He sighed. He didn't want to recall that night—or what he had been forced to do. Especially now, when he felt so close to her, so much at peace.

"O'Neill is an Irish immigrant in St. Giles. I am often called there to treat the poor—especially those who cannot obtain admittance to Bart's or who are too afraid to go to the lying-in hospitals. His wife was in labor, but unable to deliver the child. By the time I was called to her bedside, it was too late."

She listened carefully as he related what had occurred that night. Without going into graphic detail, he explained exactly what he had done. Even without the particulars it was dreadful enough, but if she were to marry him, she couldn't be protected from that part of his life. He could only pray she would understand why it mattered.

Bathsheba paced along beside him. A few times, her fingers dug into his coat sleeve but she heard him out. When he finished the sorry tale—making sure not to leave out O'Neill's accusation that he had murdered his wife—he fell silent. Bathsheba needed time to absorb what he'd told her. She needed time to decide if she could actually be the wife of a doctor—a doctor who didn't always live by society's rules.

As they left the din of Charing Cross and Cockspur Street for the relative quiet of St. James's Square, John had the unnerving sense that his future with Bathsheba hung in the balance. The bright sunshine, the warm summer air, the happy shriek of children playing in the square, it all seemed artificial as he realized with a chilling pang that he might lose Bathsheba right here and now.

"If you couldn't save her, why did Dr. Steele accuse you of engaging in dangerous medical practices?" she asked.

He hesitated, and she flicked her hand in an irritated wave.

"John, I know it is nonsense. You're a fine doctor. I understand that better than anyone. I'm trying to fathom how he could make such a ridiculous accusation."

The chill in his body fled, and he felt the summer's warmth once again.

"Men like Steele received their training years ago, and still hold fast to the methods they most feel comfortable with. But there have been great advances in the study of midwifery, much of it coming out of France. That in itself," he said dryly, "is enough to prejudice so narrow-minded a man as Dr. Steele. Instead of embracing those advances, he clings to the old ways and is threatened by those of us who seek change."

She sighed. "And he's obviously greatly humiliated by losing Lord and Lady Silverton's patronage. I'm sorry about that, John. I didn't mean to cause you so much trouble."

She looked so guilty that he could barely resist the temptation to sweep her into his arms and kiss the hurt away.

"Sweetheart, you have nothing to apologize for. Just the opposite. I'm relieved that Lady Silverton will no longer have to suffer from Steele's ignorance."

She dimpled at him, and the roses returned to her cheeks. As they walked along, she peppered him with more questions about his work. He was happy to indulge her, and relieved beyond reckoning that she found it worth talking about.

All too quickly, they reached Curzon Street. "We're here," he said, coming to a halt in front of her town house.

She gave a startled laugh. "Oh! I didn't even notice when we crossed Piccadilly. How foolish of me. Well, now that you're here, would you like to come in for a cup of tea?"

He shook his head. "I think I best get down to Bart's. I'd like to speak with Abernethy. Explain what really happened today, before the rumors grow too exaggerated."

She started to look guilty again, but he gave her cheek a light brush with his index finger.

"Hush, Bathsheba. This is what I do. I won't apologize for it. Abernethy already knows that."

She nodded, still looking worried, but let him hand her up the steps. As he reached for the door knocker, she stopped him.

"I'd like to see where you work," she blurted out. "What you do."

He frowned. "You've already been down to Bart's."

She looked more certain now, as if she had reached another decision. "No. The other places. I want to see where you work, and to know what kind of risks you have to take." She took a deep breath. "I think it's important I do."

"Bathsheba, it's not—"

"Yes. It *is* necessary. I want to know everything about you. I need to, if we're going to consider . . . well, you know," she said, giving a cautious look around.

Her face was a study of conflicting emotions—curiosity, determination, and trepidation. But mostly determination.

He nodded. "I was thinking something along the same lines, but I didn't expect you would actually want to see it. Or need to. But you're right. You shouldn't make any decisions until you know everything about me."

She smiled, but that solemn, unfamiliar air still hung about her. He knocked on the door of the town house, telling himself he could trust her—that he *did* trust her to understand his work, and why it meant so much to him

But as they waited for the door to open, he couldn't help feeling that he had just made the biggest mistake of his life.

Chapter 21

Bathsheba inhaled a deep breath, struggling to ease the tightness in her chest and throat. How could she have been so stupid as to think she could actually do this? She deserved to be locked up in Bedlam for even making the suggestion.

Silently cursing herself for a fool, she grasped John's hand and stepped from the landau onto the pavement. She couldn't control a nervous flinch as an overburdened cart lumbered past, squeezing by them in the crush of activity at this end of Drury Lane.

John gave a quick glance around the crowded street. "My coachman will remain here with the carriage. The laneways in St. Giles are too narrow for it to pass."

He ran a sharp eye over her walking dress and sturdy boots, then gave her an approving smile.

"I'm happy to see you dressed so sensibly, Bathsheba. Trust me. You'll be grateful for those boots before the end of this day."

She tried to return his smile but her cheek muscles refused to cooperate. The dread gathering somewhere in the vicinity of her heart made it impossible for her to utter a word in reply.

Her impulsive offer to join him for a trip into the stews to see him work had seemed like a good idea—yesterday. After that infuriating episode with Dr. Steele at Somerset House—and her subsequent heartfelt discussion with John—it had all made sense. And perhaps if he had been able to visit her last night, reassuring her as he always did, she would still think it made sense. But their paths had not crossed last evening. Bathsheba had returned home alone from a dinner party to spend hours tossing and turning in bed, mentally replaying the all-too-public confrontation with Steele and trying to convince herself that marriage to John wouldn't add to her long list of blundering decisions.

When John arrived at her town house this afternoon, her exhausted brain had been shrieking at her to retreat from this misguided expedition. She had seriously considered pleading illness, but she couldn't stand the idea that he would think her a sniveling coward, too afraid to catch even a glimpse of what he faced every day.

Even if it were true.

His grin faded as he inspected her face. "What's wrong?"

She swallowed past the dryness in her throat. "Nothing. How far must we walk in?"

"Not far. The house is in a laneway just off Coal Yard."

She started off in that direction, but he stopped her by grasping her elbow. "Bathsheba."

She turned back to face him, afraid he would see her reluctance through the thin netting of the veil that hung from the brim of her hat.

"It's not too late to change your mind," he said in a voice so understanding it made her skin prickle with shame. "You don't have to do this. Not for me."

"Yes, I do," she replied, more sharply than she intended. "I can't pretend that you don't do this work, or that it won't affect our future. You take risks, John. With your life, I suspect, and certainly with your career. I have to find out if I can live with that."

John stared at her, trying to read her expression through

the veil's netting. Her heart sank at the stubborn, taut line of his mouth.

"Bathsheba," he began in a grim voice.

She stopped him by touching his sleeve.

"It's all right, John. You don't have to say anything. I'll try not to disappoint you."

He shook his head. "You could never do that, my love."

She gave him a wry smile, even as her heart took a guilty leap. How wrong he might be.

John took her arm and they set off, moving quickly from the rough but cheerful bustle of Drury Lane into Coal Yard, and into the warren of tumble-down buildings. The tenements crowded along the narrow street, cutting off the sun and casting long shadows over the dirty, broken stones of the pavement.

Bathsheba soon lost her sense of direction, confused by the intersecting alleys and laneways—each one darker and drearier than the next. Her heart began to pound at the fear of being alone in such a place. If she were separated from John, she would never find her way back through the confusing tangle of courts and blind alleys. She had heard St. Giles described as a honeycomb, but this particular honeycomb had nothing of sweetness about it. Instead it oozed darkness, filth, and a heavy sense of despair.

Feeling breathless, Bathsheba huddled closer to the reassuring strength of John's muscular body. She had no one to blame but herself for the vulnerability of her situation. He had suggested bringing his student, Roger, along with them, but she had balked, wanting as few people as possible to witness her folly. And even though John had assured her that Roger could be trusted, she couldn't help thinking that the young man might be tempted to gossip about the Countess of Randolph and her rash expedition in the East End.

John gave her an easy smile, looking completely confident in their surroundings. As they penetrated ever deeper into St. Giles, he never hesitated, taking each turning with

an unerring step. Suddenly she felt less anxious. If he could
be fearless, so could she. After all, he wouldn't have taken
her into the stews if he thought it would put her in danger.
One of these days, she would have to learn to let go of her
fear and give him her complete trust. And today seemed as
good a day as any.

As she matched him stride for stride, her racing heart
began to settle. The breathless feeling faded, and she began
to take better stock of her surroundings.

There were men, women, and children in every manner
of costume—some of it scanty, most of it worn and dirty.
Many lounged in the doorways of tenements or what looked
like flash houses, eyeing them with a mixture of curiosity,
wariness, and, in some cases, undisguised hostility.

John didn't seem to notice the hostile glances, or, if he
did, he ignored them. If fact, he obviously knew many of the
people they passed—women mostly, who gave him gap-
toothed smiles and greeted him with a shy respect.
Bathsheba was both startled and impressed when he invari-
ably tipped his hat and answered them by name.

She tugged on his arm to draw his attention. "John, you
seem very well known in St. Giles. Are these people the
patients who come to St. Bartholomew's for treatment?"

He shook his head. "Most of these poor souls can't get
a referral from one of the governors. A few have managed
it, which is where they came to know of my work. They are
the ones who send for me when a neighbor or a family
member falls ill. They know I will come whether they can
pay me or not."

Her unease stirred again. "How long have you been
doing that?"

He cast her an unreadable glance. "Five years this October."

"And how often do you come down to the stews?"

"As often as I am needed."

She fell silent, dismayed. She knew about his quest to establish his own ward for pregnant women, and about his

work at Bart's. But this was different. This looked more and more like an obsession. One he would be loath to relinquish, whatever the cost to his private or professional life.

They dodged a group of barefoot, rag-clad children and turned into a small courtyard. John brought her to a halt.

"Here we are," he said.

She peered through the gloom at the house before them. Unbidden, the image of a Hogarth engraving came into her mind. Gin Lane—come to life with a sickening vengeance.

The house, three stories tall, loomed over them at a crazy angle. As in the other buildings they had passed, many of the windows were broken and stuffed with dirty rags. Mud-smeared walls and a crumbling foundation gave the impression that the entire structure could collapse at any moment.

A group of men—most of them lacking coats or even a vest—squatted on what passed for the doorstep, all clearly in various stages of inebriation. They ran their insolent gazes over her figure, making lewd comments in a local cant so thick she had trouble understanding it.

Thank God for small mercies. She repressed the urge to let out a hysterical laugh.

John squeezed her hand. "Don't be frightened. Their bark is much worse than their bite."

He stepped forward and gave the men an easy smile. "Good day to you, gentleman. I'm here to see Mrs. Butler and the new baby."

One of the men extracted a smoke-blackened pipe from his mouth and rolled his eyes. "Aye, that be the brat that wails all night long. It's enough to make a man's rod go limp, I tell you, just when he's fixin' to poke his missus."

His remark elicited a round of guffaws. After a few good-natured jests and a plea for John to fix "the little bastard," the men squeezed over to let them pass.

As she stepped over the threshold, Bathsheba smiled weakly at the man with the pipe, and he moved aside with a flourishing, mocking bow. She heard a few more indelicate comments about the shape of her backside as John led her down a dark hallway.

"There, now," he murmured as he steered her toward a staircase. "That wasn't so bad, was it?"

She was opening her mouth to make an acid retort when she got her first whiff of the stench permeating the building. It stank of drains, urine, and unwashed bodies, a choking miasma so thick she could taste it. She blinked several times as her eyes started to water.

Hastily, she groped in her reticule for a handkerchief, only to find a large square of clean linen thrust into her hand. Gratefully, she pressed it to her eyes and then covered her nose.

"You'll get used to it," John said.

She peered into his face, unable to tell in the gloom of the hallway if he was joking or not. Surely, no one could ever grow used to such degradation.

As they climbed the stairs at the end of the hall, each step groaned loudly, as if the rotting wood was about to give way. On one flight, they had to step around a pair of squabbling women who looked ready to push each other down the stairs. On the next, they clambered over a group of half-naked, giggling children making bets with matchsticks. Finally, John led her down a dank-smelling passage to a closed door.

The door opened at his knock, and he ushered her into the room.

It was brighter than the hallway, with some light from an open window and from a lamp set on a small, rough-hewn table. The room looked and smelled a good deal cleaner than the rest of the building. Cautiously, Bathsheba lowered the handkerchief and dared to take a full breath.

"Mrs. Butler, how are you feeling today?" John asked as he made his way to an old bed shoved up against the wall. A faded piece of dimity hung in the corner, and a battered tea chest sat by an empty grate. On the chest perched a man, presumably Mr. Butler, mending a shoe.

Mrs. Butler huddled under a blanket, cradling a mite of an infant—blessedly quiet for now—to her breast. The woman smiled at John as he set his doctor's bag at the foot of the mattress.

"I'm feeling so-so, doctor, and that's for sure. I don't know when a baby has wore me out so much. My girls never gave me a speck of trouble."

She smiled and seemed to nod at a spot behind Bathsheba. Startled, Bathsheba turned to find two little girls, dressed in plain dark frocks, sitting in the corner of the room and staring up at her with huge, solemn eyes. One looked no older than twelve or thirteen, the other, several years younger.

"Well, let's see what we can do to make you and little Samuel more comfortable," John said.

As he began his examination, Bathsheba stood uncomfortably by the door, wishing she had something to do with her hands besides twisting the strings of her reticule. Feeling useless, she returned her gaze to the little girls, who stared back with unblinking fascination.

"Hello," Bathsheba said, feeling like an idiot.

"Girls," began the mother. Before she could go on, she broke into a loud, hacking cough that shredded the air. She gasped for breath while John rubbed her back. After a minute, she regained her voice.

"Don't forget your manners," she wheezed. "Give the nice lady a curtsy."

The older one stood up and hauled her sister to her feet. Each gave Bathsheba an awkward bob, and the younger girl immediately broke into a cough almost as bad as the mother's.

Bathsheba clutched her reticule, forcing herself not to back away. Surely John would not bring her into a place rife with contagion, would he?

"I'm Bess and this is Amy," said the older girl. "What's your name, miss?"

"Bathsheba," she replied with a forced smile.

"You're pretty. Just like one of them lightskirts I sell my flowers to down in the market."

An amused snort came from Mr. Butler's direction but Bathsheba thought it best to ignore it, as well as the assumption that she was a prostitute.

"So you sell flowers in Covent Garden, do you?" she commented brightly. "What kind do you sell?"

"Primroses when they're in. And violets. The fancy ladies always like the violets. Lilies of the valley and green lavender, too."

The girl prattled on, happy to talk about the flower stalls in Covent Garden, and her customers and friends in the market. Her sister remained by her side, her silence broken only by her alarmingly regular fits of coughing. Every time the poor little girl started to hack, Bathsheba had to resist the urge to turn tail and flee.

Mrs. Butler finally broke in on her daughter's monologue.

"My girls are like to support us, these days," she said proudly. "Best little sellers in the market. God knows we wouldn't have a roof over our heads without them."

Bathsheba cast a glance toward Mr. Butler. He never looked up, ignoring his wife and children as he kept his attention grimly focused on the work in his lap.

"Not that my Henry doesn't do his best to feed us," added Mrs. Butler in a soft voice. "But work these days is scarce. Seems a body can't afford a pair of shoes, much less pay to get them repaired."

The woman smiled apologetically at John, which confirmed Bathsheba's suspicion that no money would change hands for his services.

John rested his hand briefly on Mrs. Butler's head before pulling the blanket up to cover her chest. With a quiet murmur he plucked the baby from her arms, gently opening the swaddling to listen to its scrawny little chest. Bathsheba's heart ached with an emotion she couldn't name, but which seemed closer to sorrow than anything else.

After carefully examining the baby, John smiled down at the anxious-looking mother.

"Samuel is doing much better. If he is well fed, he should be fine. That means that you, Mrs. Butler," he added on a stern note, "must be sure to eat as much as you can. No more doing without, do you hear me?"

Mr. Butler finally spoke, not looking up from his work.

"You leave that to me, doctor. I'll see that she eats," he said in a gruff voice.

John nodded his approval and handed the infant to his mother. She took him eagerly and set him to her breast.

"I have plenty of milk for little Samuel, Dr. Blackmore. It's my strength I can't seem to get back."

John gave her arm a soothing pat. "Once you recover from your cough, you'll feel more like yourself. I'll give you and Amy," he smiled at the little girl, "a powder to help. Make sure the girls get fresh air, and keep them out of these damp rooms as much as possible."

Mr. Butler snorted in derision. "They gets all the fresh air they needs down in the market," he said in a sour voice.

"I'm sure they do," John replied, not taking offense. As he packed up his bag, he gave a few more instructions to Mrs. Butler. After waving away her effusive thanks, he took Bathsheba's arm and headed for the door.

"Wait, miss," cried Bess. "I want to give you some violets."

Bathsheba swallowed a groan. All she wanted was to escape. If she had to spend another moment in this room— much less have to take away a reminder of this family's poverty and illness—she just might scream.

"That . . . that won't be necessary," she stammered.

"Oh, do take them, miss," exclaimed Mrs. Butler. "Since we can't pay the doctor, it's the least we can do."

She was about to refuse again when John gave her elbow a warning squeeze.

"Oh, thank you," she managed.

Bess elbowed Amy, who scurried to a ratty-looking basket tucked away in the corner. She flung back the cloth that covered it and extracted a small but vibrant bunch of flowers. But before she could hand them over, she broke into another set of hacking coughs—directly over the violets.

Once she recovered, she came to Bathsheba and held out the bouquet in her grubby little fist. Bathsheba couldn't seem to move her arm, couldn't bear the thought of touching anything that had come in contact with the sick child.

After a long moment, John nudged her.

"Um, thank you," she said, flushing with shame. She took the flowers as gingerly as she could. "They're lovely."

Amy beamed with pleasure, waving cheerfully at her as John pulled her out of the room.

"You needn't worry, you know," he said in an exasperated voice as he steered her down the hall to the stairs. "Mrs. Butler and Amy are no longer contagious. Their coughs have become chronic because of the damp and the soot."

"Are you sure?" she asked, hating herself for even voicing the question.

"Yes. I wouldn't have brought you here if I thought you could catch any kind of fever. You do realize that, don't you?"

She wanted to believe him, but all she could think about was the dirt and the stench, and how sick everyone looked. Sweat broke out on the back of her neck and her body flared with heat. With it came the memory of her recent illness, and how close she had come to dying. In this horrible place death lurked everywhere, waiting like a predator to leap on her again.

As they turned the corner of the stairwell, Bathsheba opened her hand, dropping the violets on the landing. Yes, she was the worst kind of coward, but she simply couldn't stand to touch them a moment longer.

She glanced up as he led her past the still-lounging men in the front doorway. He looked as he always did—calm and in control, as if they had just spent a pleasant afternoon in Hyde Park and not in some disease-ridden slum. How in God's name did he manage to keep his sanity?

"I'm sorry you found this so distressing an experience," he said as they left the gloomy lodging house behind. "It's perfectly understandable, but I did tell you that you needn't come. You have nothing to prove to me, Bathsheba."

She winced, fully aware of how shabby her behavior must appear to him. For all intents and purposes, she had turned this little expedition into a test—of what, she wasn't yet sure. But somehow it now seemed as if it were she who had been tested, and who had been found wanting.

"I—"

John abruptly halted, and she skidded as her feet slipped in the thick muck covering the alley. Righting herself, she was about to launch into a frustrated scold when he grabbed her by the arm and shoved her behind him.

"John, what in the world is going on?"

"Stay behind me, Bathsheba," he warned in a low, tight voice.

She peered around his shoulder to see a man standing directly in their path. The big brute's hands curled into fists, and his lips peeled back into a nasty snarl.

"Well, fancy that," he said, his voice thick with an Irish brogue. "It be the doctor. Come down to St. Giles to kill more patients." He took a menacing step forward. "My wife and son weren't enough, I reckon. You and your masters won't be satisfied till you kill off as many of us as you can."

Bathsheba gasped, and the burly man's gaze switched to her. His bloodshot eyes widened as they raked down her body.

"Now, who be this fancy little piece?" His blunt features took on a sly cast. "Your doxy?"

Bathsheba curled her fingers around John's bicep. The hard muscle flexed under her grip.

"John," she whispered. "Who is this man?"

"It's O'Neill." His voice was so calm he could have been discussing the weather, and nothing more. "The man I told you about yesterday."

O'Neill's face split into a savage grin. "Aye. That's me. I'm the one whose wife and son you murdered, you bastard. And I'm the one who's going to make you pay."

Chapter 22

Bathsheba clutched at John's arm, fighting back the panic surging through her blood. Underneath her fingers his bicep flexed, then grew as hard as iron. Tension radiated from his body as he shifted his stance to keep her behind him.

She peered around his shoulder at the man blocking their path. O'Neill was huge, with meaty fists that looked powerful enough to crush a rock into dust. While John could probably hold his own in a fight with the man—at least for a while—she doubted he could prevail against so great a brute.

John took a cautious step forward, coming within reach of the other man's fists. She gasped and clutched his arm, trying to hold him back.

"Mr. O'Neill," he said, "you have my deepest sympathies. I share your sorrow over the death of your wife and son. I assure you that I did everything in my power to save them."

O'Neill glared at John with a killing hatred. A muscle jumped in his jaw and his throat worked, as if he had to force the words from his mouth.

"You killed them," he rasped. "My Mary was fine until you put her filthy hands on her."

The muscles in John's arms bunched under Bathsheba's fingers, but he gave no other outward indication that he was alarmed by the accusation.

"Mr. O'Neill, your wife was beyond help." John's voice seemed infused with sorrow for the mother's untimely death, and pity for the man who had been left alone with his grief. "Mary's deformed pelvis was too small to allow for the baby's passage. There was nothing anyone could do to change that circumstance."

"So you cut her open, you bastard," snarled the Irishman. "Gutted her like a fish."

Bathsheba had to swallow hard as the bile rose in her throat, not only at O'Neill's sickening description, but at the fury that gave his eyes a glassy, almost insane cast. Dread crawled up her spine, and she had to resist the urge to flee blindly down the nearest alley. But she couldn't do that. She wouldn't abandon John, although heaven only knew what she could do to help him.

A growling kind of murmur penetrated the fear that had kept her attention focused on the menace blocking their escape from the stews. Glancing around, she had to bite back a groan as she took in the rough-looking crowd that drifted over from what appeared to be a gin house. Several women passing in the laneway also stopped, peering at John with expressions of concern on their careworn faces. But most of the spectators displayed an avid curiosity, as if waiting for some kind of spectacle to begin. And from the greedy expressions on their faces as they eyed her, Bathsheba doubted they could be relied on to lend them any help.

She tugged on John's arm. "Look around," she whispered.

He turned his head, making a quick but thorough sweep of the laneway. Then his attention shifted back to his adversary. Bathsheba followed his gaze.

She almost choked. O'Neill's face was mottled with red blotches of rage, and the veins bulged in his neck. She peered into his muddy-colored eyes to see a dark void as deadly as a lunatic with a knife.

John's steady voice broke the rising tension. "I tried to save your baby, Mr. O'Neill. That's why I performed surgery.

It was the only chance I had, and your wife was already gone. You know that. Why would I want to hurt either Mary or your child?"

O'Neill lowered his head, like a bull about to go on a rampage. "Because you're a bleedin' English bastard, that's why. You want to get rid of us Irish, like your kind have been doing for bleedin' centuries. We're dirt to you—fouling your streets. You'd rather see us dead than let us live in peace."

A low rumble of disgruntled agreement rose from the men from the gin house. With a sickening jolt, Bathsheba realized most of them must be Irish—probably recent immigrants who lived in the boarding houses and tenements of St. Giles. If that was the case, they would be overwhelmed in moments.

She sucked in a deep, trembling breath, pulled her shoulders straight, and stepped up to John's side. He looked down at her with shock writ large on his face.

"What are you doing, you little fool," he hissed. "Get behind me and stay there."

She glared back. "I most certainly will not."

Lifting her chin defiantly, she gave the crowd a stern warning glare—the look she leveled at impertinent young bucks and snooty dowagers of the ton. It was madness to think it would work in this particular situation, but she had to do something to help John and help extricate them from this desperate fix.

O'Neill switched his feral gaze to her. She swallowed, tasting acid, as she mentally grabbed for the tattered threads of her ephemeral courage.

"Oh, aye," he snarled. "Let your doxy come to your aid, because no one else will. Not down here in St. Giles. I knows what they call you, Blackmore. Angel of Death. Every time you show up a woman dies. That ain't no coincidence. You kill 'em, and that's a fact."

A stout-looking woman pushed her way to the front of the crowd.

"That's a lie," she cried, waving a battered red parasol for emphasis. "Dr. Blackmore saved my daughter and her baby. 'E's the only doctor who'll step foot in St. Giles. There's many a woman down 'ere that has him to thank for her life."

Several other people—mostly women—chimed in with a chorus of support. O'Neill cursed at them before turning back to John.

"What would you do if it was your woman here who died, Blackmore? What if somebody killed her?" His lunatic gaze flickered to Bathsheba. She grew cold under the harrowing intensity of that stare.

John made a low, growling noise deep in his throat. She glanced up, startled to see a sudden fury darken his countenance.

An ugly grin fractured O'Neill's face. His muddy eyes gleamed with satisfaction. "So . . . that's what you need, Doc, ain't it? A taste of your own medicine."

Bathsheba couldn't hold back a squeak as the Irishman took a menacing step forward. John shook free of her clutching hand and moved forward to block him.

"Stop right there, O'Neill," he said in a lethally cold voice. "I understand the depth of your loss, but my patience has its limits. Come any closer, and you'll pay the price."

A guttural laugh rose from O'Neill's throat and he took another step, reaching out with those horrible massive hands as if to grab her.

John thrust her behind him. As she clutched his waist, trying to pull him back with her, she caught a flash of movement out of the corner of her eye. A child darted past, skidding to a halt directly in O'Neill's path. She recognized the little flower girl, Bess.

"Don't you touch her, you big ox," the child yelled, shoving O'Neill in the stomach.

The man halted in his tracks, staring down at the furious little obstacle in his way. His face went blank, dumbfounded by his challenger's behavior, as was everyone else in the crowd.

But only for a moment.

"Get out of my way, girl," he growled.

O'Neill pushed her aside, but she spun and danced back into his path. Bathsheba couldn't hold back a cry as the girl put herself back in harm's way.

"Bess! Get back!" John tried to reach for her while keeping Bathsheba well behind him.

Bess ignored him, glaring at the hulking brute in front of her. "You leave Dr. Blackmore alone," she shouted, "or you'll be sorry."

O'Neill gave a frustrated snarl and swung his arm, sweeping the girl off her feet. Bess yelped and tumbled to the broken paving stones, while voices in the crowd gasped in outrage.

"You bloody Irish bastard," screeched the woman with the parasol. She slammed it into O'Neill's head just as he lunged for John.

His balance thrown off by the woman's attack, O'Neill's punch went wide. He staggered, then spun clumsily around to face his attacker. Undaunted by O'Neill's size or his angry roars, the woman continued to rain blows on his head and shoulders with her parasol.

In an instant, the street exploded into a violent melee. Bathsheba shrieked as someone jostled against her, then pulled her away from John. Jerked around, she found herself staring into the leering, pock-marked face of a man almost twice her size. He yanked her toward his body, reaching to paw at her breasts. His breath, heavy with gin fumes, rolled over her and she almost retched as he began to drag her across the broken pavement.

Clenching her jaw against the rising nausea, Bathsheba kicked him in the shin as hard as she could. With a howl, he loosened his grip. As she struggled to break free, a big set of hands curled around her arms and lifted her out of the other man's grasp. She gasped and looked up into John's face, his features carved with a savage anger. He shouldered her safely behind him, then drove his fist into the face of the gin-sodden lout who had seized her. The man's eyes rolled to the back of his head and he collapsed onto the muck-covered stones.

"We have to get out of here," John shouted above the din. He yanked her out of the way as two grappling combatants crashed by them.

She gaped at him. "Tell me something I don't know," she finally managed to yell back.

Unbelievably, his lips twitched into a sardonic smile, and she had to fight the sudden urge to box his ears. How could he be so cavalier at a time like this? When this foolish expedition into the stews had placed both of them in such danger? Even worse, he obviously didn't realize just how bad things could get, since he risked his life by coming down here on a regular basis. Didn't he understand that someday he could be injured or even killed?

Before she could say anything else, he tucked her under his arm and retreated to the doorway of an old lodging house. They huddled against a scarred wooden door as he scanned the laneway, searching for a path through the mayhem.

She repressed a groan. It didn't look promising. The fight was getting worse, and threatened to escalate into a full-out riot at any moment. The street was filling up fast as tenements and public houses disgorged their human contents. It would soon become impassable as men, and even some women, eagerly launched themselves into the fray. It no longer mattered what the fight was about. Violence had been unleashed and whirled like a vortex, sucking in all the anger, frustration, and drunken despair that stalked like death through this part of London.

Bathsheba stood on her tiptoes and tried to spot O'Neill. She couldn't. Tugging on John's sleeve, she pulled him close to speak into his ear.

"Where's O'Neill? I don't see him."

He pointed. "Over there. By that public house."

She followed his gaze, breathing a sigh of relief when she caught sight of him on the other side of the street, hammering away at two men. With any luck, that would keep him occupied while they slipped away.

John grabbed her hand. "We should make a run for it before it gets worse."

She gulped, terrified to leave the uncertain shelter of the doorway but knowing he was right. They began to edge their way along the rough brick wall of the building when a familiar face popped up out of the mass of bodies in front of them.

Bess. Coming to their rescue, once again.

She tugged on John's sleeve. "Here, sir. I'll get you and the lady out. This way."

With a backward glance to make certain they followed, the child slipped around the side of the lodging house.

John gave Bathsheba a grim look. "Ready?"

She reached up to straighten her bonnet and realized it had been knocked off her head, probably in her struggle with the drunkard. Repressing a curse—she didn't have enough hats anymore to go losing them in riots—she nodded and squeezed his hand. He pulled her behind him as they hurried after Bess.

The scurrying girl guided them into what appeared to be a blind alley. But as they followed her to the end, Bathsheba spied a small gate set into a brick wall. Bess ran to it and pulled. Rusty hinges protested, but when John gave it a hard yank it came free.

They all three stepped through into the quiet of an almost-deserted court. Only a few children, watched over by an old woman, played in the dirt. From there, Bess led them through another alley and small court, and finally into a paved street with shops and some respectable-looking houses. The noise from the riot had faded to a dull rumble, barely audible over the bustle of the street.

Bathsheba heaved a sigh of relief and collapsed against John's side as her legs began to tremble. His arm came around her waist, holding her securely upright.

Bess tipped her head up, her narrow face splitting into an engaging, gap-toothed grin. "We're safe now, sir. Drury Lane is just ahead. Right at the end of this here street."

John gave the child's shoulder a gentle squeeze. "Thank you, Bess. You shouldn't have put yourself in harm's way, but you have my gratitude just the same. It's a lucky thing you happened to come upon us when you did."

Her eyes widened. "T'weren't luck, sir. I followed you. Ma sent me on an errand just after you left, and I saw the pretty lady had accidentally dropped her flowers. I was comin' after you to give them back."

Bathsheba froze as Bess reached deep into the slit of her gown and extracted a bunch of limp violets.

"Here, miss. Ma and Amy would be some upset if they knew you lost them."

John's arm turned as stiff as a board around her waist. He looked down at her but she refused to meet his eye. A painful flush crept up her neck, heating her face as shame crawled over her skin. Never had Bathsheba felt so small, so worthless. And now John knew just how worthless she was, too.

But Bess, at least, didn't need to know how cruel she had been.

Bathsheba gave the girl as bright a smile as she could muster. "It was very kind of you to bring me the flowers. I never even realized that I had dropped them."

She took the violets from the girl's grubby, outstretched hand and tucked them into the bodice of her gown. They hung there, looking as bedraggled as Bathsheba's clothing, but Bess didn't seem to mind. She beamed back at her, joy making her thin face almost pretty.

Bathsheba's heart turned over in her chest. She stepped out of John's embrace, leaned down, and gave the girl an impulsive hug.

"Thank you," she whispered into the child's ear. "I don't know what we would have done without you."

She straightened, repressing a smile at Bess's wide-eyed stare. The little girl looked as stunned as if manna had just dropped from the heavens.

John extracted a few coins from his pocket and gave them to Bess, who found her tongue enough to register a weak protest.

"No, Bess," he insisted in a gruff voice. "You led us to safety. I'm sure your mother would be happy if you spent the money on fruit from the market. She has to keep her strength up, and so does Amy. Why don't you run off and do that? The lady and I can find our way back to the carriage from here."

Bess gave them that sweet, gap-toothed grin again and took off in the direction of Covent Garden.

"Be careful," Bathsheba called after her, strangely unsettled to see the child racing off by herself.

Bess gave a cheery wave and disappeared around a corner.

It hurt to watch her go. Bess was so small and vulnerable. Despite her courage and fortitude, her life of grinding poverty must be a misery. Bathsheba hated even knowing about it—hated having to think about what the girl's future would be like. How in God's name did John tolerate coming here, day after day? How did he live with the pain and frustration?

His deep voice broke into her thoughts.

"Don't worry. She knows her way around St. Giles better than men three times her age."

"I'd like to help her," she replied, forcing herself to speak past the lump in her throat. "I don't know how, but I've got to do something."

He was silent for a long moment, as if she had surprised him.

"Why?" he finally replied, his voice heavy with sarcasm.

"Because she saved your life? Was she not worthy of your notice before then?"

Her melancholy evaporated in a blaze of anger and self-loathing. She knew her own failings well enough. But she didn't think he would be heartless enough to mock her with them—especially after what they had just gone through.

"Of course she was," she snapped, glaring up into his face. His expression was cold, even judgmental. "I'm the one who isn't worthy, as is now perfectly clear to both of us."

They stood in the middle of the street, staring at each other like two wary combatants. His smoky gray eyes probed hers, as if he would pull aside a veil separating them and read her soul. Anger and latent violence swirled about his tall, lean body, as if he were expecting another fight to break out at any moment.

But, suddenly, all that boiling emotion seemed to drain away. He sighed, and the angry warrior transformed once more into the compassionate doctor. If Bathsheba hadn't been so weary and depressed, she would have smiled. She had come out much worse from this afternoon's adventure, physically and mentally, she suspected. But he looked as he always did—the calm physician who knew exactly what must be done. Unlike her, he hadn't even lost his hat.

"I'm sorry, Bathsheba," he said with a rueful shake of the head. "This is my fault. I should never have allowed you to step foot in St. Giles in the first place."

She raised her eyes heavenward, praying for strength. Would the blasted man always forgive her, no matter what sins she committed?

"Of course, John," she retorted, not bothering to hide her irritation. "Everything must always be your fault—your responsibility—mustn't it? God forbid the lady of privilege should ever admit a mistake."

"Bathsheba—"

"Not now, John. Please. All I want is a little peace and quiet, and a very large brandy."

He nodded, clearly unhappy as he took her arm and guided her out toward Drury Lane.

"The carriage is just ahead," he said. "I'll take you straight home."

Good Lord. The man could be amazingly dense. "No, we will not go straight to Curzon Street. We will go to your house first, where I can clean up before going home."

He frowned. "It's not a very good idea to call at my house without even a maid to accompany you."

She yanked on his arm, pulling him to a stop.

"Look at me." She gestured at the front of her gown. "I'm a wreck. My hat is gone and I'm sure my hair is a tangled mess. My servants are better than most, but some of them are bound to gossip if they see me like this, especially after returning home with you."

His eyes drifted over her dirt-stained bodice—the lout who mauled her obviously had filthy hands—then lifted to her hair. A wry smile touched the corners of his mouth, confirming her suspicion that her coiffure was a disaster.

"I see your point," he said in a dry voice. "We'll return to my house immediately. My servants are used to all manner of visitors, day and night. They won't think twice about your appearance."

She gave a terse nod and began striding toward Drury Lane. He caught up with her and took her hand, tucking it into the crook of his arm. She wanted to lean into him, savoring his warmth and the security of his strong body. But she stopped herself. What she had seen today had shocked her to the core, and she couldn't remember the last time that had happened. But the people down in the stews were a part of John's life, and a very important part if the risks he took to help them were any indication. Everything she knew about him, everything she had already learned about his character, told her that he wouldn't give it up. Not if he felt it was a necessary part of his work.

But if that were the case, she didn't think she could stand it. She had been married to one man with an obsession, and it had almost destroyed her. That John's obsession was for good, not for ill, didn't matter.

She couldn't sit by and wait for disaster to strike again.

Chapter 23

As John handed Bathsheba down from the landau, he caught her staring at his small but elegant town house in Market Lane. Her eyebrows arched in surprise, making it all too obvious she had underestimated him once again. In spite of all the evidence to the contrary, some part of her had insisted on believing he was little better than a simple country gentleman, barely able to make ends meet.

He took her hand to escort her up the steps of the house, feeling more than ever the emotional and social barriers she had thrown up to keep him at bay. Yesterday he had felt closer to her than any person he had ever known—including Becky. Today it felt like a chasm yawned between them.

As he extracted the key to the front door from his pocket, she gave the street an anxious scan. She needn't have worried. Businesses comprised most of the buildings on Market Lane, the main reason John had chosen this particular house. The neighborhood was genteel, but the street held few private residences, giving him and his patients freedom from the prying eyes of local gossips.

He ushered her into the quiet of the tidy entrance hall. The door leading down to the kitchen opened and Jordan hurried forward to relieve him of his hat and medical bag. His manservant took in Bathsheba's disheveled appearance in one comprehensive glance, but retained his customary bland expression.

"Good afternoon, Dr. Blackmore," he said. "Will you and your guest be taking tea in the drawing room?"

John shook his head. "This lady has met with an accident. Please bring a bowl of hot water and some towels to my study."

He eyed Bathsheba, trying to decide what else she might need to restore her appearance to the required degree of respectability. She gave a slight, exasperated shake of her head.

"A comb would be helpful," she said in a dry voice.

"Right away, madam." Jordan gave a respectful bow and retreated to the lower regions of the house.

John took her by the shoulders and guided her to his study. The small but comfortable room was situated at the back of the house, well removed from the bustle of the street. Bathsheba needed a period of quiet to regain her equilibrium. Whatever they might have to say to each other could wait.

Except, of course, for his apology for thrusting her into danger. Given her uncharacteristically silent demeanor since he had bundled her into the carriage a short while ago, that obviously couldn't wait.

He escorted her to the comfortably padded leather club chair in front of his desk. She sank down with a grateful sigh. Crossing to a trolley, he selected one of the crystal decanters and poured her a brandy. A large one. She still looked a good deal too pale for his comfort.

"Here," he said. "I want you to drink all of it."

Her emerald eyes glittered with a flash of amusement as she took the glass. "You won't have to persuade me, I assure you."

She took a generous swallow, and softly murmured her satisfaction. The muscles in her slim, white throat rippled as she drank, and he was struck once again by her delicacy. For all her determined bravado, there was so much about her that was achingly vulnerable.

His stomach clenched with a volatile combination of anger, frustration, and worry. What had he been thinking to bring her into St. Giles? She had insisted, but he had known better and he had allowed his feelings for her—his desire for her approval—to override his judgment. It was a mistake he wouldn't make again.

If only it wasn't already too late. What happened today might have ruined any chance they had for a future as man and wife.

"Bathsheba—"

A discreet tap on the door interrupted him, winding his frustration even tighter.

"Enter," he commanded. Bathsheba lifted both eyebrows at his irritated tone of voice.

Jordan glided serenely into the room and placed a tray holding a bowl of water, towels, and a comb on a low table in front of the club chair.

"Will there by anything else, sir?"

"No. Thank you, Jordan. See to it we're not disturbed."

The manservant exited the room. After the door closed, a heavy tension filled the study. Bathsheba still refused to meet his eyes, which John began to find very annoying.

"Bathsheba, I realize you're angry and unsettled by the day's events. More than I can say, I regret placing you in that position. I assure you that what happened today was not typical."

She gave him an unreadable glance, finished her drink in one swallow, and reached for the comb. With quick, jerky movements, she began to drag it through her bedraggled coiffure. He watched, barely tamping down his frustration.

"Here," he finally said, wrestling the comb from her fingers. "Give me that before you tear your hair out."

She scowled at him and tried to stand up, but he pushed her back down into the chair.

"Don't be a goose," he growled.

She subsided with a mutter and he stepped behind the

chair to untangle her hair. He worked carefully, trying not to pull, teasing the comb through the knots as gently as he could. Gradually, she relaxed, letting her head fall forward as he smoothed a soft path through her silky locks.

"Bathsheba," he said. "I know you're angry with me for what happened today, but it would be better if you talked about it."

She swatted his hand away from her head, then jumped up from the chair to face him. Her face was pale, her features pinched with tension.

"That's not why I'm angry," she cried. "Yes, I hated it, but that's not it."

He stared, baffled by her words.

Her delicate brows snapped together in a fierce scowl. "I'm angry because you expose *yourself* to such danger. On a daily basis. It's beyond foolish, and I won't tolerate it."

She glared at him, her emerald gaze sparking with fury, but he didn't fail to notice that her full mouth trembled and tears clung to the ends of her long lashes. The tightness in his chest began to ease. She was worried about him, not herself. That was something he could remedy.

"What happened today was unusual, to say the least. As for what other dangers I might encounter, a doctor always runs the risk of contracting an illness through his work. Surely you understand that, Bathsheba." He smiled, trying to take the sting out of his words.

She gave her head a violent shake, and the auburn curtain of hair swung around her shoulders. "I'm not an idiot, John. Of course I understand that. I'm talking about the danger you face every time you go into those horrible stews. The violence—"

She broke off, swallowing so hard he could hear it. He reached for her, but she waved him away. He waited patiently, even though he wanted to snatch her into his arms and soothe away the shock of the day's events.

"It's not safe," she insisted after regaining her voice. "You could be hurt, or worse. And then where would I be?" She finished on a plaintive note, sounding more like a sad and worried child than the sophisticated widow he knew her to be.

This time he did move, folding her in his arms and ignoring her weak efforts to hold him off. He gave her trembling lips a lingering kiss, then guided her back to the club chair. After she sat, he knelt down and took her hands between his.

"I assure you, love," he said as he carefully pulled her gloves off. "What happened today was an aberration. I've never encountered anything like that before. More often than not I'm treated with great courtesy and respect."

"But not always," she challenged.

He hesitated. "Where there's poverty, there's always despair and the risk of violence. Generally, though, it's not a worry. Besides," he said with a reassuring smile, "I do have my defenders, as you may have noticed this afternoon."

She chewed her lower lip for a moment before responding. He was sorely tempted to plunder her soft pink mouth with a ravenous kiss.

"What about O'Neill?" she asked. "The man is a lunatic who wants to kill you. Do you think it was simply a coincidence he found you today?"

John sat back on his heels. That question had been troubling him for the last hour, and he was no closer to an answer. "I don't know. He doesn't live near Coal Yard, but that doesn't mean he had no business in that part of St. Giles. Many of the Irish live there."

She began to absently chew on her thumbnail. He took her hand and gently pressed it into her lap. A blush rose into her cheeks, but then she frowned at him.

"He didn't seem surprised to see you there, John. I think he was following you, and what's to say he won't do it again? He's dangerous."

Damn. He didn't blame her for being upset, but there was

no point in turning O'Neill into a bogeyman who would haunt her dreams.

"You're not to worry about him," he said, determined to calm her fears. "I'll see to it that he doesn't bother you again. I promise he won't come near you."

Her eyes blazed with a sudden, surprising fury. She grabbed the lapels of his coat and yanked him forward until they were nose to nose.

"Listen to me, you stupid man! I'm not worried about myself. It's you I'm afraid for. O'Neill will come for you again. I know it. And every time you go down into the stews, you make yourself vulnerable to him and a thousand other dangers. You're reckless and foolhardy. Don't you understand you could be killed down there?"

Her passionate outburst stunned him into silence. Then tenderness filled his chest with a sweet bloom. He stroked the perfect skin of her cheek, letting the arousal he could no longer hold back spiral through his body.

"I won't let that happen, my sweet. I promise you."

Tears welled in her eyes, turning them into brilliant shards of green crystal. "You can't be sure of that, John. I—"

"Hush, now," he murmured, bending close. "Don't think about it."

When his lips covered hers, she moaned as if in pain. She clamped her hands on his face and kissed him with a startling desperation. A thought—unbidden and unwelcome—crossed his mind. Her frantic embrace felt like good-bye, and she was putting all the loneliness and sorrow of that severing into one last kiss.

His mind struck back at the horrifying image. Swiftly, before she had the chance to pull away—or even think—he lashed his arms around her waist and jerked her forward to the edge of the leather seat. With a frenzied sense of urgency that threatened to boil out of control, he mashed her slender body against his chest and devoured her soft, yielding mouth. She gave a muffled squeak but spread her legs wide to accommodate him, the material of her skirts bunching up around her knees.

John dropped a hand to her thighs and pushed her dress up to her hips. With the other hand, he threaded his fingers through her hair, angling her head to seek the sweetness of her open mouth. Then he gently pulled her hands from his face and placed them around his neck, not breaking contact as he kissed her. Their tongues stroked and tangled, tasting each other as the heat between them spun out of control.

Bathsheba moaned. That vulnerable, feminine sound dug spurs into his growing need. As he pulled her closer she wound her arms around his neck, rubbing her full breasts against his body. If she was hoping to incite him, it worked. He had to feel her hot, cinching flesh around his cock. If he didn't come into her soon—slake himself in her lush body— he would go mad with lust.

He retreated, holding her shoulders in a fierce grip. Her eyes popped open. They were soft and heavy-lidded with a dazed passion.

"Why . . . why are you stopping?" she stuttered.

His laugh sounded more like a groan. "God, Bathsheba. I couldn't stop if someone held a pistol to my head."

The muzzy look in her eyes vanished. "That's not funny, considering what could have happened to you today," she snapped.

God, she was adorable. He couldn't wait a moment longer to take her.

"Believe me, sweet. I'm not joking."

He swiftly rose to his feet, bringing her up with him. In one motion he pivoted and dropped down into the club chair. He curled his hands around her hips, holding her steady before him.

"Well," she asked in a grumpy voice. "What now?"

"I want you on top of me," he murmured, dragging her gown and chemise up around her hips. He caught his breath, captured by the smooth purity of her skin, the soft rounded curves, and the nest of auburn curls at the apex of her thighs.

Her mouth twitched. "You're a wicked man, Dr. Blackmore."

"As are you, my lady wicked. Now stop complaining and climb up here. Tuck your knees on either side of my legs."

She settled on top of him with a voluptuous sigh, letting her head fall back as he gripped the firm globes of her luscious bottom, kneading them between his hands. Never had he seen anything as beautiful as she was in this moment, as she gave herself over to sensuality. As she gave herself to him. In a strange way it made his heart contract with loneliness—the knowledge that without her in his arms, in his life, he would remain forever solitary. In some elemental way, he would be set apart at a careful distance from the rest of the world.

With that thought came fear—the fear he might still lose her. He moved his hands in a rough glide over her body, determined to possess her, to love her so completely she would never for a moment think of seeking another man's protection or bed.

Bathsheba whimpered, rocking against him as he stroked his fingers between the soft folds of her sex. She was so hot and wet, he had to clench his teeth to keep from ripping open his breeches and plunging into her. But first he needed to convince her that only he could give her the satisfaction—emotional and physical—she so obviously craved.

He slid one, then two fingers inside her tender sheath. She undulated her hips, trying to increase the pressure on the peak of her sex. But he wouldn't give her what she wanted until he received what he needed from her.

"Open your eyes," he murmured. "I want you to look at me."

She gave another throaty sigh and dragged open her eyelids. Her gaze was hot and primal. It latched onto his, possessing his soul as surely as his hands possessed her body. He stilled, and for a long moment they stared deep into each other's eyes, the connection flaring between them. Then she gave a smug little smile, draping her arms around his shoulders as she began to rock leisurely against his hand.

Vixen. As always, she sought to control the game. He wouldn't allow that—not today.

"Open your bodice," he commanded in a low voice.

Her eyes widened, and she hesitated. He pulled his fingers from her damp flesh, drawing them out in a lingering caress as he left her body. She cast him a disgruntled look, but released him and began to undo the tight buttons that marched up over her chest.

Slowly she pulled back the tailored fabric, exposing her full curves, barely covered by light stays and a thin chemise. He rewarded her by rubbing his palm across her swollen bud. She gasped, and he could feel the tremble in her thighs.

"I've got you," he murmured, keeping one hand fastened on her bottom. "Pull your chemise down. I want to see all of you."

Her small white teeth appeared, pulling on her lower lip as she untied her undergarments. With a quick yank, she pulled them down and her plump breasts spilled out, riding high over the top of her stays. Her nipples, already stiff and rosy, were ready for the tasting.

An insatiable greed raced through his blood. With a groan, he fastened his mouth over the taut point of one breast, sucking the tender flesh deep into his mouth. She gave a muffled shriek and arched back, forcing him to follow.

He did, sucking and nibbling as she writhed under his mouth, against his questing hand. He slid his fingers through the moist flesh, playing with the erect little bud before slipping into her soft, cinching channel. Every nerve ending in his body was on fire, as he filled his hands and his mouth—all his senses reveling in the texture and scent of her aroused body.

As he tongued her nipple, he could feel tiny spasms contracting her sheath. She moaned frantically, pressing his head to her breast as she sought her climax. But he couldn't—wouldn't let her reach those heights without him. The hunger he felt, the urgent compulsion to be joined with her, could no longer be denied. Never had he desired, no, needed a woman as much as Bathsheba—body, soul, everything she had to give would be his alone.

He pulled away from her breast, ignoring her soft wail of protest. Steadying her with one hand, he ripped at the fall of his breeches. She gave a hot, eager pant, gazing at him with slumberous eyes as she helped him push the fabric out of the way. Bracing one hand on his shoulder, she reached down and curled her slim fingers around his erection. He clenched his teeth, feeling like he was coming out of his skin as she gave him a short, pumping stroke. Just as he was about to pull her hand away, she positioned the tip of his erection against her soft cleft.

Their eyes caught and held. He shifted both hands to her hips. Pressing down, she sank slowly around his aching length. They both gasped as she settled around him, pelvis pressing against pelvis.

For several moments, they held that position. Her mouth sought his, their tongues mating in a sensual, moist kiss. Then she moaned and began to move. Her hips undulated, up and down, in a rhythm so languid and delicious it stole the breath from his body and stretched his control to the breaking point. He grabbed her bottom and surged underneath her, holding the firm globes in an unyielding grip as he took her with short, sharp lunges. Her breath came and went in sobbing moans as the tremors began deep in her sheath, rippling around his erection.

He gave another hard lunge, unleashing his need, finally allowing the power of their loving to pour through him. She cried out, curling her body around him as her climax broke. Contractions rippled in her soft channel, pulling on him, forcing him to completion. He poured himself into her in a hot wave, the intensity of it a heady rush that wrenched his body with a racking spasm.

After an endless, rapturous moment, she collapsed onto his chest. He pulled her tight against him, cradling her in his arms as she trembled uncontrollably. His heart throbbed with tenderness as she sobbed quietly against him.

"Hush, love," he finally murmured after his heart had found its normal beat. "All will be well. There's nothing to be afraid of."

Her breath caught on a hiccup and her slim body flexed with tension. She pushed herself up to meet his gaze. Her bewitching face was flushed from the aftermath of their love and her tears. Her eyes glittered wetly but, as he watched, they cleared and the emotion from their lovemaking was replaced with a cool determination. He recognized that look, and it usually boded no good.

"You're not still worried about O'Neill, are you?" he asked, mystified by her swift emotional retreat. "I told you I'd take care of him."

She braced her hands on his shoulders and met his gaze head-on, even as the tremors lingered in the place where they were still joined.

"And what about me, John?" Her voice was low and somber. "How will you take care of me?"

Chapter 24

Bathsheba struggled to catch her breath as she stared into John's eyes, all gray smoke and smoldering from their love-making. But that desperate blaze of passion had only been a respite, not a resolution. The obstacles standing between them still loomed as high as a Swiss Alp.

Suppressing a ridiculous urge to burst into tears, she slumped wearily against his chest. Making love had been a mistake —an almost fatal mistake. His touch weakened her, and her yearning for him wove an insidious, dangerous spell. It urged her to capitulate, whispering that all would be well. She knew from bitter experience that nothing could be farther from the truth.

She rested against him, putting off the confrontation for as long as she could. He'd wrapped his arms around her, rocking her gently as if she were a child needing comfort. His loving touch tore a hole in her heart as she thrust away the pretty illusion that safety and security lay within his embrace.

John tipped her chin, forcing her to meet his somber stare.

"I thought we answered that question, my love," he said. His voice held a lingering husky note that sent a shiver down her spine. "I'll always take care of you—and Rachel. You won't be a countess, but neither will you want for anything. Within reason, of course," he finished with a sardonic quirk of his lips.

Impatiently, she pushed his hand away. "That's not what I'm talking about."

His eyes narrowed. "Then what?"

Bathsheba took a deep breath and plunged ahead. "You must promise not to risk your life anymore on these fool-hardy expeditions into the stews. It's too dangerous. You could get hurt, or worse."

All traces of the lover disappeared from his face. Now he simply looked exasperated. "I'll try my best. I assure you, I take no foolhardy risks. But certain hazards can't be avoided. As a doctor's wife, you must learn to trust that I know what I'm about."

She forced herself to move, sliding from his lap before she did something unforgiveable—like box his ears for being so pigheaded. She had always understood that John was a man who would not be managed, but his stubborn re-fusal to see reason would drive her mad with frustration.

Awkwardly, she scrambled to her feet. His hands shot out, steadying her at the waist.

"Well, I can't trust you," she snapped, yanking her skirts down. "Not unless you stop going into the stews."

He too started to rearrange his clothing, but he paused, jerking his head up to give her a hard stare.

"Bathsheba, you worry too much. I'm sorry it troubles you, but I have no intention of giving up that kind of important work. I'm sure you'll get used to it sooner than you realize."

He sounded so bloody arrogant she wanted to scream. God, she was sick of men forcing her to give in, always having to change her life—her needs—to accommodate.

"Why can't you give it up?" she demanded as she wres-tled her bodice back into place. "You have your growing practice and your duties at the hospital. Ample work for any man, I would think."

"True, but women like Mrs. Butler need me, Bathsheba."

"Well, I need you, too," she snapped.

John's eyebrows rose in subtle disapproval. Bathsheba inwardly winced, then clamped down tight on her frustration. Losing her temper wouldn't make him listen to reason.

"And so does Rachel," she said, grasping at the fraying strands of her composure. "John, I cannot spend the rest of my life imagining the worst every time you go haring off into that rat's nest. If anything should happen to you . . ."

She swayed, feeling light-headed, as a sudden image of John sprawled bloody and lifeless in a filthy laneway sprang into her head.

"For God's sake," he muttered, rising to his feet, "sit down before you fall down."

Distracted by her terrifying vision, Bathsheba allowed him to push her into the club chair.

While she attempted to marshal her wits, John gave her a grim, assessing perusal. Tension radiated from his tall frame, charging the air between them with the menace of a gathering storm. Gradually, a hard control settled over him, casting his features into stonelike relief. Even his eyes seemed to grow pale, as if some harrowing process had stripped away their silvery sheen.

As she gazed up into his face, Bathsheba's throat tightened. Something ugly had slouched into the study with them—something that made her want to bolt from the room.

"I had a sister once," he said in a flat voice. "Her name was Becky, and she knew me better than I knew myself."

Bathsheba's heart collided painfully with her ribs. In all their weeks together, John had never mentioned a sister. Whatever he had to tell her, it was going to be bad.

"Go on," she managed to say in a thin voice.

He turned away, moving over to lean against his bookshelves. She sensed that he had retreated to a place far away from his austerely appointed study.

"I was the youngest of three children," he began. "Two

boys and a girl. My brother was considerably older, but Becky and I were only a few years apart. As children, we were inseparable. We roamed the countryside for hours on end. To my mother's everlasting dismay, Becky was something of a hellion—as brave and reckless as any boy. We got into more trouble than you can possibly imagine."

Bathsheba swallowed around the lump in her throat. Rachel had been much the same as a child—a veritable whirlwind—before the fever struck her down.

John's lips curled into a rueful smile. "My mother used to say we were little better than heathens, but Becky had such a sweetness about her. She grew up into a beautiful woman and fell in love with the local squire's son. My parents wanted her to look higher, but Becky refused. She loathed the idea of going to London and having a Season. Everything she wanted, everything she loved, was right at home. Eventually, my parents capitulated, and Becky married her sweetheart. She was more than content with her lot in life."

John paused and his expression grew dark, his mouth twisting into a disdainful sneer.

"I, on the other hand, couldn't wait to escape that boring country life. After finishing my studies, I moved to London to establish my practice. Becky wanted me to return home, but I couldn't bear the thought of it. The life of a country doctor, doing the same thing, day after day . . ."

He lapsed into silence, gazing at the floor with an almost baffled look.

Bathsheba let him brood for a minute before prompting him to continue. "Then what happened?"

He lifted his head, his gaze clouded with dark and bitter memories.

"Six months after I moved to London, Becky became pregnant. From the beginning, she had a difficult pregnancy. More than once I intended to go north to see her, but the demands of establishing my practice kept me too busy." He hesitated, casting a hooded glance her way before continuing, "And other things distracted me, as well."

A dull red glazed his cheekbones. Suddenly, she understood. There had been a woman involved, one who had enthralled him—so much that he had neglected his own sister. With a stab of jealousy, Bathsheba wondered if John had loved that woman more than he loved her. She found herself hating that shadowy rival for making him forget the people who loved and needed him most.

A jolt of dismay took her breath and cramped her stomach. Was she not doing much the same thing? Trying to convince him to give up what he wanted to do—for her?

Hot tears welled in her eyes but she blinked them back and focused on John. He studied her with a narrowed, intent gaze. She flushed, certain he could read every guilt-ridden thought spinning through her brain.

"Do you want to hear the rest?" he asked softly.

She nodded, not trusting her voice.

"Becky wrote to me several times, asking me to visit," he continued in a flat voice. "Finally my mother wrote, all but ordering me to return home. This time I did go, but the weather and the roads were against me. By the time I got there, Becky was near death. She had gone into labor and struggled for two agonizing days to deliver twins. Neither of the infants survived, and my sister died a few hours after I arrived home."

Bathsheba pressed a hand to her heart. Sweat prickled along her brow.

"I'm so sorry," she whispered.

John gave her an absent nod, then began to prowl the confines of the small room. His fingers brushed the leather-spined books on neatly arranged shelves.

"My mother blamed me, although she never said a word

to that effect. Father didn't—he always thought the best of me. But Becky's husband . . ."

He came to a halt in front of her. His shoulders hunched under the weight of a guilt he couldn't, or wouldn't, relinquish. Bathsheba understood because she lived with the same kind of useless emotion every day. But that kind of guilt never fixed or changed anything. John didn't deserve to be punished any longer for his sister's tragic death, and Bathsheba would be damned if she let him throw everything away—including their only chance for happiness—on a well-meaning but dangerous and ultimately foolish quest for redemption.

She took a deep, calming breath. Now she understood how much she needed him in her life, more than anything that had ever come before. She needed him to love her, and to care for her and Rachel. It had taken her days to acknowledge what should have been clear long ago—he belonged to her as surely as she belonged to him. And she wouldn't give him up without a fight.

"John, you can't know that you would have been able to save your sister," she said in a quiet voice. "Even if you had arrived in time, the outcome might well have been the same."

He shrugged, almost as if he didn't care. Tendrils of icy panic wrapped around her throat. He was already slipping away from her.

"I know you think you failed her," she continued, fighting to keep the desperation from her voice, "but you've made up for it a thousand times over. The work you do at Bart's, your plans for a new wing at the hospital. You already do so much. No one could ask more of you."

He met her gaze, and despair hollowed out her chest. His clear eyes, hard as flint, were full of a determination so obsessive that she knew she had little hope of winning him to her side.

"No, Bathsheba," he said. "All that is still not enough. I

made a promise on my sister's grave that I would help those who most needed it. I intend to keep that promise."

She gaped at him. "A promise to a dead woman is more important to you than I am? I can't believe your sister would want you to ruin your life like this."

He jerked back as if she had slapped him, and then anger flared in his eyes. She felt sick that she could utter such cruel words, but if he didn't come to his senses they were lost. His work would always come between them, eventually destroying everything, including him.

"I made the promise to myself," he ground out in a harsh voice. "But if Becky were alive she would never forgive me for turning my back on those who needed me."

"You mean you could never forgive yourself for not being able to save her," she retorted.

His eyes burned, but his face grew as cold as a stranger's. After a searching glance that swept her from head to toe, he turned away. Bathsheba sprang up, grabbing his arm with frantic haste.

"John, how can you know what your sister truly wanted? Do you really think she would be happy knowing you risked your life every day going into the rookeries? Would she want you to endanger your practice, your position at the hospital?"

He grimaced, but some of the anger drained from his face. Gently, he pried her hand from the fabric of his sleeve, holding her cold fingers in a comforting grip.

"Bathsheba," he said patiently, "you must understand—"

"I can't," she choked out. "But I do understand that your sister must have loved you very much. She would have wanted you to be happy, and not throw your life away because of guilt and some self-destructive promise you made to yourself."

He grasped her shoulders, gazing into her eyes. Tension and determination etched sharp angles into the contours of his face. Still, he kept his voice low and patient, and his hands drifted across her collarbone in a soothing stroke.

"Becky would want me to do what was right. After you recover from the fright you had today, you will, too. Bathsheba, you're stronger than you think you are. You can do this. For me, and for all those women who have no one else."

Shame twisted in her gut, giving her the strength to wrench away from his loose grasp.

"No, I'm not. You're a fool to think I am. And, in case you've forgotten, I have a sister, too. One you promised to support and care for, if we were to marry. What would I do—what would Rachel do—if anything were to happen to you? We would be penniless, with no one to support us."

John swore under his breath, shaking his head with frustration.

All the pulses in Bathsheba's body throbbed, matching the driving beat of her heart. Why couldn't he understand what she needed from him?

"John," she pleaded, sick with the thought of losing him, "I've already had one husband who nearly destroyed my life, leaving me with almost nothing. I can't go through that again. I need to know I can depend on you."

Shock, then fury, blazed on his face.

"Jesus Christ, Bathsheba! Do you really have the nerve to compare me to that bastard?"

She hated herself, but she had to say it. "You leave me no choice," she flung back. "You refuse to see the danger in what you do, and you're willing to risk everything, including my future, and Rachel's."

He stepped forward to loom over her. Inwardly she quailed, but she stood her ground. When he spoke, his mouth barely opened, so tightly did he clench his teeth.

"I'll always take care of you. And Rachel. You have my word."

She shook her head. Misery surged through her veins and swirled through her body, snatching the air from her lungs.

"You won't. You're convinced that you will, but your work, your . . . your mission will always come first. I won't be able to stand that. I must come first, John. Before anything else in your life."

"You *will* come first. Always." He spat each word out, as if the taste of them was sour.

Bathsheba covered her eyes, blocking out the sight of his fury. Her heart fluttered in her chest, beating against her ribs—against fate. She desperately searched for a way out.

There wasn't any.

"I don't believe you," she whispered.

Silence fell between them. The air in the small room grew stifling and heavy, settling around them like a shroud.

Finally, John stirred, letting out a great sigh. "Bathsheba, what in the name of God will convince you?"

She dropped her hand. He gazed down at her, implacable and stern.

"You know very well. Give up your work in the stews."

He shook his head. "If you truly loved me, Bathsheba, you wouldn't ask that of me."

Shame and grief strangled her. But then resentment welled up, swamping those other feelings. How many times in her life would a man insist she give up everything in order to prove her love?

Her determination came flooding back.

"Perhaps not," she replied. "But I will not risk my security, or Rachel's, for any man. Not even for you, John."

He stared at her in disbelief. "Then where does this leave us?"

She defiantly tilted her chin. "You will not stop?"

He gave her one, last searching look. "No."

Her heart folded in on itself. "Then I can't marry you, John. I hope you can forgive me."

She walked stiffly to the door, every muscle in her body screaming with leaden misery. As she reached for the knob, she glanced over her shoulder. John stood in the center of the room, still as a statue.

"And I hope you can forgive yourself," she whispered.

Chapter 25

"Lady Randolph," intoned a deep masculine voice. "May I have a moment?"

Bathsheba glanced up, meeting Lord Silverton's azure gaze as he descended the imposing marble staircase of his town house. Handing her parasol to a waiting footman, she conjured a friendly smile and stepped forward to greet him. He didn't return it, regarding her instead with a cool distrust.

Inwardly, she sighed. The last thing she needed was another confrontation with a hardheaded, arrogant man. She'd had enough of that lately to last a lifetime.

At the thought of John and their awful encounter, her smile wavered. Her spirits were low, and she was exhausted from lack of sleep, but she still believed she'd been right to reject him. At least that's what she told herself when she crawled into bed every night, her heart aching with loneliness and regret. But what other choice had the stubborn man given her?

"My lady, are you well?"

Silverton's voice, sharp with concern, brought her back to her senses.

"Quite, thank you," she said in a cheerful voice as she gave him her hand. "It's just this terrible heat. It makes one feel quite out of sorts, doesn't it?"

"To say the least," he said, his handsome face easing into a cautious smile. He gave a quick nod to the footman, who retreated to the front door.

"Allow me to escort you up to my wife," he said, giving her an elbow.

She took his arm, praying she wasn't in for a lecture. Lady Silverton—Meredith—might like her, but Bathsheba had no illusions her husband felt anything for her but disdain.

"I was very happy to receive Lady Silverton's note this morning," she said pleasantly, trying to lighten the tension. "I hope it means she's feeling better, if she's able to have visitors."

Silverton led her to the staircase. "I'm afraid not," he replied heavily.

Bathsheba studied him more closely and was startled to see him looking pale and heavy-eyed, as if he too hadn't slept well in days.

"I'm sorry to hear that," she said. "I hope Dr. Blackmore has found nothing seriously wrong."

She had to force herself not to stumble over John's name.

Silverton hesitated as they reached the top of the stairs.

"Lady Randolph, I'm sorry to say that Dr. Blackmore is no longer my wife's physician."

"What?" she blurted out, stunned by his words. "How is that possible? Please tell me you haven't brought Steele back to attend her. The man's a pompous ass."

She winced as soon as the words left her mouth. His lordship would undoubtedly escort her right back down the stairs and toss her into the square.

"I beg your pardon," she apologized. "I had no right to say that."

To her surprise, he gave her a smile, and not one of the chilly social ones he employed to keep people at a distance. This one was broad and warm, a dazzling grin that sent a ripple of pleasure up her spine. If not for her demented obsession with John, she might have fallen in love with Silverton right on the spot.

"That smile of yours is lethal, you know," she said, shaking her head. "I hope you realize that."

He laughed. "I'll take that as a compliment."

Taking her arm, he guided her down a hallway to the back of the house. His smile faded.

"As it happens," he said, frustration etched on his features, "I share your opinion of Dr. Steele. Unfortunately, Dr. Blackmore has declined to treat my wife. He sent a letter yesterday withdrawing his services. I called on him immediately and asked him to remain on her case, but he refused. No argument I could make was able to change his mind."

Bathsheba's stomach twisted into knots. Surely John wouldn't do something like this to punish her. There had to be another reason. "Did he say why?"

Silverton's eyebrows shot up. "You haven't heard?"

The ominous question kicked her heart up into her throat. "No. I . . . no, I haven't heard anything about Dr. Blackmore. Please tell me."

He stopped in front of a door at the end of the hallway. "I'll let my wife do that. She's eager to see you. If I hadn't agreed to send her note 'round to your house, I think she would have stolen a carriage and driven there herself."

Despite her anxiety, Bathsheba couldn't help smiling at Silverton's aggrieved expression. "I'm happy she sent for me. And I'll be glad to help in any way I can."

He paused, his hand on the doorknob as he perused her face. "I'm sure you would," he said softly. "You've surprised me, Lady Randolph. I don't mind telling you that."

"Don't let it bother you. I frequently surprise myself."

After a brief flash of that devastating smile, he turned serious again.

"Meredith tires easily. I would ask you to be aware of that. If she is not watched carefully, she tends to exhaust herself."

Impulsively, Bathsheba laid a hand on his arm, giving it

a reassuring squeeze. "I promise, my lord. Your wife is safe with me."

He opened the door and gestured her in. Bathsheba stepped into a sunny, delightful sitting room painted in shades of blue and pale lemon. The marchioness reclined on a large velvet sofa, her ample form wrapped in a crimson silk shawl.

"My love," the marquess said in a cheerful voice. "Here is Lady Randolph to visit you."

As Meredith struggled to get up, Bathsheba dashed to her side, several steps in front of Silverton.

"Lady Silverton," she scolded as she helped Meredith into a sitting position. "Don't you dare get up. You know very well you needn't stand on ceremony with me."

The marchioness drew in a shallow breath and flopped back onto the cushions. By this time, Lord Silverton had come behind her, gently inserting some extra pillows behind her back. Although looking wan and exhausted, she managed to give him a loving smile. Bathsheba had to bite back a foolish pang of jealousy.

After settling herself, Meredith extended a hand in greeting. "If we're not standing on ceremony, then you must call me by my given name, remember? And I promised to call you Bathsheba."

"I remember," Bathsheba replied. She snatched up the silk shawl from where it had slithered onto the floor, and draped it around Meredith's shoulders.

Lord Silverton dropped a kiss on the top of his wife's head. "I'll leave you ladies alone. Don't forget, Meredith," he admonished tenderly, "you're not to wear yourself out."

Meredith sighed as her husband left the room. "Honestly, I think this whole thing has been harder on him than on me."

"That I doubt," Bathsheba said, sitting down on a dainty Sheraton chair across from the sofa.

"You're right," Meredith replied morosely.

Bathsheba laughed. Meredith blushed and gave her a

shy smile, already looking better than she had just a few moments ago.

"I'm so glad you came to see me," the marchioness said. "Since Silverton saw Dr. Blackmore yesterday, I've been longing to speak with you. It's so unfair," she flared, her silver eyes glittering with outrage. "The hospital board had no right to treat him so shabbily."

Bathsheba's heart thudded at Meredith's alarming words. "I'm sorry. I'm afraid I don't know what you're talking about. I was indisposed for the last several days, and kept to my house."

She hadn't been sick at all, of course, unless one counted being sick at heart. But after her fight with John, she hadn't been able to stand the thought of re-embarking on her campaign to find a husband, or rattling about town. Not only had she driven away the only man who ever really loved her, she was right back in the same ugly situation she had been in a few weeks ago—under the hatches, waiting for the debt collectors to pull her to pieces.

Meredith's eyes opened wide with surprise and consternation.

"It's all right," Bathsheba said. "You can tell me."

The marchioness hesitated only a moment, but it was enough for Bathsheba to realize she should brace herself for the worst.

"The Board of Governors at Bart's informed Dr. Blackmore a few days ago that his services were no longer welcome," Meredith explained. "Apparently, a man living in St. Giles went to Bow Street and swore out a complaint with the magistrate. He claimed that Blackmore murdered his wife and newly born child."

"O'Neill," Bathsheba whispered, stunned that her fears had come true so quickly.

"I beg your pardon?"

Bathsheba shook her head impatiently. "Go on."

"Dr. Blackmore was brought into Bow Street for questioning. It was all nonsense, of course, and he was released, but the director of the hospital was furious."

Bathsheba clenched her gloved hand into a fist. "That would be Dr. Abernethy."

"Correct. He insisted the board dismiss Dr. Blackmore on the grounds that his conduct reflected poorly on the hospital and the board."

Bathsheba leapt up, unable to sit still a moment longer. "That's a lie! He's the best doctor they have."

"I'm sure he is," Meredith replied in a calming voice. "But apparently there were also concerns about his work in the East End. It would seem Dr. Abernethy had already warned Blackmore that his practice of going into the stews was damaging to the hospital's reputation. Dr. Abernethy took his concerns to the Board of Directors and, unfortunately, they agreed with him."

Bathsheba began wearing a path across the plush carpet, not caring if she looked like a madwoman. Furious with John for not heeding her warnings, she was even more furious with Abernethy and the fools on the board for their cavalier treatment of him.

Meredith watched her with sympathy, and something rather more perceptive. But she held her tongue.

After a few moments trying to expend her futile rage, Bathsheba came to a halt, more questions springing to mind.

"I understand John's anger," she said. "But why won't he treat you? How does what happened at the hospital affect his practice?"

Meredith grimaced. "You've really not heard any of the gossip these last few days?"

Bathsheba shook her head.

The marchioness sighed. "Dr. Blackmore has some powerful enemies. Word of his dismissal from Bart's, and rumors about the murder accusation, spread like fire through the ton. Silverton heard that the worst gossip was started by physicians jealous of his success. I don't need to tell you how quickly this kind of thing can destroy a person's reputation. Sadly, most of Blackmore's patients abandoned him immediately. His practice is in ruins."

Bathsheba sank back into her chair. Her anger drained away, replaced by a suffocating despair.

"We both know how unforgiving the ton can be," she said. Then she straightened up, frowning. "But I still don't see why John won't treat you. You don't care about the rumors, do you?"

Looking forlorn, Meredith spread her hands over her enormous stomach. "Of course not. Silverton pleaded with him, but Blackmore wouldn't be persuaded. He's closing his practice, and in a few days' time will move north to be near his family. Since my babies aren't due for another month, I must find someone else to treat me."

"I . . . I don't know what to say," Bathsheba stuttered. She never would have believed John would abandon a patient, no matter the circumstances. But surely not Meredith, a woman whose pregnancy must remind him of his sister's.

The marchioness gave a fatalistic shrug. "Dr. Blackmore told Silverton that the sooner he left London, the better. The gossip would fade more quickly if he did, with less damage to his reputation. Fortunately, he knows someone who can take over my case—Dr. Wardrop, his colleague."

Even though anguish shredded her heart, Bathsheba tried for a reassuring smile. "Dr. Wardrop is an excellent doctor. He'll take wonderful care of you and the babies."

Meredith sighed. "That's what Blackmore assured Silverton, but Dr. Wardrop is away from London until Tuesday. His assistant promised to have him come to Grosvenor Square immediately on his return."

Bathsheba suddenly noted Meredith's white face and drawn expression. Further discussion of John's situation would do the marchioness more harm than good. Besides, there would be plenty of time to brood over the whole mess later.

"Well," Bathsheba said in a bracing voice, "that's a relief.

I'm certain you'll like Dr. Wardrop. He's a most engaging man, and quite an outrageous flirt. Not that you would care about that, with a husband as charming as Lord Silverton."

Meredith narrowed her eyes, ignoring her conversational feint. "You're not fooling anyone, Bathsheba. You might as well tell me what happened between you and Blackmore."

Bathsheba's heart skipped several beats. "What . . . whatever can you be talking about, Meredith?"

"You refer to him as John," Meredith replied dryly. "Although I can tell simply by looking at your face how you feel about him."

Bathsheba slumped into her chair with a sigh. "It's that obvious, is it?"

"To me it is. But I doubt my husband would notice. He's hopeless when it comes to this sort of thing."

Bathsheba laughed. More of a choke, really, but it made her feel a bit better.

"You love him, don't you?" Meredith asked in a kind voice.

"I do," Bathsheba admitted, feeling more wretched by the second. "But I don't know what to do about it."

"Does he love you?"

Bathsheba nodded. "He asked me to marry him."

"Then what is the impediment? His current situation is distressing, but surely he can establish himself elsewhere. Money is no object for you, since you're already wealthy. Why can you not go north with him?"

Bathsheba shook her head, unable to force any words past the tears clogging her throat.

Meredith hesitated, then spoke warily. "I've been told you despise the country, and rarely leave London. But surely that can't be the reason. If you truly love each other, you could be happy anywhere."

Her mind a whirlwind of conflicting thoughts and emotions, Bathsheba couldn't find her voice.

"Forgive me," Meredith finally said in a cool voice. "I

have no right to pry. I'm sure you'll make the right decision, whatever that might be."

Bathsheba's heart took a sickening plunge. If Meredith thought she was that shallow . . .

"It's not that," she blurted out. "I'm afraid you don't understand my situation. I'm not rich at all. In fact, I'm poor. And if I don't do something soon, I'll lose everything."

She clapped both hands over her mouth, horrified by her impulsive confession. Why could she never learn to keep her blasted mouth shut?

"Oh, my dear, I had no idea," said Meredith, her cool demeanor evaporating instantly. "You must be consumed with worry. What can I do to help?"

In the face of such heartfelt sympathy, especially from a woman with her own troubles, all Bathsheba's defenses crumbled. She poured out everything—her dire financial situation, her wrenching estrangement from John. She even told Meredith about Rachel. Words rushed out, leaving her breathless. The marchioness listened quietly, her beautiful face alight with understanding, her silver eyes glistening with tears.

"Is that why you've entertained Sir David's advances?" she enquired when Bathsheba finally paused for breath.

"Of course. I hate the thought of it now, but it seemed sensible at the time. Sir David is kind, and he seems generous, but . . ."

"But there's Miss Roston." Meredith nodded. "I can't imagine the two of you living under the same roof."

Bathsheba rubbed her temples. Her head throbbed and her heart ached, but she felt strangely relieved. She had bottled up her feelings for so long that telling another person eased the burden.

"You're right." She sighed. "Miss Roston would make life difficult. But what choice do I have?"

"There's always a choice," Meredith said, her eyes going misty. "But sometimes one can't see it straight away."

"And sometimes one can, but it still doesn't help," Bathsheba replied bitterly.

Meredith grimaced and shifted awkwardly on her cushions.

Bathsheba studied her with concern. "Good Lord, Meredith! Why am I bothering you with my foolish tale of woe? Your husband will have my head if I tire you out."

"I'm fine," the marchioness replied, though she looked anything but. "It's just that my back hurts like the devil. But that doesn't matter. What matters is you, and what you're going to do about Dr. John Blackmore."

"There's nothing more to do. He'll go north and start a new life, and I'll marry Sir David," she said firmly, hoping to close the discussion. "It's not what I truly want, but at least I won't be poor. And I'll be able to care for Rachel. That's what matters most."

"Yes, but—" Meredith broke off on a shuddering gasp as she hunched over her belly.

Bathsheba shot to her feet. "What's happening, Meredith?"

The marchioness looked up, her face ashen and pulled tight with pain. "I'm not sure, but I think I might be in labor."

Chapter 26

Meredith squeezed Bathsheba's hand in a punishing grip, doubling over as another contraction slammed through her body. Bathsheba held on tightly, forcing back a surge of panic. The marchioness had been in labor for over thirteen hours, and still she made no progress.

As the long day crawled into night, Meredith had grown weaker and weaker, each contraction driving her closer to exhaustion. Fear had crept into the spacious dressing room where the portable birthing bed had been set up. Even the monthly nurse, the redoubtable Mrs. Griffiths, had begun to look anxious.

Bathsheba winced as Meredith's fingernails clawed into the soft flesh of her palm. It hurt like the devil, but she thanked God the marchioness retained some of her strength. If only the blasted doctor would arrive, all might yet be well. Perhaps it was even normal for there to be so much pain when birthing twins.

As the contraction passed, Meredith collapsed onto the pillows. Her younger sister, Annabel, stationed on the other side of the bed, gently sponged her face with a cool, wet cloth.

"There, darling," the girl murmured, "you did splendidly that time. I'm sure those little babies must be getting very close to being born."

Meredith gave her sister a weary smile. Bathsheba couldn't help smiling at Annabel, too. The slender, sweet-faced girl—young woman, really—had a strength of character and calm presence Bathsheba had come to appreciate over the course of the drawn-out, difficult day.

"Good Lord, I hope you're right," Meredith croaked. "I don't know how much longer I can stand this."

Bathsheba glanced over at Mrs. Griffiths, crouched at the foot of the bed. The nurse slid Meredith's shift up to her knees and took a quick look. After a moment, she hissed out a tight breath and switched her gaze to Annabel, giving a quick shake of the head.

Bathsheba's heart plummeted. "Where is that blasted pig of a doctor?" she grumbled without thinking. Annabel gave a surprised squeak, and Meredith's eyes snapped open.

"Oh, my fool mouth, again," groaned Bathsheba. "Ignore me, Meredith. I'm sure Dr. Steele will be here straight away. Everything is going to be fine."

Meredith managed a thin laugh. "Don't apologize. I think he's a pig, too, but I'd put up with a whole roomful of barnyard animals if only someone would get these babies out of me."

Mrs. Griffiths snorted and Annabel giggled, easing the tension in the room.

"I'm sure they'll be out soon enough," soothed Bathsheba as she massaged Meredith's hand. "And then you can spend the rest of your life scolding them for making such a troublesome entrance into the world."

Meredith cast her a grateful smile. "I'm so glad I asked you to stay with me today. You've been such a comfort."

Bathsheba's throat closed with emotion. She had to work not to let tears well up into her eyes. But she would be damned if she gave into them, at least not until this was all over.

"I'm quite sure no one's ever called me *that* before," she said in a teasing voice. "I must ask you to put that in writing, else no one will believe it."

"Well, you have been a marvelous help," Annabel defended stoutly. "I wouldn't have believed it if I hadn't seen it for myself."

"Annabel," Meredith protested. Bathsheba laughed.

Their short respite ended as another fierce contraction seized Meredith's body. This one lasted even longer than the previous one, and it wrung every ounce of strength from the marchioness's body.

Meredith flopped back with her eyes closed, sweating and as gray as death. With a nod, Bathsheba motioned Mrs. Griffiths to follow her to the door. Annabel stayed where she was, fighting back tears as she dabbed her sister's forehead.

"Has Dr. Steele been sent for again?" Bathsheba asked the nurse in a quiet voice.

"Yes, Lady Randolph," the nurse whispered back. "I told Lord Silverton an hour ago that my lady needed the doctor. I'm worried. I'm sure one baby's head is lodged against Lady Silverton's pelvis." She cast an anxious glance toward the bed. "I know Dr. Steele had to attend another delivery, but the housekeeper downstairs told me Lady Winbury had her baby hours ago. Her cousin works in the Winbury household, and she sent word right away."

Bathsheba cursed quietly. The entire day had been one frustration after another. When Meredith went into labor, the household had sprung into action. Mrs. Griffiths had been summoned, and Silverton had dispatched a footman to fetch John. But the footman had returned with the distressing news that John had gone to visit a poor patient in the East End. Only his kitchen maid had been at home, and she had no idea how to find him or when he would return.

After two more attempts to find Blackmore, Silverton had reluctantly sent for Dr. Steele. To his credit, the older man had come quickly and had refrained from disparaging John. But he had scowled when Silverton told him that Meredith was pregnant with twins, and had sharply demanded to know how that fact had been ascertained. But when the marquess leveled his quizzing glance at him, the doctor had flushed a mottled red and murmured an apology, hastily turning his attention to Meredith.

"There's no cause for alarm, my lady," Steele had pronounced after examining her. "Your pain is in no way out of the ordinary, I assure you. But you must be patient. Nature must take her course, and no amount of prodding on our part will do any good."

Bathsheba had been tempted to put the idiot in his place for that unfeeling statement, but Annabel had hastily stepped in, asking the doctor what they should do in the meantime.

"Simply ensure her ladyship is calm and comfortable," he had replied. "Mrs. Griffiths will know what to do. I'll return later this afternoon to check on her progress. Lady Winbury is also in labor, and I must attend her immediately. After all," he had said with a hearty chuckle, "she is the daughter of a duke, and a duke trumps a marquess any day of the week."

With that appalling comment, Dr. Steele had sailed from the room.

When he returned later in the day, he checked Meredith and then cheerfully pronounced she had many hours of labor ahead before she delivered. He had taken himself off again, promising to return after calling on another patient. At that point, Silverton had been ready to throttle him, but a few quiet words from Annabel had defused the worst of his anger.

But it was now well into the evening, and Steele had yet to return. Casting a worried glance at Meredith's pale, perspiring face, Bathsheba opened the door to the bedroom.

"I'm going to find Lord Silverton," she said to Mrs. Griffiths. "I'll be right back."

She hurried down the staircase, following the sound of voices into the drawing room. Not waiting for the footman, she threw open the door and halted on the threshold.

Robert Stanton and his grandparents, General and Lady Stanton, sat huddled at one end of the room. They turned at the sound of the door opening, and the general and Robert glared at her with undisguised hostility. Lady Stanton, however, simply appeared tired and anxious.

Bathsheba swallowed a sigh, and advanced into the room. "Forgive me," she said. "I'm looking for Lord Silverton."

"He's gone out to find that quack Steele," barked the general. "The man should have been here hours ago. A pretty turn of events when a marquess has to scour the town to find a blasted physician."

Lady Stanton gave her husband a quelling glance. "Do come in, Lady Randolph. Sit for a moment. You must be tired, and we would be grateful for any news."

Bathsheba hesitated, but Lady Stanton's offer seemed genuine. She sank onto the settee next to Robert, who immediately inched away from her. Repressing the urge to roll her eyes, she dredged up a smile for the older woman.

"I'm afraid I have little to report," she said apologetically. "Nothing much seems to be happening, and that causes Mrs. Griffiths some concern. I intended to double-check to ensure Dr. Steele had been sent for."

"Of course he's been sent for," retorted the general. "Do you think we're all sitting around down here like a bunch of addlepated boobs?"

Lady Stanton actually did roll her eyes, and Bathsheba had to choke back a laugh.

"Not at all, General," Bathsheba managed to reply in a calm voice. "Please forgive me for seeming impertinent. My actions are a reflection of my own anxiety, I'm sure."

The general subsided with a grumble, looking slightly mollified.

"How is Meredith holding up?" Robert asked hesitantly.

There was no point in lying, but neither did Bathsheba want to unduly worry them. "She's in quite a bit of pain, but I would think that's perfectly natural when having twins."

Lady Stanton smiled. "It's perfectly natural when one is having a baby, period, my dear."

Bathsheba was about to agree when she heard voices in

the entrance hall. She jumped up and hurried out to see Lord Silverton and Dr. Steele handing their hats and walking sticks to the butler.

"My lord, Dr. Steele," she exclaimed in a low voice. "I'm so happy to see you."

Anxiety flashed through Silverton's eyes. "Is Meredith all right?"

"Yes, but she continues to be in a great deal of pain. Mrs. Griffiths is anxious to see you, Dr. Steele."

The physician gave her a jovial laugh. "Nurses always tend toward the hysterical, Lady Randolph. I'm sure everything is perfectly fine. Frankly, it's too bad Dr. Blackmore had already engaged Mrs. Griffiths. The nurse I work with— a most respectable woman—is a paragon of good sense."

"Mrs. Griffiths came highly recommended," Silverton replied dryly. "By the Queen, among others."

"Oh, quite," Steele huffed, flushing a dull shade of red.

Silverton led the way upstairs, his long legs taking the risers three at a time. Bathsheba hurried after him, while Steele trudged along behind with offended dignity.

By the time Bathsheba reached Meredith's dressing room, Silverton had already crouched down by her side, stroking her tangled hair from her brow. She breathed a sigh of relief that the marchioness looked a bit stronger than she had only a few minutes ago.

"Well, now, Lady Silverton," exclaimed Steele as he came into the room. "I have a report that you are in pain. Surely you know that a little pain in childbirth is no cause for alarm."

Meredith gave a weak snort, but held her tongue. Annabel didn't.

"It's hardly a little pain, my good sir," she exclaimed. "She almost fainted after her last contraction. Not that you would know, since you weren't anywhere to be seen," she finished in a sarcastic voice.

Steele began to bluster, but Silverton cut him off with a hand gesture.

"Annabel," the marquess said in a kind voice, "why don't you go down and sit with Robert and your grandparents. They're most anxious to see you."

Annabel looked outraged. "I have no intention of leaving Meredith."

Her sister reached for her hand. "I insist, darling. You've been up here for hours. I don't even know when you've eaten last."

"I'm fine," growled Annabel, even though she was almost as pale as her sister.

Bathsheba stepped up to the bed. "Annabel, go sit with your family and have something to eat. I'll stay with Meredith."

The girl looked mulish, but Bathsheba crossed to help her up from the floor. "Once you've eaten, you can come back up and take my place. I'm sure I'll be famished myself by then."

"Well, all right," Annabel grumbled. "But I'll be back in half an hour."

"I'll be waiting," Bathsheba promised.

The girl left and Bathsheba sat next to Meredith, taking her hand in a reassuring clasp.

"Now, Dr. Steele," Bathsheba said, "perhaps you might get to work and deliver these babies."

The doctor gave her an offended look—the man appeared to be perpetually offended—but positioned himself at the foot of the bed.

"Lady Silverton," he said with a frown, "why aren't you lying on your left side?"

"It hurts when I do that. Lying on my back causes less pain."

Grousing to himself about newfangled ideas, Dr. Steele reached under the marchioness's shift and began examining her. Meredith gasped and bit her lip, squeezing Bathsheba's hand. Silverton stroked her face and murmured comforting words into her ear. His blue eyes glittered with emotion, but his voice was steady and warm with affection.

Under his calming influence, Meredith began to relax. She stared up at him, and even though her eyes were dull with pain and her skin slicked with perspiration, her obvious love for Silverton made her seem almost serene.

Bathsheba dropped her gaze, struggling to swallow the lump in her throat and push back the sense of terrible loss that threatened to swamp her. She would never again know the kind of love that flowed with palpable energy between Meredith and Silverton.

Taking a deep breath, she forced her attention onto the doctor. Her heart stuttered at the grim look on his jowly face.

Mrs. Griffiths leaned over and whispered into his ear.

"Yes, yes," he responded irritably. "I realize the situation. I don't need you to explain it to me."

Silverton's head came up. "What's wrong?"

"My lord," the doctor said, "may I talk to you in the other room?"

"No!" Meredith's voice was surprisingly forceful. "You will talk to us both, Doctor. Is something wrong with my babies?"

"My lord," responded Steele, now looking very nervous. "It would be more appropriate if I spoke to you first."

Silverton hesitated, looking down at his wife. Anguish pulled his handsome features into a tight mask.

Meredith groped for his hand. "My love," she said, "whatever it is, we'll get through it together."

He gazed at his wife for a moment, then nodded. "Whatever it is you have to say," he said, never taking his eyes off Meredith, "you can say to both of us."

"Very well," Steele replied stiffly. "One of the babies is lodged tightly against Lady Silverton's pelvis. I cannot turn it, and no amount of pushing will free the head. It's . . . it's stuck. I'm sorry."

Meredith groaned and dropped her head on Silverton's shoulder.

"Good God, man, don't apologize," snapped Bathsheba. "Tell us what is to be done. Her ladyship can't take much more of this."

"There is only one thing to do, under the circumstances. We must act to save Lady Silverton's life. If we are very lucky, we might be able to save the second child. But even then, the chances are slim."

Bathsheba froze, and both Meredith and Silverton gaped in horror at the doctor. The marquess found his voice first.

"Are you absolutely certain of that?"

"Quite, my lord. This is not the first such case I've seen."

"No," Meredith cried, thrashing her head on the pillow. "You must save my baby."

"My lady," pleaded the doctor. "There is no other way, I promise you. I must crush the baby's head and extract the rest of its body. If I don't, you will die."

Meredith's protesting wail filled the room. Black dots danced in front of Bathsheba's eyes as a wave of shock washed over her. She clenched her teeth and gripped Meredith's hand as she forced her head to clear.

Silverton snapped his attention back to Meredith and tried to soothe her, even though he looked enraged and terrified, all at once. He clearly had his hands full with his distraught wife.

Bathsheba rose to her feet, keeping a firm grasp on Meredith's cold hand.

"Dr. Steele," she said in a hard voice. "There must be something else you can do. I refuse to believe this is your only alternative."

He began to bluster about all his years of experience, but Bathsheba's eye was caught by Mrs. Griffiths, who stood behind him, vigorously shaking her head.

Bathsheba cut Steele off with a sharp gesture.

"Mrs. Griffiths, do you have something to say?" she asked.

Steele fell silent, apparently stunned by Bathsheba's question. The nurse cast a worried look between Steele and Meredith, who was now sobbing quietly in Silverton's arms.

"Go on. Please," Bathsheba encouraged the nurse.

"Well, my lady," Mrs. Griffiths began, "I've seen Dr. Blackmore—"

"This is outrageous," Steele roared. "That you would even think to place my word against that quack, that . . . that murderer."

Bathsheba gasped with outrage, but Silverton's voice—cold and deadly—sliced through the room.

"Dr. Steele, you will shut your mouth or I will shut it for you. Do I make myself clear?"

Steele gaped at him, but then gave a weak nod.

"Good," said the marquess. "Mrs. Griffiths, please continue."

"As I was saying, sir, I've seen Dr. Blackmore save more than one mother and child in this situation, using forceps."

"Forceps!" exploded Steele.

Another look from Silverton sent Steele into a fuming silence.

"Yes, forceps," Mrs. Griffiths said defiantly. "Those that know how to use them can save many lives, and Dr. Blackmore knows what he's about. He's the best man-midwife I've ever worked with."

Steele wiped beads of sweat from his purpling forehead. "Lord Silverton, I beg of you. This is the only way. You must trust me. It is madness—"

Meredith's voice came low and harsh from the bed. "Get out of my house. Now."

Bathsheba swung around, her mouth falling open at the sight of the marchioness. She'd pushed herself up on her pillows, her black hair a wild tangle around her head, and her silver eyes blazing with hatred. She looked like an avenging goddess, and Bathsheba could almost believe she was about to rise up and throw Steele out on his ear.

"But, my lady," whimpered Steele.

"You will not hurt my babies," spat Meredith. "Get out."

Silverton stood and took a menacing step toward the doctor. "You heard my wife. Leave now."

Shocked, Steele took his bag and fled out the door.

A stunned silence filled the room. Then Meredith doubled over with a keening wail of pain. Silverton sank down beside her, gathering her up in his arms. He lifted his face, now drained and pale with fear, and stared at the nurse.

"Are you sure about this, Mrs. Griffiths?"

"I am, sir. If anyone can save those babies and Lady Silverton, it's Dr. Blackmore."

He switched his pleading gaze to Bathsheba, who was already scrambling to grab her reticule and bonnet.

"Don't worry," Bathsheba said as she yanked on her bonnet, all askew. "I'll find him. If I have to search every blasted alley in St. Giles to do it."

"Take Robert with you. He can help," called Silverton as she rushed to the door.

Mrs. Griffiths followed her. She gripped Bathsheba's arm.

"Hurry, Lady Randolph," she whispered. "I don't think she has much time."

Chapter 27

Trying to keep her face dry, Bathsheba ducked her head as Robert handed her from the carriage and onto the slippery pavement of Drury Lane. In keeping with their wretched luck all day, it had started to rain—a steady downpour that would soak them in minutes. Worse, the foul weather would hamper their search. Fortunately, at least they now had some notion where to seek John out.

After rushing from Silverton House, Bathsheba and Robert had headed to Market Lane in the faint hope that John had returned to his town house. He hadn't, but his manservant Jordan was there. He told them John had been called some hours ago to St. Giles to treat two patients—a young woman in labor and an elderly man dying of consumption.

Bathsheba had been horrified at the idea of searching the tangled laneways of the rookery, especially at night. But when Jordan explained that the pregnant woman lived in the same slum as the Butler family—the flower girl, Bess, and her parents—Bathsheba's spirits lifted. She just might be able to recognize the tenement where Bess lived, if she could manage not to get them hopelessly lost or murdered first.

After a hurried discussion, she and Robert developed a plan. Jordan would go with them to St. Giles. He knew where the dying man lived, so he would look for John there. Bathsheba and Robert would try to find John's other patient. Although the prospect of searching the stews made her grow faint, the only alternative was to wait for John to return to Market Lane. By then, it might be too late for Meredith. Much worse to confront the terrors of the rookery than to face that possibility.

Bathsheba waited impatiently as the coachman unhooked a lantern from the carriage and handed it to Robert. Jordan had already faded into the night, disappearing into the shadows of Coal Yard like a wraith.

"Are you sure about this, Lady Randolph?" Robert asked, casting the lantern light onto her face. "You could wait here with the horses, and the coachman could come with me. I'm sure I could find the right building if you gave me directions."

She snorted and turned her back on him. "We're not going for a stroll in Mayfair," she flung back over her shoulder as she strode into the darkened laneway. "You'll never find the place without me."

Despite her bravado, her legs trembled so badly she wondered how she managed to stay upright. More than anything, she longed to climb back into the carriage and huddle in the corner, leaving the men to search for John. But only she could find the place they were looking for in the confusing mass of tumble-down structures that made up this part of the stews. Letting her nerves get the best of her was unacceptable. She was Meredith's only hope—she and John, together.

Robert scrambled to catch up with her. "No need for sarcasm, Lady Randolph," he grumbled. "And I suggest you let me go first with the lantern. It's dark as pitch in there. If you run head-first into a wall and knock yourself out, don't expect me to pick you up."

She gave a surprised choke of laughter. "How very rude of you, Mr. Stanton. Whatever would your grandfather say?"

"I expect he would agree with me," he retorted.

"You're probably right," she said absently, scanning the buildings in the fitful light cast by the lantern.

She reached out and grabbed his sleeve, jerking him to halt at the junction of a laneway and two alleys. Her heart raced with fear and frustration as she tried to remember which way to go. She cursed, unable to make up her mind. Robert took her hand in a reassuring clasp.

"Take a deep breath and try not to think too hard for the answer," he said. "That usually works for me when I've forgotten something, or when I'm afraid."

She gave an irritated sigh but did as he suggested, closing her eyes and trying to let the tension fade away. Gradually, her pulse slowed and her mind cleared. Then she opened her eyes and let them wander where they would. Suddenly, she knew exactly where to go.

"That way," she exclaimed eagerly, pointing to an alley branching off to the right.

Robert pulled her forward, holding the lantern high above their heads. The rain hissed down and spattered off broken pavement. She stumbled into a muddy hole, but Robert held her upright in a sturdy grip.

They made steady progress into the nightmare landscape and, strangely, Bathsheba grew ever more confident. Despite the rain and gloom, she began to recognize landmarks. As frightened as she'd been that day with John, she'd obviously kept enough of her wits to know where they were going.

They rounded a corner. After a brief hesitation, she led them through a deserted courtyard. She jumped when something scuttled by, brushing against her skirts. But that was the only living creature in the place. The rain, at least, had done that much for them—kept the most dangerous predators in the rookery safely in their lairs.

"That was a good trick," she said to Robert as they hurried through the courtyard. "Thank you for helping me."

"My grandfather taught me that. It was a trick he used during battle, when fear threatened to get the best of him."

They exchanged brief smiles, then clasped hands tightly as they plunged into the black maw of another laneway. A few candles flickered here and there behind broken windows or tattered curtains, but darkness loomed on all sides—thick and suffocating. If not for the light cast by the lantern, they would have been lost in the encompassing gloom.

As they emerged from the alley into another courtyard, a rough murmur of male voices brought them up short. Robert hissed out a warning and pulled her into a deserted doorway. He peered cautiously around the edge of the door frame, keeping the light well behind him.

He muttered a curse under his breath.

"What is it?" she whispered.

"There's a group of men in front of that building," he returned. "Lady Randolph, you must stay back. I don't like the looks of this."

"Robert, please stop calling me Lady Randolph. It's annoying and ridiculous under the circumstances."

"I most certainly won't," he huffed. "No need to lose one's manners simply because one could be knifed by a ruffian at any moment."

"Do get out of the way," she ordered, shoving past him. "I can't see anything."

She peered through the rain at the knot of men gathered under the sagging portico of a tenement. Her heart thumped with relief and excitement.

"I know those men! We found it."

"Lady Randolph—Bathsheba, wait!" Robert cried.

Ignoring him, she raced across the courtyard and skidded to a halt in front of the men. They gaped at her, stunned into silence. All but one. He calmly removed a blackened pipe from between his teeth and ran his gaze over her sodden figure.

"You be lookin' for the doctor, I reckon. Must be a terrible lot of trouble you're in for you to be riskin' your pretty neck in this part of town."

It was Mrs. Butler's neighbor—the one who had complained about the squalling baby.

Robert came up behind her in a rush, thrusting himself between Bathsheba and the men.

"Here," he said loudly. "You stay away from her, you lout."

A growl rumbled up in concert from several throats. Her pipe-smoking friend, however, barely gave the young man a glance.

"Do stop acting like an idiot, Robert," Bathsheba snapped, elbowing him out of the way. "This man is a friend of John's. He can help us."

The men's grumbles turned into laughter, and several ribald jokes were made at Bathsheba's and Robert's expense. The pipe smoker waved them to silence.

"You speak rightly, missus. How can I help you?"

"Is Dr. Blackmore here? With the woman having a baby?"

The man's rough face split into a grin. "That he is, and that be my grandson he delivered a few minutes ago. Safe and sound. And my daughter, too."

Bathsheba staggered as a wave of relief washed through her, so strong that her head spun. A meaty paw shot out and gripped her elbow.

"Careful now, missus. Don't want to fall and bust your pretty head."

She sucked in a wavering breath and found her balance. "Can you take me to the doctor? It's urgent."

He knocked his pipe against the building and stowed it in his pocket. "It always is when there's a doctor involved, ain't it?"

Jerking his head for them to follow, he led them into a dingy hall and to the back of the building. Bathsheba's heart thudded with an erratic and painful beat, both at the thought of seeing John again and that they had found him so easily. With a little luck, they would be back in Grosvenor Square less than an hour after they left.

Their companion threw open a door and nodded for them to step through. Bathsheba blinked in the bright light cast by several branches of candles and a lamp. After a moment, the dancing motes in her vision cleared and a tall, broad-shouldered figure swam into focus.

John.

He cradled a swaddled infant in his arms as he spoke in a low voice to a tired-looking young woman on a cot in the corner. Bathsheba stumbled forward, fighting the impulse to burst into tears.

At the sound of her footsteps, John's head came up. He froze, staring at her with a blank expression. She gave him a tentative smile, but before she could say a word his silver gaze blazed into furious life.

"Jesus Christ, Bathsheba," he said with a growl. "What the hell are you doing here?"

Bathsheba stood as if nailed to the rotten floorboards, the half-smile curving her plush lips fading away. John had thought never to see her again, and yet there she was. Rising before him like a beautiful apparition—an enticing dream, one that had tormented him every night, just as the memory of her heartless rejection had dogged him during the endless hours of the day. When he wasn't being hauled off on murder charges, that is, or seeing his life's work crumble into dust. The fact that Bathsheba had been right about that last one, too, had made it a cruelly bitter potion to swallow.

She stared back at him, her slender throat working, trying to force words up into her mouth. The fashionably dressed young man beside her took her arm in a possessive grip, glowering at John with open suspicion.

Jealousy clawed deep in John's gut. "Who are you?" he demanded.

The young man bristled. He did a good job of it, given his sodden state.

"I'm Robert Stanton," he said. "Are you Dr. Blackmore?"

John nodded, then gently handed Sarah Repton her baby. It had been a difficult labor for the girl, and the last thing she needed was two dripping strangers causing a scene.

Even if one of them was Bathsheba.

"Let's go out into the hallway," he said.

He stalked across the room, running his gaze over Bathsheba as he did so. Her soaked walking dress clung to every curve, putting her ample charms on brazen display.

"What were you thinking coming down here, especially in this weather?" he snapped as he jerked her away from Stanton and pushed her into the hallway. "You could have been killed—or worse. And you're drenched. Have you lost your mind?"

Bathsheba yanked her arm away and glared up at him. She looked like a bedraggled waif, and a furious one at that. Yet he still wanted to plaster her body against his and cover her lips with a smothering kiss.

What a fool he was.

"I came looking for you because I had no other choice, you tiresome man," she said through clenched teeth. "We've been to your house twice today, but you couldn't be found. Because you were too busy running away from your responsibilities!"

Fury exploded inside him. "What the hell do you think I was doing with that girl and her baby? Playing whist?"

She grabbed his waistcoat and came up on her toes, shoving her face right up to his. "We needed you, John . . . I needed you. And you couldn't be found." Then she burst into tears.

Baffled and stunned, he wrapped an arm around her

shoulders and looked at Stanton, who stared at them with a bemused expression on his face.

"What's this all about?" John asked as Bathsheba sobbed into his chest.

"It's Lady Silverton," the young man replied. "She's gone into labor. Something's wrong. Steele wanted to—"

"Steele? Why the hell is he with Lady Silverton? She's not his patient!"

Bathsheba gave a hiccup and pushed out of his arms. "No, she's not. But you abandoned her, and Wardrop is out of town. Lord Silverton couldn't find anyone else but Steele."

"I didn't abandon her," retorted John. "You know that, Bathsheba. Or you would have, if you hadn't abandoned *me*."

She gasped with outrage and jabbed a finger into his chest. "Why, you—"

"Excuse me," interrupted Stanton in a testy voice. "Meredith is in trouble. We've got to get back to Silverton House before it's too late to save her."

Bathsheba looked stricken. "It's true, John. One of the babies is lodged against her pelvis. Mrs. Griffiths thinks you're the only one who can save them."

John cursed as frustration sliced through him. He'd been certain Lady Silverton wouldn't give birth for at least three more weeks. Once again he'd misjudged, letting his own life get in the way of his patient's well-being, just as he had all those years ago with Becky.

"I'll get my bag. You can tell me the details on the way to the carriage."

He charged back into the room and gathered his instruments. Bathsheba hovered in the doorway, looking anxious, while Stanton peered over her shoulder.

"Lady Ran—Bathsheba," Stanton said in a ridiculously loud stage whisper. "Are you sure Dr. Blackmore's up to this? He looks like the very devil."

"Oh, do shut up, Robert," Bathsheba replied. "He's the best doctor in the city."

Stanton looked mortally offended, but John couldn't hold back a grudging laugh.

"He's right, Bathsheba. I do look like the devil, which I have you partly to thank for."

She starched right up, ready to argue, but he cut her off.

"Enough," he said. "We'll have plenty of time to fight later."

Dick Repton, Sarah's father, had been watching their little scene play out with a lively interest. He finally took his pipe from between his lips to speak.

"Anything I can do to help, Doc? Like throw that young pup out on his ear?"

"That won't be necessary, Mr. Repton. Just keep a close eye on Sarah and the baby. I'll be back tomorrow."

John closed his bag and headed for the door, grabbing Bathsheba as he went. After giving Dick Repton a scowl, Stanton followed them, grumbling under his breath.

They hurried down the hallway and out into the courtyard. The rain still teemed, and they had to splash their way through puddles as deep as their ankles. John cast a worried look at Bathsheba, but he had to hope she was strong enough to fight off any ill effects of the dank night. Regardless, he'd deal with that later. Lady Silverton must come first.

He raised his voice over a rumble of thunder. "How long has her ladyship been in labor?"

Bathsheba held onto his arm as she hurried to keep up. "I've been with her—"

She broke off and gave a strangled shriek as something jerked her backward and away from him.

John spun around and his heart seized. O'Neill had appeared out of nowhere, his rage-distorted features illuminated by a flash of lightning. He clutched Bathsheba tight against his body, one massive arm clamped across her chest.

And he pointed a pistol at her temple.

John froze. If she moved even a fraction, the pistol could go off and blow her skull to pieces. She stared back at him with huge eyes, her face pulled tight with fear.

Stanton slid to a halt off to the side. "Who the hell is he?" he yelped.

John laid a restraining hand on his arm, but Stanton shook it off.

"Look here, fellow," he said to O'Neill in a sharp voice, "if it's money you're after, I'll give you my purse. Let the lady go and we'll be on our way."

O'Neill slowly backed into the courtyard, dragging Bathsheba with him. She said not a word, only staring at John with a pleading look on her face. His soul wrenched with anguish, but he pushed down the fear that threatened to choke him. If O'Neill saw how much she meant to him, Bathsheba would be done for.

"Let her go, O'Neill," he said. "She means nothing to you. It's me you want."

Robert bit back an oath, but had the sense to keep his mouth shut.

"Aye, Doctor," the big man growled. "I want you dead. I've been following you, biding my time. I was going to kill you tonight, but when I spied your doxy here, I got me a better idea."

John's heart threatened to beat its way out of his chest. "She means nothing to me," he managed in a calm voice. "She was just delivering a message."

O'Neill pulled back his lips in a travesty of a grin and nudged the pistol against Bathsheba's head. Her eyes opened even wider, but she didn't make a sound.

The Irishman laughed—an ugly, echoing sound that rang off the walls of the tenements. "You won't bamboozle me anymore. You killed Mary and my boy, and now I'll have my revenge."

John opened his hands wide and took a step forward.

O'Neill jerked back, hauling Bathsheba to the center of the courtyard.

"You've already had your revenge, O'Neill. I've lost everything—my position at the hospital, and my practice. I'll be leaving London in a few days, completely ruined. Isn't that enough for you?"

"No! It's not enough," O'Neill snarled. "Fool I was to listen to that bloody cove in the first place . . . the one that told me to swear out that bleedin' complaint. You toffs never get what you deserve. It's only the likes of me that swing from the end of a rope."

John frowned. "What cove? What are you talking about?"

"Steele, his name was. He saw me at the hospital, with that other one—the old doctor who runs the place."

"Steele saw you with Abernethy?" John asked, hardly able to take it in.

"Aye, that's him. Steele came after me that day and told me to go to the magistrate. Said you would hang for killing Mary." O'Neill turned his head and spat. "Shoulda known better than to trust an Englishman."

Rage burned in John's gut, but he thrust it aside. He couldn't afford to be distracted by Steele's calumny.

"I understand your need for revenge," he said. "I'm willing to do whatever you want, O'Neill. Just let the woman go."

Out of the corner of his eye, John caught young Stanton slowly inching along a wall, moving behind O'Neill. Fortunately, the other man was too focused on John to notice the movement.

"See, now, that's the beauty of it." O'Neill sneered. "I'll have my revenge. I'll kill your lady, like you killed mine. And you'll spend the rest of your life knowin' she died because of you."

John inhaled a deep breath, willing himself to remain calm. Every muscle in his body screamed for him to lunge at O'Neill, but that would surely mean death for Bathsheba.

"No," he finally said. "I can't let you do that." He took

another step forward. As he'd hoped, O'Neill swung the pistol away from Bathsheba and pointed it straight at him.

"John, don't," she shrieked. "Meredith needs you. Just go to her!"

"Shut your gob," O'Neill snarled as he crushed his arm into her chest. She gasped in pain, and John again had to beat back the urge to fling himself at O'Neill.

"It's all right, Bathsheba," he said. "I'm not leaving you. I won't ever leave you."

By now, Stanton had circled behind O'Neill. He crouched down and stealthily picked up a rock.

"John, don't be a fool—" Bathsheba choked out. But her voice died as he gazed at her face. A silent moment of communication passed between them. Her trembling mouth firmed with determination.

"I won't let you kill her," John said, taking another step forward. "And you're not going to kill me, either."

O'Neill practically frothed at the mouth, maddened with rage. "No? Just watch me."

He cocked the pistol and John launched himself through the air. At the same time, Bathsheba jostled O'Neill's arm with her free hand.

The pistol discharged and the shot rang off the pavement as John barreled into the Irishman, knocking them all to the ground in a heap. As he wrestled with O'Neill, the two of them slipping about in the mud, he felt rather than saw Stanton pull Bathsheba to safety.

O'Neill roared out an oath and swung a massive fist at John's chin. John jerked his head away, but the heavy blow landed on his shoulder. Pain blurred his vision, but he shook it off and wrapped his hands around O'Neill's skull, banging it into the pavement.

The crazed man barely seemed to register the blow. After a short, desperate struggle, John found himself on his back with O'Neill's crushing weight on top of him. Beefy fingers clawed at his throat, trying to find purchase. John wedged a hand under O'Neill's chin, shoving with all his might, but the man didn't budge.

Suddenly, he heard a sickening thud. O'Neill stared down at him, his pupils dilating in shock. A moment later, his eyes rolled in his head and he collapsed, half on John's body and half on the water-slicked, broken pavement.

John heaved O'Neill's body aside. Gasping for breath, he looked up and met Bathsheba's gaze. She stood over him with a rock clutched in both hands.

"John, are you all right?" she exclaimed in a shrill voice.

He took a deep breath and sat up, resting his forehead on his knees for just a moment. Then he looked at her and smiled.

"Yes, my love. Thanks to you."

She dropped the rock and reached a hand down to him.

"Please get out of the mud, John," she said, snuffling back tears. "I can't hug you if you're lying down there. I'm dirty enough as it is."

He gave a weary laugh and scrambled to his feet. As soon as he was up, she launched herself at him, curling around him in a fierce hug. Her body trembled in his arms.

"Shh . . . everything's fine," he murmured as he wrapped her in a tight embrace. She had almost died because of him, but her courage had saved them both. Bathsheba didn't know it yet, but he intended to spend the rest of his life making it up to her.

If only he could convince her to give him a chance.

The sound of running footsteps cut through the pounding rain. Dick Repton and several men from the tenement raced toward them.

Repton peered down at O'Neill's body and whistled. "Sweet Jesus, what the hell is this? We heard a pistol go off, and we come running. You all right, Doc?"

Young Stanton loomed out of the darkness. "This ruffian tried to kill the doctor, but we managed to incapacitate him."

Bathsheba shifted in John's arms and glared at the young man.

"Well," he amended. "Lady Randolph managed to incapacitate him."

"That's better," she grumbled.

"Mr. Repton," said John. "I have a patient who urgently needs me. Can I ask you to send someone to Bow Street to fetch the Runners, and then keep an eye on this man until help comes? Mr. Stanton will stay behind to explain matters to the magistrate."

"Me?" Stanton protested. "I haven't a bloody clue what's going on."

"Robert, someone has to deal with this while John sees to Meredith," Bathsheba said testily. "I'll explain the situation to your grandfather and send him to Bow Street as soon as we get back to Silverton House."

"Very well." Robert sighed. "But I'll want a full explanation later, mind you. It's not every day a fellow gets set upon by a madman."

"Not to worry," Repton said to John. "We'll take care of it, guv. And I'll see to it myself that the young lad gets safely back home."

John gave him a grateful nod, then looked down at Bathsheba. "Ready?" he asked.

She pulled out of his arms and headed at a brisk pace across the courtyard. "Come along, John," she tossed back over her shoulder. "We haven't a moment to waste."

Chapter 28

Bathsheba and John dashed up the steps to Silverton House. At their knock, the door flew open. Wig askew, a frazzled-looking footman waved them into the entrance hall. Servants clustered at the foot of the marble staircase. Dread shimmered in the air, a palpable, sickening presence.

A cry, loud and long enough to raise prickles on Bathsheba's nape, drifted down from the family apartments. One of the servants, a sturdy-looking older woman, burst into noisy tears and threw her apron over her head.

Astoundingly, John smiled at Bathsheba. "That's a good sign. It means Lady Silverton still has the strength to push."

Before she could answer him, the doors to the drawing room crashed open and General Stanton stalked out, followed by his wife.

"What's going on out here?" he barked at the servants. "Don't you have anything better to do than stand around like a bunch of old women? Return to your duties."

Despite his harsh tone, the general gave the butler a kind pat on the shoulder, while Lady Stanton spoke soothingly to the woman with the apron. In a few moments, order was restored and most of the servants returned below stairs.

The general transferred his hawklike gaze to them. "I see you're finally back," he said to Bathsheba. "Took you long enough, young lady. And who is this disreputable-looking character you brought with you? Not the doctor! Surely you can't think I would let him lay a finger on my niece!"

Bathsheba yanked off her sodden bonnet and shoved it at a waiting footman.

"Really, General," she snapped, having run through her limited store of patience. "You're as bad as Robert. This is Dr. Blackmore. He's dirty because . . . oh, I'll explain in a minute."

She turned her attention to John, who was struggling out of his wet coat with the help of the butler.

"Why don't you go straight upstairs," she said. "I'll tell the general about Robert and then come right up."

He nodded and headed for the stairs.

"What about my grandson?" the general exclaimed as Lady Stanton anxiously clutched his arm. "Has something happened to him?"

Bathsheba silently cursed her hasty tongue. "Robert is fine, I assure you. Please step into the drawing room and I'll tell you everything that's happened."

Minutes later, the general had stomped out the front door on his way to Bow Street and Bathsheba was racing upstairs. As she hurried down the hallway to Meredith's bedroom, she began to pray. She hadn't prayed in a long time and had almost forgotten how, but she couldn't stand the thought of Meredith or her babies dying. Bathsheba would have bargained with old Scratch himself, if she thought it would make a difference.

She crossed through the bedroom to the dressing room, steeling herself for what might lay on the other side of the door. With a trembling hand, she twisted the doorknob and stepped inside.

Into the quietest room in the house. Bathsheba blinked to see Meredith sitting on the edge of her low bed, sipping . . . a glass of brandy? Next to her, Silverton rubbed her back, and Annabel had just opened a window to let in the fresh air of the rain-swept night. Mrs. Griffiths stood in front of an armoire, laying out John's medical instruments on a clean piece of toweling.

"There you are, Lady Randolph."

Bathsheba whirled around at the sound of John's voice. He stood in front of a washbasin, drying his hands and arms. He'd stripped down to his shirtsleeves, and his hair was mussed where he'd obviously run a towel through it to soak up the wet.

She hurried to him. "What's going on in here? Is Meredith drinking brandy? Why is she out of bed?"

"Brandy calms the nerves and eases the pain, and sometimes moving about helps, too."

Even though John appeared completely at ease, she couldn't miss the grim expression in his eyes. Her heart sank.

"Is she going to be all right?" she whispered.

He gave her shoulder a reassuring squeeze. "I think so, but it's a good thing you came for me when you did," he said in a quiet voice. "You most certainly saved her life."

Throwing the towel aside, he strode to the bed. Gently, he removed the tumbler from Meredith's hand.

"Are you ready, my lady?"

The marchioness lifted her head, and Bathsheba had to swallow a gasp of dismay. Meredith's pallor was a sickly gray, and her eyes were dulled and sunken with pain. For a horrible moment, it seemed it might be too late, after all.

Bathsheba desperately locked her gaze on John, and the tightness gripping her throat began to ease. He looked confident and calm, ready to take on the world—a miracle after that scene in St. Giles. She had always known him to be a good and kind man, but tonight she realized how truly extraordinary he was. He held deep reserves of character and strength, and unflagging courage.

And this extraordinary man had decided she was the woman for him. That was another miracle, one she didn't deserve.

Her heart aching with love, she watched John help Meredith swing her feet up onto the bed.

"I had better be ready, hadn't I," replied the marchioness in a weak voice. "It's not like I have a choice. I don't mean to complain, but I'm so tired."

"I know," John replied. "But you're strong. We'll get through this together." He bent over and gazed into her eyes, silver meeting silver. "You must trust me, my lady. You have nothing to fear. I promise."

Slowly, Meredith's lips curved into an answering smile. Tension seemed to flow from her body and dissipate on the cool evening breeze.

"Yes," she replied in a clear voice. "I do trust you."

"Good. Lord Silverton," directed John, "would you please sit on the bed behind her ladyship? She'll be more comfortable if she can lean against you."

Silverton knelt on the bed and tenderly eased Meredith back against his chest, while John stationed himself at the foot, perching on a low stool.

"Ah, the head is lodged, all right," he said, after examining her. "I'll wager that's your son who doesn't want to come out, my lady. What a stubborn little fellow he is."

Meredith's smile was more like a grimace. "Well, tell him he doesn't have a choice."

John nodded but didn't answer, his brow knit in concentration. "Mrs. Griffiths, please hand me the forceps."

Bathsheba wandered over to stand next to Mrs. Griffiths, feeling helpless, frustrated, and scared to death. All she could do was pray. She repeated the same prayer over and over—a desperate, incoherent plea for mercy.

John glanced up at Meredith. "You'll feel pressure and pain, but you must not push until I tell you to."

The marchioness drew in a trembling breath, preparing herself. Silverton wrapped his arms about her, murmuring soothing words of love in her ear. Suddenly, Meredith gasped and bit her lip, going rigid in her husband's arms.

"Hang on," John breathed. "Hang on . . . now, push!"

Meredith bore down, her face screwing up and turning crimson with the effort. A low moan surged from the back of her throat and built into a scream.

"I've got him," John exclaimed, and a moment later he was easing a messy baby onto the sheets. Meredith collapsed against Silverton, panting and drenched with sweat.

"The baby, is he . . . ?" Silverton asked in a hoarse voice.

John cleaned out the infant's mouth and nostrils and rubbed his little chest. A moment later, a thin wail filled the room.

"Very much so," John said with a grin. "Now, let's get that other baby out."

He handed the boy to Mrs. Griffiths, who bustled off to clean and swaddle him. A few minutes later, with surprisingly little fuss, an infant girl, pink and round as a berry, entered the world.

Bathsheba sniffed, wiping away the tears she had just realized were drenching her cheeks. Meredith fell back into her husband's arms, sobbing openly with joy and relief. Annabel, who had been silently gripping her sister's hand throughout the entire ordeal, bent her head, her slender shoulders heaving with silent tears.

"Well done, Lady Silverton," John exclaimed as he inspected the mewling baby girl. "You have two beautiful children, and they look healthy to me." He turned and nodded to Mrs. Griffiths. "Griff, please give the boy to Lady Randolph, and take this little one while I attend to her ladyship."

With trepidation and wonder, Bathsheba carefully took the boy in her arms. She hadn't held a baby since Rachel was an infant but, somehow, it seemed as natural as breathing. He had a squished little face and a sweet, grumpy frown, and her heart melted as she cradled the sturdy bundle in her arms. When he opened his tiny mouth and yawned, joy filled her chest and she broke into laughter.

John looked up for a moment and smiled, then returned to his work.

Mrs. Griffiths gave the baby girl to her aunt Annabel, and bustled over to help John clean up and organize the bed. A few minutes later, Meredith, dressed in a clean nightgown, was reclining comfortably on fresh sheets. She looked exhausted, but the pink had returned to her cheeks. With a radiant smile, she held out her arms to Annabel, who carefully placed the baby girl in her mother's arms.

With a nod from John, Bathsheba approached the bed.

"Your son, Lord Silverton," she said as she gently transferred the baby to his father's arms. Silverton gazed at the bundle with a bemused expression on his face, but when the mite blew out an air bubble, he gave a soft laugh.

He looked at John, his eyes glittering with unshed tears.

"Thank you, Dr. Blackmore," he said, "for saving my family. I can never repay you."

"I was happy to be of assistance, my lord. Your lady's safety is payment enough."

Silverton gave him a solemn nod. Then he cradled the baby in one arm and seized Bathsheba's hand.

"And you, Lady Randolph." His voice grew hoarse, and he paused. "I . . . thank you," he finished.

She squeezed his hand. "Call me Bathsheba, please. And I was happy to help."

"I think Lord and Lady Silverton might like a few moments alone with their children," John said as he turned down his shirtsleeves. He smiled at the couple, already lost in love with their new babies. "I'll return in a few minutes to check on you."

"Heavens, yes," cried Annabel, leaping up. "I must go tell Grandmama. How could I have forgotten to do that?" She dashed out of the room in a flurry of skirts.

John waited at the door for Bathsheba. She walked through, suddenly feeling crushed with weariness, and shaking from the accumulated stresses of the harrowing day. She stumbled to a well-padded chair placed against the wall and collapsed onto it. John didn't even bother to make it to one of the chairs a few feet away. He just set his back to the wall and slid down to the floor next to her.

"Good God," he said, rubbing the back of his neck. "This is a day I would be thrilled to forget."

Then he looked up at her, his tired, bloodshot eyes filling with a slow heat. "Well," he amended. "Perhaps not all of it."

The warmth in his eyes flooded every inch of Bathsheba's body. Suddenly, she didn't feel nearly so tired. She reached out and stroked his damp, tumbled hair.

"You were magnificent, John. We would have been lost without you."

He took her hand and turned it over, pressing a kiss to the inside of her wrist. Her pulse jumped, and tingles shot along her nerves and flowed through her veins.

John's eyes, no longer weary, shone clear and silver bright with emotion. "And you were beyond magnificent, my love. You were willing to risk everything for me. I will never forget how you told me to leave you—to save Lady Silverton instead of yourself."

Bathsheba swallowed a sudden rush of nausea. Reliving that awful moment made her light-headed. "I can't believe I did that. I must have been out of my mind."

"Nonsense," he scoffed, rubbing her hand against his rough, bristled cheek. "You're the bravest woman I know."

"I'm not brave. I'm a coward of the worst order. And a fool. I want to lock myself in a closet every time I think of the things I said to you that day in your study. Can you ever forgive me?"

In a fluid movement, he rose to his feet. She made to get up, but he surprised her by going down on one knee in front of her chair. Her heart began to flutter in the most ridiculous, girlish fashion.

He studied her with a grave expression on his lean, aristocratic features, but a hint of mischief lurked in his gaze.

"I would consider forgiving you, my lady, under one condition."

"And what is that, Dr. Blackmore?" she said pertly, just to show him that she wouldn't melt at his feet like some foolish miss.

"That you marry me, Lady Randolph. Then I'll have to forgive you."

She sucked in a breath, too full of emotion to reply. After the way she had treated him, all the cruel things she had said . . . he was giving her a second chance.

When she didn't answer—because she would have started blubbering if she even opened her mouth—a worried look crossed his features.

"It won't be what you're used to, Bathsheba. I know that. You won't be a countess anymore. But I'm not poor. I'll be well able to take care of you. In fact," he said with an encouraging smile, "I already have a position. When I wrote Dr. Littleton to tell him that I was leaving London, he begged me to return to Ripon. He's ready to retire, and would very much like to turn his practice over to me."

Joy mingled with horror in Bathsheba's breast. For a moment, horror won out. "Move back to Yorkshire? You must be joking! How will I ever bear it?"

His handsome face split into a relieved grin. "I'm sure Miss Elliott will be happy to give you whatever support and advice you need."

She groaned and dropped her head into her hands. "That's what I'm afraid of."

"Bathsheba," he said, tilting her chin up. "There's something else."

"Now what?" she sighed. "I can't take much more."

The grin faded from his lips and his eyes grew solemn. "Your sister . . . I've been thinking about how we could manage that."

She took his hand and held it between her own. All she

had to do was look into his eyes and she knew exactly what to do.

"It's all right, John. I've been thinking about that these last few days. I believe it's time for Rachel to come home. She's been away from her family long enough." She shook her head, sick with shame that she had allowed it to go on for so many years. "God knows I should have insisted upon it when I married Reggie. I don't know what you must think of me."

Understanding and compassion filled his gaze. "You did what you had to do to survive, and you always made sure Rachel was taken care of," he said. "But are you sure? It won't be easy."

"I know. But Boland will help. We'll manage. And as long as I have you, everything will be fine."

He took a deep breath and closed his eyes, his face pulling tight with . . . what? Guilt? A frisson of panic rippled along her nerves.

"John, what is it? Tell me."

"I must confess something, as well," he said, finally opening his eyes. "What you said the other day, that I was needlessly risking my life—you were right. I allowed guilt for Becky's death to consume me. On some level, I didn't care what happened to me. I needed to punish myself, but I was punishing you, too, and putting you in danger. I couldn't see that—not until tonight."

She clutched his hands, aghast that he might doubt himself.

"But your work is important," she said earnestly. "I see that now. You mustn't ever stop—not on my account." She gave him what she hoped was a confident smile. "I promise I'll do my best to support your work."

He planted a light kiss on her brow. "Yes, my love, it is important, and I thank you for saying that. But the need for skilled physicians is just as great in Yorkshire as it is here, and there is much I can do to help those who are most vulnerable—even in a smaller town like Ripon. Others will continue my work in London. My student, Roger, for one. He's been training with me for the last two years, with the intention of opening a dispensary in St. Giles."

John gave her a sly grin. "And while Lord Silverton is feeling in such a giving mood, I believe I'll have a word with him about funding that new wing at Bart's. The Board of Governors wouldn't dream of turning down so powerful and wealthy a patron."

Bathsheba didn't know whether to laugh or cry, so great was her relief that he wouldn't turn his back on the work that meant so much to him. Of course, she was silly for not realizing that he never would.

John's expression softened as he tenderly captured her face in his hands. "But I want you, Bathsheba. You're the most important thing in my life. I'll never be happy without you."

His features blurred, and she had to blink away tears before she could see again. He was grinning at her now, a world of devilment—and love—shining in his eyes.

"Well, then," she said, putting on a mock scowl. "Will you listen to me from now on, and promise you won't run off into danger at a moment's notice?"

He laughed. "I'll try, my darling. What I will promise is that I will always return home to you. You're my life, Bathsheba. You're everything I've ever wanted."

Then he swooped in, taking her mouth in a kiss so sweet, so hungry, that it made her head spin and her toes curl in her boots.

"Well," she gasped, when he finally lifted his head, "as long as you try. I suppose that will have to be enough."

Of course it was more than enough. It was everything.

Epilogue

Nidderdale Cottage, Yorkshire
November 1817

John glanced up from his correspondence as the landau rumbled by his study window and pulled to a halt in front of the house. Dodger, the half-grown spaniel puppy asleep at his feet, twitched awake, tail thumping in anticipation. As usual, the puppy sensed that his new but already beloved mistress had arrived home. Bathsheba pretended to regard Dodger as nothing but an infernal nuisance, only tolerating him for Rachel's sake. She lied, of course. Bathsheba would constantly slip Dodger treats under the table when she thought no one was looking, and she would croon baby talk to him as he followed her around the house, close on her heels.

Dodger yipped as several thumps sounded out in the hallway, followed by clomping noises on the stairs. Then peace reigned again. The study door opened, his wife stepped into the room, and Dodger launched himself at her.

"Oh, do get down, you ghastly beast," Bathsheba ordered. The puppy ignored her stern command, romping around her skirts. With an exasperated sigh, she picked him up and cuddled him before dropping into the chair in front of John's desk.

He rose to greet her and tipped her chin to plant a lingering kiss on her soft mouth. As always, she melted into him, opening her lips in sweet surrender—until Dodger thrust his bony little head between them.

"Bad dog," she scolded as she deposited him on the floor. The unrepentant puppy gave her a doggy grin, his pink tongue lolling out of his mouth.

John untied the ribbons of her bonnet, tossing the hat onto his desk. "How was your visit to Compton Manor, my love? I trust you found Lady Randolph and her lord in good health?"

She rolled her eyes. "I still can't get used to calling her *Lady Randolph*. She'll always be Miss Elliott to me, especially when she starts lecturing. But I must admit that Matthew has never been happier, and the manor house looks beautiful. I shouldn't be surprised if the repairs are completed by Christmas, because all the workmen are scared to death of her. I'm sure they can't wait to escape her clutches."

He laughed. "And what about Rachel? Did she have a pleasant visit?"

"It's the oddest thing, but Rachel adores Lady Randolph. She attaches herself to her as soon as we walk in the door, and refuses to leave her side. Today, Lady Randolph tried to teach her to make scones. It was a disaster, of course."

Bathsheba gave a wicked chuckle, the one that always made John want to take her upstairs and ravish her into exhaustion.

"There was more flour and milk on Rachel and Lady Randolph than in the scones," she said. "Rachel certainly tried her patience, but Lady Randolph never loses her temper with her, which certainly surprised me."

John smiled. The former Miss Elliott and the former Countess of Randolph would never have tolerated each other, but Lady Randolph and Mrs. Blackmore had reached a tacit agreement to let old quarrels rest, for the sake of their families.

"And did you help with the scone-making?" he enquired, enjoying himself.

She wrinkled her nose. "I tried, but Lady Randolph said my lack of enthusiasm was apparent to everyone. She made me leave the kitchen. I did not protest."

John couldn't help laughing. Bathsheba was a lamentable housekeeper, and he suspected she always would be. But she had other talents as a loving wife and sister that more than made up the difference.

She grinned at him and settled more comfortably into her chair. Dodger gave a contented moan as he flopped down on her feet.

"Well, Dr. Blackmore," Bathsheba asked, "what have you been doing with yourself while I was being tortured all afternoon by Lady Randolph?"

"Attending to my correspondence. Wardrop wrote me a lengthy missive about the outcome of O'Neill's trial."

She instantly turned solemn. "And?"

"Thanks to my intervention, he will escape the gallows. Wardrop says he'll be deported to New South Wales in the next few days." He shook his head, feeling the old guilt tug at him. "Despite everything, I can't help but feel sorry for the man. He lost all that he loved in the world. Little wonder he struck out at me so violently."

She took his hand in a comforting grip. "You're not to blame for what happened, John. You did everything you could to help that poor woman and her baby. Besides, you always tell me to let the past remain in the past. You've done what you could for that man, and it's more than he deserves."

He nodded, knowing she was right. It served no purpose to speak about O'Neill, especially when Bathsheba found the subject so disturbing. She still experienced nightmares about that harrowing rainy night in St. Giles, although they came less frequently now that they were settled in their comfortable house in Ripon.

"What else does Wardrop have to say?" she asked. "Any news of Dr. Steele? Is he still on staff at Bart's?"

"For now, apparently. But Lord Silverton has made Abernethy and the Board of Governors aware of his displeasure with Steele. I shouldn't be surprised if we soon heard that Steele will be retiring from public life."

"Well, I should hope so," Bathsheba scowled. "I also received a letter today—from Meredith. She says that Silverton is determined that no woman or child will ever suffer at Steele's hands again."

"I'm sure Lord Silverton will prevail," John remarked dryly. "But enough of that subject. Tell me how Lady Silverton is doing. And your godchildren—are they well?"

"Very well, although Meredith says she no longer remembers what it's like to get more than a few hours' sleep. Little Bathsheba, of course, is a perfect angel, but young Stephen thinks nothing of keeping his mother up half the night. Oh, but I haven't told you the best part yet," she said excitedly. "Meredith and Lord Silverton are going to donate two thousand pounds toward the building of the new hospital here in Ripon, and General Stanton and Robert Stanton equal amounts. It took some doing to convince the general, but I finally managed it. Six thousand pounds! Isn't that wonderful?"

She beamed at him, her beautiful face alight with triumph. Once given the chance, Bathsheba had thrown herself enthusiastically into meaningful work—including his scheme to persuade the local town fathers to build a public hospital and dispensary. True, they still sparred over what Bathsheba deemed his tendency to take unnecessary risks when going into the unsavory parts of town to treat patients. But she held fast to her promise to do everything she could to support him and his work.

Their arguments never bothered John, since their resolution often took place behind the closed door of their bedchamber. Bathsheba's passion for debate was more than equaled by her passion for lovemaking, and for that he was exceedingly grateful.

"John, aren't you going to say something?" she demanded, her lips pursing into an adorable pout. "I thought you'd be thrilled."

"My darling, as always, your talent for managing the male of the species renders me speechless."

She glowered at him with mock irritation. He captured her face in his hands, more than ready to show her how thrilled he could be. Her eyelids drooped as he leaned in to kiss her.

A tap sounded on the door. "Oh, blast," she muttered as he reluctantly drew back.

Boland sailed into the room with the tea tray. John took it from her and set it on the desk.

"Is Rachel coming down for tea?" he asked.

"Not today, Doctor," Boland replied as she prepared a cup for Bathsheba. "Poor thing is plumb worn out from her visit to Compton Manor. I put her to bed for a nap. She should sleep until dinner."

"I'm not surprised," Bathsheba said, hiding a yawn behind her hand. "Lady Randolph would exhaust anyone."

"If you don't mind my saying so, my lady," Boland said with a stern look, "you could use a nap yourself. You've been on your feet all day."

"I haven't done a thing today, and you know it," protested Bathsheba. "And, Boland, you really must stop referring to me as *my lady*. I don't think the current Lady Randolph appreciates it. Nor does my husband, I would imagine."

Boland shot him a look so guilty and apologetic that John had to laugh.

"It's quite all right, Boland. I sometimes still think of her that way, too. As for wearing herself out, I'll see that Mrs. Blackmore gets some rest."

"Honestly," Bathsheba huffed after Boland left the room,

"you two fuss over me like I'm an old lady. I'm as healthy as a horse, and you know it."

"And I intend to keep you that way," he said, pulling her out of the chair and into his arms. Dodger gave a little growl in protest, but they both ignored him.

"Boland's right," he murmured, skimming his mouth along her delicately angled cheekbone. "A nap is a capital idea. But first, I think an examination is in order. A very private examination. In our bedroom."

A sultry smile curved her perfect lips, and her emerald eyes glittered with a knowing heat. "Doctor's orders?" she asked as she nestled her lush body against him.

John's heart filled with a boundless joy even as lust surged through his veins. He captured her mouth, too swept up by his need to love her to bother with words.

After a short but ravenous kiss, Bathsheba broke away, her eyes shining with mischief.

"As I've told you many times before, my darling husband," she said, pulling him eagerly to the door, "I always follow my doctor's orders."

HISTORICAL NOTE

When I first decided to create a hero who was a physician and an accoucheur (man-midwife), little did I know how complicated a task that would be. The study and practice of midwifery during the Georgian and Regency periods was fraught with scientific and political complications, as different groups of practitioners, including midwives, surgeons, and physicians, fought for dominance in the profession. The history of the use of forceps is but one example. Invented by the Chamberlen family in the early seventeenth century, their design and use was carefully guarded as a family secret until about 1700. Forceps were then used quite extensively throughout the eighteenth century. Toward the end of the century, however, there was a swing away from the use of forceps, as many physicians strenuously advocated non-intervention in the birthing process. Heated discussions about the appropriate use of forceps and other medical interventions went on for years, as childbearing became increasingly the sphere of male doctors rather than of female midwives and family members. Finding my way through this complicated history would have been much more difficult without the assistance of Franzeca Drouin, researcher and librarian. Any errors or medical mishaps in the telling of this story, of course, are mine.

Part of my book takes place in Ripon, a town in Yorkshire, and certain events take place around the celebration of a local festival to celebrate St. Wilfrid. I am indebted to Roy

Waite of the Ripon Historical Society for information about the town and the festival. Although it is unlikely that the festivities to honor the saint were quite as lively in 1817 as the one attended by John and Bathsheba, celebrations of that type did occur in towns like Ripon during the eighteenth and nineteenth centuries. I drew on those traditions to create the scenes in my book.

GREAT BOOKS, GREAT SAVINGS!

When You Visit Our Website:
www.kensingtonbooks.com
You Can Save Money Off The Retail Price
Of Any Book You Purchase!

- **All Your Favorite Kensington Authors**
- **New Releases & Timeless Classics**
- **Overnight Shipping Available**
- **eBooks Available For Many Titles**
- **All Major Credit Cards Accepted**

Visit Us Today To Start Saving!
www.kensingtonbooks.com

All Orders Are Subject To Availability.
Shipping and Handling Charges Apply.
Offers and Prices Subject To Change Without Notice.

Books by Bestselling Author
Fern Michaels

___The Jury	0-8217-7878-1	$6.99US/$9.99CAN
___Sweet Revenge	0-8217-7879-X	$6.99US/$9.99CAN
___Lethal Justice	0-8217-7880-3	$6.99US/$9.99CAN
___Free Fall	0-8217-7881-1	$6.99US/$9.99CAN
___Fool Me Once	0-8217-8071-9	$7.99US/$10.99CAN
___Vegas Rich	0-8217-8112-X	$7.99US/$10.99CAN
___Hide and Seek	1-4201-0184-6	$6.99US/$9.99CAN
___Hokus Pokus	1-4201-0185-4	$6.99US/$9.99CAN
___Fast Track	1-4201-0186-2	$6.99US/$9.99CAN
___Collateral Damage	1-4201-0187-0	$6.99US/$9.99CAN
___Final Justice	1-4201-0188-9	$6.99US/$9.99CAN
___Up Close and Personal	0-8217-7956-7	$7.99US/$9.99CAN
___Under the Radar	1-4201-0683-X	$6.99US/$9.99CAN
___Razor Sharp	1-4201-0684-8	$7.99US/$10.99CAN
___Yesterday	1-4201-1494-8	$5.99US/$6.99CAN
___Vanishing Act	1-4201-0685-6	$7.99US/$10.99CAN
___Sara's Song	1-4201-1493-X	$5.99US/$6.99CAN
___Deadly Deals	1-4201-0686-4	$7.99US/$10.99CAN
___Game Over	1-4201-0687-2	$7.99US/$10.99CAN
___Sins of Omission	1-4201-1153-1	$7.99US/$10.99CAN
___Sins of the Flesh	1-4201-1154-X	$7.99US/$10.99CAN
___Cross Roads	1-4201-1192-2	$7.99US/$10.99CAN

Available Wherever Books Are Sold!
Check out our website at **www.kensingtonbooks.com**